The Highwayman is Born

"Who are you? What do you want?" Tarkus Breen said, the confidence long gone from his voice.

"I am . . ." Bransen paused as if awakening from a dream, as if for the first time actually realizing what he had done. While his body had come in here, fighting perfectly, his thoughts were stalled back at the tree. But what was he to say?

"I am the Highwayman," he said, hardly considering the implications.

Breen's knife slashed left to right then back again, but Bransen retreated and veered so as not to trip over Cadayle. Bransen's hand pushed the strike out wide, but then his attacker surprised him by breaking off and turning back to Cadayle.

Tarkus Breen stabbed the knife out toward her.

He never got close to connecting.

Bransen rushed back to Cadayle, catching Breen's wrist with his left hand. He lifted Breen's arm and went under it, turning it and forcing the bully to come up straight. Bransen kept twisting as he stood up straight. He lifted his right arm and drove his elbow against Breen's.

The snap of bone sounded like the breaking of a thick tree branch.

TOR BOOKS BY R. A. SALVATORE

The Highwayman
*The Ancient**

*Forthcoming

R·A·SALVATORE

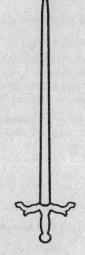

THE
Highwayman

A Novel of Corona

TOR
fantasy

A TOM DOHERTY ASSOCIATES BOOK
NEW YORK

THE HIGHWAYMAN

Originally published in 2004 by CDS Books.

A Tor Book
Published by Tom Doherty Associates, LLC
175 Fifth Avenue
New York, NY 10010

www.tor.com

Tor® is a registered trademark of Tom Doherty Associates, LLC.

Text design by Holly Johnson

ISBN-13: 978-0-7653-5870-7
ISBN-10: 0-7653-5870-0

First Tor Edition: October 2007

Printed in the United States of America

0 9 8 7 6 5 4 3 2 1

CONTENTS

PART III: GOD'S YEAR 74

MAP OF
HONCE AND
BEHR

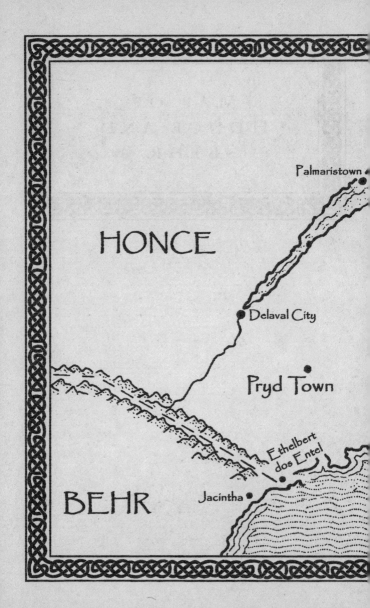

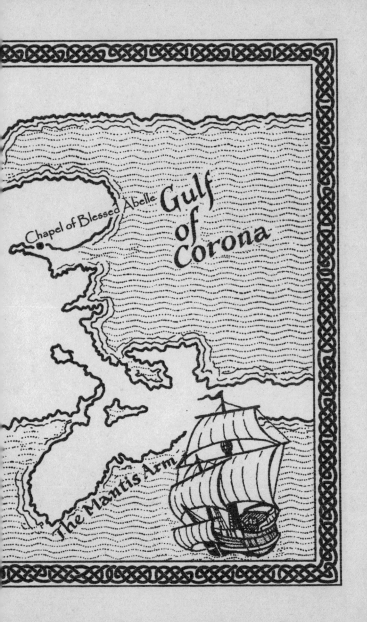

Chapel of Blessed Abelle

Gulf of Corona

The Mantis Arm

GOD'S YEAR 74

Seventy-four Years after the Death of Blessed Abelle

Harkin cracked his whip with an urgency wrought of terror. Orrin slumped next to him, a spear buried deep in his side, bright blood flowing freely, staining his brown woolen tunic a dark and ugly red black.

"Come on, run!" Harkin urged his team, and he cracked the whip hard again. He couldn't help but consider the terrible irony of it all. He had been transferred from the front lines of battle—in a war that had been raging since he was a young man—to the seemingly safe job of driving Prince Yeslnik about the growing lands of Greater Delaval. And now this—to be caught and killed on the road!

The horses dug in and pulled hard, but an undeniable drag slowed the coach. "Orrin, you hold on!" Harkin cried to his injured friend, and he shifted his hands just enough so that he could pull back the slumping man, who seemed as if he would tumble from his seat.

Harkin glanced all around frantically. He heard Prince Yeslnik shout, though the words were lost in the tumult. He heard Prince Yeslnik's wife, Olym, scream in fear. When the coach hit one straight, flat stretch of the tree-lined road in the southeastern reaches of Pryd Holding, Harkin dared to stand quickly and look back. The coach was dragging a tangle of logs. "Ah, you cunning beasts," he lamented, for the bloody-capped powries had hit the coach with some sort of grapnel, affixed by rope to the logs.

Harkin's mind tumbled through the possibilities. He knew that he had to do something; it was only a matter of time before those bouncing logs caught on a tree or some other obstacle at the side of the road and either stopped the coach or, more likely, tore it apart. He couldn't go back to free the grapnel while they were charging along, and he couldn't stop. He knew the truth. He had seen the bright red berets. He had heard the grating voices and the guttural shouts. These were powrie dwarves, and powries showed no mercy.

"Come on," he called again to his straining team, and he cracked the whip once more.

Good fortune got them through the straight section of road without any serious entanglements, but Harkin knew that the flagstone path twisted and wound around many stones and trees, down into dells and into sharp-cornered turns over ridges. "Bah!" He snorted in dismay, and he pulled back hard on the reins, bringing the coach to an abrupt halt. Before the wheels had even fully stopped turning, Harkin looped the reins about the bench seat and leaped to the ground. "Stay inside, my prince!" he cried to Yeslnik as he ran past the door's open window and around the back of the coach.

He followed the rope to the grapnel, and found it secured underneath the carriage. Cunning powries, indeed! They hadn't hit the coach with a spear or anything like that, but rather had set a trap in the road to hook it from beneath.

Harkin started to bend and even dropped to one knee, starting under the coach frame to free it, but the thought of crawling on the ground, so vulnerably, with powries closing, had him gasping for breath. Instead, he drew out his short bronze sword and began hacking at the rope with all his might.

"You fool! What are you doing?" cried the prince, leaning out and hanging on the now-opened door. "Why have you stopped? I am the nephew of the Laird of Delaval!"

"We cannot go, my liege," poor Harkin tried to explain. He hacked with all his strength, and finally the rope snapped. Yeslnik saw it and cried out in dismay, and then he saw a spear come arcing in and hit the coach near Harkin.

"Get back in, I beg you, my liege!" Harkin cried, and this time Yeslnik didn't argue.

Harkin scrambled around the coach and back up into his seat. If he could just get them moving . . .

The reins were not there.

Harkin's gaze went forward to the nervous team, and there, between them, he saw his doom. For there stood a powrie, a smile on its leathery and wrinkled face, white teeth showing behind the long hairs of an overgrown red mustache.

"Ye lookin' for these, me lord?" the dwarf asked, and he held up and jiggled the reins. "Aye, but ain't yer horses tired from yer stupid run?"

Harkin could hardly draw breath as he heard other dwarves moving around the sides of the coach, for the powries' reputation preceded them. They were not here for treasure, other than human blood.

The dwarf in front dropped the reins and drew forth a long, curving knife with a wicked, serrated edge. "If ye don't fight, it won't hurt as much."

Harkin's mind whirled—he didn't want to die, certainly not like this! "Wait!" he cried as he heard the coach creak behind him and knew that a dwarf was beginning to climb on it. "I got something for you. Something that'll get you all the blood and money you want!"

The dwarf in front held up his hand, and the one creeping near Harkin stopped.

Poor Harkin heard the coach door open, and a moment later, he heard Prince Yeslnik's wife scream, followed by a protest from the prince himself.

"Aye, that one," Harkin improvised. "He's noble blood, and his laird'll pay whatever you want to get him back. Money and people—it won't matter to Laird Delaval, as long as he gets the safe return of his precious nephew."

"Hmmm," the dwarf in front mused.

Harkin could hear more movement and shouting from behind, but no sounds of battle yet joined. The dwarves were waiting, he believed and prayed.

"What're ye thinking, Turgol?" asked the one in front. "Ransom? That be our game?"

"Nah," said the dwarf to the side and behind Harkin, and he nearly fainted when he realized how close this second one actually was. "Lots o' work in that, and we're to rile up a laird? Nah, kill 'em now, I say. Three humans to brighten me cap."

The dwarf in front began to nod and smile all the wider, and he opened his mouth to speak.

"Oh, wrong answer," came a voice from above—a human voice and not the grumbling chant of a powrie. Harkin and the dwarves turned, their gazes flying up, up to the high boughs of a wide oak tree.

And there he sat on a limb, a smallish man dressed head to toe in a black outfit of some exotic fabric. He wore a mask black as night that covered more than half his face, with holes cut out for the eyes.

"If it was just a business deal—a good one—then perhaps I could have wandered along on my way without interfering," the mysterious man said. "But since you insist . . ."

As he finished he shoved off the branch and came flying down at the coach.

"By the gods!" Harkin cried, and he fell back, throwing his arm up in front of him, expecting the man to go crashing through the coach.

The powrie behind Harkin shrieked but instead of retreating, lifted up a heavy battle-axe.

The dwarf roared and swung trying to bat the man in black out of the air. But amazingly, the axe whipped below the descending man, as if he had somehow slowed his fall. And he didn't crash through the coach roof—as he should have after falling from so high—but rather touched down firmly on it right behind the swinging blade. He fell as he hit, absorbing the impact with a forward roll following the swing of the axe, and he came up tangled with the dwarf—at least as far as the dwarf was concerned. For the man's balance as he rolled fast to his feet remained perfect, and as he leaped down from the coach his hands caught the dwarf so that the dwarf had no choice but to go flying away with him.

Again the man landed in perfect and easy balance, as the powrie crashed down hard beside him, sprawling on the ground, its axe flying away.

"Not a graceful sort, now is he?" the man asked a pair of powries standing before him, their mouths agape. He jabbed his elbow back as he spoke, for he had cleverly landed right beside the open coach door, and a simple shove from that elbow had it swinging closed. "I beg your pardon, Prince Yeslnik, but would you please remain inside while I finish my business out here?"

The two dwarves recovered, roared, and charged; and the man sprang into a forward somersault right over them. He touched down, running, turning as he went, and drawing from over his shoulder the most magnificent sword that any of them—man or dwarf—had ever seen. Its blade gleamed silver, shining in the morning light, and tracings of delicate vines ran the length of it. Most wondrous of all was the hilt, all silver and ivory, the pommel shaped as the head of a hooded serpent.

The powries swung and rushed right in, one thrusting a spear, the other stabbing with its own sword, a weapon of bronze.

Two quick, sharp raps turned both those weapons aside. The man retracted his blade to his right, spun it end over end suddenly, and it disappeared behind him.

The foolish dwarves kept coming.

Out from the left now stabbed the silvery sword, forward, a quick tap to the side to push the dwarf's sword wide, and then ferociously ahead to stab the powrie in the chest. The man came forward at the same time, turning at the last second so that the thrusting spear flashed past him. He caught that spear shaft in his right hand as he stepped closer to the dwarf, tearing free his sword from its falling comrade. Too close to use the weapon effectively, the man tossed the sword up into the air, and predictably, the powrie's eyes followed its ascent.

The man hit the powrie with three short left jabs—short but amazingly hard. The dwarf staggered back a step, dazed.

The man caught the sword as it fell, and his hand flashed out, smashing the snake pommel into the dwarf's face. He had to turn as another dwarf came at him; and as he did, he flipped the sword and stabbed straight behind him, plunging the magnificent blade through the stunned dwarf's chest so forcefully that its tip exploded right out through the creature's back.

The man let go of the hilt again, his hands moving in a side-to-side blur before him to confuse the next attacker. Somehow those flashing hands evaded the stabbing powrie sword. The man's right palm slapped the blade out to the dwarf's right, while the lightning-fast fighter brought his left hand under the dwarf's arm, backhanding it out even further. Suddenly he grabbed the dwarf's wrist and pulled it between them. His right hand bent the dwarf's wrist, overextending the ligaments and bringing a howl of pain. A sudden brutal jerk took the strength from the dwarf's fingers, and the man slid his hand down, pulling free the powrie's sword.

"You only get one chance," he said, throwing the dwarf's arm out wide, slapping him across the face with his left hand, then grabbing the powrie by the hair, and forcefully tugged it back.

The dwarf growled and started to punch, but his forward movement only served to present the man with a clear line to an exposed throat.

The sword slid in, turning the growl to a gurgle, and the man pushed on.

The dwarf wasn't punching anymore but was frozen in place, staring up at the morning sky, its arms out to the sides and twitching.

The man was gone, leaving the powrie's sword in place.

Another dwarf pursued, with several more circling as if to cut the man off, for it seemed as if their enemy were unarmed now.

The man remedied that as he came upon the dwarf he'd skewered with his sword. The man dove into a sidelong roll right over the dwarf, catching his sword's hilt. When he landed on his feet on the other side, with two powries rushing up in front of him, he had his sword in hand. He put it to sudden and devastating work, launching a series of short back-and-forth slashes, striking their weapons in succession. Somewhere in the side-to-side blur, he thrust out, once and then again, and one of the powries staggered back, bright blood erupting from its shoulder and chest.

Now the man's sword went into a tight circular motion around the remaining dwarf's sword. He had the dwarf watching the dazzling display: he knew from its spinning eyes.

A fatal mistake.

The sword then changed its angle, and, with a sudden shove and a cry that came from somewhere deep inside, the man threw the dwarf's weapon out wide and stiffened the fingers of his free hand as he stepped forward, thrusting that hand straight out, his fingers driving into the powrie's windpipe.

The dwarf shuddered and staggered back, all its body jerking in death spasms.

"Who shall be next?" the man asked, spinning and bringing his sword into a series of left and right diagonal cuts.

But none of the remaining dwarves wanted anything to do with him! They were off and running, scattering to every direction.

The man laughed and looked at the coach, where the Prince of Delaval was peeking out and slowly opening the door and where the unnerved driver was staring at him from above. "They always run when half are down," the man calmly explained. "If only they would play it out to the end, they might find me growing tired."

As he finished, he launched into a series of leaps, twisting and striking out with his sword, a barrage that would have likely taken down any ten enemies standing too near.

"Or perhaps not," the man said with a salute.

"Who are you?" Prince Yeslnik asked.

"My reputation has not preceded me? I am wounded."

"The Highwayman," Harkin said.

"Thank you for that," the man in black replied. "I would hate to think that all my hard work these past months has been for naught."

Prince Yeslnik slid out of the coach. "Your reputation does not do you justice, my friend."

"Why, thank you."

"You will be rewarded." Behind the prince, the Highwayman could see his female companion staring out at him from the coach, leaning toward him eagerly.

So predictable a reaction from these fair ladies of court.

"And pardoned," the excited prince went on, "for any crime of which you have been accused. You will live the life of a wealthy and free man, from one end of Honce to the other."

"As if that was yours to give," said the man. " 'Tis a big place."

"Then in Delaval Holding at least," Yeslnik said. "You may walk freely in Delaval."

"I have no desire to travel to Delaval."

"Well . . ."

"But a reward does sound fine, and so I will take it . . . now."

Yeslnik seemed unsettled, but he composed himself quickly and turned to the packs tied on the back of the coach.

"A hundred silver coins, then," Yeslnik offered.

"I prefer gold."

The prince glanced back at him, a momentary flash of anger betraying his true feelings. "Gold, then, a hundred pieces."

"Surely you have more than that. You did come to collect your uncle's taxes from Pryd Holding. You know—we both do—the burden Delaval places on the people of Pryd in exchange for keeping them free from the advances of Laird Ethelbert."

Prince Yeslnik stood up very straight. "Name your price then."

"Why, all of it, of course," the Highwayman said.

The prince looked shocked.

"You see, I lied when I told the powrie that it gave the wrong answer. I agree with it! Taking you hostage for ransom would be a terrible choice."

There was no missing the threat in those words, and Yeslnik's bluster seemed to melt away.

"All of it," the Highwayman repeated, "and be glad, stupid prince, that I have no need for human blood. My mask is black, you see."

He walked over past the prince and right up to the woman who was hanging half out of the coach. How her green eyes sparkled as he neared, and her breasts heaved with excitement.

He reached up as if to stroke her face.

And tore the bejeweled necklace from her neck. She gave a little shriek and lifted her hand over her tiny mouth, and her eyelids fluttered as if she would swoon.

"Surely a beauty as radiant as your own needs no baubles," he said sweetly.

She stammered and tittered, and the Highwayman glanced back at Prince Yeslnik, offering a look of pity.

"Such substance," he said as he turned back to Olym, masking his sarcasm beneath a voice that seemed husky with awe.

She sucked in her breath and brought her hand up before her mouth again; and this time, the Highwayman took a closer look at the shining emerald ring she wore. He took that hand in his own and kissed it.

Then he took the ring.

She didn't know whether to protest or to swoon, and behind him, the Highwayman heard the growls of Prince Yeslnik. He offered a salute to one and then the other, then stepped behind the coach where he freed two packs bulging with coins. Slinging them over his shoulder as if they were weightless, he seemed to fly away, with a great leap that brought him to the top of the coach. He glanced at the driver and his slumping companion, then moved closer to inspect the wounded man.

The Highwayman closed his eyes and placed a hand on the wound. His focus brought warmth to his hand, and that warmth brought some healing to poor Orrin.

"You turn and get him to Chapel Pryd," the Highwayman instructed Harkin. "The brothers will help him—his wounds are not as grave as they seem."

Harkin nodded stupidly.

The Highwayman bowed to him, turned and bowed to Prince Yeslnik, then leaped again, even higher, back to the low branches of the tree from which he had come.

In a matter of only a few minutes, he had arrived, rescued, robbed, healed, and vanished.

PART I

—

GOD'S YEAR
54

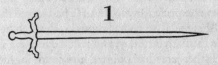

1

WALKING IN THE CLOUDS

Brother Bran Dynard stepped out of his room into the brilliant morning light. The sun reached down through the few patches of cloud, which were really no more than jagged lines of white torn by the fast winds. Bright flashes dotted the terrace and the bridges, as puddles from the night's rainfall caught the rays of morning and threw them back into the air with exuberance.

Brother Dynard walked across the landing to the waist-high railing and leaned over, looking down at the clouds that drifted across the mountainsides below him, then looking past them to the valley floor, hundreds and hundreds of feet below. Though he had grown up just north of the mighty Belt-and-Buckle mountains, though he had sailed around the eastern fringes of that great range, right under their shadow, Dynard could never have imagined looking down on the clouds.

Looking down on them!

He noted the sparkle of the river snaking through the valley, weaving around the sharp stones and red-streaked rock that seemed to grow right out of the mountains. In the six years he had been here, this view of the strange land that the nomads of Behr called Crezen ilaf Flar, the Mountains of Fire, had never ceased to amaze Dynard and had never ceased to send his heart soaring with the possibilities of . . .

Of anything. Of everything.

When he had left Chapel Pryd of the Honce holding of the same name on his *Journey Proselyt* (as the monks called their evangelical missions) seven years before, weary Brother Dynard had never expected any of this. He had served the Church of Blessed Abelle well, so he had thought, through his twenties and past his thirtieth birthday; and it had come as a surprise to him when Father Jerak had pointed him south for his mission. "Go to the desert of Behr," the elderly Jerak had told him one cold and wet winter's day in God's Year 47. "If we can turn the good people of Honce from the dark pagan ways of the Samhaists, then surely even the beasts of Behr will not be beyond the call of Blessed Abelle."

"The beasts of Behr," Dynard quietly mouthed, and how many thousand times had he sarcastically repeated that denigrating phrase used by the fair-skinned people of Honce when referring to the darker-skinned people of the great desert to the south of the Belt-and-Buckle. The Behr were nomadic tribesmen, wandering the windblown sands of the desert from oasis to oasis, from the sea in the east to the steppes far in the west. They rode misshapen beasts—humped horses—and spoke in gibberish, so said the men of Honce who knew them. An excitable lot, they were, by all reports, quick to laugh and quicker to anger, and fierce in battle—as would be expected of any animal, so the general reasoning in Honce went.

Thus it was with great trepidation that Brother Dynard had sailed on one of the small, shore-hugging fishing boats from Laird Ethelbert's domain. He hadn't known what to expect of the southerners; could these people even properly communicate? Were they merely savages or animals?

His string of surprises had begun before he had stepped off that fishing boat, for the structures of Jacintha, the largest settlement in Behr, exceeded anything Brother Dynard had ever before seen, even in the great Honce city of Delaval. White towers topped with brightly colored pennants captured his imagination that morning on the boat. And to this day, what he most remembered about Jacintha was the colors of the place, the brilliant hues and dazzling patterns of the clothing and the rugs. So many rugs! The city seemed to be one sprawling marketplace, anchored by the great houses of the tribal sheiks, more elaborate and beautiful than any of the castles of Honce, and shining pink and white with polished stone. The city bristled with energy, with life itself; and it was there that Brother Dynard believed he truly began his journey and found his heart once more. Before Jacintha, he had walked with weariness, dour and depressed, but a few weeks in that place had him alive again and ready to spread the good word of Blessed Abelle.

He spent many weeks in Jacintha, learning the ways and the language of Behr and coming to recognize the ridiculousness of the labels his people placed upon these civilized and cultured people. Then came the months when Brother Dynard had traveled with the nomads through the stinging, windblown sands and in the shadows of the great dunes. He spoke with the tribesmen about his faith, of the great Blessed Abelle who had found the sacred isle and the gemstone gifts of God. He showed them the gemstone powers, using the gray hematite, the soul stone, to heal minor wounds and afflictions. And they had listened, and they had been amused and tolerant, though not amazed at all, to Dynard's surprise. A few even seemed genuinely interested in learning more about this wondrous prophet who had died nearly a half century before. From those potential converts, Dynard had heard of this place, Crezen ilaf Flar, and of the mystics who lived here, the Jhesta Tu.

According to his guides, these mystics could perform feats of magic similar to those Dynard had displayed, only without the use of any props, gemstone or otherwise.

And so, on a blistering summer day nearly six years before, Bran Dynard had arrived in the valley below his present perch, in the dry bed where the spring waters now ran as a river, at the base of the magnificent staircase, built into the mountain wall, that wound up to the lower terraces of this mountain monastery, the Walk of Clouds.

Thinking back to that day now, it seemed to Dynard to be

a lifetime ago. And indeed, in the six years since, he had learned more about himself, about the world, and—he truly believed—about God, than in the three decades he had lived before that.

And he had learned about love, he silently added as his gaze drifted to the solitary figure who had come out on the open walk to perform her morning exercise ritual. Warmth flooded through Dynard as he gazed upon SenWi. Ten years his junior, with delicate, birdlike features and shining black hair that hung to her shoulders, the brown-skinned woman had won his heart almost upon first glimpse. She smiled often—continually, it seemed!—and filled her steps with a bounce and twirl that made her movements more of a dance than a walk.

Dynard watched her precise turns and twists now, as she wove her limbs gracefully and slowly through the ritual of practice, stretching her muscles and playing one against the other in moves to strengthen. The wind gently ruffled her loose-fitting clothing—the off-white ankle-length pants and her rose-colored shining shirt, decorated with intricate embroidery of flowery vines. The light material rippled and whipped, but beneath the clothing stood the anchor of a solid form.

For there was a strength about SenWi, though she wasn't much more than half Dynard's weight.

How could she ever love me? Dynard wondered as he looked down upon the beautiful creature, with her round face, dark brown eyes, and her delicate lips, perfectly shaped and balanced and brought to a pouting peak so that a hint of her white teeth showed when she assumed her typical expression, as if she were always smiling.

How different she was than he, how much more beautiful! Brother Dynard could not help but make these comparisons whenever he looked at her. Her nose was a button, his a hawkish beak. Her body was smooth and flowing, her every movement like the bend of a willow in the wind, while he had ever been a stiff-legged and somewhat hulking figure, with one shoulder forward. His black hair was thinning greatly now, more and more each day it seemed, and his once sharp jawline now possessed ample jowls.

SenWi had not fallen in love with him at first sight, as he had with her. How could she have, after all? But she had listened to his every lecture and participated in every discussion with him in those first months after his arrival, often staying late after all the others had retired, to press Dynard for more stories of the wide world north of the mountains. Dynard could still remember the moment when he had realized that her interest went beyond curiosity in what he knew and had seen, when he had realized that she wanted the stories, not for what they revealed about the world but for what they revealed about him, about this strange white-skinned man from another world. Through Dynard's tales, SenWi had discovered his heart and soul, and somehow—miraculously as far as he was concerned—had fallen in love with him and had agreed not only to formally wed him but also to travel with him back to his home in Pryd.

But first they had their respective tasks to complete.

The thought brought Brother Dynard's gaze to the row of clay pots lining the back of another terrace. The mere sight of the pots, wherein pieces of iron had been placed with wood chips, brought to mind all the condescending and dehumanizing slurs of these southern peoples that Bran Dynard had heard throughout his lifetime. "Beasts of Behr" indeed!

These southern people had found a new way to prepare iron, to strengthen it considerably by transforming it into a metal they called silverel steel. The process was difficult, the items made of it very rare. For a Jhesta Tu mystic, one of the very highest trials was to take this steel and to craft with it a light and mighty sword.

SenWi had been working on hers for years—every day, one fold a session. Brother Dynard remembered the day her work had begun, marked by a grand ceremony that had all the four hundred mystics of the Jhesta Tu assembled on the terraces, praying for her success. Amid the hum of their intoning, the blessed roll of silverel steel had been borne up the mountain stairway by the younger members of the sect. Thin enough to ripple in a gentle wind, the piece was just under four feet wide and, if unrolled, nearly twenty feet long.

Great heated stone wheels had pressed the metal to this thin state, so thin that the entire roll weighed but a few pounds. It had to be light, for this roll—all but the tiny pieces that would be trimmed at the end of the process—would become SenWi's sword, one inch at a time. That was her task: to take this piece of marvelous metal to a specially designed table that had been constructed within her private rooms for the single purpose of crafting her weapon. Many times had Brother Dynard asked about that secret process—asked SenWi and all the masters of the Walk of Clouds who had so warmly welcomed him into their home.

But, alas, this was one secret they would not tell.

Dynard couldn't complain, for the generosity of these mystics had been more than he could ever have imagined. They listened to his stories of Blessed Abelle, of his Church and its precepts, of his hopes of spreading the word. They didn't deny him the opportunity to preach his beliefs to any in the Walk of Clouds, for these mystics saw Bran Dynard as a source of increasing their knowledge, and to them that was all important. In return for his gifts of the gospel of Abelle and his instruction in the use of the magical gemstones, the Jhesta Tu had taught him their disciplines spiritual, mental, and martial—though he hadn't become very accomplished in the latter! They had welcomed his questions and welcomed, too, the blossoming love between this strange man from the northern lands and one of their own.

And they had given Dynard perhaps the greatest gift of all: they had taught him to read their language, which was quite different from that of Honce. And they had loaned him a copy of the Book of Jhest, their defining tome.

So many of their secrets were revealed within the pages of

that massive tome: the lessons of concentration, of movement memory, the dance of the fighter, the dance of the lover. It was all there, and the Jhesta Tu masters offered it freely to this visitor from afar. They had provided Dynard with a similar-size and length book, but one whose pages were as yet unlettered, and had bade him to copy the work so that he could take the duplicate back with him when he returned home, and share it with the people of the northern kingdom.

"But would that not compromise your tactics and understanding of battle?" a shocked Dynard had asked when he had been presented with the intriguing prospect.

Gentle old Master Jiao had answered without hesitation, "Any person capable of understanding our martial dance will have first taken the time to learn the language of Jhest. Even then, the words are meaningless unless one first absorbs the wisdom of the Book of Jhest. Without that wisdom, without that totality of understanding, there is no power; and in one who finds that totality of understanding, there is no threat."

Every day, as SenWi went to her work in which she would accomplish but a single one of the thousand folds that would form her sword, Brother Dynard retired to his own room and sought to precisely copy a few lines of the weighty tome. He had done quite a bit of similar scribing in his first years as a follower of Abelle and always before had approached the task with trepidation, though with devotion. For bending over the table, quill in hand, had brought him aching shoulders and neck, and had left his eyes bleary. His new friends, though, even had an answer for those maladies, in the form of the morning exercises they had taught him, the gentle stretches and the connection to the earth beneath his bare feet.

He stared down at SenWi, glad that she was not aware of him at that moment of her own sweet dance. She rose to the ball of one foot, lifting her arms gracefully as she did, extended her other leg, and used it to send her in a slow turn. As she came around, her left arm swept across, with her right following, fingertips to the sky, moving straight out from her chest.

Her balance shifted and she smoothly landed on her other foot. A series of shoulder twists followed, each arm coming forward in turn, hands sweeping in a rotating motion as they retracted to the opposite shoulder, then slicing back across her chest and rolling forward once again.

She went down in a sudden waist bend, her feet turning, and then she rotated back to her right, where she repeated the motions.

It looked like a dance, a graceful celebration of the wind and the earth and life itself, but Brother Dynard understood it to be much more than that. This was the basic martial training of the Jhesta Tu, and each pivot was designed to put the warrior face-to-face with another opponent. The form on which SenWi was now working, *sing bay wuth,* was designed to defeat three opponents; Dynard had watched it in fierce practice sessions and had come to appreciate its worth.

Even if it had been but a dance, the monk from the north could not deny its simple and graceful beauty.

Nor could he deny the beauty of the dancer, whom he loved beyond anyone he had ever known.

SenWi ended her exercise, standing perfectly erect and still. She closed her eyes and steadied her breathing.

Dynard understood the posture. She was aligning her *ki-chi-kree*, the line of spiritual energy the Jhesta Tu believed ran from the top of one's head, the *ki*, to the groin, the *kree*. To the Jhesta Tu, this *chi* was the line of power, of balance, of strength, and of spirit—the very energy of life itself. Finding perfection of that line, complete alignment, as SenWi was now, was the key to true balance.

She finished by lifting her arms up, thumb tips touching, index fingers touching, in a salute to the morning sun. And then she bowed low as she brought her arms back to her sides, her whole body perfectly still except for the bending at her waist.

Brother Dynard gave a great sigh as the woman walked back into her private quarters to resume work on her sword. Then he, too, faced the rising sun and went through his practice. Not nearly as proficient as SenWi, of course, he neverthe-less managed to get through *sing bay du*, a routine designed to battle two opponents, front and back, with some measure of grace. Then he came to the part he most enjoyed: the stance of the mountain. He found his line of *chi*, head to groin, and con-sciously extended that life energy down his legs and through his feet, rooting himself to the stone of the wide terrace. A strong gust of wind blew by, but Dynard didn't budge. He felt the strength of the earth grasping him, becoming part of him, and felt as if he wouldn't flinch if a large man charged into him at full speed. Once he had achieved the posture, he allowed himself to absorb the sensations of the morning: the smell of the flowers, the warmth of the sun, the soft feel of his light clothing brushing his skin.

He saluted the sun, he bowed, and he went inside to his work.

He couldn't help but notice his old clothing hanging on a rack just inside the door. Like all the common folk of Honce, each of the brothers of Abelle wore a simple woolen tunic that reached to the knees and was typically belted at the waist with a leather cord. The brothers also added a coarse woolen traveling cloak, dark brown in color. Dynard considered that tunic and cloak, then looked at the silk clothing the Jhesta Tu had given him.

"Beasts of Behr," he said with a chuckle and a shake of his large head.

The monk rubbed his face and moved to the desk, where two books sat open and quills and inks of various colors waited.

As she had advanced through the ranks of the Jhesta Tu, SenWi had found her private quarters moved forward and forward, and now, as a budding master, the young woman's rooms were at the very front of the house and cave complex built so high on the mountainside. Several windows lined the front wall of her two-room abode, facing south and east. They were open holes in the stone wall, but SenWi usually kept the heavy drapes pulled aside, except on the coldest of winter nights and when she was at her private work.

Fresh from her morning exercise, she moved to close those drapes, but paused, catching a glimmer of slanting morning sunlight streaming in to illuminate the ivory and silver hilt and crosspiece of her sword. SenWi walked over and gently stroked the carved piece, fashioned to resemble the flared, curving neck of one of the great hooded vipers known in the steppes of To-gai. Shiny silver and smooth white ivory intertwined through the length of the hilt, an artwork in and of itself. SenWi let her fingers trace the crafted lines, taking satisfaction in the solid grip she had created beneath the illusion of beauty. The neck tapered just a bit down to the crosspiece, which was comprised of two thinner rods of shining steel. Even these had been worked intricately by SenWi so that they bent at their respective ends to form snake heads. Above the crosspiece was a steel rod, just under three feet in length.

SenWi looked across the room, to the roll of thin metal, much of it already folded to form the sword's blade. Those first few folds had been critical, for SenWi had to leave an exact opening into which this center pole could be inserted, joining blade to hilt.

SenWi released the hilt and stared at it, hardly believing that years had passed since she had begun this process, since she had crafted the hilt. She remembered the day when the masters had returned it to her, smiling all, with the news that she could begin to craft her sword.

How many thousands of hours had she toiled in this one pursuit, this singular goal? Only now, with the end clearly in sight, did SenWi appreciate how well spent those hours had been. For she had learned so much about herself in these last few years. She had found the limits of her discipline, had learned the patience of a true craftsman. She couldn't help but smile as she recalled days, weeks even, when she had managed to craft only a single line of scales on the serpent-headed hilt.

And now she worked on the blade no less meticulously, bending one by one the hundreds of folds that would comprise it. Each one of those folds consumed the working hours of a single day.

Even on those days when SenWi was able to complete the single fold easily, she could not then go on. There was no "getting ahead" in the crafting of a Jhesta Tu sword. There was only the process, methodical and disciplined.

The woman drew the heavy curtains closed and moved across the small room to the special metal table and the rolled steel. She felt the heat more profoundly with each step forward, for under the table was set a small oven, which she had fired up before going out to her morning exercise. She picked up another block of coke, slipped a heavy glove onto her left hand, and used an iron poker to pull open the small round hatch. She tossed in the fuel, then paused and watched as the orange glow increased, as lines of smoldering fires ran like living caterpillars across the face of the new block. Above it, waves of heat climbed, funneling into the seams of the furnace and table so that it would be properly distributed.

SenWi closed the furnace hatch and moved to the side of the table. To her right lay the beginnings of the shaped blade, with the unfolded metal sheet running to her left like an unwound bolt of silk. Just past the blade, farther to the right, was a raised edge, the apex of the heat zone, slightly glowing in the dimly lit room.

A small diamond-edged rule and cutter, fashioned with a concave edge designed to fit tightly against the edge of the blade facilitated the next part of the process. When SenWi slowly and precisely ran it across the thin sheet, it drew the line of the next fold and also drew a lighter line indicating the breadth of the overlap area. With her bare hand, she lifted the blade and brought it up and over, using all of her focus and discipline to set it precisely in place, so that the scratched line rested perfectly along the raised and heated edge.

Then she removed her glove and let the metal sit, while she

went across the room and prayed, finding her center of focus, aligning her *ki-chi-kree*. When the appropriate time of heating had passed, she took up a pair of tiny hammers and moved back to the table.

SenWi began to sing softly, finding a rhythm and cadence. She began to dance around the table, her hands working slow circles, tap-tapping the metal atop the raised edge, but gently, so as not to tear the already thin sheet. It went on for nearly an hour: the soft singing—chanting really—the graceful steps, each bringing her arms in reach of a different point of the crease; and the continual tapping. Never once in all the days of her work had the woman touched the formed blade with those hammers, despite their proximity. That was the discipline of the dance and the movements, to strike precisely along that single, definitive line.

When she was done, she dropped the hammers and quickly put on the heavy gloves. Moving fast now, she folded the blade back over the raised bar with even pressure, so that the fold line was perfectly in place with the edge of her previous work. She pulled it as tightly as her honed muscles would allow and held it there, squeezing, for a long moment. Satisfied, breathing heavily, SenWi then poured water over the length of the blade, smiling at its hissing protest.

She was equally quick to dry the blade, thus hardening the fold.

Then she prayed some more, and added more coke to the oven.

Then she prayed some more, and when she judged that the table surface was again hot enough, she hoisted a long, thin block of heavy stone and set it in place atop the blade. And another, and another, until the whole blade was covered, the weight of the stones forcing the folded metal tight against the blazing metal surface.

SenWi went to take her morning meal. She hoped that she would see her lover there, though she knew that he was nearing the end of his scribing and was working furiously so that his finish would coincide with her own. Bran Dynard wanted them to be on the road in late spring or early summer at the very latest.

Her work this day wasn't nearly done, of course. When she returned, she had to remove the stones and cool the blade, and then she would use a diamond-encrusted file to finish the tip of the last fold, scraping it down, hour by hour, so that it fell into exact place of the triangular sword tip.

Tomorrow, she'd do it again, exactly the same way.

Enough tomorrows would produce the sword. And they would give her the sense of accomplishment and ownership: that she had taken a simple sheet of metal and so crafted it into a beautiful weapon, a true work of art, an extension of her martial training.

He wasn't shivering with cold—winter was surely loosening its grip on the land—but his fingers trembled so badly that he had to stop.

Brother Dynard sat back, gave a frustrated snort, then stood up, abandoning the moment that he thought would bring him triumph. He paced away from the desk, determined not to look back.

But he did glance over his shoulder, to see the large volume, the Book of Jhest, opened wide, with all but one of its many pages turned over to the left now.

Only one to go. Half, actually, for in the second book similarly opened on the slightly inclining desktop, that last page was half written. Half a page to copy of all the great tome—except for the still-blank two opening pages, which were customarily left so that the scribe could preface the work after completion with a letter to its intended recipient. Up to this point, Dynard had been moving on a roll, momentum gained for the final push and with the hope and expectation that this morning would mark the last day of his copying.

Then had come Dynard's moment of doubt. For the first time since he had embarked upon this task of expanding his boundaries of understanding and spirituality itself, the monk from Honce had come to realize that this particular part of the journey would be a finite thing: that his work here would end.

For months, Dynard had been lost in the swirls of the Jhesta writing, the gracefully curving lines and symbols drawing him into contemplation as surely as any chanting ever could. The concentration of exact copying brought him into that same trancelike and prayerful state of meditation. For months, his work had been his purpose and his life; he knew that he could not underestimate the importance of this. This tome that he would bring back to the north could change the very scope of the Church of Blessed Abelle.

Those thoughts weren't the source of his trembling now, though. With the end of this part of his spiritual journey so clearly in sight, Brother Dynard had finally begun to look toward the next road—the physical road—across the deserts to the coast and north to the mountains and, finally, the sea.

He knew well the perils of that road: the robbers and knaves, the warfare between the rival tribes of the Behr, the snakes and great cats and other monstrous animals, the dreadful and often vengeful power of the sea itself. Even if he arrived back in Honce, around the mountains and into Ethelbert Holding, the road inland to Pryd was a graveyard for foolhardy travelers.

Dynard looked back at the book. Had he done all of this, had he buried himself within the curving lines of understanding and enlightenment, had he created this copy, this artwork, only to have its illuminated and illuminating pages rot in a gully in the rain? Or to have those soft pages used by some ignorant knave to wipe the shite from his arse?

His chest heaved in short gasps. He closed his eyes and told himself to calm down. In a sudden fit of nervous energy, the monk raced out of the room, down the hallway, then out onto the terrace.

The wind blew fiercely this day, dark clouds rushing overhead. Few of the Jhesta Tu were outside, no clothes were drying on the lines, and most of the flowers had been brought inside. His fears churning his stomach, his arms and legs trembling,

Brother Dynard walked to the far edge of the terrace, to the rail and the thousand-foot drop to the valley below. His knuckles whitened as he grasped that railing, partly to secure himself and partly out of anger—anger at himself for being so weak in the face not of failure but of triumph.

"I am surely a fool," he said, his words whipped to nothingness by the gusting wind. A self-deprecating chuckle was similarly diminished, as the monk considered the simple humanness of his failure. He recalled a day from his youth in Chud, a small village across the forest from Pryd. With his father, mother, and two sisters, young Bran Dynard had been walking the forest path, a pilgrimage of sorts, to see the new stone chapel being built by this new Church that was sweeping the land, and sweeping the Samhaist religion before it.

Bran's father had never followed the Samhaists and held some anger against them that young Bran did not understand. Not until years later, after his father's death—indeed at the occasion of his father's funeral in Chud—would he learn that his father's twin brother had been sacrificed by the Samhaists; they always killed one of any twins, considering the second born to be an appropriate offering to their gods.

On that road that long-ago day, the family had come to know that they weren't alone. Sounds to the side of the path, in the shadows of the forest, had warned them of robbers, or worse. They moved more swiftly—the smoke of Pryd's fireplaces was in sight up ahead. Bran had seen the sign of danger first, a flash of red in the dark shadows, and on his call of "Powries!" his father had gathered up his younger sister, his mother had grabbed the hand of the other girl, and all had sprinted for the village. For powries, the bloody-cap dwarves, were not ordinary thieves seeking gold or silver—of which the family had none. They sought only human blood in which they could dip their enchanted blood-red berets.

To this day, Dynard didn't know whether or not there really were powries on that forest road. Perhaps it had been a red-headed bird or the bright behind of a wild tusker pig. But he remembered that flight and the sensations that had accompanied it. Barely into his teens, he had dutifully taken up the rear, his father's spear in hand, and had even lagged behind the others so that his engagement with the powries would not force any of them, particularly his father, into the battle. What Dynard remembered most keenly was that he had not been afraid. At that first sighting of the red, he had been terrified, of course; but during the run, his helpless family before him, he had felt only a sort of elation, the pumping of his blood, the determination that these monsters would not wash in the blood of his loved ones, whatever he had to do.

It wasn't until the very end, his family already reaching the wooden gates of Pryd and with only fifty yards left before him, that young Bran Dynard had felt the return of fear, of a terror more profound than anything he had ever known. He was not carrying the spear, but he didn't even know at the terrifying moment that he had dropped it.

By the time he reached the gates, his cheeks were wet with tears, and he stood there before his family and the townsfolk who had come out to see what the commotion was all about, trembling and sobbing and feeling a failure.

A couple of the townsfolk had laughed—probably not at him, though it seemed that way to the teenager. His father, though, had clapped him hard on the shoulder and tousled his hair, thanking him for his courage over and over again.

Bran hadn't believed him and felt himself a coward, but then one man dressed in cumbersome brown robes had come forward and had wrapped him in a hug. He pushed Bran back to arms' length and saluted him. That was when Bran Dynard had first met Father Jerak of Chapel Pryd.

"Is it not strange that only at the end of our run, when the goal seems attainable, that we allow our fears to surface?" Jerak had said to him, and those words echoed now in his mind as he stood on that balcony of the Walk of Clouds.

The monk stepped back from the railing and turned into the fierce wind. He spread his feet shoulders' width apart and brought his arms up before him, entwining his fingers and lifting them high over his head. He found his center of energy, his *chi*, as the Jhesta Tu had taught him, and he extended that line of power down through his legs and feet and into the stone of the terrace.

He stood against the breeze, rooted as firmly as any tree, as solidly as any stone. With his internal strength, he denied the wind, and while his light clothing flapped wildly, Brother Bran Dynard did not move the slightest bit.

In that place and in that time, he found again his heart. Some time later, he went back inside, back to his work; and before the last rays of the sun disappeared from the light of his western window, he closed both books, his task complete.

Only reluctantly did SenWi relinquish her hold on the diamond-faced file, laying the wondrous tool, one of only three such items in all the world, down at her side.

There was no need to continue; the sides of the triangular tip were smooth and even, and no amount of working them would make them more perfect.

The tip was done. The wrapping was done. The final heating and beating of the metal was done, including the attachment of the blade to the hilt and crosspiece. Earlier that same morning, SenWi had finished her own scribing, marking the lines, both delicate and bold, of the flowering vines enwrapping the length of the blade. These symbols, so precise, tied the sword back to the Hou-lei traditions, the warrior cult from which had long ago sprung the Jhesta Tu. There could be no mistaking one of these blades, for there was nothing like them in all the world. The wrapped metal ensured that the blade would only sharpen with use, as layers wore away to even finer edges.

Looking at her sword now, this weapon of few equals, crafted with her own hands, SenWi felt a sense of her past, of her kinship to those who had come before, perfecting their methods, defining the very nature of her existence in their accrued centuries of wisdom. She appreciated them now, more fully perhaps than ever before.

With hands moist and trembling, SenWi lifted the sword and felt its balance. Assuming a two-handed grip on the hilt, she stepped into a fighting stance and brought the weapon slowly through a series of thrusts and parries, as she had done so many thousands of times with wooden practice blades on the terraces of the Walk of Clouds.

She knew that a wondrous journey was before her, with the man she loved, on a road that would lead her farther from her home than she had ever imagined.

Holding this sword, this tie to her past, this tangible reminder of all that she had learned, SenWi was not afraid.

In a display of dazzling colors and sound, of snapping pennants and richly colored clothing, the entire body of Jhesta Tu mystics stood on the terraces, flying bridges, and walkways of their mountain monastery. They sang and played exotic instruments: carved flutes, harps small and large, and tinny, sharp, and strangely melodious four-stringed instruments the like of which Bran Dynard had never before seen.

Sounds, smells, and colors everywhere greeted the couple as they made their way along the terraces. Propelled by the dance-inspiring music, Brother Dynard picked up the pace as they neared the end of that last terrace, the entrance to the long stone stairway that had been carved into the mountain wall eons ago. As they approached, SenWi paused, holding his hand and holding him back.

The monk looked at his new wife and recognized the myriad emotions flowing through her. This was the home she had known for most of her adult life; how terrifying it must now be for her to walk down these steps, knowing that perhaps she would never again make that long and arduous climb.

Dynard waited patiently as the moments slipped past, as the celebration continued around them. He noticed the great masters of the Jhesta Tu, standing in a line beside the stairway entrance, and he saw SenWi's stare focusing that way.

One by one, those masters nodded and smiled, offering both permission and encouragement; finally SenWi glanced over at Bran, smile widening, then pulled him along.

Down the couple went, away from the Walk of Clouds. Neither of them would ever return.

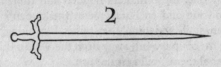

2

MY DEAR BROTHERS

My Dear Brothers of Blessed Abelle,

I had no idea how wide the world really was. I thought that in my studies I had learned the truth of our lands, of God and of Man. I believed that within the tomes of the philosophers and the fathers, and within the writings of Blessed Abelle himself, I could find the entirety of human existence and purpose, and the hope of ascension beyond this physical experience.

This is what we all hope, of course. This is our prayer and our faith and our reason. These truths shown us by Blessed Abelle have loosened the fear-inspired hold of the Samhaists, and rightly so!

Knowing all of this prepared me for my *Journey Proselyt*, so I believed. With wisdom in hand, I could travel the world secure in my beliefs and in the notion that I could extend those truths to those I encountered. My confidence in the teachings of our faith lent me confidence in the validity of my mission. And, of course, such conviction of the ultimate truths of our faith also bolstered my own courage, for my understanding of what will ultimately befall me, of the existence my spirit will find when my physical being is no more, grants me freedom from fear of the specter of death. Faith led me out of Chapel Pryd. Faith allowed me to place one foot before the other, to travel through lands unknown and dangers unforeseen, though surely anticipated. Faith allowed me to meet peoples of other cultures and lands, and to tell them with confidence of the revelations of Blessed Abelle and the sacred gemstone gifts of God.

With all that knowledge and all that confidence, I hardly expected to find, out there in the world so wide, cultures and ways beyond my expectations. With all the surety afforded by the supreme calm of blessed insight, I hardly expected that I would find my horizons widened even more!

I pray to Blessed Abelle, as do we all, and to the God he showed us; and there is no tremor in my voice—not of doubt, at least!—unless it is the usual shakiness I feel when I attempt to communicate to those so far greater than I.

And yet, my brothers, for all the beauty of Blessed Abelle and for all the completeness of serenity in his teachings, I found myself with eyes wide and heart opened once more. For I have discovered that we who follow the words of Blessed Abelle are not as alone in our faith as we assume. For I have traveled among the Jhesta Tu, generous in spirit and wise in nature. The Jhesta Tu, who understand the same sacred powers offered by our godly gemstone gifts. These mystics, ancient in their ways, are as akin to Blessed Abelle as any man might be. They, too, have found the strength of God, not from gemstones falling from heaven to the shores of holy Pimaninicuit Isle, but within themselves! With energy internal, they replicate the beauty of godly magic.

Are these Jhesta Tu who we shall become?

I do not know, and I do not elevate them above Blessed Abelle, surely. And yet I must insist that from these Jhesta Tu we will find a continuation of our own road to understanding. We must learn from them as they will learn from us—and they have already shown the willingness and the hope that such will occur.

Thus I have copied the Book of Jhest, the foundation of understanding of the Jhesta Tu. In the final measure of my mission, this will prove the most fundamental and important accomplishment of all. Study the Book of Jhest, I beg each of you, with eyes wide and heart open. Infuse yourself with its wisdom and blend the revelations within with the truth we know from Blessed Abelle.

I walked a road with sure strides, but I had no idea that the road would take my spirit to places it had not yet tread. I walked a road to enhance the lives of those pagans I encountered, but I had no idea that the road would brighten my own understanding. I am not afraid of these revelations and the greater scope of miracle, and neither should you be.

Turn these pages with reverent hands. Bask in the words of wisdom of the Jhesta Tu, and find in them enough similarities to show us that the only falsities in our understanding of the truths of Blessed Abelle are the limitations that we naturally place upon those teachings. This was my wont, for never did I imagine the true width of faith's horizon.

Penned this day of Bafway, God's Year 54
Brother Bran Dynard, humble servant of Chapel Pryd

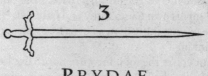

3

PRYDAE

With backs stooped from hours and hours of heavy labor, the peasant workers building the road south of the holding of Pryd were most commonly seen with their hands placed firmly on their aching lower backs. They didn't look behind them often as they dug and smoothed the ground between two forested hills, for if they did, they would see the stone tower of Castle Pryd, red pennant emblazoned with the black wolf waving in the brisk breeze above it: a poignant reminder of how short a distance they had actually gone in these weeks of brutal labor and how inconceivable—to the peasants, at least—a distance they had yet to go.

Work had begun on the project in the summer of the previous year. The road itself was not an elaborate affair, merely a widening and smoothing of the existing southern cart paths, with the ground pounded flat and strategically reinforced with wide flagstones. Laird Pryd had been quite pleased with the progress made in the late summer weeks and those of autumn, but all those involved—particularly the peasants pressed into this hard labor—had been quite dismayed to find, when the snow had at last relinquished its grip on the land, that much of their work had been damaged by the frost heaves of the unusually harsh winter.

"At least I won't be needing to clean under me fingernails," one man griped to another as they stood beside the road in a moment of respite, their heavy flagstones set on the ground before them, upright and leaning against their bare, badly bruised, and always scuffed shins.

"That's because ye got no fingernails," the other replied, and he held up his own hand, filthy and battered. "By the time we make the mountain shadow, all of us'll be missing more than that, I'm thinking."

"Bah, but you're the fool, for we're not to live long enough to ever cool in the shadows of them great mountains."

"Come on, then, the two of you," came a call from up the road. The pair turned to see a soldier of Pryd, splendid astride his tall horse and in his shining breastplate of bronze. With each pace of the mount, the hard sheath of the short sword on the soldier's hip made a clapping sound against the iron studs of his leather skirt. "They're needing stones up front. Now get about it."

Both peasants sucked in their breaths, bent their knobbly knees, and hooked their arms under the bottoms of the large stones, then hoisted them and began waddling away.

"Weren't that Doughbeard's boy?" one gasped to the other when they had moved beyond the soldier's range of hearing.

"Aye, and ain't he looking all pretty up there on his fine horse?"

"So many o' them young and strong ones do, while our old bones creak and crack."

"Creak and crack! And swim in the mud and horses' shite."

"And work all the day and all o' the night," said the other, taking up the cadence and the nonsensical rhyme.

"Until them soldiers be out o' our sight!" the other went on, and he cackled with laughter between the grunts.

His friend started to cackle as well, but broke off, feeling an impact and the sound of a sharp rap against the front of the stone he was carrying. He staggered back a step, managed a "what?" and then lost his words and his breath as he recognized what had struck his stone was a stone-headed throwing axe now lying on the ground before him.

Had he not been carrying a flagstone against his chest like some unintended breastplate, that axe wouldn't now be on the ground, he knew.

"What are ye about?" his friend asked, staggering to a stop

and turning. He followed the ashen-faced gaze of the stunned man to the weapon.

"Bloody caps!" the man shouted, and he dropped his stone and ran back toward his friend, who still stood there, holding the stone that had saved his life, and staring slack-jawed at the axe.

"Go, old fool! Go!" the fleeing man shouted, grabbing his friend's shoulder as he raced past, turning him; but as he did, his friend lost his grip on the stone and it crashed to the ground, clipping his foot and bringing a great howl from him.

The fleeing man didn't wait, didn't slow at all. He ran back up the road, toward that fluttering pennant, screaming "Bloody caps!" at the top of his lungs.

"Your scouts were correct," young Prince Prydae said to the guard captain standing beside him. They had moved secretly into place, under the cover of the brush and trees to the side of the road. A hundred yards or so farther down the road, all the workers were running and waving their arms frantically, the calls of "Powries!" and "Bloody caps!" filling the air.

The nobleman slid his leather gauntlets onto his hands and stepped into his chariot—the most magnificent war cart in all the holding. It was bordered on three sides by waist-high walls of hard oak and leather, a running black wolf painted on either side, silver trim running the length of it. The wheels were heavy and sturdy, with spokes as thick as a strong man's forearms, and hubs set with scythe blades that stuck out for more than a foot. The pulling team, a pair of Laird Pryd's strongest horses, pawed the ground, eager to run.

To any onlookers, young Prince Prydae did not appear out of place there. He stood strong and tall, his blue eyes set with determination in a face not unaccustomed to scowling. When he did so scowl, Prydae's thick brow furrowed such that it formed a triangular chasm atop his long, thin nose; and people in all the region for many years had known to beware the "sharp shadows of anger" from the men of the line of Pryd!

Prydae's other features were no less powerful: a strong chin and high-boned cheeks that bespoke his noble heritage. His black hair was neatly trimmed about his ears; and thick sideburns ran down to touch the thin jawline beard, which blended in with a thin goatee and mustache, as was the fashion of the day. He wore a bronze breastplate, fitted perfectly to his muscular frame, leaving his arms bare. Many nobleman warriors had taken to wearing iron instead of the softer bronze, but Prydae preferred this piece precisely because the soft metal had allowed his craftsman to decorate it with grand designs. Right at the ridge below the breasts was a line of running wolves, three across and nose to tail. The back of the piece boasted clever swirls and geometric shapes, and even contained the "fisted P," a letter formed from an upraised forearm and cocked and balled fist, the emblem of the line of Pryd.

Prydae did use iron for his open-faced helmet and for the metal greaves overlaid onto thick leather breeches. His belt was leather, too, wrapped in a bright red sash of fine fabric; and complementing that, a red ribbon was tied about Prydae's right upper arm, a black one tight about his left biceps, a sign of his station in the Holdings of Pryd. Only Prydae or his father, Pryd, could by law wear such distinctive armbands within the holding.

"Well, my friend, shall we go and remind the peasants of the importance of the House of Pryd?" the young nobleman remarked, turning a sly smile at the garrison captain.

"Indeed, my liege."

"Take care the powries, for they are no easy foe."

"Yes, my liege."

Prydae gave a nod to his trusted soldier, a man hand-picked by his father to watch over him, then cracked his whip. The horses burst from the brush, charging up the short incline to the road and thundering down onto it, the chariot bouncing wildly. Prydae held his stance securely, urging the galloping horses on even harder.

He cracked the whip above his head and waved the peasants out of the way—and how they scrambled, diving from the road!

Prydae soon came in sight of the one mounted soldier who had been at the forefront of the work area and was now bringing up the rear of the fleeing peasants, shouting at them to run for their lives. The man was lurching, one shoulder forward, and Prydae noted the flash of red behind him, the telltale shimmer of the blood-soaked berets.

More peasants dove to the side; one was not quite fast enough and got clipped by Prydae's team and sent flying from the road. Before the young nobleman, the wounded soldier seemed hardly in control of his mount anymore, but the well-trained horse veered out of the way just in time, leaving the racing chariot a straight line to the charging bloody-cap dwarves.

Those powries were odd little creatures, each standing under five feet, with a broad, thick torso and shoulders at least as wide as those of a large man, but with spindly little limbs, whose size was exaggerated by the bulky, padded, and metal-stripped armor the dwarves wore around their barrel-like torsos and by the fact that the powries were almost always bearded, with bushy, wild-flying hair sticking out from under their caps. Prydae was seasoned enough not to underestimate the strength in those spindly limbs, though—as he was reminded now by a dwarf, near the front of their charging line, who carried an iron-headed axe so huge and bulky that few humans could have wielded it.

With typical ferocity, the ten bloodthirsty dwarves didn't turn from the sudden appearance and charge of the prince and his entourage.

Prydae grasped one of the small iron-tipped spears set at the front of his chariot, and hoisted it high. Before him, the powries parted ranks, some scrambling wide, others barely sidestepping the charging horses, no doubt to try to strike at him as the chariot raced past. Prydae let the scythe blades of his wheels handle the immediate threat, the spinning weapons slicing deep into the surprised dwarves, taking a leg from one, disemboweling another, and hooking the leather tunic of a third, who was trying to scramble aside, pulling it along in a bone-crunching tumble. Then the prince threw his spear deep into the chest of a powrie at the side of the road.

He had no time to grab another spear, for a dwarf at the left side of the road before him was already launching an axe his way. Prydae shifted his reins to his right hand and cracked his whip at the dwarf with his left. He felt the thump as the axe smacked against his breastplate and bounced aside, clipping his chin and drawing a line of blood.

Prydae growled through the pain and pulled hard on the reins, wanting to slow his team, wanting to get back around in time to repay that particular dwarf before his soldiers killed them all.

As the chariot slowed, Prydae let go of the reins altogether and grabbed his shield and leaped from the chariot back, drawing his sword as he went.

The powries were scattering now as the full force rolled over them; in those initial moments of combat, more than half were down. Prydae did not lose sight of the axe thrower in that turmoil, noting the dwarf scrambling toward the trees. Running full out, Prydae's longer legs chewing up the ground, he caught up to the wretch in the shadows of the nearest boughs.

The powrie spun to meet the charge, an axe in either hand. It wasted no time, but came forward wildly, slashing left and right.

Prydae dodged back, avoiding one cut, and got his shield out in front to block the second. His arm went numb under the force of the heavy blow, and good luck alone prevented him from having his arm cloven, for the axe crunched right through his wood and leather shield, hooking in place.

Prydae retracted the shield arm hard, tugging the axe along with it. The powrie started to tug back, but it saw the danger as Prydae stabbed ahead powerfully with his iron-bladed sword.

Metal rang against metal as the powrie cunningly parried with its free axe. But the dwarf lost its grip on that second, trapped axe, with the prince spinning and tugging it free. Prydae threw his arm out behind him, dropping his shield and hardly interrupting his momentum as he charged forward, stabbing again and again.

The powrie frantically slashed with its axe, clipping Prydae's sword, though the prince was already retracting it anyway. The powrie managed to retreat enough so that the prince's next strike fell short of the mark.

More important to Prydae was that he saw his attacks were keeping the dwarf moving and dancing, preventing it from reaching for its third axe that Prydae saw strapped behind its left shoulder. Fortunately, since its left hand was the empty one, the dwarf could not both fight and retrieve the remaining weapon.

And Prydae was determined not to give the creature a chance. He stepped boldly ahead, and the powrie's axe rang out against his thrusting sword. He stepped and slashed; the powrie darted back to his left, just under the blow, then riposted hard with a slash and back slash of the axe, forcing Prydae to throw back his hips. When the powrie tried to use this apparent opening to toss its axe to its left hand, freeing the right so it could easily reach its other weapon, Prydae came forward again.

The powrie had barely caught the axe in its left hand. Recognizing its own vulnerability, it simply threw the weapon forward.

But Prydae didn't flinch, ignoring the dull metallic ring as the axe bounced off his breastplate. The powrie had its right arm back, reaching for the axe, presenting Prydae with a fine opening through the armhole of its jerkin.

The nobleman warrior took that opening. He slammed in hard against the dwarf, wrapping his free arm around the beast to keep its arm trapped between them, while his sword sank deep through the armpit.

The pair went down hard, the impact of the ground only furthering the sword's bite. His face barely inches from the powrie's grimace, Prydae heard its growl and groan. He felt the wretched little creature tense beneath him, tightening every one of its muscles as if it meant to simply crush the sword within it!

And still the powrie growled long and low, a rumbling breath of denial.

It went on and on and on, and Prydae did not let go, did not lessen the pressure on the stabbing blade. He tried to turn his sword, which brought a different pitch to the powrie's groaning protest, and the vicious dwarf even tried to bite Prydae's face.

But there was little energy in its lunge, and gradually Prydae felt the powrie's muscles relax. The growling stopped and the dwarf lay very still, eyes wide and staring at Prydae with hatred.

They were dull eyes, though, with no life behind them.

Prydae pulled himself off the dwarf and yanked his sword free. He stood and surveyed the area. One fight was still raging, but his soldiers seemed to have it under complete control, with several of the mounted warriors surrounding a single dwarf who already had at least five spears sticking from him.

"Seven of ten dead, my prince," a soldier reported, trotting his mount up beside the blood-spattered nobleman. A shriek rent the air, and the pair glanced over to see the surrounded powrie finally go down. When it tried to rise, one of the soldiers guided his horse over and had the beast stomp the dwarf flat.

"Eight," the soldier corrected. "Two have fled to the forest, but we will hunt them down."

Prydae nodded, then moved toward his abandoned chariot. "And what of my people?"

The soldier quickly dismounted so that he would be walking beside his prince and not towering above him. "A few minor injuries," he explained. "One man dropped a heavy stone on his foot as he tried to flee. That might be the worst of it. With all the talk of powries of late, the peasants were well prepared to run away."

"Double the guard along the road," Prydae ordered as he reached the back of the chariot. He paused and reconsidered. "Nay, triple it. We have no need for another display of force anytime soon. The peasants understand that we protect them; their complaints will be fewer. So let us dissuade the fierce dwarves or any other monsters that might be about from even beginning such a battle."

"Aye, my liege."

Prydae waved the man away and pulled himself up into the chariot. The well-schooled team had not continued after he had leaped from it, nor had they veered off the road. Prydae turned them around until he had them trotting back down the road toward the castle of his father.

He kept his eyes straight ahead, a look of "royal calm"—as Laird Pryd liked to call it—upon his face as he guided the magnificent chariot past his soldiers and the gathering of appreciative peasants. The soldiers fell into ranks behind him, adding to his splendor; the peasants called his name, cheering.

Prydae held his royal calm and slowly paced his team past them all. The battle had gone exactly as he had hoped it would. When reliable reports of powries gathering in the area had come to him, along with many reports of grumbling among the workers, he had seen the potential of quelling both problems. And so he had lain in wait with his choice warriors, and with one decisive charge they had defeated the powrie threat as well as the chorus of complaints. And not a soldier was badly injured, and the few injured peasants would likely heal.

It had been a good day's work.

Chapel Pryd, a stone structure that could hold nearly four hundred people in its wide and long nave, was only a short walk from the much more dominating stone structure of the holding, the castle of Laird Pryd itself. But to old Father Jerak, the number of required paces to go from one building to the other seemed greater and greater each day.

He could count those paces, too, and easily for the increasing stoop of his back had his eyes looking at his feet, and it was only with increasing effort that he was able to look up. He didn't complain, though, as he and Brother Bathelais made their way up the narrow stair to Castle Pryd's portcullis and then past the guard towers and up a longer flight of stairs to the audience halls of the laird, which were set more than halfway up the tall tower that served as the principal keep.

They were welcomed without question and admitted without formal introduction, for visits to Laird Pryd of the two presiding holy men of his holding were not uncommon and of late had become a more-than-weekly matter.

As usual, Laird Pryd was sitting on his huge oaken throne, its arm rests gilded, its high back bejeweled. He was the same age as Father Jerak, and, indeed, the two had known each other for more than forty years, since the then-young Jerak had been assigned to Pryd Holding after his training in the mother chapel of Abelle, along the coast to the north. Unlike Father Jerak, though, the laird didn't so obviously show his age. He sat straight and tall; and while his hair was now more salt than pepper, and perhaps his blue eyes did not hold their previous luster, he kept his shoulders squared, his jaw high, and his beard and hair meticulously trimmed.

Behind him and to the side stood another aged man, with hawkish features and a scowl that only intensified whenever the monks of Abelle entered the room. Jerak paid Rennarq, Laird Pryd's close adviser, no heed, but Bathelais always took note of that scowl. Rennarq was rumored to be a staunch Samhaist, though not openly, of course.

The two monks moved up before the throne and bowed to their laird. Jerak was glad that Bathelais held his arm, for without that support, he feared that he would have tumbled at Laird Pryd's feet.

"You seem rather tired today, old priest," Laird Pryd remarked, and at his side, his sentry snickered.

"Our work has been long, Laird," Brother Bathelais answered.

"That is the way of things."

Jerak forced his eyes up to meet those of the laird. Whenever Pryd made that particular remark—"That is the way of things"—his tone became dismissive. "That is the way of things," Jerak understood, meant that there was nothing Laird Pryd meant to do to remedy it.

"We have come to discuss the matter of your son," Father Jerak said.

"The matter? Whatever matter my son might have is hardly a concern of yours."

Father Jerak bowed in deference at the not so subtle reminder that he and all the brothers of Abelle were allowed and recognized in Pryd Holding at the sufferance of the laird. Again, the old monk was glad of the physical support of Brother Bathelais.

"He drives the peasants hard, Laird," Jerak said.

"Their work is important."

"We spend all the night with the soul stones, Laird, alleviating their aches and trying to mend fingers cracked from digging and hammering and carrying those huge flagstones."

"I am grateful for your efforts, I assure you. But that is your duty, is it not?"

"Their maladies outpace our abilities to heal them," Father Jerak began to explain, trying to keep his voice steady in the face of Pryd's continuing dismissive tone.

"Winter will come soon enough, we all know, and they will have the quiet months in which to recover."

"My laird—"

"This business only aids your Church, as well, can you not agree?" Pryd interrupted. "My son, serving as my voice, shows the peasants the way to a better life through their toil. That toil begets suffering, of course, and so you serve a heroic and healing role, one that no doubt enamors the peasants of your Blessed Abelle. I believe that my son's tactics serve you well in your continuing duel with the Samhaists for the souls of the people." He offered a smile that sent a shiver coursing along Jerak's spine, and Jerak glanced past him to note the scowl of Rennarq.

"Ah, those marvelous and sacred gemstones," Pryd went on. "So much more convincing must they be when you put them to use in such a practical and helpful manner as healing the injuries and maladies of dim-witted peasants!"

It was a joke, of course, and one that had Laird Pryd and all his guards laughing, but only with great effort was Father Jerak tactfully able to join in.

"Perhaps there is a compromise to be found," the old monk suggested.

The smile disappeared in a blink from Pryd's face. "All the lairds have agreed on the construction of these roads, and for good reason."

Before he could go on, a side door of the audience chamber banged open and Prydae strode into the room, still wearing his battle gear and still with the stains of powrie blood and of his own, where dried blood had crusted on his beard.

"Powries," he explained. "A band on the road."

Father Jerak gasped.

"Our healing skills will be needed at the chapel," Brother Bathelais said.

Father Jerak noted the dismissive look young Prydae turned on the holy men at that moment, a typical response from the prince, whom Jerak believed viewed the Church of Abelle as a rival to the power and wealth of his forthcoming inheritance. No doubt, Jerak supposed, that crafty old Rennarq often whispered disparaging remarks into Prydae's ear.

"Yes, some of the peasants were injured," Prydae said, looking back at his father. "Unfortunate."

"As they often have been injured since you began your work on the roads," Father Jerak dared to say, and Brother Bathelais gave his arm an insistent squeeze.

"Truly, I should think that you would wish the roads completed," Prydae was quick to reply, "that you can spread the word of your God and bring more and more folk under your control."

"They are not under our control, young prince," Father

Jerak corrected. "They serve beside us because they, too, see the truth of the word of Blessed Abelle and the hopes of eternal life and redemption."

Behind the throne, Rennarq snorted.

"As you will," Prydae said with a bow.

Father Jerak stared at the prince a moment longer, then turned back to Laird Pryd and gave a stiff bow. He and Brother Bathelais took their leave immediately, knowing that they had much work to do.

"Step lightly with the brothers of Abelle," Laird Pryd warned his son as soon as the holy men had gone. "Their Church is displacing the Samhaists in the hearts of the commoners and is fast becoming a dominant force in all Honce. It would not do your aspirations well to turn them against you."

"You overstate their hand, my laird," Rennarq dared to put in.

"And you have stubbornly denied the obvious for more than a quarter of a century, my old friend," Pryd replied.

"The lairds rule Honce, not the Church," Prydae remarked, and then pointedly added, "Not either Church."

"And the wise lairds will see the Church of Abelle for what it is and use it to their best designs," Pryd went on, directing his words to his son. "There is talk of unity in the land, the likes of which I have not heard in my lifetime, the likes of which have not been known in Honce since the Samhaists ruled both body and soul." He looked back at Rennarq again, and teased, "The golden age of Honce?"

Rennarq couldn't help but smile at that, and he didn't voice his belief that such an estimate might not be far from the truth.

"That talk is fostered by the agreement to build the roads," Prydae observed. "What laird has refused his resources in this endeavor?"

"None of the thirty," Pryd answered. "Because the driving force is that Delaval City, on the Masur Delaval, has proceeded with their road building, with or without our agreement."

"I have heard the marvels of the Delaval roads," said Prydae. "Lined in iron, so say the traveling skalds."

"Indeed, and in this endeavor, if we are behind, we risk irrelevance. The world is changing before our eyes and it is up to us to determine where we will fit into those changes. Think of the trade when the roads connect! And we will be better able to move our armies."

"To drive the powries from the land."

"And to exterminate the goblins," Laird Pryd said, his old eyes gleaming, for he still felt the pangs from a wound in his hip, an injury received in his youth from a goblin spear. "We may tame the land, at long last, but only if we are able to work in coordination with the other lairds of Honce and only if we can keep the peasants content through the years of trial they will no doubt face.

"And that is where the brothers of Abelle will prove their usefulness. Their gemstones heal the wounds even as their promises of eternal life strengthen the spirit. The Samhaists ever ruled by fear, but the brothers of Abelle have found a greater means. They guide with promises that no man or woman could resist. See the light of Abelle and you will find eternal rest. Hear the words of Abelle and you will one day be reunited with your loved ones who have died. What mother could deny her desire to one day see again her lost child?"

"These promises have been made before, many times," Rennarq reminded.

"But the brothers of Abelle strengthen such promises with the gemstones," Laird Pryd explained. "They have the gifts of God to prove their words."

Prydae looked at his father, studying the man from head to foot. "You believe them," he said at length. "You believe the way of Blessed Abelle."

Pryd shrugged, but he wasn't quick to offer a denial.

The prince looked back at Rennarq, whose expression clearly showed that Prydae's words had hit the mark.

"Would it be so bad a thing if Abelle were proven right?"

Laird Pryd replied. "If his promises were true? You are a young man yet, my son, and do not concern yourself with questions of what might follow this life. Even in your battles, you do not believe that death will find you. But I am old—every day I awaken to feel the creeping of age in my bones and in my heart. Many are the nights that I close my eyes and wonder if I ever shall open them again."

Prydae walked to the edge of the dais and sat down. He had never heard such words as this from the unshakable Laird of Pryd before. A frown creased his face as he considered the words of his father and mentor.

"The peasants cheered you in your splendid armor?" Pryd asked.

Prydae glanced back at him, and did manage a smile. "Four powries fell to my hand—my soldiers will claim that I killed six single-handedly. Of course the peasants were appreciative."

"As they should be. We offer them protection. We give them their very lives, every day. And we ask little in return."

Laird Pryd gave a chuckle as he considered his own words. "Nay," he corrected, "we ask nothing of them. We demand what we must, and they have no choice but to comply. That is the way of it."

"They would be wandering sheep, fodder for the powries, without us," Prydae reminded, and his father nodded.

"As it has always been and as it will always be," the laird remarked.

"The young one is brash and headstrong," Bathelais observed, not for the first time, when he and old Jerak finally walked out of Castle Pryd's main gates.

While Bathelais's words were spoken in a jesting and almost dismissive manner, Father Jerak didn't share his amusement. "And we both know that the wretch Rennarq whispers in his ear," he said. "Prince Prydae cares nothing for the suffering of the peasants. I wonder if he even hears their groans."

"Like so many noblemen, he views the world beyond the concerns of the individual," reasoned Bathelais. "He sees the gains the roads might bring to all of us, beyond the pain some might suffer in creating them."

"That is the place of the laird, it would seem," said Jerak. "What, then, might be the place of the Church of Blessed Abelle?"

The seemingly simple question set Bathelais back on his heels, so much so that the old monk walked right past him and continued alone for many moments. For in that seemingly simple inquiry, Bathelais saw many deeper questions. Was Father Jerak insinuating that it was the place of the Church to work against the lairds, as the Samhaists had done, often and futilely, in their string of miserable failures? Though it had made great gains in its seventy years of existence—particularly in the fifty-four years since the death of Father Abelle and the creation of the new Honce calendar—the Church of Abelle was still in its infancy. Missionaries armed with gemstones had traveled far and wide, and every holding in Honce had a chapel of Abelle of one sort or another. And yet it was clear to Bathelais, as it had been earlier to Jerak, that their very existence was under the sufferance of the individual lairds.

With a wave of his hand, Laird Pryd could order the Chapel Pryd dismantled, stone by stone, and all of the brothers expelled from his holding. Or worse.

Bathelais hurried to catch up, and found Father Jerak talking away, as if he hadn't even been aware of his companion's absence.

"The people will love us because we salve their wounds," Jerak remarked, and he picked up his pace, for he could hear the crying and groaning within the chapel now and knew that the wounded were waiting. "We must remain worthy of their trust, that they can trust, too, in the message we bring. But we cannot feed them, can we? We cannot protect them from the monsters of the world, can we?"

"Then what are we to do?"

Jerak stopped and slowly turned to face the younger brother, straining his stiff neck so that he could look Bathelais in the eye. "In serving the lairds, we serve the people of Honce," he said. "Never forget that."

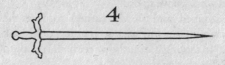

4

SAILING TO CIVILIZATION

It was comforting to smell the salty air and to see the dark swells of the Mirianic again, and with good fortune on the road, Bran Dynard and SenWi made the city of Jacintha at just the right time of year, barely a week before the summer solstice, when the fearsome ocean could be well navigated. The spring storms were behind them and the dark waters had calmed somewhat.

Even in the summer, it was not easy to find transport around the eastern spurs of the Belt-and-Buckle mountains and to the land of Honce. All of the boats sailing around Jacintha were coastal vessels, and the coastline to the north was rocky and treacherous. Still, for those daring enough to try the journey, there were fine profits to be had in Honce.

Dynard and SenWi wound up on a merchant vessel, a square, flat-bottomed, and high-sided craft set with a single square sail and rows of five oars on either side. Though he could use the extra hands at the oars, the merchant sailor, a man so leathery and wrinkled and hunched over that some questioned whether he was human or powrie, had been reluctant to take them on. Only after Dynard had used his soul stone on the sailor's blistered feet, alleviating the man's pain, had the deal been struck; and even with that, Dynard and SenWi found themselves laboring at the oars almost continually throughout the journey.

"And if we see some sharks, you're sure to be the ones getting fed to them!" the sailor said every time he passed the couple, always offering a wide and ridiculous two-toothed smile.

Given the sword SenWi had beside her, Brother Dynard rather doubted that.

The small craft had to swing so wide of the coast to avoid the treacherous rocks that the journey from Jacintha to Ethelbert Town, a mere fifty miles as a bird might fly, took them nearly a week. But they got onto the sandy beach that lined the harbor without serious incident, and with just the cracked lips and sunburned skin that any extended stay on an uncovered boat guaranteed.

"Lucky ones, aren't you, that we saw no sharks?" the wrinkled sailor cackled as he walked between the couple, and he gave SenWi an exaggerated wink. Then he stopped and turned, assuming a pensive posture.

"Once more with that stone of yours?" he asked, lifting his bare foot up.

Brother Dynard was in too fine a mood to resist, so he produced the hematite, the sacred soul stone, and brought it before his eyes, quietly reciting the prayers that would allow him entrance to the gray stone's depths. He continued to pray for some time, then pressed the stone against the sailor's battered, sea-soaked, and rotting appendage. Dynard felt the stone's magical energies reaching out even before the old sailor gave a moan of relief.

The boat slid against the sand beneath the shallow waters then, and the sailor pitched backward, though with the extraordinary balance that only a seaman could ever achieve, he caught himself before he tumbled to the deck. He gave another cackle and stomped his healed foot hard on the deck, then even did a little dance of appreciation.

Dynard and SenWi dropped off the side of the boat, into water that came halfway between Dynard's knee and waist. They hardly noticed and hardly cared, for they were on dry land in seconds, navigating through the crowd that was coming down to see the southern boat and its exotic wares.

"It is one of the greatest cities of Honce," Dynard was explaining to SenWi as they moved up the slope of the beach and more and more of Ethelbert came into view. Many cottages were spread about the lower reach of the community, which was built on several layers climbing into the foothills of the great mountains.

Brother Dynard paused and spent a long while more fully surveying the scene, then closed his eyes and tried to compare it to the vision of Ethelbert he had known as he had sailed out of the place nearly ten years before.

"The city has grown," he remarked, as much to himself as to SenWi. "When I last journeyed through here, most of the folk of Ethelbert lived in those caves up there." He pointed to the south, where the ground climbed sharply and where many cave openings could be seen at many different levels, connected by ladders, most with balconies carved in the stone before them.

"It is not as primitive as it might seem," Dynard quickly added as he considered the view, and how the structures of Ethelbert paled beside the marvels of Walk of Clouds or the great man-made stone structures of Jacintha.

SenWi offered him a comforting and nonjudgmental smile.

To the southwest of their current position, Dynard pointed out Castle Ethelbert dos Entel, though he hardly needed his guiding finger to show SenWi the structure, which so dominated the landscape. It was built against the cliff wall; indeed, the bulk of the place was within the cliffs themselves, tying into the natural limestone caverns common at the lowest levels. But this castle, worked and expanded generation after generation, was much more external than internal, with huge round towers, sweeping walkways, and a magnificent gatehouse that seemed as if it alone could hold all the people of the town.

"Come," Brother Dynard bade her, taking her delicate hand in his own. "Let us see if Laird Ethelbert will grant us audience."

Focused on that thought, his mind spinning as he came to

fully comprehend that he was back in his homeland, Brother Dynard hardly noticed that the farther he and SenWi got from the beach, the more curious grew the stares of the Honce folk.

Similarly, when Dynard approached the sentry at Castle Ethelbert and introduced himself and stated his wishes for an audience, and the man responded, "You come bearing gifts, brother monk?" it almost escaped Dynard that the sentry was looking directly at SenWi.

Several flights of stairs later, Dynard paused by a tower window to take in a wider view of the land. Only then could he comprehend how dramatically Ethelbert Holding had grown in the last decade. Out to the west of the city, the great forests had been felled to make room for many more houses—and even more striking—for tracks of land for farming.

The sentry led the pair through a short corridor that took them into the smoky inner chambers of the complex, where stone walls were mostly covered by ancient tapestries of sailors and great battles, and sculptures of the line of Ethelbert lairds decorated every hallway. The couple soon found themselves before the present laird of the holding, a burly, sun-hardened man with curly black hair and eyes the color of the sea under a blanket of gray clouds. He was older than Dynard by a dozen years, but seemed fit enough to travel the world, battling goblins and powries every step of the way.

"Greetings, Laird Ethelbert," Dynard began with a bow. "I doubt you remember me, but once have I come before you."

"Yes, yes," the older man said. "From . . . Pryd, was it?"

Brother Dynard looked up, smiling widely. "Indeed it was, my laird. I am Brother Bran Dynard of Chapel Pryd, returned from the desert of Behr."

"With a fine trophy, I see," said Ethelbert, tilting his head to regard SenWi.

"My wife, SenWi," Dynard said. He looked at SenWi as he spoke, so he didn't see Ethelbert widen his eyes at the declaration that the two were married.

"Greetings, L—Lair . . . ?" She looked at her husband for support.

"Forgive her, Laird Ethelbert, for her command of our language is not yet complete." He draped his arm over SenWi's shoulders and pulled her close. "I am teaching her, but it was much more important for me to learn the southern languages during my years there."

"I see," said Ethelbert, his tone a bit flatter. "Well, what might I do for you, good brother? I am sure that Father Destros would wish to speak with you. Do you know Destros?"

"Was he Brother Destros when last I came through?"

"Yes, that would be right. Only recently has he assumed leadership of our chapel. Poor Father Senizer was forced aside by issues of his health, I am sorry to say. You might speak with him, as well, but I fear that he will not comprehend your presence and will have no memory of your previous visit."

"Your holding has grown greatly since my last journey through, Laird," Dynard remarked. "I congratulate you."

"No less than has grown your Church, good brother. The teachings of the brothers of Abelle, and those marvelous stones you command, have put the Samhaists in retreat throughout the lands of Honce. Every holding has a chapel now, of course."

Dynard couldn't contain his smile at that. He squeezed SenWi close again and grinned at her.

"And now we are all hard at work on the roads," Laird Ethelbert went on. "You will find your traveling far easier on the trails just west and north of my holding, and though you will have to pass through lands still wild, you will again find solid roads awaiting you as you near Pryd, if that is where you plan to go."

"It is indeed. My mission is ended, more successfully than I could ever have imagined. Have you word of Father Jerak and Pryd Holding?"

"None of Jerak," said Ethelbert, "but Laird Pryd is well, and his son is making quite a name for himself in driving back the powrie threat."

Dynard nodded and smiled, though the news did catch him a bit off his guard. Prydae had been a mere boy when Dynard had left the holding, after all, and the sudden realization that the boy was now a man came as a stark reminder to him that he had been gone a long, long time.

"I will see to it that you are escorted to the borders of my holding when you are ready to go," Laird Ethelbert said. He came forward in his seat and motioned to the nearest sentry, indicating that the audience was at its end. "Is there anything more you would ask of me?"

"No, Laird, you are most generous," Bran Dynard said with a bow. He started to walk away with SenWi and the guard, but Ethelbert waved him back suddenly.

"Approach closer," the laird said, waving him right up to the throne.

Brother Dynard glanced back at SenWi, who kept looking at him over her shoulder and at the guard, who kept pulling her along to the doors.

Ethelbert put his hand on Dynard's wide shoulder and pulled him close.

"Have I offended you, Laird?" the confused monk asked.

"Me? No, no. But I offer you now a word of advice. Call it my respect for the Church of Abelle, or perhaps it is merely that I am fond of a man such as yourself who dares travel the world. I traveled extensively in my own youth, you know."

"Indeed, I had heard as much, Laird."

"To the desert of Behr on several occasions," Ethelbert explained. "I would tell you then, with worldly knowledge and a better understanding than you possess, perhaps, of man's failings, that you would not be wise to so openly announce this dark-skinned creature as your wife."

Brother Dynard reflexively pulled away, staring hard at the laird. "Am I to be embarrassed?"

"Of course not. Her beauty cannot be denied. But you must understand that Ethelbert Holding is unique among the lands of Honce in our understanding and acceptance of the southern race of Behr. You'll not find . . ."

The laird paused and smiled warmly, if a bit resignedly.

"Well, take my advice as you will, good brother. I congratulate you on your safe return and on the knowledge and happiness you have seemingly discovered."

"For so long, I feared my journey to Behr," Dynard admitted. "I had been taught that the people south of the mountains were animal-like, and so you can imagine my surprise when I witnessed the beauties of Jacintha, and when I . . ." He paused, seeing that Laird Ethelbert was holding up his hand.

"Again I congratulate you, good brother, and take pleasure in welcoming you home. I pray that you will find your forthcoming journey through the lands of Honce as enlightening as your travels south seem to have been." He waved to the now-closest guard as he finished, and Brother Bran was escorted out of the room to rejoin SenWi.

"What did he want?" SenWi asked, using the language of Behr.

"Nothing important at all," Dynard assured her, and he leaned in and kissed her on the forehead. "A private welcome for a returning countryman."

Dynard was not so blind as to expect that SenWi believed that explanation, but she did accept it.

As she accepted the curious stares of those they had passed on the way up to the castle, he supposed.

5

LONG ROOTS

With great effort, his limbs wearier this night than usual, old Father Jerak pulled on the brown robes set with the red trim that marked his station in the Church of Abelle. The news had just come in to him that an adulteress had been caught, and now, predictably, old Bernivvigar was demanding his rite of justice. Father Jerak could well imagine the scene of eager onlookers, and he had personally witnessed the look upon the Samhaist Bernivvigar's face several times in the past: the satisfaction, a calm so profound that it reeked of savagery, as if this act of brutal retribution and the willingness of the laird and the people to go along with it somehow denied the changes sweeping through the land with the ascendant Church of Abelle.

There came a soft knock on Jerak's door, and it creaked open. He turned to see brothers Bathelais and Reandu.

"Are you ready to go, father?" Bathelais asked, his tone appropriately somber.

"If anyone can ever be ready for such a journey as this," Jerak replied, and he started toward the door.

"The legacy of Samhaist justice," Bathelais said with a shrug that made it clear to Jerak that the younger man was not so upset by the rite.

"The woman is guilty," young Reandu declared rather bluntly, and both of the other monks turned their surprised gazes upon him. Reandu—a short man with close-cropped black hair and a solid, if diminutive, frame—shrank back beneath those looks.

"There is always the question of proportion, brother," Father Jerak quietly offered. "In this case, the proportion of sin to punishment was determined long ago, and it has not been within our province to modify its balance. Someday, perhaps, we will see a different measure of things and convince the lairds of our enlightened position. For now, though, our duty is to acquiesce to the law humbly and to bear witness to its legitimacy."

Jerak paused, as if considering his own words. "But it is a long journey."

The three monks swept up four other brothers before they had exited Chapel Pryd. By the time they had gotten outside, they could see the bonfire marking the ancient Stone of Judgment already burning brightly.

"Try not to reveal your enjoyment of the spectacle, if indeed you do find it amusing," Laird Pryd said to his son. Lying on his goose-down bed and wearing only a cotton nightshirt that reached to his ankles, the Laird of Pryd Holding didn't seem quite so formidable this particular evening. Laird Pryd had taken ill that very day, and now his eyes were sunken and darkly ringed, contrasting starkly to the chalky color of his face.

"You are the eyes of Pryd this night," the laird went on. "Your presence sanctions the event under the laws of the holding."

Prydae, dressed in his full military regalia, bronze breastplate and all, bowed.

"You need do nothing but bid Bernivvigar to commence," Laird Pryd explained. "Take your seat and bear witness; the old Samhaist will preside over the course of events. He takes great pleasure in these things, you see."

Prydae felt a bit of hesitance, leading to an expression that his perceptive father did not miss. "This will not be a crime paid for with coin," Pryd said.

Prydae looked at his father directly and nodded.

"Bernivvigar is not to allow that in these times," Pryd went on. "The Samhaists feel the press of the Church of Abelle, you see, and what have they to offer the peasants but the surety of order contained within their codes of strict justice?" Pryd raised a hand and dropped it on Prydae's forearm. "You are prepared for this?"

Prydae shook his head at the whole question. "I will not disappoint you, father," he said, and he gave a low bow.

Laird Pryd waved him away.

As he exited the room, castle guardsmen sweeping up in his wake, Prydae considered the events. There could be little doubt of how the evening would proceed, given the claim of the wronged husband that he had actually caught his wife in the arms of another man. And, as his father had said, Prydae's role was minimal; he was just there to give the weight of law to the proceedings.

Prydae hardly even realized that he was rubbing his hands with anticipation as he moved out into the warm summer night.

Whatever he might feel while witnessing this particular form of punishment, it would surely be exciting.

He noted that the brothers of Abelle were already at the clearing. Old Father Jerak and the others stood and sat off to one side, many with their heads bowed and hands folded in prayer. Not far from them stood Rennarq. Prydae knew that the man had come out here, though Rennarq was not acting as an official of the laird this night. Prydae's father wouldn't allow that, for where the Samhaists were concerned, he didn't consider Rennarq to be possessed of objectivity.

Most of the townsfolk were in attendance as well, even many of the children. That surprised Prydae for a moment, but then he realized the point of it all. Harsh justice demonstrated civilization, of course, and reinforced societal expectations of behavior. Let the children learn these lessons young, and learn them well, and perhaps fewer of them would find themselves in the same situation as the guilty woman.

The guardsmen set the chairs they had brought from the castle in the proper place at the left side of the large, flat stone that old Bernivvigar would use as his dais, the customary spot for the Laird of Pryd to bear witness. When Prydae took the chair center and forward of the others, the customary seat of his father, the gathering predictably began to murmur and whisper among themselves.

Prydae stood up and stepped forward. "Laird Pryd is taken ill this night," he said loudly, silencing them all, then he offered a reassuring smile and patted his hands in the air to calm the gasps and fearful exclamations. "A minor case of the gripe, and nothing more. Laird Pryd has bidden me to serve as the voice, the eyes, and the ears of Castle Pryd this evening."

Nods of assent and even some scant cheering came back at Prydae, and he took his seat once more. He recognized the importance of this night then, all of a sudden. He was the obvious heir to Pryd Holding, as his two older siblings were female. There were rumors of half brothers, but they were all by women Laird Pryd had never formally recognized as wives, and so had no claim to the throne. No, it was Prydae's to hold, and soon, too, he believed. Often of late he had seen the weariness in his father's face when the formalities of the day had ended. Prydae's exploits in battle were helping to smooth the way to his ascent but presiding over so important an event as this, he realized, was no less vital. The people of the holding had to believe in him as their protector and as their adjudicator.

Only then did Prydae understand the significance of his father's advice to not reveal his amusement at the spectacle.

The crowd stirred and went quiet as the minutes turned to an hour. The bonfire marking the clearing before the stone— the signal from Bernivvigar of the significance of this night— burned low, casting them all in dim shadows.

Finally, a tall, lean figure made its way down the forest path and out onto the flat stone. The Samhaist did not bend with age, as did Father Jerak and even Laird Pryd. And Berninvvigar was taller than almost any other man in Pryd, standing above six and a half feet. He had wild, almost shaggy, gray hair and a long, thin beard that reached halfway down his chest. He wore his simple light green robe, the Samhaist habit, and sandals that revealed his dirty feet and his red-painted toenails. He carried an oaken staff that was nearly as tall as he, with a knobbed end that made it look more akin to a weapon than a walking stick. A necklace of canine teeth framed his beard and clacked when he walked or when he turned quickly to settle his sharp gaze on one or another of the onlookers.

He looked at Prydae only once, gave a slight nod, then squared up to face the general gathering and lifted his arms high.

"Who claims grievance?" he called. The crowd went completely silent, all eyes turning to the left of the stone, near where the monks were sitting.

A young man, his face covered in snot, his cheeks streaked with tears, stepped forth from that area and staggered up before the stone and the Samhaist, which put his head about level with Berninvvigar's feet. "I do," he said. "I seen them." He brought his arm up and wiped it across his dirty face.

"Bring forth the accused woman," Berninvvigar commanded.

The crowd parted and a group of men—soldiers of the Laird all—forced a young man and woman forward, prodding them with spears and slapping them with the flat sides of bronze swords. Another man, a commoner, bearing a sack in one hand and a pole ending in a small noose in the other, came out after them and moved toward the low-burning fire.

Prydae gave a profound sigh at the sight of the accused. He knew them, the woman at least, and understood that they were young—younger than he at eighteen by two or three years. Callen Duwornay was her name; he knew her family. Startled, Prydae realized that Callen was the daughter of one of Castle Pryd's stablemen.

She was quite a pretty young thing, and Prydae had many

times thought of taking her for a night of his pleasure, as the laird and his offspring were wont and legally entitled to do. Her soft hair was the color of straw, and it hung below her shoulders, cascading from her face in silken layers. Her eyes were not the customary blue of the folk but a rich brown hue—not dark, but true brown. Her smile was bright and even, and often flashed—there was a life and lustiness about her, a scent of womanhood and enthusiasm that all fit together, in light of these charges, to Prydae.

Such a waste, he thought, and he worked earnestly to keep his expression impassive. He was bearing witness and not passing judgment. Some traditions overruled even the desires of the son of the laird.

As soon as her hands were untied, Callen brought them up to brush back the hair from her face, but since she was looking down, it fell right back.

"And the other?" Bernivvigar instructed.

A young man, barely Prydae's age, his blue eyes darting about like those of a terrified animal, stumbled through, jabbed hard by a spear and off balance because his hands were tightly tied behind his back. He seemed as if he could hardly draw breath or as if he were about to burst into tears at any moment.

"Are these the two?" Bernivvigar asked the cuckold.

"Aye, that's the one," said the wronged husband. "Oh, I seen him. Right on top o' her! And I paid good money for her. Silver coin and three sheep."

"Which will be repaid in full—nay, thrice—of course," Bernivvigar said, aiming his words and his glare at the cheating young man. "Thrice!" he repeated strongly.

"Y-yes, yes, me lord," the man stammered and he tried to bow, but tumbled against the hard facing of the stone that served as the Samhaist's platform, then fell. The crowd began to laugh and taunt, but the monks kept praying, and Prydae did well to keep his composure.

"You will be working for years to pay off the debt, you understand," Bernivvigar said.

"All me life, if need be!"

"Then you admit your crime?"

The man, up on his knees now, chewed his bottom lip, then looked from the old Samhaist back to Callen.

Prydae watched him with great interest, noting the emotions tearing at him. The man obviously loved that young woman, and he knew of course what his admission would do to her. He would be branded and indebted, but that paled beside Callen's fate.

A long minute passed.

"We will need two sacks this evening," Bernivvigar said loudly, and the crowd cheered.

"Yes, I did it!" the accused man suddenly blurted, and he started to cry. "We did. Oh, but she bewitched me with her charms." He fell forward, facedown on the ground. "Pity, me lord. Pity."

On a nod from Bernivvigar, a pair of guards moved over and roughly pulled the groveling man aside.

"Have you anything to say, woman?" the Samhaist asked.

Callen didn't look up.

She knew she was doomed, Prydae observed. She had gone past hope now, had settled into that resigned state of empty despair.

"Now comes the fun," Prydae heard one of the guards standing behind him remark.

They took the guilty man first, throwing him roughly to the ground. Two men sat on him to hold him still, while another pulled off his trousers. The cuckolded husband, meanwhile, went to the bonfire, where a flat-headed iron brand had been set in place, its end now glowing. By the time he lifted it in his gloved hand and turned, the guilty man was staked to the ground. He lay on his back, naked from the waist down and with his legs spread wide and held firmly in place by leather ties.

Gasps of excitement and even appreciation, accompanied by a few sympathetic groans, marked the husband's stride as he moved between those widespread legs. The guilty man began to whimper, and all the louder when the cuckolded husband waved the glowing iron before his wide, horror-filled eyes.

"P-please," he stammered. "Mercy! Mercy! I'll pay you four times, I will! Five times!"

The glowing brand went in hard against the side of his testicles.

Prydae had seen several battles in his eighteen years. He had watched men chopped down, squirming and screaming to their deaths. He had seen a woman get cut in half at the waist by a great axe, her top half falling so that she could see her own severed legs, standing there for a long moment before toppling over. But never in all the battles had the young nobleman heard a shriek as bloodcurdling and earsplitting as that from the man sprawled before him.

The man jerked so violently that he yanked one of the stakes from the ground. That hardly did him any good, for as he tried to kick his leg over in an attempt to cover up, he merely brought the tender flesh of his inner thigh against the side of the hot iron.

His face locked in a fierce grimace, the wronged husband pressed harder and slapped the flailing leg away. Finally he stepped back, and the wounded man, sobbing and wailing in agony, flipped his leg over again, trying to curl up.

The guards pulled him up from the ground, and when he tried to duck, one kicked him hard in the groin. He doubled over and fell back to the ground, and so they grabbed him by the ankles and unceremoniously dragged him away, through the jeering and laughing crowd, many of whom spat upon him.

When finally it settled again, Bernivvigar turned his hawkish gaze upon Callen once more. "Have you anything to say?"

The woman sniffled but did not look up.

A nod from him had the guards eagerly stripping off her clothing.

Despite the gruesome surroundings, Prydae couldn't help but take note of the pretty young thing's naked body. Her breasts were round and full and teasingly upturned, and her belly still had a bit of her girlish fat, just enough to give it an enticing curl. Yes, he should have taken her for a night's plea-sure, Prydae realized, and he sighed, for now it was too late.

Again the aggrieved husband went over to the fire, where the handler was preparing the adder, exciting it and angering it by moving it near the hot embers. With a wicked grin, the dirty man handed over the catch stick, its noose now securely holding the two-foot-long copper-colored snake right behind its triangular head.

The husband glanced back when he heard Bernivvigar say, "This is your last chance to speak, woman. If you have any words of apology or remorse, this is the moment."

Callen started to lift her head, as if she wanted to say some-thing. But then she slumped back, as if she hadn't the strength.

Prydae watched the husband, noting his wince as the guards drew the large canvas bag over his wife's head, pulled it down, then pushed her roughly to the ground and forcing her legs inside. Now she flailed wildly and struggled, until one of the guards kicked her hard in the back.

They drew the drawstring of the sack, and kicked her again for good measure, and she lay there, sobbing quietly.

The crowd began to murmur, urging the husband on; and, indeed, there was a hesitation to his every step toward her.

Prydae watched him intently, seeing him pause and imag-ining the tumult of feelings that must be swirling within him. That hesitation seem to break apart all of a sudden, as the cuckold painted a scowl on his face and moved to the sack with three quick strides. One of the guards pulled up the tied end, and the other pulled open the mouth of the bag.

"Don't ye miss," the guard holding the open end said, and he gave the cuckold an exaggerated wink.

The cheering grew louder; the husband looked around. Then he thrust the catch-stick forward, shoving the adder's head far into the bag. With quick hands, the guards helped him force the rest of the squirming snake in, and the husband released one of the drawstrings and pulled back the empty catch-stick.

The guard drew tight the string and tied it off, then jumped back, letting the sack fall over.

The crowd hushed; Prydae found himself leaning forward in his chair.

For a long while, nothing.

There came a slight movement as the snake began to stir. The woman screamed, and the sack began to thrash.

They heard her cry out, and a sudden and violent jerk of the sack brought every onlooker to hold his breath and seemed to freeze the scene in place. The sack held still for a moment, then came another jerk, the woman within no doubt reacting to a second bite.

And again and again.

It went on for many minutes, when finally the bag went still.

The snake handler cautiously moved over and slightly opened the tied end, then jumped well back.

Sometime later, the adder slithered out.

Prydae sat back in his chair, chilled to the bone.

"Stake her up at the end of the road," he heard Bernivvigar say, "that all the workmen might be reminded of her crime."

With that, the old Samhaist turned and walked away, and the crowd began to disperse.

"It'll take her two days to die, unless an animal gets her," Prydae heard his guard say behind him.

"Aye, and with the poison burning her, head to toe, all the while."

The prince sat very still watching the sack. One delicate bare foot had come out of the end and was twisting slowly in the dirt and twitching.

Prydae finally managed to turn his eyes and consider the monks. Father Jerak was staring at the departing Samhaist, his expression obviously uncomplimentary. The prince noted the young and stern one, Bathelais, had his arms crossed over his chest, eyes set determinedly. Bathelais seemed the most accepting of the group, standing in particular contrast to the monk beside him, a young man Prydae did not know, whose look of horror and distress was so pronounced that the prince had to wonder if the man's eyes would freeze open. Obviously, most of the monks had no liking for this severe Samhaist justice, but they hadn't the power to do anything about it. In times past, the adulteress would often have been spared the sack, with a confession and if she were properly broken of spirit before going in. But now, Prydae understood—as did his father, as did Bernivvigar and the monks of Abelle—this scene was about much more than the life of one pitiful little peasant girl.

It was about an old Samhaist's declaration of his continuing importance.

This was justice in Honce, in God's Year 54.

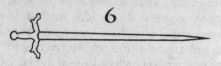

6

ALONG THE RIM OF
TIME'S CIRCLE

They traveled the wide and smooth way out of Ethelbert Holding for many miles to the west, then turned to the north, where the road fast dwindled to a simple cart path, a pair of wet, muddy ruts in the grass.

"Laird Ethelbert is more interested in pressing forward to Delaval City than to my home of Pryd, apparently," Dynard said with a laugh, for the work on the road extended beyond their vision to the west.

"I prefer the untamed lands," SenWi said, and when she glanced at Dynard, she had a little sparkle of excitement in her dark eyes that the monk could not miss.

He tightened his grip on her hand and strode more boldly forward. Soon after, the couple had left all signs of the road behind them and moved along an even less defined trail, where underbrush obscured the cart ruts and great trees crowded overhead.

"I know the land, even after all these years," Dynard assured her. "In two weeks' time, we will find Chapel Pryd. We'll not get lost."

"Little is the care if we do," SenWi replied. "The unknown road oft brings unexpected joys."

Her reference to Dynard's own journey brought a blush to his cheeks. "And oft brings unexpected dangers," he replied. "The land is rife with powries and goblins, so said Laird Ethelbert. Even when I left, the beasts were all about."

"I am Jhesta Tu," SenWi reminded him, the words drawing Dynard's eyes back to the ivory and silver hilt of the sword that pointed diagonally above her left shoulder.

He squeezed her hand again, and they strode off along the forested trail.

Later that same night, on a hill open to the stars above, SenWi ran her hand over the sleeping Bran's shoulder. The air was warm, but the evening breeze carried a slight chill that amplified and tingled as it moved across the perspiration that still clung to SenWi's naked body.

Bran slept soundly, his chest rising and falling in a smooth, contented rhythm. Their lovemaking had been particularly energetic that night, with Bran almost ferocious in his advances, and as urgent in the act itself as he had been in their first encounter, years before in the Walk of Clouds.

Was he trying to reaffirm his love for her to himself? SenWi had to wonder. Was his insistence of action a way for him to defy the obvious disdainful glances that he knew the two of them would face among his unworldly, even intolerant, people?

SenWi smiled the thought away, not over concerned. Had her beloved Bran Dynard felt any more at ease during his first days in Jacintha or among the xenophobic tribes in the desert of Behr? Had he not been a curiosity of sorts when first he had come to the Walk of Clouds, with his chalky skin and strange ways, his words of Blessed Abelle and magical gemstones?

SenWi understood. In making love to her that night, under the stars in the summer breeze, Bran had tried to prove to her that he loved her beyond anything else and that there could be no severing of that tie. And he had tried to prove to himself, she presumed, that the curious and doubting expressions of other people mattered not at all.

His sleep was not restless.

"My love," SenWi whispered, her words floating on the evening breeze. She bent low over Bran and kissed him, and he gave a little grumble and rolled onto his side, drawing yet another amused smile from SenWi.

She held faith in his love for her, and never doubted her own for him, and she was doubly glad of that now.

For she knew.

With her Jhesta Tu training, her senses attuned so well to the rhythms of her own body, the mystic knew.

She brought a hand down to her belly.

"That is it?" SenWi asked in a halting voice. She was gaining a better command of the Honce language, for she and Dynard had been speaking that alone for the last week of traveling. She moved around the side of the rocky jut on the hillside to stand beside her husband, and followed his gaze to the distant dark shape of a formidable castle, anchored in the back by a wide, round tower.

Dynard's grin gave her the answer before he verbally confirmed, "Castle Pryd, home of Laird Pryd, who hosts my chapel." He glanced to the west, and noted the sun, now more than halfway to the horizon.

"This night only if we travel long after . . . *bokri*," SenWi answered his unasked question.

"Sunset," Dynard translated. "*Bokri* is sunset, as *bonewl* is sunrise." He extended his hand to her. "Tomorrow morning, then. I am anxious to return to my home, 'tis true, but I will miss our time alone."

SenWi took his hand and followed him and didn't disagree at all with his observation. The weather had been fine and the company better over the days since they had left the bustle of Ethelbert Holding. It had rained just once, a light sprinkle one dark night, but even in that, SenWi and Bran had huddled and laughed under the sheltering lower boughs of a thick pine, and barely a drop had touched them.

The Jhesta Tu mystic had enjoyed the journey as much as her companion. They had laughed—mostly Dynard laughing at her as she struggled to master the language—and basked in the scents and sights of the unspoiled Honce wilderness in the late summer. They had been fortunate thus far, for the only monster or dangerous animal they had encountered was a single adder that slithered into their campsite one night. Dynard had reached for a stick, but SenWi had intervened, moving low to face the serpent and swaying her hands rhythmically to calm it and entrance it. With a lightning quick strike, the Jhesta Tu had caught the adder in her grasp right behind its head, and had gently carried it far from the camp, where she then had released it.

She remembered now the image of Bran Dynard when she had returned to the camp, as he sat there, shaking his head and grinning widely and chuckling with obvious admiration. "You have learned *ki-chi-kree*," she had said to him. "You, too, could have calmed and caught the serpent."

To that, Dynard had laughed all the louder and had equated his own command of the Jhesta Tu understanding to that of SenWi's grasp of the language of Honce.

Since they had agreed that they need not make Castle Pryd that night, they walked leisurely and on a meandering road, with SenWi often rushing to the side to further explore some interesting sight or sound. For their camp, they chose a bare-topped hillock, and from its apex as the sunlight began to fade they could just make out the southernmost reaches of the new and expanding road, less than a mile away.

"Your world is changing," SenWi remarked as they stared down at that significant development.

"Greatly, I would guess, when these roads are connected. But for the better," Dynard added, turning a grin SenWi's way. "Better to spread the word of Abelle. Better to take the healing powers of the soul stones to the ends of the land."

"Better to move about your armies?"

"If in the pursuit of the monsters that plague the land, then yes."

SenWi nodded and let the conversation go at that. She was Jhesta Tu, and so she had studied the history of the southern lands of Behr extensively. Many times over the centuries had empires arisen, building roads and marching their armies all about. Most of those roads were lost again now, as were the empires, reclaimed by the desert sands. History moved in circles, the Jhesta Tu believed, a hundred steps forward and ninety-nine backward, so the saying went; and that understanding was based on solid evidence and a collective, often bitter, experience. How many people through the ages had thought themselves moving toward a better existence, toward paradise itself, only to be thrown back into misery at the whims of a foolish ruler or by the stomping of a conquering invader?

SenWi wondered then if the roads of other empires had crossed this land of Honce, ravaged by time and swallowed by regrown forests. She expected as much.

She fell asleep comfortably in Bran's tender embrace that evening, her vision of the stars above and thoughts of eternity taking her to a quiet and peaceful slumber. Like all Jhesta Tu, she had trained her body to remain alert to external stimuli even in the deepest sleep, and she awakened sometime near midnight to the distant sound of coarse laughter, drifting on the summer breeze.

SenWi extricated herself from her husband's arms and slowly rose to her feet, staring off to the north, toward Pryd. She saw the flicker of a torch through the trees, perhaps halfway to the firelight glow showing in the windows of Castle Pryd. The commotion and new lights were somewhere down by the end of the road, she figured.

She heard Dynard stir and crawl over beside her, where he wearily rose to his knees. "What is it?"

Some more laughter filtered through.

"A party?"

"No," SenWi quickly answered, for she recognized that there was little joyful mirth in that grating sound. It was more taunting and wicked in timbre. "Not a party."

She began to dress, and not in the flowery white clothing she typically wore through the days, but in a black suit of silk—the dress of a nighttime hunter.

"You mean to go down there through the darkness?"

"In this instance, the darkness might prove our best ally," she replied in a grave voice. She started off down the northern side of the hillock, pulling her silken shirt about her as she went.

Dynard grabbed his clothes and rushed after, not wanting to lose sight of SenWi in the night. The woods could be confusing and disorienting, he knew, but he knew, too, that his wife could find her way unerringly.

A few minutes later, the monk found himself crouching behind a bush beside SenWi. She motioned for him to hold his place, and she crept forward toward the flickering torchlight and harsh-toned conversation. The hairs on the back of Dynard's neck were standing on end now, for he could recognize the language of the speakers, if not the words, and knew them to be powries.

He felt SenWi tense before him, then he moved past so that the scene came into view. A group of five powries stood at the end of the road, prodding, poking, and taunting a young woman, naked and battered, who had been strung up by her wrists, her feet a foot off the ground.

One powrie said something Dynard could not understand, and the others began to laugh.

"Ack, but ye're a pretty one, ain't ye?" the spindly-limbed little dwarf then said to the woman, speaking in the language of Honce. She didn't even groan in response, just hung there, twisting slowly and seeming very near to death, if not already there. The powrie poked her naked belly, sending her into a little swing, and the others laughed again.

"Pretty and with bright blood, eh?" the powrie said, and with a sudden movement, the dwarf brought a knife up and across the inside of the woman's thigh, opening a large wound. Now she did cry out, softly and pitifully, and she tried to wriggle away, but the powrie caught hold of her and slapped his beret against the flowing blood.

The other dwarves hooted.

SenWi leaped out of the brush, bringing forth her magnificent sword.

"Be gone from here!" she commanded.

The powries stared at her for just a moment, then howled and lifted their own weapons.

SenWi's sword spun over in her right hand, went behind

her back, and reappeared on the other side, and she thrust her left hand forward, taking the powrie with the fresh blood on its beret in the side and sending it away with a shriek. She retracted her sword immediately, then flashed it left to right, parrying a swinging powrie axe. SenWi let go and left the sword out there, engaged with the axe, as she spun a tight circle, catching the blade back in her right hand as she came around. Using her momentum, she slid the blade hard across the axe and thrust ahead, forcing the powrie to suck in its belly and scramble back.

SenWi couldn't finish the move, for another powrie came in hard at her side. Across went her sword, slashing the tip from the iron-headed spear and forcing the newest attacker into an overbalanced posture.

The other powries came in hard. She spun and she leaped, kicking out and punching as often as thrusting her sword. Blades came at her from every angle, but she bent and swerved, dodged and parried, with precision.

Brother Dynard had hardly registered that his wife had even moved! Still crouched in the brush, he tried to make sense of this whirling and furious combat before him, tried to call out to SenWi. But he couldn't hope to find his voice, and didn't know whether to cheer or to scream in terror at the wild melee, the slashing swords, the ring of metal.

Up SenWi went above a pair of thrusting spears, and she kicked out, scoring solid hits on the faces of each attacker. But the dwarves didn't fall, and one of the tough creatures even began to laugh at her.

Dynard knew that he had to help. As wondrous a warrior as SenWi was, she couldn't hope to win against five powries!

He started to come forth, but stopped cold, wondering what in the world he might do. He had no weapon, and even if he had, Dynard understood all too well that he was no match for the average powrie. He scrambled about, his eyes glued to

SenWi's continuing flurry, and finally settled one hand into his belt pouch.

Dynard brought forth the smooth gray stone and held it up before his eyes.

The soul stone.

Her fighting was completely defensive now. SenWi ducked and turned from weapons that came in at her from every side. The dwarves coordinated their attacks well, leaving her little opening, but one of the five was lagging, she noted. In her initial attack, she had hit him hard, her sword digging a deep wound. He was trying to keep up with his four friends, but his thrusts shortened every time, as he winced and curled over that torn side.

SenWi wanted to focus on him and finish him off, but the other dwarves had her turning continually. She leaped over one swiping axe and threw her leg out wide to avoid the stab of a spear. As she landed, she brought her forearm up to accept the smack of the spear she had beheaded, for the dwarf was now using it as a club. As her arm connected, she shoved it out wide, then stepped in and stabbed at the dwarf with her sword.

But again, she had to pull up short and spin to deflect the charge of another, the dwarf lowering his shoulder and trying to bowl her right over. She hit him with three short jabbing punches to turn him, then crossed hard with the snake hilt of her sword, cracking his jaw.

The tough little creature staggered backward but did not fall.

Brother Dynard chanted and clutched his soul stone, trying to find his concentration and his center, seeking his *chi* so that he could send it fully into the swirling gray depths of the magical stone. He heard SenWi's breathing, heard the growls of the ferocious dwarves.

He heard his love grunt as a powrie connected with the wooden shaft of its spear, and he opened his eyes.

He snapped them shut immediately and concentrated again on the issue at hand. He couldn't go out there physically, he knew, for his appearance and incompetence would likely hinder SenWi more than aid her. Thus, he had to go out there spiritually. He had to find his center and free his spirit through the use of the soul stone.

The sounds of battle grew distant suddenly, and Dynard felt as if he were falling through cool water. And he was standing there, looking back at himself, on his kneeling physical body.

His spirit turned and willed himself forward into the fray. He denied his trained revulsion as he approached one powrie and accepted the invitation of its corporeal form.

In he went, against his understanding that this usage of the soul stone—insinuating himself into the body of another free-willed creature—was among the most trying and repugnant possibilities offered by the gemstone. To possess another was the temptation of the stone and the danger of the stone, and was an act frowned upon by the brothers of Blessed Abelle, an act specifically damned by Abelle himself in his writings.

But this time, with SenWi in so difficult a position, Dynard accepted the danger and the moral ambiguity and fought past his revulsion. His spirit dove into the powrie.

He sensed the creature's surprise and horror, and he knew that it would instinctively react to possession with a fierce battle of willpower. But for just a moment, the powrie was off guard, confused, and in that split second, Dynard took control. He saw through its eyes; he felt its limbs as if they were his own.

He made the dwarf throw its axe to the ground, turn, and leap upon the dwarf nearest him, bearing both to the ground.

Then Dynard felt the sudden attack upon his spirit, the rebound of the dwarf's free will. He envisioned a dwarvish shadow tearing at the fabric of his own spiritual silhouette.

But he held on stubbornly, with willpower and with the dwarf arms he controlled.

SenWi had no idea what had just happened, why one of these vicious dwarves would tackle another, but she didn't pause to ask questions. Her sword went out to the right to block a spear, then she rolled her blade about the weapon repeatedly in rapid succession.

Instead of retracting, the dwarf came forward, but SenWi had anticipated the move. She retracted her arm, then struck straight out, like a serpent, once, then again and again.

The dwarf staggered backward.

SenWi sprang into the air, tucked her legs, and went right over backward as the dwarf opposite her, the wounded one with the knife, charged in with a roar. She landed lightly right behind the creature as it stumbled past, a perfect opportunity to strike hard.

But she didn't, diving sidelong instead at the remaining battling powrie, who was obviously thinking to follow her in pursuit of the knife wielder.

SenWi's sword whipped over, coming in diagonal down strikes at the too-slow dwarf, slashing shoulder to hip one way, then the other.

The dwarf tried to get its axe up to block, but SenWi seemed one movement ahead of it each time, her sword coming across and down repeatedly.

The dwarf's tunic hung ragged, with lines of blood beginning to show, and the dwarf continued its futile efforts to block. Not once did it hit SenWi's sword, and it began to retreat—to inevitably stagger backward.

SenWi's sword blazed in diagonal circles, each one scoring a hit.

And she stopped suddenly, reversed her grip on the sword, and thrust it out behind her, just in time to meet the roaring charge of the knife wielder. He came forward anyway, for he couldn't break his momentum, and ran right up against SenWi. For a moment, he seemed frozen in time, impaled to the hilt on her blade, and then his eyes slowly turned up to meet hers.

He roared and tried to strike, but SenWi whirled and ducked under the blow, moving out to the side of the dwarf, where she gave a great tug on her sword.

Powries were made of tough stuff indeed, but so was the steel of SenWi's sword, and strong was its impeccable design. The blade tore through the powrie's innards and ripped out the side, and the dwarf staggered. It tried to cry out, but only a thick flow of blood rushed out of its mouth.

SenWi spun her sword, using its momentum to center her own balance once more as she turned.

That dwarf was down and dying; as was the one she had slashed so many times; as was, she was glad to see, the one she had poked thrice. That one was still alive, kneeling and groaning. The other two were up again, off to the side, staring at her incredulously.

They turned and ran off.

SenWi took one step to follow, but stopped at once, turning to regard the hanging woman, then glancing over at the bushes where a shaken Dynard came stumbling forth, soul stone in hand.

"I—I possessed him," the stumbling monk explained.

SenWi responded with an absent nod, but was already focusing on and moving toward the woman. She looked up at the rope and then at her sword, but then snapped the sword back into the scabbard across her back, recognizing that the woman was too near death to handle the trauma of a fall.

The Jhesta Tu brought her palms together before her and again fell into that line of energy, that center of power, that ran from the top of her head to her groin. With a deep exhalation, SenWi breathed that power forth into her arms, coursing down to her hands and her trembling fingertips.

She felt the heat building in her hands even as she reached out to the dying woman.

She placed a hand on the tear in the woman's thigh and sent forth her healing energy, and accepted the woman's pain as her own.

She felt something then, in the blood, some uncleanliness.

But she didn't relent, forcing her energy into the woman, lending her strength.

A soft groan escaped the battered woman's lips.

"SenWi, do not," came a sharp cry behind her, drawing her from her concentration. She glanced over her shoulder to see an ashen-faced Dynard staring at her wide-eyed. "Leave her alone."

SenWi's jaw drooped open in disbelief.

"She is an adulteress," Dynard explained, "or some other such sin."

"This is how your order deals with sinners?"

"No, no, not the brothers of Abelle. But this is not our province. This justice is the tradition of the land, since long before Blessed Abelle walked the ways of Honce. In the half century of our Church, we have made some gains and offered some concessions. This is the doing of the Samhaists, who once presided over all the folk as the clerics of Honce. The lairds have not seen fit to change."

"This is justice?"

The accusatory tone had Dynard back on his heels. "It is the way of Honce. The woman was convicted, no doubt, and given to the snake."

The snake. SenWi's head snapped around, and only then did she fully realize the other wounds; fang marks. She understood then the sensation of uncleanliness in the blood, for it was rife with poison.

She swallowed hard and stared at the woman, who seemed more alive, just a bit, as if the healing hands had made some progress. The poor, battered girl gave another little groan.

"I will not watch her die," SenWi declared.

"It is not our place."

"Choose your own place as you will," she granted. "I will not watch her die." She folded her palms and fell into her *chi*, then went back to her healing work with renewed energy.

A moment later, to her great relief, Brother Dynard was beside her, soul stone in hand. With a look and helpless smile at SenWi, he pressed his free hand against the woman and began his own healing, using the magical stone.

A few moments later, the two looked at each other again, and SenWi nodded and motioned for Dynard to grasp the woman. SenWi then pulled forth her sword and leaped into the air; and with a sudden and swift strike, she cut the woman free.

She helped Dynard guide the poor girl to the ground.

"Your cloak," SenWi instructed, and Dynard shed his woolen robe, and he and his wife managed to wrap it about the shivering woman. Then Dynard picked her up gently in his arms. "Come along," he instructed SenWi. "The powries might return with their friends."

He started off into the forest, to the side of the road. "We cannot take her to Pryd, for they will merely throw her in the sack with the snake again and hang her once more," he explained. "But there may be a place."

"Chapel Pryd?"

Dynard nearly laughed aloud at the notion, for he knew well that Father Jerak, kindly as he could be, would not go against Laird Pryd in this matter. Nor would Dynard, in all good conscience, even involve the others of his order in this crime.

No, this burden was his own.

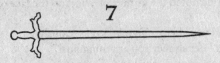

7

TO THE SIDE OF THINGS

The middle-aged man stared out the partly open door for a long and silent moment, then finally seemed to breathe again and stepped back, pulling the door wide. "Can it be?" he whispered, and he held up a candle before him. He was of medium build, a bit shorter than most men, with a shaggy head of black and gray hair, and with several days of beard evident on his face. One of his eyes was quite dead, showing only milky white, but the other held a lustrous blue-gray sparkle.

Brother Dynard put on a wide smile. "Garibond, my heart fills with joy at seeing you alive and well." He stepped inside the dimly lit stone house, and in doing so, stepped out the lake, for this stone structure was constructed on a rock out in the water, a dozen feet from the shore along a sometimes submerged, sometimes revealed, shoal. The house was built in two parts, with this, the lower level, right at the lakeside, and a higher, drier structure a dozen feet above and farther from the shore, on the higher rocks. Even with the two structures, connected by a cave and stone extension, there was little elaborate workmanship showing about Garibond's home, just two stone-walled rectangles with thatched roofs.

"Bran in the flesh! Back from his travels around the world!" Garibond Womak replied. He stepped forward and clapped Dynard hard on the shoulder, then wrapped him in a great hug, which Dynard comfortably returned.

Garibond leaped back. "Come in," he bade. "Come in! You must tell me every detail." His enthusiasm melted almost at once, as he noted the grim expression on the face of his long-lost friend.

"I need your help," Dynard said seriously.

"Have I e'er shown you anything but?"

With an appreciative nod, Dynard stepped back outside and splashed across the shallows to the shore, returning a moment later with the unconscious young woman in his arms.

Garibond's good eye went wide.

"We found her at the end of the new road," Dynard explained.

"Where Bernivvigar left her to die, with the blessing of Laird Pryd."

Dynard nodded.

"Are you mad?" Garibond asked. "The woman was convicted and executed. She met the adder in the sack—to the joy of the folk who went to watch, I am certain," he added, his voice taking a sour note. "You cannot—"

"I could not leave her out there. I—we—met powries dancing about her, ready to take her blood."

"Dead is dead. Probably better that way than from the slow poison of the snake."

Dynard just shook his head and moved to the side, gently laying the woman down on a thick bearskin rug elevated on a wooden frame near the still-warm hearth.

"You had to know the truth of her predicament," Garibond protested. "You've seen old Bernivvigar's work before."

"I could not leave her."

"They'll put you in her place, you fool," protested Garibond. "You cannot go against the word of Laird Pryd. Your own brothers of Abelle were there in attendance, bearing witness."

Dynard held out his arms helplessly, and Garibond gave a great sigh.

"You said 'we,' " Garibond remarked. "Who was with you, and more important to your own skin, where is he now?"

The smile returned to Brother Dynard's face and he stepped back outside and motioned off into the night. A moment later, SenWi appeared at his side in the doorway. "Not he. My wife."

Garibond's good eye went wide again, and widened even more as he came to understand the truth of SenWi's exotic heritage. "But she's a pretty one," he managed to say at length.

"Will you help us?"

"What would you have me do?" Garibond answered skeptically. "I'm no healer."

"Just let us stay here for a bit, that we can tend the girl and keep her safe and warm."

"You're to be the death of me."

"I know you can hide her—can hide us," Dynard said with a grin, and Garibond gave a sigh. "He has tunnels beneath this house," Dynard explained to SenWi. "Keeps him safe from powries and goblins." He turned back to Garibond and, with a wide grin, added, "Though I thought you'd have slowed enough by now for them to catch you before you got your old arse into the hole."

"Bah, them stupid ones don't even come around here. If they did, I'd be more likely to stand and kill them all before I'd run like a child into the tunnels!"

Dynard knew the truth of the bluster, but he didn't press the point.

Garibond's smile proved short-lived. "Tunnels or no, she won't be safe if Lord Pryd—or worse, his son, Prydae—discovers that she is missing," Garibond said.

"Prydae?"

"Aye, Prydae. A boy when you left. A man now. A young warrior with as much fight and metal as the father ever knew, who makes his reputation daily against the goblins and the powries."

Again Dynard was reminded of how long he'd been gone. He looked at SenWi and gave a helpless laugh and shake of his head. "The world moves on without me, it would seem."

"Young Prince Prydae would not take well to your disruption of old Bernivvigar's holy ritual."

"Murder is holy ritual?" SenWi asked, her eyes going wide, and she looked up at Dynard for support.

"Not murder," the monk tried to explain, but he found little heart for the distinction he offered. "The Samhaists carry out the executions and other punishments of convicted criminals."

"This young girl was a murderess?"

"An adulteress," said Garibond.

SenWi looked to Dynard, who explained the crime in the woman's native tongue. That explanation did little to alleviate either her confusion or her disdain, however.

"Appeasing the Samhaists has always been important to the lairds," Garibond reminded Dynard. "You know that."

Brother Dynard paused to study his friend before answering. "But you will allow us the use of your home?"

"Shut the damned door, old fool," Garibond said. "And come along to the upper house where it's more dry—and bring along a log or two to throw upon the fire. I've some stew I can heat." He gave another sigh and looked at SenWi. "And for you, pretty one . . ." He turned to Dynard with his pause.

"SenWi," the monk explained.

"Yes, SenWi, pray you go behind that curtain and find more blankets for the poor girl."

"Prince Prydae will see the powrie tracks and think no more of it," Dynard assured his friend.

"Or he will follow your own to my house, and Bernivvigar's next ceremony will feature four sacks."

That brought a laugh from Dynard, though he knew well that Garibond was hardly joking.

A short while later, with SenWi tending Callen by the hearth in the upper house, Dynard and Garibond sat opposite each other in comfortable chairs of wood and skins a few feet back, telling the woman of Behr the tales of their long friendship. The two had been fast friends since childhood, and Garibond had even tried to enter the Church of Abelle at the same time as Dynard. But the court of monks had seen that Garibond's motivation was strictly one of loyalty to his friend and not wrought of any sincere belief in the Church and its precepts, and so he had been refused even before Dynard had set out from Pryd Holding to the mother chapel in the north.

Their friendship had not been as tight when Dynard had returned a few years later, the two explained to SenWi, and they both blamed circumstance and no lessening of their almost-brotherly love. Dynard had been busy in the town and chapel, right up to the time when he had departed for the southland, after all; and Garibond only very rarely went to the town, preferring the solitude of his small farm east of the community.

"Sometimes it is easy to forget those things that are truly most important to us," Dynard reflected.

"And this one has always been getting me in trouble," Garibond said suddenly, and he jabbed his accusing finger in the air Dynard's way.

"Or the other way around!" Dynard argued.

" 'Twas your own idea to take the ripened tomatoes from farmer Filtin."

" 'Twas my idea to take only the ripened ones after you dragged me to his fields," came Dynard's not-so-subtle correction.

The two laughed, and SenWi did as well, until Garibond began to pat his hands in the air and whisper for quiet, reminding them that his house wasn't that far out of town, after all.

"What are you doing to her?" Garibond asked SenWi then, for she had bent over the gravely injured younger woman and slid her hands under the blanket around the poor girl's midsection.

"She is offering her healing powers to the poor girl," Dynard answered.

"Callen," said Garibond. "Callen Duwornay. She was indeed guilty of the accusation of adultery, from what little I heard, but she's not deserving this fate. Poor girl indeed."

He studied SenWi as she slid her hand back out and shifted to put it back from a different angle. "She uses no soul stone," he remarked.

"SenWi is Jhesta Tu," Dynard replied.

Garibond shrugged. The name likely meant nothing to anyone north of the mountains, Dynard knew.

"Just one of the many marvels I have to share with you," the monk said, and he began recounting his journeys then, from the road to Ethelbert to the sea voyage around the Belt-and-Buckle and all through the wild deserts of Behr to his culminating exploration at the Jhesta Tu monastery. He spoke with passion and true admiration as he detailed those years spent at the Walk of Clouds with the devoted mystics, and his story lasted until the eastern sky had begun to lighten with the coming dawn. Garibond didn't point out the lateness of the hour and neither did SenWi, whose work with Callen was hardly finished.

"What are you going to do?" Garibond asked somberly when at last Dynard settled back in his chair.

"In the morning, I return to Chapel Pryd with SenWi."

"Take care," Garibond warned. "Things have changed in the ten years since you left, my friend."

"How so?" Dynard asked, responding to the alarm in his friend's voice.

"The work on the road is hard on the people; and Laird Pryd, like all the lairds of Honce, is determined that his holding will not be outdone in this endeavor. But the land is not tamed—less so than even when you left, I would say."

"Laird Ethelbert spoke of goblins and powries."

"The powries are as thick as trees, as you saw for yourself," said Garibond. He paused and looked curiously at his friend. "How did you get rid of the beasts? You've never been a warrior."

Dynard led Garibond's gaze to SenWi.

"Interesting," Garibond remarked.

"So you are not surprised to hear that we encountered powries?"

"The bloody caps are all about," Garibond explained. "They've left me alone, for the most part. I don't know why. Mayhap they think my dirty old blood will soil their berets."

"Or it could be those tunnels beneath your house," Dynard said with a wink.

"Perhaps you should move closer to the town," SenWi offered in her halting command of the language.

"Ah, that would kill me sooner than any powries ever could!"

"Fie the day that we granted them the safety of our coast," Dynard added, and Garibond nodded.

"A group of powries came to the shores of Honce many years ago," Dynard explained to SenWi. "Perhaps a score of years ago now. The lairds chose not to confront them, but parlayed instead, granting the dwarves a region of the coast as their own. We have come to regret that generosity."

"Your own Church did not oppose the decision," Garibond reminded, to which Dynard could only hold up his hands.

A long pause ensued, and Garibond's last statement led Brother Dynard back to the meetings he would face in the morning. "How fares Father Jerak?"

"He is getting very old, and looking even older. Rumors say that Brother Bathelais has assumed most of his duties now."

That news saddened Dynard but did not surprise him; Jerak had already been an old man when Dynard had set out on his mission, after all. Nor did it alarm him in any way. He and Bathelais had been friends before he had left, and, from what he knew, Bathelais was possessed of a good heart and a clear mind.

"More important is the passage of the title of laird," Garibond explained. "Laird Pryd is robust yet, so many say, but he was not at Bernivvigar's court last night. Day by day sees the rise of Prydae."

"A good man?"

Garibond shrugged. "That would hardly be my place to judge, though I have heard nothing contrary to that. His courage against the powries cannot be dismissed, and the soldiers of Castle Pryd follow him with great loyalty. He is as proud as he is fierce, some say, but whether that will prove a strength or a weakness in these days of change, who can know?"

It occurred to Dynard to ask about how this young and rising prince might view the Church of Abelle, but he held the question private. Garibond wouldn't likely know the inner workings of Pryd's Church of Abelle, since he wasn't one to visit Chapel Pryd. Had he ever gone to the place after the monks had turned him away, except on that one occasion to see Dynard off on his mission?

The conversation drifted away then, and so did the three companions, falling into light sleep right where they sat. Sunlight awakened them soon after, though, streaming in through every crack and opening in Garibond's old house.

"And what am I to do with her?" Garibond asked when Dynard and SenWi moved immediately to collect their packs.

Dynard looked to SenWi.

"She will not likely awaken today," SenWi said with confidence.

"And we will return to you this very night," Dynard promised. He looked all about, then reached into his pack and pulled forth his most-prized possession, the transcribed Book of Jhest. He stared at it for a few moments, wondering whether he should reveal it to Father Jerak immediately upon his return to Chapel Pryd. A nagging thought in the back of his head, undefined but forceful, made him reconsider, and he glanced all around. He moved to the back of the two-roomed upper house and pulled open the partially hidden trapdoor, revealing a narrow shaft. He tenderly wrapped the tome and went down the hole with it. He returned a moment later without the book, to see his two companions, particularly Garibond, watching him intently.

"More trouble you're bringing to my house?"

Dynard looked at his friend. "It will not remain here for long," he promised, and Garibond merely smiled and shook his head—a familiar look that sent Dynard's thoughts careening back to the garden raids of their youth.

"First sign of the laird's men, and Callen's going down the hole, as well," Garibond warned.

"Gently, I trust."

"Quickly."

Dynard smiled, knowing the truth of his compassionate friend.

Another fine, warm summer day surrounded Dynard and SenWi as they moved back to the end of Pryd's lengthening road. Workers and soldiers were all around, some studying the myriad tracks, others looking to the empty pole where Callen had been strung.

"To think that they meant to work all day under the shadow of the hanging woman," Dynard quietly remarked as he surveyed the scene, while he and SenWi were hidden from the sight of the crew. He noted that the powries had apparently returned after the fight and retrieved the bodies of their fallen. Still, the signs of the struggle clearly remained, a puzzle that the folk milling about the area were trying hard to decipher.

"Are you ready to meet them?" Dynard whispered. He couldn't suppress a helpless chuckle when he regarded his wife, who seemed so uncomfortable dressed in a typical Honce woolen tunic. The dress was normal for the land, true, but wearing it, SenWi hardly seemed like any normal Honce citizen.

SenWi looked up at him, her typically calm expression telling him all he needed to know. He took her hand and rose, then crossed out onto the open ground before the work area.

Calls for them to "stand and be counted!" assailed the couple almost immediately, and soldiers drew out their short swords.

Dynard couldn't help but grin as he noted those weapons, of bronze and iron, and compared them to the sword that SenWi had strapped across her back.

The soldiers approached cautiously, fanning out to flank the couple.

"Be at ease, soldiers of Laird Pryd, for I am of your town, returned now to my chapel," Dynard said to them.

"That's Bran Dynard!" one of the workers yelled out, and a host of murmurs erupted.

"Indeed," said the monk. "The time of my mission is ended, and so I return to Pryd."

"I do not know you," said the nearest soldier, a large man with knotted muscles and a broad and strong chest. Although hardened like a seasoned veteran, he was less than twenty years of age, by Dynard's estimation, perhaps no more than sixteen.

"I am of Chapel Pryd," he explained. "You would have been no more than a boy when I departed."

"It is that monk," said another of the soldiers, and he slid away his sword and moved closer. Nods of agreement came from all around and the warriors relaxed.

Dynard's relief was short-lived, though, for he noted their expressions as they scrutinized SenWi, showing a range of emotions from lewd to curious to dismissive, as one might view a goat or a cow. It was that last expression, offered by the powerful younger warrior, that most unnerved the monk, showing the warrior's complete disregard for the dark-skinned southerner.

" 'Twas powries who ran off with the girl," Dynard said, drawing them all back to him.

"What do you know of it?" asked one, apparently the leader of the group, a slender, tall warrior of about Dynard's age whom the monk thought he recognized, though he could not recall the man's name.

"Captain Deepen," the man introduced himself, and Dynard nodded his recollection.

"We came upon them last night, and did battle," the monk explained. "They were too numerous for us to retrieve the girl, but we drove them away."

"And yet you escaped?" Deepen asked, obvious doubt in his tone.

"Because of your gemstones, no doubt," another remarked.

"More the work of my wife," Dynard explained, looking to

SenWi, and he didn't miss the horrified expressions all around him as he proclaimed this diminutive woman, the stranger to Honce, this "beast of Behr," as his wife. Dynard steeled himself against that response and recounted the battle in full, dramatizing SenWi's prowess and sword work, and leaving out only the not-so-small detail that he and SenWi, and not the powries, had run off with poor Callen.

"Laird Pryd will hear of this," Deepen decided and he reached out as if to take Dynard by the arm.

The monk recoiled. "I am for Chapel Pryd straightaway. Too long have I been out on the road. I will speak with Father Jerak, and will come to the summons of Laird Pryd, of course, if I am so called."

The captain eyed him suspiciously, then at SenWi as well, but he did back away a step, clearing the way to the road.

"Where'd you find that . . . one?" the young and powerful warrior asked Dynard, and the man strode up to study SenWi more closely.

"She is my wife, from Behr," he replied, and the man gave a burst of laughter.

"And your name is?" Dynard asked.

"Bannagran," said the warrior, and he looked at Dynard, chuckled again, then walked away.

Dynard took SenWi by the arm and led her along quickly before the soldiers could reconsider, before they perhaps grew more interested in, and concerned about, the weapon strapped across her back.

In short order, the couple were long out of sight of the workmen and the soldiers, walking quickly down the road. Dynard slowed their pace when they came to the outskirts of Pryd Town and in clear sight of Castle Pryd, considering again the expressions on the faces of those folk at the battle scene, looks from soldier and peasant alike, as they regarded his foreign wife.

How might his brothers of Abelle respond to her?

He wondered if perhaps he should have left SenWi with Garibond.

"By the Ancient Ones, it is impossible!" Garibond said to Callen when he came back from his chores to find the woman sitting up in bed, the blankets wrapped about her shoulders. "The poison had you, girl."

Callen kept her head bowed, but Garibond saw her brown eyes glance up at him from behind the screen of her wheat-colored hair.

"The woman—of Behr no less!—saved your life, girl. She gave you healing." He shook his head in disbelief.

Callen rose, unsteady for a moment. "Have you clothing for me?" she asked, and the tremor in her voice reflected the ordeal she had suffered.

Garibond nodded at the foot of the bed, where a tunic and traveling cloak were set out.

"I will be gone this morn," Callen said, and she moved to the clothing and began to dress, discarding modesty in the face of necessity.

"Now, take your time," Garibond said. "Where will you go?" He started for Callen, but held back until she had slipped the tunic over her head.

"Where will you go?" he asked again when she turned back to him.

"I've family in the west," she answered. "They will see to me."

"You've friends here," Garibond replied.

Callen stared at him for a few moments, then tightened her lips and shook her head. She was afraid, he could plainly see. She knew that she was a danger to any who showed her kindness.

"You need food and rest," Garibond remarked, and he rushed across the way and pulled open a cabinet and began searching for some food he might offer. "You cannot go out there now, not so soon. They'll see you and guess the truth of it, don't you see? You should let all the whispers of Callen Duwornay die away before you venture out anywhere where you might be seen. Memories are short, don't you worry, and soon enough, strong and with all health returned, you'll find your way." He finished hopefully, and turned with a loaf of bread in one hand and a cooked chicken in the other.

But the door was open and Callen was gone.

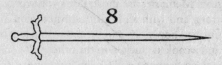

8

FORWARD LOOKING

With a great and steadying sigh and a glance back to SenWi, Brother Dynard pulled open the large oaken door of Chapel Pryd and walked inside. Like all of the Abelle chapels in Honce, the place was dimly lit and smoky, with few windows and many candles set about.

"May I help you, brother?" said a younger monk Dynard did not know. The man moved up to him, his posture open and inviting, for obviously he had recognized Dynard, in his brown tunic and robe, as a fellow brother of Abelle.

Before Dynard could answer, he heard his name called out from across the way, through the inner doors of the chapel and in the main area.

"Dynard!" cried Brother Bathelais. "Is it really you?" The monk came rushing out from those doors to stand right before the returned brother, and he took Dynard's hands.

"Greetings, Brother Bathelais," Dynard replied, and he was glad that Garibond had mentioned this man the night previous, for he would not have recalled the name otherwise. "Long has been my road, across ocean waters and through desert sandstorms! It is good to be home."

"Father Jerak will wish for a full recounting as soon as is possible."

"Of course."

"You are Brother Bran Dynard, who went to Behr?" the younger monk asked. "I hope to serve my own mission soon in that same land!"

"And better will you be if you are so blessed," Dynard said to him.

"You have brought back trinkets and insights, perhaps?" asked Bathelais. "And tales of conversion?"

The unintended irony of that last statement was not wasted on the transformed monk.

"I have tales more wondrous than anything I expected," Dynard answered, smiling with sincerity. How he longed to show his brethren the beauty he had seen and insights he had gained. How he hoped that his journey to Behr, and more particularly to the Walk of Clouds, would help transform the Church of Abelle into something more wonderful and insightful.

With that thought in mind, Dynard turned from Brother Bathelais and called out for SenWi.

He turned back in time to see the astounded expressions of both the monks when his beautiful Behrenese wife walked into the chapel. Bathelais even made the sign of the evergreen before his chest, a triangular movement that was fast becoming a staple signal of devotion among the followers of Blessed Abelle, for Blessed Abelle had reportedly lived for three years sheltered under the boughs of the sacred evergreen tree.

"This is SenWi," Dynard introduced as the woman moved up beside him, and he casually draped his arm across her shoulders and pulled her close to his side. "My wife."

He saw Brother Bathelais fighting hard, but with only limited success, to keep the incredulity off his face.

Brother Dynard didn't think much of it at that time—how could the man not be surprised, after all?

Little did Brother Dynard understand.

"Three dead powries, so he said," Captain Deepen told Prince Prydae. "Who can know what powers the beast of Behr brought with her?"

"Bah, but Prince Prydae killed five in the last fight!" one of the other soldiers in the room blurted.

Prince Prydae accepted that accolade with a nod, though all in the room, including the speaker, knew it to be an exaggeration. Prydae could claim only four kills in that particular fight, and three of those would more correctly be credited to his chariot than to his battle prowess. While he would accept the compliment, the prince recognized that if the returning Brother Dynard had spoken truthfully about the foreign woman's exploits, they were well worth noting.

He saw one young, promising, and amazingly strong warrior, Bannagran by name, looking at him almost apologetically.

"You did not see her sword?" the prince asked Deepen.

The captain shrugged. "Just the hilt of it, and that alone was impressive."

"The peoples south of the Belt-and-Buckle are well known for their crafts," Prydae admitted. "On my last journey to Ethelbert Holding, I saw this clearly. Keep a close watch on this visitor. I would know her movements."

Captain Deepen bowed. "She is with Brother Dynard now in Chapel Pryd."

"Any news of Callen?"

"The powries took her, so said Brother Dynard. If that is the case, then we'll never find enough of her corpse to bother about."

"Make sure that you take down the hanging pole early in the morning," Prydae instructed. "It may serve to remind our workers of a powrie presence, and I'll have no such distraction at this time. We have far yet to travel and much more road to construct before the season's turn, and many are already grumbling that they must be back to their fields before harvest."

Captain Deepen bowed again, and Prydae motioned that it was time for him and the others to go. As soon as he was alone, the prince took up his favorite mug and filled it with mead, which he drank quickly. Then, not satisfied, he moved to a small cabinet across the castle room. He pulled open the door and sorted through the metal flasks within, at last settling on one nearly full of a light brown liquid, a fine Vanguard whiskey.

Again he filled the mug, and he wasn't slow to drain it.

All the while, Prydae kept glancing at the door on the right-hand side of the audience room, the portal to his father's wing of the castle. Pryd was still in bed and still feeling ill, and Prydae was beginning to worry that perhaps his father was more sick than he was admitting.

That notion elicited a myriad of thoughts in the ambitious young man. He was ready to assume the mantle of laird of Pryd Holding, so he believed—indeed, that was a day he had anticipated for most of his life. But Prydae had hoped for a more gradual transition. There were so many nuances to every duty, it seemed, such as his attendance at the trial and sentencing of the adulteress and her illicit lover. Laird Pryd understood these subtleties quite well; he knew how to make the peasants love him even as he broke their backs with difficult labors or took the bulk of their crops and coins.

Prydae cocked his arm back and only at the very last moment stopped himself from throwing his mug across the room.

He would never rule with that type of tact and wisdom, he feared. He was not possessed of his father's diplomacy.

He finished the whiskey in one large gulp, then tossed the mug aside and stormed through the door to Pryd's private chambers. He found his father in bed, lying on his back, his eyes sunken and circled by dark rings. Prydae was struck by how frail the laird appeared. Only a few days before, Laird Pryd had ridden in the courtyard, inspecting his soldiers, and at that time it seemed as if the laird could have led them all into battle and would have claimed the most kills of all with his fabulous sword. He had started to cough a bit that same day—just a tickle in his throat, he insisted—and it had sounded as if it was nothing serious.

And now he lay in bed, coughing and pale, his bowels running as water and his breath smelling of vomit.

"How fare you today, father?" Prydae asked, kneeling beside the bed.

"I curse my age," the old man said with a laugh that sounded more like a wheeze.

"One of the monks who had gone off on his mission has returned," Prydae explained. "A Brother Bran Dynard, back from Behr—I do not remember him."

"A man of little consequence, no doubt."

"He brought with him a brown-skinned woman with strange eyes."

With great effort, Pryd managed to lift one hand and offer a slight, dismissive shake.

"Yes, it does not matter," Prince Prydae mumbled. "Powries took the executed adulteress," he started to say, for he cut himself short, realizing that this event would mean little to his father.

He took his father's hand and kissed it, then clasped it. He felt no strength there, and little warmth, little sense of life at all. He knew that he had to get the healers back in here with their soul stones, and had already arranged a meeting with Brother Bathelais for that very night.

Prydae also understood the limitations of those healers.

Again the prince had to follow two diverging lines of emotions, for beside his fear and pain at watching his father's diminishing health, there was another type of fear, one rooted in ambition and eagerness. He gave his father's hand a slight squeeze, then placed it back atop the old man's chest. He was held there for just an instant, staring at his father and feeling the hints of coming grief, and then he was propelled away by the hints of coming responsibility.

By the time he reached the room where Brother Bathelais waited, his step was brisk and alive.

"There is word that Laird Pryd does not fare well," the monk said as soon as Prydae, after glancing both ways in the corridor to ensure that no one was watching, entered the private room.

"Age wins," the prince dryly returned. He took a seat across the hearthstone from the monk.

"I will send Brother Bran Dynard, who is only just returned, to his side posthaste."

"Not that one," Prydae quickly replied. "Nor his exotic concubine."

"You have heard, then."

The prince nodded.

"And you do not approve?"

"The Church of Abelle approves? You would open your texts and hearts to a beast of Behr?"

Bathelais let the sarcasm go with a resigned shrug. "Perhaps I should tend to your father myself."

"To what end?" the prince asked. "Will Laird Pryd again feel the vitality of youth?"

Bathelais looked curiously at the young man.

"For that is what we will now need in this changing world," Prydae went on. "The roads will connect us all—perhaps as early as the summer after next. What challenges might Pryd Holding find in that new reality, when cities coalesce in a myriad of alliances?"

"Your father's experience—" Bathelais started to say.

"Is founded upon the old reality of individual holdings," Prydae interrupted. "It is time for all of us to look forward."

Bathelais settled back in his chair, his eyes widening as Prydae continued to stare hard at him, driving the implications of his point home with the intensity of his gaze.

"Yes, perhaps Brother Bathelais should be the one to tend ailing Laird Pryd," Prydae remarked.

The monk wiped a hand across his mouth but did not, could not, blink.

"How fares old Father Jerak?" Prydae asked.

Bathelais jerked in surprise at the abrupt change of subject. "H-he is well," he stammered.

"For such an aged man."

"Yes."

"His successor will be determined as much by the laird as by the Church of Abelle, of course."

Bathelais sucked in his breath, and Prydae smiled, marveling at how easily he had taken control of this meeting. The prince settled back comfortably in his seat. "Tell me more of this Brother Dynard fellow and of the exotic goods that he brought back from his journeys through the wild lands of Behr," he bade, his wide smile showing interest, amusement, and most of all an understanding that Bathelais was in no position to refuse.

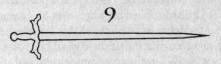

9

THE DANGEROUS
CONCUBINE

"There may perhaps be a place for your concubine here at the chapel, though I warn you that your behavior is unseemly," Father Jerak said.

"She is my wife," replied Brother Dynard, biting his emotional response back. He knew that Jerak's error was neither benign nor a simple misconstruing of his relationship with the woman of Behr.

"Your concubine," the old monk bluntly stated, confirming Dynard's understanding.

"She is as much a part of my heart as any wife could be," Dynard protested. He looked across the small room at Brother Bathelais for support, but found none forthcoming on the icy visage of the monk. "Any ceremony—and of course I agree to such!—would be a formality, following the vows of marriage SenWi and I already exchanged in southern Behr."

"Vows unrecognized by the Church of Abelle."

"True enough, father, and so I say again that I willingly submit—"

"Your concubine will agree to forsake the ways of the Jhesta Tu?"

The question nearly knocked Brother Dynard from his seat.

"For, of course, no brother of Blessed Abelle can enter a sanctified union with a woman who is not devout in her faith to Blessed Abelle. Would you not agree, Brother Bathelais?"

"Of course, Father Jerak. The logic is self-evident."

Brother Dynard rubbed his hands over his face and tried to sort out his thoughts in response to this unexpected barrage. He had always recognized that there would be some resistance to the exotic SenWi, resistance from within and without the Church, but he had never imagined gentle Father Jerak to be so stubborn, determined, and apparently prejudiced against the Jhesta Tu.

"Well?" Father Jerak asked.

"Well?" Brother Dynard helplessly echoed.

"Will this woman, SenWi, willingly renounce the ways of her current religion and devote herself to understanding and following Blessed Abelle? Do you suppose that to be the case?"

Brother Dynard couldn't find the words to answer, but he was already shaking his head anyway.

"Nor do you believe that she should move away from this cult, do you, brother?" Jerak accused.

"Father, there is a joining here of beauty and possibility," Dynard started to explain.

"In you and SenWi?"

"In Abelle and Jhest," Dynard continued.

"Brother, you went to Behr to enlighten, not to be enlightened."

"But if such was an unintended consequence—" Dynard started to argue, but Father Jerak held up his hand to cut him short.

"Brother," the old monk said gravely, "do you ask me to detail the possibilities before you if you have moved away from the teachings of Blessed Abelle?"

Brother Bran found it hard to breathe. How could he explain to Father Jerak and to doubting Brother Bathelais that he had not moved away from Blessed Abelle through learning the ways of Jhest, but rather that he had enhanced his understanding of magic—gemstone and other—and thus of godliness? How might he best illustrate to these suddenly hostile brothers that, far from being a threat to the glory of Blessed Abelle, the ways of the Jhesta Tu would only enhance the beauty of the Blessed One's teachings?

After a long pause wherein Brother Dynard could merely shake his head and mumble under his breath helplessly, Father Jerak cleared his throat.

"There may be a place for your concubine here at the chapel," he said. And he sat back and smiled, as if he seemed to think that he was acting quite generously. "I would ask for a measure of discretion, though. You, we all, must serve as examples to those around us, after all, and while your physical needs are understandable and perhaps undeniable, you would do well . . ."

Brother Dynard wasn't listening, for his mind had wandered down a sand-swept Behrenese road and to a place that he realized he badly missed at this terrible moment. Had he erred by returning to Honce? To his Church and his home?

Father Jerak's voice trailed off, and Dynard, thinking that his inattentiveness might have caught the man's attention, hurriedly glanced back up.

There sat Jerak, seeming perfectly content, having had his say.

Brother Dynard simply had no answer and no argument.

"I trust her not at all," Prydae told his father. "The idea that a dangerous and armed beast of Behr is living right beside Castle Pryd bodes nothing good."

"Rest easy, my son," Laird Pryd replied. He seemed his old self again after his week-long bout with sickness—through no fault of Brother Bathelais, who had done little in the way of real healing, Prydae knew. "This Brother Dyn— what was his name?" the old man asked Rennarq, who stood in his customary spot behind the throne.

"Brother Bran Dynard, my laird," Rennarq dutifully replied. "A man of little consequence, so I was told. By you, I believe."

"But this woman—" Prydae started to say.

"Yes, she would indeed seem more formidable, my laird," Rennarq agreed. "By all reports, she slew several powries in fair combat in a single fight."

Prydae did not miss the man's emphasis on the notion of "fair combat," the subtle reference Rennarq was making to his own exploits in an armored chariot.

"She is in the care of the monks?" Pryd asked.

"Yes," Prydae answered before Rennarq could, drawing Pryd's gaze back his way. "Brother Bathelais has informed me that this beast of Behr will likely remain in the chapel as a worker."

"What would you have me do in that case?" asked Pryd. "Am I to deny her my trust when the brothers of Abelle have seen fit to take her in?"

"It is not within their province to deny your claim," Rennarq put in; the harshness of his tone served as another reminder of his general feelings toward the brothers of Blessed Abelle.

"She should be surrendered to the laird until her disposition can be properly determined," added Prydae.

"You fear her," Laird Pryd remarked as if suddenly realizing it. "Or is it, perhaps, that you fear that her reputation will outshine your own?"

Prydae narrowed his eyes and crossed his arms over his chest, one foot tapping on the stone floor. A moment later, Laird Pryd laughed at him.

"Forgive me, my son." The old man was quick to explain, "I have seen this creature from Behr from afar, and she is but a wisp of a thing."

"Who slew several powries in combat," said Rennarq, for no better reason, apparently, than to thicken the tension in the air.

Laird Pryd stopped laughing and turned to offer a stern glance to his longtime friend, then turned back to his son.

"Would you have a stranger, a foreigner, a beast of Behr capture the hearts of the peasants as a hero?" Prydae asked. "A foreign creature who is allied with the brothers of Abelle and not with the Laird of Pryd Holding?"

Put like that, Prydae's words seemed to have a greater effect on his father. Laird Pryd settled back in his chair and assumed a pensive pose.

"She should be surrendered to Castle Pryd at once," Prydae pressed now that he had his father's sudden interest. "Father Jerak is not over fond of her anyway, from what Brother Bathelais has told me. I doubt he will argue against your request."

"You would have me take her into Castle Pryd, and what— imprison her?"

"Until we can understand her true nature and her intent in being here, yes."

Laird Pryd paused and took a couple of deep breaths, then looked back over his shoulder at Rennarq, who merely shrugged.

"I will go and speak with Father Jerak," the laird agreed, and with some effort—a lingering weakness from his illness, perhaps—he pulled himself off his throne.

A wave of dizziness had SenWi leaning back in the cool shadows of an alcove, broom in hand, when the main door banged open and Laird Pryd and his entourage entered the chapel. The woman watched him with interest, measuring his strides and recognizing that something might be amiss here.

SenWi had been uncomplaining, accepting the position offered her by Brother Bathelais as a cleaning servant in the chapel. Dynard had not been pleased of course, but SenWi had counseled him to patience. At least the two of them could spend some time together by this arrangement, which was much better than an alternative that had him serving in this dark place, with her somewhere away. As a disciplined Jhesta Tu, SenWi didn't fear work, after all.

Without apparently noticing the woman hidden by the shadows, the laird and his escorts swept through the room and down the side corridor toward Father Jerak's private quarters.

SenWi stepped out of the alcove and glanced all around. She knew that this was an unusual visit, and she sensed something deeper, some notion that the secular leader's presence here had something to do with Bran Dynard's return. Seeing no one watching her, SenWi leaned the broom against the wall and moved off, silent as a shadow. She headed down the corridor, turning the corner to see the laird enter Jerak's private room. SenWi paused at the wall and gathered her concentration, then lifted her *chi*, lightening her body weight as she scaled the decorated wall.

She crawled sidelong atop a ledge, moving right above the now-closed door to a transom, so she could look down upon the private meeting. They were exchanging formal greetings, and SenWi reconsidered her course. What was she doing here? What business was this of hers? Shaking her head at her foolishness, she began to ease away, but stopped short, when she heard Laird Pryd say to Jerak, "It would not be wise for the brothers of Abelle to harbor a dangerous animal."

"We are assessing her," the old monk replied.

It hit SenWi then that they were speaking of her. As she quickly moved away, she heard Laird Pryd say something about the need for proper security during such assessments.

She hit the ground running, slipping back into the main area of the chapel and then out the door. She thought that she should go to Dynard but wasn't sure where he might be. In the tiny prayer rooms, likely, but he would not be alone.

SenWi went out and around the corner of the building, moving into the alleys between the chapel and the castle. She found a quiet, secluded spot and leaned back against the brown stone wall, overcome by lightheadedness.

Her hand went instinctively to her belly, to the child growing there.

"They are going to tell you that I must be turned over to Laird Pryd," SenWi told Dynard, in the language of Behr.

"They will not—" Brother Dynard started to argue, but he

stopped short and leaped forward, grabbing his suddenly swaying wife. "Are you all right? SenWi!"

She put her hand comfortingly on his shoulder and managed a weak smile. "I am with child," she explained. "I am pregnant with your child."

Suddenly it was Dynard who needed the support to stand.

He gasped out a few unintelligible sounds, then, his eyes moist, he hugged his wife close, burying his face in her black hair and wondering if anything in the world could be more wonderful.

Finally, after a long while, Bran managed to move back to arm's length. "My Church will sanction our marriage only if you disavow the teachings of the Jhesta Tu."

SenWi's expression went cold immediately.

"Which of course you cannot do," Dynard quickly added. "Nor should you. I embrace Jhest as wholly now as I did in the Walk of Clouds."

"But your brethren will not approve."

"Not yet," he admitted. "These things take time. I will show them the truth, SenWi. It is my place in the world now—well, that and serving you as husband and our child as father." He couldn't suppress a grin, but his smile did not soften SenWi's concerned expression.

"I will teach them and persuade them," he promised her, taking her by the shoulders so that she had to look at him directly, had to see his determination.

"They will insist that I am handed to the charge of Laird Pryd," SenWi countered. "I heard them myself. He fears me, for some reason."

"Or he wishes to learn from you. Might it be that Laird Pryd has heard of your exploits against the powries?"

"He likely would have, since you boasted of it to his soldiers."

"Then perhaps he wishes to have you teach his soldiers or his son."

SenWi's lips went very tight and she shook her head.

Brother Dynard hadn't expected any different reaction, of

course, for he understood that the Jhesta Tu weren't about to divulge their secrets of combat. To the southern mystics, the learning of martial arts was part of the process of learning the Book of Jhest, and to remove the specifics of combat from that overall process went against everything they believed. Dynard had made the suggestion of intent only to place a less menacing twist on the laird's apparent interest in SenWi, to try to lighten their shared fears.

"I just mean—" he started to explain.

"I am vulnerable now," SenWi interrupted, and she took Bran's hand and placed it on her belly.

He could hardly draw breath. He turned his hand over and clasped SenWi's tightly, pulling her close. He looked up at the sky as late afternoon turned to twilight. "Come," he bade her. "We will get you out to Garibond's house, where you will be safe. I will tell my brethren that you have departed for Behr, that you could not accept the terms of their demands." He was thinking as he went, improvising. "And I will remain steadfast in my support of your choice. I will teach them—I *must* teach them. I see my duty now to my brethren as clearly as Blessed Abelle must have seen his own when he discovered the glories of Pimaninicuit and the sacred gemstones. This is my place in life." He looked back down at SenWi's delicately curving belly and added, "My place in the wider world."

The couple went out soon after, as darkness fell across the land.

Before the dawn, Brother Bran was on his way back to Chapel Pryd, clutching the Book of Jhest, his expression one of complete determination.

He would teach them.

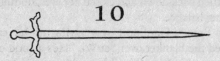

10

THE LOSS OF CONTROL

SenWi awakened with a start and immediately tried to rise. A wave of nausea sent her tumbling back to the cot, and she gave a little cry.

As soon as she saw Garibond coming through the door toward her, she realized where she was—in the tunnels beneath his house—and she remembered her last conversation with her husband. Dynard had wanted to return at once to Chapel Pryd with the Book of Jhest. He was convinced that he would sway the brothers of Abelle, that he would enlighten them as he had been enlightened.

SenWi didn't believe it for a moment. She had counseled Bran against returning—or at least against returning with the book.

But he was angry, livid over the dismissal of their marriage by his brethren and outraged at the notion that SenWi would be "turned over" to anyone.

The discussion had gotten heated, SenWi remembered, with Dynard shaking his head so violently that it seemed as if he were using the movement to physically deflect her naysaying.

Then, in the excitement of the moment, the dizziness had returned, had knocked SenWi off her feet. She remembered being carried to a cot and gently laid on it by Dynard. She remembered his bending low and kissing her, and leaving her with the promise that he would make them understand.

She settled back down and closed her eyes, finding her center and inner balance.

"Trust Bran," Garibond was saying as he came and straightened the blanket over SenWi. "He's a good one. He'll let them know the truth of it all."

SenWi kept her eyes closed and remained focused internally, though the man's words did register with her. She didn't doubt Garibond, nor did she lack faith in the abilities of her husband—hadn't he won over the entire enclave of the Walk of Clouds? But SenWi understood, where these other two apparently did not, that the monks at the chapel—Father Jerak and Brother Bathelais—already understood the truth, at least from a practical point of view. They understood perfectly well that Dynard honestly believed that he had found an extension of their religion, a supplement that strengthened and did not diminish the words of Blessed Abelle.

SenWi believed the same thing.

But she also recognized that the folk of Honce would not likely open their ears to that call. Nor would the monks, nor could they at this time when their religion was vying for the approval of the lairds.

She was desperately afraid for her husband, but SenWi couldn't hold her focus upon that. She was Jhesta Tu, attuned to the rhythms of her body, and she was beginning to understand that something was very wrong inside her. The lightheadedness, the overwhelming weakness, the nausea—all of that could be explained simply because she was with child. But there was something more, she understood. It wasn't just the symptoms but the intensity of them. She had seen other Jhesta Tu women through their pregnancies, women who were not nearly as accomplished in the way of Jhest as she, and they had almost always been able to use their *chi* to overcome any and all symptoms.

That was the problem here. When SenWi tried to find her center, to align her thread of life energy, she could not. It was as if that line of energy were somehow creased and unbalanced, and the problem went far beyond the normal bounds of what a pregnancy might cause. SenWi knew that, but she had no answer.

She did have a guess, though. She thought back to the poor battered girl hanging by her wrists from a pole at the end of the road.

SenWi put a hand over her face and fought hard against her welling tears.

"He'll be all right," Garibond said softly, and he stroked her black hair. "You must trust Bran."

She started to shake her head to explain her deeper concern, but it didn't matter.

Brother Bathelais wasn't opening up. Brother Dynard could see that clearly as he sat across from him. Dynard clutched his precious Book of Jhest to his chest, huddling over it like an eagle protecting its kill.

"You presume much, brother, to think that we are in need of further enlightenment," Bathelais said slowly and deliberately. "The teachings of Blessed Abelle are not open-ended and inviting of addition."

"But even Blessed Abelle was ignorant of the truths of the Jhesta Tu," Brother Dynard said before he considered his words. As soon as they left his mouth, Bathelais widened his eyes and recoiled, and Dynard knew that he had erred.

"Th-those truths are extensions," Dynard stammered, trying to bring back a level of calm that seemed fast eroding. As he spoke, he uncurled from around the book and slowly presented it to Bathelais. "Contained herein are beauteous revelations that enhance all that Blessed Abelle has taught us."

"Then you are saying that Brother Abelle was not God inspired? You are saying that the words God spoke to Brother Abelle were not revelations of divine truth but merely revelations to him of a truth that already was known to man?" Bathelais shook his head, a sour look on his face. "A truth already known to the beasts of Behr?"

Brother Dynard forced himself to continue to present the book. He even leaned closer so that Brother Bathelais couldn't ignore the large tome.

Finally, his face a mask of suspicion, Bathelais took the great book and set it upon his lap. Still looking at Dynard, his eyes narrow, he flipped the cover open and read Dynard's letter—a two-page introduction that was virtually the same argument that Dynard had been making to him for more than an hour now. When he finished Bathelais paused and looked back at the hopeful Dynard—and to the enlightened monk, Bathelais seemed more bemused than intrigued.

Could his mind be so closed? Brother Dynard wondered. Was his heart so encased in absolutes that he would not allow for an expansion of the beauty he had learned?

Brother Bathelais turned the next page and glanced down, perplexed. "What is this?" he asked.

"It is written in the language of Jhest, one similar to that of Behr," Brother Dynard tried to explain.

"I did not know the beasts could write."

The continuing racism struck hard at the heart of Brother Dynard. He wanted nothing more than to reach across and grab Bathelais and give him a good shake! He wanted to tell Bathelais about the culture of the southern people, about the intricacies of their language—which in many ways was superior to that of Honce—about their clothing of silk, and the fabulous colors of their rugs. He wanted to describe artifacts he had seen, hundreds of years old, predating any known art in all Honce. He wanted to tell Bathelais about the architecture of Jacintha, an ancient and wondrous city. He wanted to do all of that; he thought it imperative that his brethren came to see and appreciate this reality.

All he could do was point at the book, although emphatically.

"What would you have me do?" Bathelais asked. "Admire the curvature of your lines?"

"I will instruct you in the language."

"Could you not have simply translated the work?"

"It would not be exact," Brother Dynard explained. "And it was a condition of the Jhesta Tu that any who would peruse their secrets do so in their language—learning the language is part of the discipline required to truly appreciate the knowledge contained within, you see."

"A condition of the Jhesta Tu? They do not willingly share their insights?"

"They do not proselytize, no," Brother Dynard replied. "Theirs is a light that must be attained by the willing, not forced upon the reluctant."

"Are you not proselytizing right now?"

The question had Brother Dynard nonplused. He finally managed to string a few words together in a coherent fashion. "I am not Jhesta Tu."

If Brother Bathelais was convinced of that, his expression did not show it. "What are you, then?"

"I am your brother," Dynard insisted. Though he believed that with all his heart, he could not infuse his voice with any strength under the increasingly hostile stare of Bathelais.

Brother Bathelais looked back at the cursive and stylized writing on the page, then gently closed the book as his eyes rose to regard Dynard once more. "And you will teach us how to read this language of the Jhest?"

"I will."

"And when we read this book, we will learn that Blessed Abelle was not wholly correct?"

The form of that question left it unanswerable by poor Dynard.

Brother Bathelais stood up, the tome wrapped in his arms. He looked hard at Dynard for a moment longer, then gave a curt nod, turned, and left the room.

Brother Dynard sighed and slumped in his chair, glad of the reprieve. He held no illusions that this initial discussion of the delicate subject had gone well.

She stood before the rising sun, her breathing perfectly even, her stance completely grounded, not a muscle twitching.

She focused on the sun, climbing slowly above the eastern horizon. She imagined its rays permeating her, linking with her *chi*, and she used the vertical climb of that burning orb to focus her inner strength on the vertical line of her *ki-chi-kree*. In the sun, SenWi found balance. In the sun, she found inner warmth.

As slowly as the great ball rose, she lifted her arms before her. As so many minutes passed and her arms lifted before her face, she brought her hands together, linked six fingers, and pressed both thumbs together and index fingers together in salute.

The sun continued its climb and her arms moved as if lifting it. She meant to stand here until noon, until her arms above her head were in complete concert with the heavenly cycle. But she didn't make it. As her hands began to lift above her forehead, SenWi felt a stretch in her belly, constricting at first and then suddenly so painful that it had her doubling over and clutching her midsection.

The line of her *ki-chi-kree* could not hold the straightened posture; her life energy had been wounded, and badly—and not just her own, she feared.

"The snake venom," she whispered, her teeth clenched. She understood it all then. When she had healed the poor girl, her own inner-heated hands had taken the venom of the adder into herself. But how had that so wounded her? A Jhesta Tu mystic could do this, with little danger, for the Jhesta Tu mystic could overcome poison with ease.

And then SenWi understood; and her breath came in short gasps and she wanted nothing more than to scream in outrage.

A Jhesta Tu mystic was possessed of the inner discipline to defeat poisons. But the unborn child of a Jhesta Tu mystic . . .

He knew as soon as Father Jerak entered the room with Brother Bathelais that things had not gone well between the two of them, for the old man's face was locked in such a scowl as Brother Dynard had never before seen.

"You have come to question Blessed Abelle?" Jerak asked, and it seemed to Dynard as if he were trying, quite unsuccessfully, to keep the bitter edge out of his voice.

"No, father, of course not," Brother Bran answered.

"And yet, there is this," Father Jerak said, and he turned, extending his open hand toward the Book of Jhest that Brother Bathelais still held close to his chest.

"Father," said an exasperated Dynard, "as I tried to explain to Brother Bathelais, this book, these truths of Jhest, are no threat to our order or the teachings of Blessed Abelle. If we are to believe in divine inspiration, then are we to claim sole province over it?"

"And thus you believe that this ancient order—" again he indicated the book "—received this divine inspiration many years before Blessed Abelle?"

Brother Dynard felt as if he were sinking. He could clearly see on their faces that they had made up their minds. They weren't questioning him now in hopes of understanding. No, they were allowing him to damn himself and nothing more. "It is not . . . There is no threat here," he tried to explain. His frustration turned to hopelessness when a pair of armed soldiers of the laird appeared in the doorway.

"Where is the woman?" Father Jerak asked.

When Dynard continued to stare incredulously at the soldiers, Jerak repeated his question in even sharper and more insistent tones. Then Dynard did look at him, and old Jerak's scowl seemed even more pronounced.

"Where is she?" he asked again.

"She left." Dynard's thoughts were swirling. He tried to concentrate, reminding himself that he had to cover for SenWi at all costs, that he had to be convincing! "She could not tolerate the prejudice and the unwillingness."

"The unwillingness?" came Father Jerak's sharp reply. "To convert to her heathen ways? Did you expect to come here with some false prophet from the land of beasts and undo the blessings of Abelle's teachings? Did you believe that your revelations of a few tricks from these . . . Jhesta Tu creatures would turn us aside from our path to spiritual redemption? Brother Dynard, did you truly believe that one misguided brother—"

"No!" Dynard shouted, and he sat back and went silent as the soldiers at the door bristled, one even drawing his bronze short sword halfway from its sheath. "No, father, it was never my intent."

"Your intent? Wherever did you come to the conclusion that your intent meant anything, Brother Dynard? You were given a specific mission, entrusted with a duty to spread the word of Abelle to people deserving, though ignorant. You were sponsored by and of the Church of Blessed Abelle. You were sent by our arrangements and with our money. You seem to have forgotten all these things, Brother Dynard."

Dynard couldn't give voice to any objections. For he could not argue with Jerak's reasoning. He thought the man's perceptions skewed, to be sure, but in looking at all of this from that viewpoint, it struck Dynard for the first time that these brothers of Abelle were afraid of the Book of Jhest.

Truly afraid.

"You misunderstand," he finally found the courage to reply. "The Jhesta Tu—"

"Are heathens in need of enlightenment," Father Jerak finished.

The silence hung in the air like the crouch of a hunting cat.

"Do you not agree, Brother Dynard?" Jerak said.

Dynard swallowed hard.

"Where is your concubine?"

"She is my *wife*," Dynard insisted.

"Where is your concubine?" Jerak asked again.

Dynard's lips went very tight. "She left. This place, this chapel, this town. This land of Honce itself. She could not tolerate."

"She would go south and east then, back toward Ethelbert Holding," Father Jerak reasoned, and he turned toward the soldiers as he spoke. Both men nodded. He turned back to Dynard. "She'll not get far."

Panic coursed through Dynard and he licked his lips and glanced all around. "Leave her alone," he said. "What reason . . . She has done nothing."

"Be easy, Brother Dynard," Father Jerak said. "Your concubine is in no danger as long as she has truly departed this holding. Laird Pryd has promised me this."

"What are you saying?" Brother Dynard demanded, and he leaped out of his seat and moved to tower over the stooping Jerak. But Bathelais was there, staring him down. The soldiers came forward suddenly, interposing themselves between the furious Dynard and Jerak.

"Brother Bran Dynard, it becomes apparent to me that you have lost your way," Father Jerak said, stepping back to give the soldiers access to him. "Perhaps you are in need of some time alone to consider your true path."

On a nod from Jerak, the soldiers reached for Dynard, who roughly shrugged them away.

"She is my wife," Dynard stubbornly insisted, and he started to take a bold step forward. But before he could shift his weight, the pommel of a sword slammed him hard on the back of the neck. One moment, he was moving for Father Jerak, the next, he was staring at Father Jerak's sandals. And he felt as if the stone floor beneath him was somehow less than solid, as if it was rising up, its cool darkness swallowing him.

He knew not how much time had passed when he at last awoke, cramped, in the dark. The dirt was muddy beneath him, the ceiling too low for him to even straighten up as he sat there. He heard the chatter of rats and felt some many-legged creature scramble across his foot.

But all he could think of was SenWi.

What had he done to her by bringing her to this place?

What had he done to their child?

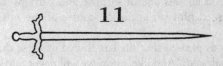

11

THE POWER OF THE
WRITTEN WORD

Father Jerak sat quietly in his private chamber, staring at the troublesome book. It pained him to see his former student so seduced. He had been overjoyed when he had first heard that Brother Dynard had returned to Pryd Holding from his mission in the wild southland, for many monks were not returning. The world was a dangerous place, after all, and Behr was considered one of the wildest regions. In his last visit to the mother chapel in the north on the rocky coast of the Gulf of Corona, Jerak had learned that of those brothers who had gone to spread word of Blessed Abelle outside Honce—to Vanguard or Alpinador across the gulf to the north or to Behr in the south, less than one in three had returned. Even if every traveling brother not already confirmed dead came back to his respective chapel, that number would not exceed one half of those who had gone forth.

Thus, Jerak had been pleased to learn that Bran Dynard, ever a favorite of his, had come home alive and well.

No, not well, Jerak reconsidered, and he looked again at the book on the small table. To Jerak's thinking, it would take a monumental effort to ever get the wayward brother well again.

There came a soft knock on his door, and Brother Bathelais entered.

"He is contrite?" Father Jerak asked hopefully.

"He has not spoken since we put him in the dungeon," said Bathelais. "He hardly registers our presence when we go to him with food and drink. The only reaction I have seen from him at all was one of surprise and perhaps satisfaction when I asked him yet again the course of the missing Behr woman."

"He was pleased that she has eluded us these three days," Father Jerak said. "And likely now we will never find her."

"Perhaps that is for the best."

Father Jerak didn't disagree, though he doubted that Laird Pryd or Prince Prydae would agree. Those two had urged him forcefully on this decision regarding the disposition of Brother Dynard. Never would Jerak have imprisoned Dynard— certainly not in the wretched and muddy substructure of Chapel Pryd! As angry as he had been, and remained, over Dynard's transgression concerning these southern mystics, Father Jerak had hoped to gently persuade the man back to the fold. He had even for one moment considered having Brother Dynard teach a younger brother, Bathelais likely, to read the flowing script in that cursed book, that he might then expose to Dynard the fallacies of the text.

But Father Jerak understood well that he and his brethren were secure and welcomed only under the sufferance of Laird Pryd. Though Jerak had seen a threat in Dynard's failings, Laird Pryd had seen more. Or perhaps this anger at Dynard was more the working of the laird's proud son, Jerak mused. There were rumors that the heroic prince hadn't taken well to the tales of the Behrenese woman's battle prowess.

Either way, it didn't matter—not now. The die was cast, and appropriately so, Father Jerak believed, though perhaps it had been thrown a bit harshly.

"I fear that if we await contrition before releasing Brother Dynard from his cell, then he will die in there," Brother Bathelais said, drawing the older monk from his contemplations. "Though perhaps that would be the best course for all."

Father Jerak answered that with a scowl.

"Better even for Brother Dynard," Brother Bathelais quickly added. "His path is a road to eternal damnation. Perhaps he has not yet transgressed too far for divine salvation."

"Unrepentant sinners are not welcomed by Blessed Abelle, who sits at the feet of God," Father Jerak tersely reminded.

Father Jerak paused, then, and studied Bathelais, but the man did not respond.

"Keep him incarcerated another week," the old monk ordered. "By then we should know the more about the missing woman."

"And if she has not been found?"

"I have no desire to see Brother Dynard dead in our filthy dungeon. If the woman is not found and our wayward brother has not repented, we will accommodate him more comfortably in a room within the chapel proper."

"A cleaner cell?"

"But a cell nonetheless," said Father Jerak. "I am willing to spend as much time and energy as we can afford to bring Brother Bran Dynard back into the ways of the order, but he will not proselytize this bastardized version of the message of Blessed Abelle. That is not a point of debate."

"Laird Pryd will agree to this?"

Father Jerak shrugged, unsure, and especially if the missing woman was not found. "Laird Pryd will see no threat in Brother Dynard as long as we keep our reins on him tight. And I assure you, Brother Bathelais, that Brother Dynard will know no freedom until he sincerely repents." That last statement chilled Father Jerak's bones even as he spoke the words. He hadn't thought of this matter in those drastic terms before— not to their obvious conclusion. That conclusion loomed before him now, powerfully so. Brother Dynard was more than merely a wayward brother in need of repentance or, absent that, of excommunication from the order.

Brother Dynard, by bringing the Book of Jhest, by his insistence on blurring the lines between the Church of Blessed Abelle and this mystical southern cult, was a threat to the Church—one the fledgling religion could ill afford, particularly with the continuing pressure of the Samhaists.

Threats to the Church could not be tolerated.

A week later, SenWi had not been found, to the increasing frustration and anger of Prince Prydae. But, true to his word, Father Jerak had ordered a haggard and ill Brother Dynard brought from the dungeon and placed in a secure room in the chapel. Dynard had lost a great deal of weight, and his body was covered in sores from the standing water and mud. His muscles had already begun to atrophy, and it took two brothers to help him up the stairs and into his new prison: a windowless room on the chapel's second floor.

That night, Father Jerak went to him, the Book of Jhest in hand and Brother Bathelais in tow. He dropped the book on a table near the bed where the ragged-looking Brother Dynard was half sitting—and it seemed as if only the wall was holding the battered heretic up.

"Have you something to say to me?" Father Jerak asked.

Brother Dynard looked up at him, then at the book. "You wish me to translate the tome for you?"

Father Jerak's expression grew very tight and he scowled at Brother Bathelais. "He is to have no visitors. His chamber pot will be replaced every morning and he will be served meals in accordance with the other brothers." He spun back to face Dynard. "But you will not leave this room. Understand that edict, foolish brother, if a brother you remain. Upon pain of death, you are not to leave this room."

Brother Dynard's expression didn't change, the fallen monk didn't flinch as he sat there staring at Father Jerak, though whether that was through stubbornness or a simple lack of strength the old monk couldn't tell. Father Jerak snatched up the book, motioned to Bathelais to follow, and stormed out of the room.

"You did not even ask him about the woman," Brother Bathelais remarked when they were out in the hallway and Bathelais had locked Dynard's door.

"You heard his response."

"A misconception regarding your request? He may have

thought that his release had been incumbent upon our lessening our opposition to this supposed knowledge he has brought back."

"The mere fact that he still harbors any uncertainty concerning that tome, or that he still holds, as his tone evinced, any desire to share the words confined within its pages, is all the proof I need that our wayward brother has not come to the truth. Let him fester through this season and the next. When winter's first winds blow against the walls of Chapel Pryd, we will return to him."

Brother Bathelais did wince at the harsh sentence, but only momentarily, and he said nothing, deterred by the power of Father Jerak's scowl.

She was having a good day, relatively speaking. SenWi had found some measure of energy and strength that morning, and after nearly three weeks of seclusion inside Garibond's house, she had dared to go out into the sunshine. She stayed close to the cottage by the lake, though, well aware that the authorities of Pryd Holding were seeking her.

She managed her Jhesta Tu training ritual that day, as well, and though a light-headed weakness did return, SenWi pressed through the ritual to completion. She was still outside, sitting in the shadow under the eaves of the house, when she saw Garibond approaching, returning from one of his rare visits to the town. She rose unsteadily, but quickly found her balance and her center, and moved to greet the man with a hesitant hopefulness.

She saw from his expression that things in town were not well.

"Where is Dynard?"

"You should not be outside," Garibond remarked, and he glanced around. "They are still looking for you."

"Where is Dynard?" He started to go by her, but she caught him roughly by the shoulder and held him back. "Tell me."

"He is alive but under guard in the chapel, so I heard. You and Brother Dynard are the talk of all the town, of course."

"They are not mistreating him?"

"Who can know what the brothers do," Garibond replied, and he gave a frustrated sigh. "I doubt you'll be well treated if Prince Prydae and his soldiers find you, and that is our main concern."

"No."

"Yes! There is nothing we can do for Dynard, and do not forget that it was his choice to return to Chapel Pryd. I promised him that I would look after you, and I'm not about to go back on my word."

SenWi's expression clearly revealed that she wasn't buying the argument.

"This is likely part of the process," Garibond went on more forcefully. "Dynard knew that it would be no easy task to persuade the monks."

"Where is the book?"

Garibond shrugged.

SenWi looked out toward the distant keep tower, her thoughts spinning as she suddenly came to recognize the potential depth of this problem. "You must return to town, to the chapel itself," she improvised. "I will know more of Bran and of the Book of Jhest. You must do this for me, at once."

"And mark my house for suspicion?" Garibond argued. "Shall I pause and visit Castle Pryd before my return and simply tell Prince Prydae that the woman he and his soldiers seek is safely hidden in the tunnels, or will you remain outside to greet them?"

With her limited command of the language, it took SenWi some time to understand the sarcasm in the remark.

"I cannot do it, girl," Garibond said bluntly.

SenWi didn't argue any further, for her thoughts were already moving in another direction. With her returning strength came the return, she understood, of her responsibilities to her husband and to the prize he had carried from the Walk of Clouds. So deep in contemplation was she that she hardly noticed that Garibond had moved to the door and had pulled it open.

"Come along inside, then," he said. "I've brought some fine spices. I'll make us a stew."

SenWi didn't argue.

Long after supper, with darkness spreading across the land, SenWi sat across from Garibond as he half sat and half reclined before a roaring fire. She said nothing, and brushed off his feeble attempts to begin a conversation. She watched and she waited, and when at last he nodded his head in slumber, she went to her travel sack and rummaged through it, producing the suit of black silk.

She changed and went out into the night, dark and silent, trotting swiftly toward the town and Chapel Pryd. She spent a moment trying to recall its layout, then moved to the base of the northern wall. There was only one window here, set high up.

SenWi fell into herself, grasping the energy of her *chi* and twisting it so that it battled against the natural pull of the ground. Then she picked out handholds in the wall and began to climb, moving steadily and easily—almost as if she were weightless. She arrived at the window in short order and squeezed through, entering the bedroom of Father Jerak himself.

SenWi resisted the urge to awaken him with a choke hold that she might force the information from him. No, such a bold course could prove catastrophic for her husband, she knew. She slipped across the room and through the door to the antechamber, and before she took another step, she saw one of her missing prizes.

The Book of Jhest lay there right before her, opened upon a wooden pedestal beside the low-burning hearth fire. Many other books were set haphazardly on shelves flanking that hearth; and even from this distance, SenWi could see the dust that had gathered on them. Was that the fate that awaited the product of Bran's long toil?

Her fingers trembled as she felt the smooth pages of the

opened book, and she promised herself that she would come back through here on her way out after locating and securing the release of her dear husband.

She moved away, but before she even reached the door, a renewed wave of nausea washed over her and nearly buckled her legs beneath her. Black spots flitted before her eyes, and it was all that she could do just to stand there and not fall over. Instinctively, SenWi clutched at her belly and it took all of her considerable willpower to bring her breathing quickly back under control.

"Bran," she whispered helplessly, and another wave brought her to one knee. She knew that she was in trouble. Her physical exertion in running all the way out here and, even more so, her mystical exertion in scaling and levitating up the wall, had been too much, she only now realized. She thought of the days she had spent in Garibond's house, incapacitated beyond anything she had ever known, barely conscious and without the strength to even stand. What might it mean for Bran if she fell ill here?

With that troubling thought in mind, SenWi glanced back at the Book of Jhest. Then she looked past it, to the shelves and the piled, disheveled tomes. Glancing all around, improvising as she went, SenWi searched the deepest recesses of the shelves and found a book of roughly similar size to the one sitting on the pedestal. She meant to tip the pedestal to the floor toward the open hearth, and nearly did so as she swooned, but fortunately, she caught herself at the last moment.

She didn't want to make a ruckus that would awaken Father Jerak and half the chapel, after all!

Regaining her balance and a measure of her strength, SenWi placed the Book of Jhest off to the side, then gently lowered the pedestal to the floor, lining it up with the hearth. She then opened the other book, taken from the shelf, and placed it on the embers, and after blowing on those orange coals for a bit, managed to set the book aflame.

SenWi glanced back at the crowded bookshelf and wondered how effective the ruse might prove. For good measure and taking care not to obviously disturb the dust, she jostled the remaining books on the shelf to better hide the theft. With no other options before her, she gathered up the Book of Jhest, and with a rueful glance at the room's other door—the one that would lead her deeper into the chapel and hopefully to her imprisoned husband—she staggered back the other way, back into sleeping Father Jerak's bedchamber.

She squeezed out onto the windowsill and glanced down the twenty feet or more to the ground. SenWi told herself how important this was, reminded herself of the grim consequences of failure—for her, for Bran, and for the precious book. She felt inside herself again, found the line of *chi*, and tried again to free herself from the bonds of gravity.

Father Jerak stirred behind her, and she knew she could wait no longer. She turned and slipped down from the windowsill.

And then she was falling.

She arrived at Garibond's house many hours later, after the dawn, dragging one broken leg, barely conscious, and trembling violently in the grip of a high fever.

She was still clutching the book.

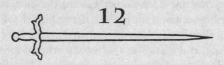

12

THE INSPIRATION OF
THE SEASON

She heard the birds singing every day but never did she open her eyes at their inviting call. She felt the movement around her and knew it to be Garibond, and occasionally heard his whispers.

But it too was distant, and nothing that could bring her forth from the damaged shell of her physical body.

She tasted the cool water and warm broth when he managed to get some into her mouth, but they were sensations of another time and place, of another world altogether, it seemed.

For most of SenWi's thoughts remained inward, sharing herself with her unborn child, offering her love and her warmth, watching the awakening of consciousness. It seemed to her such a beautiful and comforting thing that a piece of Bran and a piece of herself should create an entirely different and independent little being. She felt its presence keenly within her own corporeal coil, and knew after a time that it sensed her as well.

One morning, SenWi heard the birds more distinctly, though it seemed to her as if they were fewer in number. Hardly aware of the movement, she blinked open her eyes. Curtains covered the room's small window, but the brightness stung her nonetheless, and it took her a long time to resist blinking her eyes tightly closed.

She lay there as time passed. She knew not how long— hours perhaps—before the door was finally pushed open and Garibond, looking weary and downtrodden, walked in.

He moved by the bed, a small cup in hand, and it wasn't until he was even with SenWi's head that he noticed her looking back at him.

He jumped back, his eye opened wide, and he nearly dropped his cup, his hand suddenly shaking so violently that its contents splashed over its sides. Finally he managed to set the cup down on the small table by the bed, and he nearly fell atop SenWi, scrambling to get close.

"Are you there?" Garibond asked.

"Garibond," she replied, and with great effort, she managed to bring one hand up to stroke the man's strong, hairy arm.

"By God, I thought you'd never awaken," Garibond whispered. "All these days and weeks . . ."

His admission of time's passage struck SenWi hard, and she, too, opened her eyes more widely. "How long?"

"You've been away from me for almost five weeks."

SenWi found her breath hard to come by. "Bran?" she gasped.

Garibond's smile comforted her.

"I saw him just two days ago," he explained. "Every passing week, the brothers at the chapel afford him more liberties, though he is not yet able to move about unrestricted, and certainly not out of the chapel. He longs for you—I heard that in his every word! But he cannot come to you, for fear that you would be discovered. Laird Pryd and that son of his are a stubborn lot."

SenWi had no idea what he was talking about at that blurry moment, but she was thrilled that her dear Bran was apparently alive and well. "Some day," she replied, and left it at that.

Garibond nodded and started propping up her pillows. "Let us sit you up a bit," he explained. "You have to get some food in you."

SenWi's face scrunched up, for the thought did not appeal to her, but that only prodded Garibond on more forcefully.

"For the sake of the child in your swollen belly," he said,

and SenWi felt his hand touch her there. When she looked down to regard that gentle hand, she saw that she was beginning to show her condition. "A woman with child has to eat," Garibond insisted. "You're feeding two!"

SenWi nodded and didn't resist as Garibond helped her to sit up, and then he put the cup to her lips and let her sip its broth contents. Before long, she had drained the vessel, and Garibond smiled and went out to get her some more.

That, too, she drank, and she was feeling better with each sip of the warm liquid that washed down her parched throat.

"We will get you a solid and hearty meal as soon as you're able," Garibond assured her. "I promised Dynard that I would take care of you, and I'm not about to let your stubbornness get in the way of that."

SenWi even managed a smile, albeit a weak one.

Brother Dynard's eyes and thoughts were fixed on the wider world beyond Chapel Pryd's open gate as he swept the falling leaves from the courtyard's paths. It was late morning, and already he had been out longer this blustery autumn day than he had in many weeks.

SenWi was somewhere out there, pregnant and ill. Every fiber in Brother Dynard urged him to run off to her bedside, to hold her and kiss her, to tell her that he loved her, and to help her back to him. Nothing else in all the world, not even his beloved Church, seemed to matter beside that image of stricken SenWi, for though Garibond had assured him in their brief meeting that she was strong and would pull through, Dynard had heard the undercurrent of fear in his seemingly confident tone. SenWi was in trouble, and for her own sake and despite his every desperate desire, Dynard could not go to her.

He was gaining some measure of freedom here, at least. He had only recently learned of the accident in Father Jerak's chamber and the destruction of the Book of Jhest, and while his spirit sank at the great loss to his brethren, and while his heart ached at the thought of his most precious work undone, all that paled in comparison to his fears for SenWi and his unborn child.

Until very recently, Brother Dynard had believed that his greatest contribution would be that book he had so painstakingly transcribed. But now he knew the truth: his greatest achievement would not be measured in copied words but in living flesh, in his child.

He prayed that SenWi would fight through this illness that had befallen her and that one day he would be able to see their child and hold their child.

Ironically, Dynard recognized that the destruction of the book had probably facilitated his best chance in seeing SenWi or his child again. From what he had learned over the last weeks of his increasing freedom, Father Jerak had visibly relaxed since the book had burned. Perhaps Jerak saw in its destruction the threat of wayward Brother Dynard lessened, or perhaps he was just growing tired of his vigilance. Either way, it didn't matter to Dynard, as long as the result put him back where he belonged, in SenWi's loving arms.

Brother Bathelais called to him, and that reminded him to keep the broom moving. He glanced back to his superior, who was standing on the chapel's stone stoop. When Dynard returned his focus fully to his sweeping, Bathelais called to him again, bidding him to come inside.

Dynard moved into the shadows within the chapel door tentatively, for he had caught a hint of anger in his superior's tone. Bathelais, waiting for him just inside, stood impatiently, tapping his foot on the stone, his arms crossed over his chest.

"Yes, brother?" Dynard asked, keeping his head bowed and his gaze to the floor.

"We have received word concerning you from Chapel Abelle," Bathelais explained.

Dynard's gaze came up, eyes wide. Was it possible that his return had attracted the notice of the leaders of the great mother chapel itself?

"Of course we dispatched a courier to Chapel Abelle with word of your return and your surprising cargo, book and human," Bathelais explained. "Your fall from the teaching of Blessed Abelle is no small thing—not as inconsequential as your death might have proven."

Dynard accepted those stinging words without argument.

"The brothers at the mother chapel will speak with you," Bathelais went on. "As soon as winter lessens its grip upon the land, you will travel north to deliver a full accounting of your journeys in the land of Behr. A pity that the book does not survive, for I am certain that it would have proven of great interest to our brethren."

Brother Dynard felt his knees grow weak beneath him, and it took all his control to stop from falling over. "W-when?" he stammered, for all of Bathelais's words beyond that first simple statement had flowed right past him.

"At the first onset of spring," Bathelais repeated, "as soon as the roads are clear."

"How long? I mean . . . where will I . . . will I return to Chapel Pryd?"

He saw from the expression of Brother Bathelais that his panicky questions were inciting more than a bit of curiosity, and it was only with great effort that Brother Dynard managed to find some measure of control. Behind the placid façade he managed to paint upon his face, his thoughts were swirling and tumbling. He had to get word to SenWi, had to find some way for her to meet him on the road. How could he not? How could he walk away from this place, from her, from his child?

His child!

If he were to depart in the early spring, the baby would have just been born. How could he leave?

How could he not? he realized a moment later. Even if he turned away from the Church of Blessed Abelle now, he would hardly be a free man, and certainly not free from their suspicion and watchfulness. If he went to SenWi, then SenWi would be found.

"Is there something wrong, Brother Dynard?" he heard Bathelais say, and when he looked at the man, he recognized that the question had likely been asked several times already.

"No, no," he blurted, and he took a deep breath and forced himself to calm down. "No, Brother Bathelais, of course not. It is just that I am weary of the road."

"The knowledge you brought back with you from Behr is important to us, of course. If we are to send any more brothers into that vast southern land, as we surely will, then the information you provide may help keep them safe."

"There are fewer threats to us in the southern lands than you believe," Brother Dynard dared to reply, but he did so absently, his mind still caught on the horrible notion of this impending separation from his dear SenWi. In the silence that ensued, Dynard felt the gaze of Bathelais upon him and looked back at him.

"I offer this as your friend," Bathelais sternly said. "When you are before the brothers of Chapel Abelle, you would do well to adjust your thinking more clearly in compliance with the edicts of the Church concerning the people of Behr. You would do well to remember, Brother Dynard, that you went there to teach them, not to be taught by them."

Brother Bathelais stared at him hard a few moments longer, then spun on his heel and stormed away.

Dynard leaned heavily on his broom, needing its support.

It wasn't until nearly a week after awakening that SenWi realized just how badly her leg had been injured. The limb would not hold her weight. Even using her Jhesta Tu powers of healing and concentration, SenWi knew that it would be a long time before she walked again, if ever.

That wasn't her primary concern, however. Her body was in such a weakened state that she could hardly find her line of *chi*, and even less so, that of the child within her. The battering she had taken, from that day she had used her powers to draw the poison from the poor condemned girl on the road, went too far, SenWi feared. Now every day was a struggle—to get enough nourishment in her to keep her child alive, to keep herself active so that her muscles would not atrophy any further, to regain her focus and enough strength so that she could get herself and the child through the trials of labor and birth.

She spent many hours sitting by the window, admiring the beauty of the vibrant coloring appearing on the leaves of the deciduous trees. SenWi had never seen anything like the autumn foliage or the dance of the leaves as they tumbled from the trees, catching the wind and spinning through every unpredictable fall. Bran Dynard had told her of the seasons in his homeland, something unknown in southern Behr, and Garibond had expanded upon that information now that he had the visual elements showing clearly before them. The leaves would fall and the trees and the land would go dormant through the winter season, with its blowing snow and bitter cold. And then in the spring, the buds would bloom anew, renewing the cycle of life.

SenWi found that notion comforting through the long days, and she used it to bolster her resolve at those dark times when she felt as if she must fail.

All would be better in the spring.

"They believe the book destroyed," Garibond said to her, surprising her as she sat deep in thought by the window one blustery day, the air alive with spinning leaves. "Even Dynard."

SenWi looked at him, tilting her head, not sure of how she should take that.

"He is devastated by the thought that his work of all those years is no more," Garibond went on, and SenWi nodded.

"But you did not tell him."

Garibond shrugged. "I would do anything to lessen his pain at this time—and most of that pain comes from his separation from you and not from the loss of the book. But, no, I did not tell him. I feared that someone might be listening."

SenWi turned her head, scrutinizing him all the more. "You feared that he would be foolish enough to again try to foist that book upon them."

Garibond didn't answer.

"He is a stubborn one," SenWi admitted with a laugh. She

leaned over to the side then, bracing herself through every inch of the difficult motion. She slipped her hand under the bed and with great effort brought forth the Book of Jhest. "Do you read?"

"I am one of the few outside the Church of Abelle who does, yes," Garibond replied. "I learned very young, alongside Bran."

SenWi set the book on her lap and drew it open. "Come, then," she said. "I will teach you the language of Jhest. You will see what your friend has spent the last years of his life creating."

Garibond hesitated.

SenWi didn't allow herself to blink. Her duty was coming clear to her now. She didn't know when or if her beloved husband would return to her, and she could hardly be confident of her own health throughout the ordeal of this pregnancy.

She needed someone to trust.

Her child needed someone to trust.

"Come," she insisted. "We've not much time." When Garibond reacted to that comment with obvious discomfort, she added, "The sun is already nearing its apex."

Garibond stepped back out of the room, but only to retrieve a second chair.

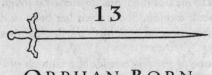

13

ORPHAN BORN

Searing lines of fire ran through her ravaged body, but SenWi did not cry out. They were down in a smoky tunnel where Garibond thought that they would be safer during this trying and noisy process. Up above, the air crackled with energy as bolts of lightning split the sky; and the sulfuric residue, that peculiar smell and tingle of a thunderstorm, permeated even down here.

Garibond continued talking about the weather, about how unusual it was for a thunderstorm at this time of year. Winter had barely let go, with little snow remaining and three weeks left until the equinox. "These storms are usually for the middle of spring," Garibond explained, trying to sound excited and engaging. His voice trailed away, for he saw clearly that SenWi wasn't paying him any heed, that she was locked in a life-and-death struggle against the waves of agony.

Never had he felt so helpless. He hadn't ever watched a woman give birth before, and now here he was, serving as midwife, as the only support, and her pregnancy had not been going well for many months.

He bent low and whispered, "What can I do for you?"

SenWi didn't answer, other than to take his offered hand and squeeze hard.

Inside her, SenWi felt as if someone were grabbing her line of *ki-chi-kree*, pulling and jerking it back and forth. She tried to find some sense of center, some focus of energy, but there simply was none. Spasms shot through her as if they were drops of acid being splashed within her.

She reached with all her powers to try to touch her child, to try to find its life energy. And there was something strong in her womb, a powerful force. But it was not aligned, she understood; it felt as if the thread of this one's *chi* had been frayed.

SenWi couldn't pause and consider that. The pain and sense of urgency were too great. They tore at her and pressed the air from her lungs. She transferred all her pain to her breathing and used that as her focus, puffing in short gasps, gradually developing a rhythm that she transferred to her thumping heart.

And she felt Garibond's hand, a tangible connection to the physical world. She squeezed that hand with all her strength and let the pain flow through her clutching fingers to dissipate beyond her corporeal being.

But more pain built within, faster than she could let it flow from her; and deeper within, the pressure built against the inside of her birth passage. She felt her skin ripping, felt a sudden surge of agony and a contraction of her muscles so powerful that she was certain they must be tearing themselves apart. It went on and on, and she had no sense of time's passage.

Garibond wasn't holding her hand anymore, and she had to fight off a wave of panic, thinking that she must have fallen away from all the world.

She felt him between her legs, then and heard his shout. "Push!"

He called to her again and again, and each repetition gave the failing woman a little bit more to hold on to. SenWi gathered all her strength, all her energy, and all her disciplined focus. She lifted the thread of her *chi*, balling it into a formidable force just above her struggling child. Then, as surely as if she were pushing with her hands or legs, she forced that energy down, down.

Her skin ripped a bit more, and then she felt a rush of

sudden coolness, a great release of pressure, and all her lower body went comfortably numb.

She lay there for some time in the cool darkness of semi-consciousness, her body falling into a deep state of relaxation, muscles sinking into the bed as if she were being swallowed by it—and that was a sensation that the battered and exhausted woman welcomed. Moments slipped past in blissful emptiness, with not a spot of light marring the blackness or a whisper of sound defeating the silence.

Not a whisper of sound.

Not the beating of her heart.

Not the cry of a newborn baby.

She was dying. She knew that, and she didn't fight it. Not then. Perhaps it was time for her to surrender.

Her child was not alive. SenWi realized that her child was not crying, was making no sounds at all. She concentrated her life energy and grabbed at her heart, forcing it to beat. She sent her thoughts back through that blackness, as if she were climbing out of a deep hole, and she finally saw a glow of light. She raced for it, desperately now, as she realized that her child was not yet alive.

Her eyes opened and the room came into focus. She saw Garibond standing off to the side, the child on a table in front of him, blue and still. He glanced back at her, and SenWi could see his tears.

Garibond shook his head.

SenWi rolled off the bed and to her feet. She swayed and staggered and nearly fell. She felt the warmth of her own blood running down her legs, and knew that she was bleeding too heavily. But she forced herself into a stumbling walk to the table, where she placed both her hands on her child.

It was a boy, a beautiful boy, a perfect boy.

His life force was so weak, barely a sliver of energy in his little body. Nor was that thread of energy straight, the typical and expected line of *ki-chi-kree* from forehead to groin. No, she sensed that her child's life line was interrupted at many points, was wavering where it should have been straight and solid. He was not perfect, SenWi realized with horror. He was damaged, badly so; and SenWi knew that it was from the snake venom she had willingly taken into herself when she had healed the condemned girl. As the venom had attacked her, so it had assailed her defenseless infant.

That realization didn't slow her in the least. Garibond grabbed one of her arms and cajoled her to relent and go lie down. He might as well have been grabbing at iron.

Was it guilt driving her? Was it anger?

SenWi didn't care. All that mattered to her was that her baby wasn't breathing, that her baby was damaged, perhaps fatally. She found the connection to his life energy and threw her own into him, offering herself fully to him. She let her *chi* energy flow out of her and into the child.

The blood splashed down her legs. Garibond's cries became more insistent. "Lie down, woman!" he shouted in her ear. "Your blood's running!"

He tugged and tugged futilely at her. "Too late for the little one!" he insisted.

SenWi felt him let go, and then he came back with a thick cloth and placed it hard against her, trying to stem the blood flow. It didn't matter, she knew by then, and she accepted the sacrifice as she came to feel the life force of her child strengthening.

The baby opened his eyes and gasped his first breath, and then he began to cry.

To SenWi, that sounded like the sweetest music ever sung.

She felt her own life energy spasm, a wild dispersal of strength and reflex that jolted her away from her child. She staggered back a step and would have fallen.

But Garibond was there, gently catching her and laying her back down on the bed. She tried to ask for her baby, but was too weak to give voice to her words. Garibond understood, though, and he took up the child and gently placed it on her chest.

SenWi heard the baby crying. She wanted to tell him that it was all right. She managed to hold the baby in her arms and feel his softness and the warmth of his breath against her neck. And suddenly, he wasn't crying anymore, but had settled in comfortably.

The torch-lit room began to darken once more, the black tunnel's sides rising around SenWi. Regret filled her for just a moment as she considered all that she would miss. She threw that emotion aside at once and considered that her baby was alive, that she had given him existence and then had breathed life into him.

To SenWi, there was no price too great for that.

She let the blackness rise, because she knew that she could not resist it. She felt the baby's breath and softness to the last.

He hated leaving the child alone, but Garibond didn't know what else to do. Dynard had to know of the babe and of the fate of SenWi, whom Garibond had buried on the small island on the lake, the island where a younger Garibond and Bran Dynard had spent many of their finest childhood days.

Two weeks had passed since the child's birth, and Garibond still had not named him. He couldn't bring himself to do it. The baby seemed healthy enough, if very frail and thin.

Garibond hurried all the way into town that cold and wet late winter day. He concocted a story of illness, a general soreness in his legs, that would get him into Chapel Pryd, begging healing from the brothers. So when he got in sight of the town, he slowed and began walking awkwardly, favoring one leg.

He found no resistance at the chapel doors. The common area was nearly deserted this day. Garibond limped in and took a seat.

"May I be of service to you, friend?" asked one of the brothers, a younger man Garibond knew as Brother Reandu.

"The cool rain's got into my bones," Garibond explained. "I've come to beg a bit of healing, if that is possible. I'll be putting my crops in soon enough, but I doubt I could bend over to work the ground."

The monk nodded. "I have not seen you regularly in church—it is Master Garibond, is it not?"

"Aye, that is my name. Garibond of Pryd. I live a long way out, brother, and with my weakened knees, the journey is painful. Perhaps if you gave some healing to me, I would be a more frequent visitor in the chapel, bringing donations, what little I have, every time."

The monk smiled at him—a look of sarcasm and not warmth.

"Brother Bran Dynard, he promised me some healing if I could return to Chapel Pryd after the snows," Garibond insisted. "He did, your—our God as my witness."

The doubting smile only widened.

"Go and get him, then!" Garibond insisted. "Go and tell Brother Dynard that his old friend Garibond is here. He'll take that cleverness from your face, I do not doubt."

"That would be a rather long walk for me, friend Garibond," Brother Reandu replied, "for your friend Brother Dynard is not here. At the bidding of Father Jerak, he has gone north to Chapel Abelle. I doubt that he will return before the next winter."

Garibond fought hard to keep his eyes from widening with shock and fear. What was he to do now?

"Shall I ask Father Jerak to come and speak with you? Or tend your sore knees, perhaps?" Reandu asked.

Garibond scowled. "Have you any healing to offer my old bones?" he asked.

"The gifts of God are not without recompense," Brother Reandu recited. "You would find Chapel Pryd more accommodating to your pains if you more regularly attended the sermons of Father Jerak and Brother Bathelais."

With silver coins ready for the passed basket, Garibond thought. He turned his gaze from the useless Brother Reandu and slowly rose. He continued to limp slightly as he made his way out of the chapel, then hardly at all through the rest of the town. Once past the gates, Garibond picked up his pace steadily until he had broken into a run, propelled by fear more than anything else.

SenWi was gone. Dynard was gone.

Leaving him with a child to raise, at least until the following winter.

Brother Bran Dynard huddled under his heavy cloak, bringing his hands to his chest. He had wrapped his fingers in fur, but that was hardly sufficient against the biting cold wind. Head bowed, leading a donkey, the monk plodded along. Only a week out from Pryd, with perhaps a hundred miles behind him, Dynard had found that winter had not yet let go. All the shady areas near the road were still covered in snow, and the road itself was icy in many places. More than once, Dynard had slipped and fallen hard to the ground.

All that he had thought about when leaving the chapel was SenWi and Garibond. She would be close to delivering the baby now, he knew, if she had not already.

How he wanted to go to her!

But he could not, for he had left Chapel Pryd escorted by soldiers—Prince Prydae had arranged an escort to the northern edge of the holding. Even after that, Dynard had been aware of eyes watching his every move, scouts for the prince and for Father Jerak, no doubt. If he turned in the direction of Garibond's house, he would give it all away.

Thus he had continued along the northern road, hoping only that he would reach Chapel Abelle and be done with his business quickly.

"Ack, ye let me have yer cloak then," he heard a harsh voice cutting asunder the smooth notes of the wind. Dynard straightened and looked up, left and right; and as one patch of blowing snow thinned before him, he saw a diminutive but undoubtedly solid figure standing in the road.

"Ye give me yer cloak now," the powrie—for of course it was a powrie—said again.

Brother Bran swallowed hard. He kept as still as possible,

but his eyes darted all around. Where there was one powrie, there were usually more.

"Come on then. I'm freezing me arse off out here," the dwarf insisted, taking a step forward. "Ye let me use the cloak a bit, and then I'll let yerself wear it in turn, and both of us'll get through this wretched storm. Come on then."

Poor Dynard didn't know what to do. He thought of attacking the dwarf, but his hands were so cold he doubted he could grasp a weapon.

He knew that he shouldn't trust a powrie, but still . . .

This was not a normal circumstance.

Dynard reached up and undid the tie about his neck, then pulled the cloak back from one shoulder.

"There ye go, giving me a good target," said the dwarf.

Dynard didn't see the sudden movement, but he saw the spear flying his way. He tried to dodge or duck, but he was too late.

The spear drove into his chest.

He was only half aware that he was sitting. He was only half aware as the dwarf pulled his cloak from him, laughing.

He was only half aware when the dwarf wiped its beret across the bloody wound in his chest.

Then the powrie kicked him in the face, but he didn't feel it.

All he felt was the cold wind, slowly replaced by the colder chill of death.

PART II

—

GOD'S YEAR
64

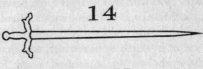

14

TAMING HONCE

Heavy rain poured down, ringing against the metal armor and running in sheets across the steep slopes of the rocky coastline. Bright flashes of lightning rent the air, their accompanying thunder reverberating through the stones.

Prydae looked down across the jagged, blood-soaked rocks and shook his head, his long brown hair flying. The warriors had dislodged the powries again but had gained only a few score yards of ground. The dwarves had merely retreated to the next defensible high ground in this up-and-down terrain of one fortresslike stone ridge after another. And there they were digging in, no doubt, and preparing the next ridge after that one for their next retreat, forcing the humans to battle for every inch of ground.

Bannagran walked up beside his prince and dropped a trio of berets at Prydae's feet. "You claim them as your own, my liege," he said.

Prydae looked at his dear and loyal friend. Bannagran was a giant of a man, not so much in height, though he was several inches taller than the norm, but in girth. His shoulders were nearly twice as wide as Prydae's—and Prydae was no small man—and his bare arms were as thick as a man's thigh, with the corded muscles one would expect on the hammer arm of a blacksmith. His black hair was long and dripping in the rain like Prydae's, and though he tried to keep his beard short and his cheeks clean shaven, as was the style of the day, the long days and difficult conditions were allowing that beard to get away from him. Even with that scraggly look, however, Bannagran kept a youthfulness about him, with a broad and often-flashed toothy smile and cheeks that dimpled. His face often turned red, either in mirth or battle lust, and that set off his dark eyes and eyebrows, which seemed, really, like a single thick line of hair.

Prydae glanced down at the berets. So Bannagran had killed three more in the latest fight; he was making a reputation for himself that would resound from one end of Honce to the other before this campaign was done. Who could have known the prowess this warrior would come to show or the strength? In the early days of their adventuring, a few years before in Pryd Holding, Prydae had always outshone his friend. No more, the prince knew. Prydae was more than holding his own, despite the loss of his prized chariot and fine horse team in the first week of fighting, but Bannagran had caught the notice of every laird in attendance, and no champion wanted to challenge this one.

"Take them," the warrior said again. "More than a few here're complaining openly about the mud and the rain and the shit and the blood. They're needing a hero to keep them steady on the line when them dwarves come back at us—and you know the vicious little beasties will do just that."

It was hard to argue with that. Prydae looked around, following the moans and sharp shrieks of the wounded. So many wounded and so many dead. The folk of Pryd Holding who had accompanied the prince on this journey to the eastern coast had been away from home for more than two years now—and nearly half, at least, would never be returning.

"Bloody caps coming!" came a cry from far to the right, and Prydae and Bannagran looked down the line to see a wave of dwarves swarming over the crest of a stony ridge and charging toward the human line. Archers let fly, but their barrage hardly seemed to slow the fierce dwarf advance. Prydae scooped the three berets and tucked them into his belt in plain sight.

"Right beside you, my liege," said Bannagran, and he moved in step next to Prydae.

The prince was glad of that.

"They're going against Ethelbert's line," Prydae remarked as the dwarves bunched together at the base of one ravine and began scrambling up. Above them, the men of Ethelbert Holding threw rocks and launched arrows, but the dwarves growled as one and pressed through the volley.

"Take the men down," Prydae said suddenly.

"My liege?" came the surprised response.

"Bring the men of Pryd into the gully. We'll cross below the fighting and when Ethelbert drives the powries back, they will find the metal of Pryd Holding blocking their retreat." Prydae turned, a tight grin on his face. "Yes, they'll have the high ground coming against us, but they'll have no coordination across their line."

"Yes, my liege," Bannagran replied, and Prydae recognized and understood the hesitation in his voice, but also the loyalty. Bannagran immediately began calling the men of Pryd to order.

"Onward!" Prince Prydae cried, and he lifted his sword high into the air and led the charge straight ahead and down the rocky slope. They swept into the gully, then turned south.

"Find defensible ground!" Bannagran ordered. He sent a couple of men up the slope in the east, farther from the battle, to ensure that no more powries could rush to join the fray. Wouldn't the Holding of Pryd bury more than a few of her menfolk if powries on ridge lines east and west caught them holding the low ground in between!

Before Prydae's forces could position themselves, the dwarves above to the west, apparently seeing the vise closing about them, began to break ranks and came charging back down the slope.

"Tight groups!" Prince Prydae cried. "See to your kin!"

Half the dwarves tumbled in their flight down the steep ground, but if that bothered the hardy, barrel-chested folk, they didn't show it. Like stones rolling, they hit the lines of the men of Pryd.

One dwarf came up before Prydae and launched an overhead swing, but Bannagran, standing beside his friend, brought his own axe across to intercept, catching the dwarf's axe just under its head and holding it fast.

Prince Prydae wasted no time but stabbed straight out through the opening, driving his sword deeply into the powrie's chest. The dwarf staggered back but did not fall.

Prydae jerked hard on the sword, then pulled it free and struck again, a fountain of powrie blood washing over his arm.

But still the dwarf didn't fall, and the vicious creature even tried to swing its axe now that Bannagran had retracted his blocking blade.

Bannagran was the quicker, though, his axe thumping hard into the dwarf beside the embedded sword. The powrie staggered backward, sliding off Prydae's blade and stumbling to the ground.

Prydae turned to congratulate his friend, but the words caught in his throat as he realized that Bannagran was in trouble: a pair of dwarves were stabbing and slashing at him, forcing him to stumble sideways. Without even considering the danger, Prydae swept past his friend, his short sword stabbing hard at one powrie and driving it back. Across he swung, his iron blade ringing against the bronze sword of the other dwarf, which snapped at the hilt.

The powrie threw the pommel against Prydae's face, but the prince only shouted all the louder and charged in, stabbing with abandon.

He felt Bannagran rush behind him to finish the other dwarf.

When both powries finally fell, Bannagran clapped Prydae on the shoulder, and the two spun, looking to see where they could fit into the continuing brawl. One group of Pryd men nearby was sorely pressed by a trio of dwarves—until the prince and his champion leaped into the fray.

Prydae paused and glanced up the slope, to see the men of

Ethelbert Holding cutting the remaining dwarves into smaller and smaller groups. More and more of those powries broke and ran. "Come along then, Laird Ethelbert," Prydae muttered under his breath, for if the army of the southeastern holding didn't immediately pursue, he and his men would be even more sorely pressed.

And at first it did seem as if the men of Ethelbert would hold their defensive position on the high ground.

"Come along!" Prydae shouted in frustration, for he knew that every second of hesitation would cost a Pryd man his life. "Come along!"

Laird Ethelbert himself appeared among the ranks on the ridge line, scanning the unexpected fighting down below. He locked eyes with Prydae then. Smiling and nodding, he ordered his men down to the aid of their Pryd comrades.

Their charge shook the ground, a continual thunderous rumble amid the flashing storm. Powries broke left and right; some tried to cross the ranks of Prydae's men, all in a desperate effort now to get away.

And many did escape, but many did not, their blood running with the rainwater along the stones of the gully.

Through it all, Bannagran and Prydae kept on the move, joining wherever the human line seemed in danger of breaking, standing strong over fallen friends to keep the deadly dwarves at bay.

When it was done, Bannagran held a handful of berets out to Prydae, but the prince smiled and shook his head. "I have enough of my own this time."

Bannagran returned that smile and nodded. Between his work and that of his liege, nine powries had been sent to the otherworldly halls of their ferocious gods.

"Take the ridge to the east!" Bannagran ordered the men of Pryd. "No retreat to the west! One less gully to cross on our march to the sea!"

Those men who were able trudged up the slick eastern slope and began settling in among the many large rocks. Prydae remained in the gully, moving among the injured, offering comfort and calling for brothers of Abelle to come with their healing gemstones. He stayed with one gutted man—a boy, really, of about fifteen winters. Prydae took the boy's hand in his own and locked stares. He could see the terror there.

"I'm dying, my prince," the boy gasped, blood accompanying every word out of his mouth.

"Priests!" Prydae cried.

"Won't do no good," said the boy. "Prince Prydae, are you there? Prince Prydae?"

"I am here," Prydae yelled at the boy, who no longer seemed to be seeing in the land of the living. Prydae clutched the hand tighter and called again, desperate to let this young warrior know that he would not die alone.

"Oh, but it's cold, my prince," the boy cried. "Oh, where'd you go, then?" His hand fumbled, clasping and pulling Prydae's. Prydae tried to call back to him, to offer some words of comfort, but his voice caught behind the lump in his throat.

"My prince, it's so dark and so cold. I cannot feel my feet or my arms. It's all cold."

A shiver coursed Prydae's spine.

The boy rambled on for a short while, grabbing frantically at Prydae's arms, while the prince tried to soothe him and tried hard not to let his voice break. Then suddenly the lad quieted, and he opened his eyes wide, his face a mask of surprise, it seemed. He gripped Prydae so tightly that the prince feared he would crush his forearm, but then that grip relented, and the boy's hand fell away.

A monk of Abelle arrived then, soul stone in hand. "Too late," Prince Prydae said to him, and he placed the boy's hand on his chest.

The monk stared at the Prince of Pryd. "I'm sorry," he said. "I was tending another. . . ." He started to point back along the gully, but Prydae stopped him—and when he grabbed the monk's arm, the prince saw that his own hand was dripping with blood.

"You could have done nothing for him anyway," he said as

if it did not matter, and in his heart, Prince Prydae knew that he could not allow it to matter. "The wound was too great."

"I am sorry," said the monk, and Prydae nodded and rose. He started to walk away, but hesitated there for some time, looking at the dead boy, remembering his own past adventures a decade before, when he was more slender, when his eyes held a youthful luster, and when he thought he could conquer the whole world.

"We lost seven more, though it could go as high as a dozen," reported Bannagran, coming to his side. "And I am thinking that we should surrender that eastern ridge and pull back to the west, for we're out in front of the rest of the line."

"The southern men did not advance?"

"Laird Ethelbert retreated as soon as the last of the dwarves went out over the eastern ridge," Bannagran explained.

Prydae scanned to the west, his lips going very tight.

"And probably wise that he did," said Bannagran. "None of the other lairds saw fit to advance, and we'd all be sticking out like a spur begging to be clipped."

Prydae looked at him.

"Those powries are not fools, my liege. They could use the same twist on us that we just used against them. Sweep in behind us and cut us from our kin."

Prydae looked all around and heaved a frustrated sigh. "Make sure that all the wounded and the dead are brought back behind Laird Ethelbert's lines," he ordered. "Then bring our charges all back to the crest north of Ethelbert. A fine fight, but no ground gained."

"No ground lost, either," Bannagran reminded him, eliciting a strained smile from his friend.

And a short-lived smile, as Prince Prydae continued to scan the rocky area. Wet, cold, and aching from head to toe, he was weary of this campaign. The combined armies of Honce had chased the powries to the coast in short order, but it had been day after day and week after week of fighting since.

"One ridge at a time," he muttered.

"That was among the most daring maneuvers I have ever witnessed, Prince Prydae," came a voice that drew both Prydae and Bannagran from their private thoughts. The two turned as one to see Laird Ethelbert walking his warhorse down toward them. He cut an impressive figure on the armored stallion, but it didn't escape Prydae's notice that the old man was not covered in the blood of his enemies nor in mud. Prydae had to wonder if Ethelbert had even drawn his sword. Was there a single nick along its iron edge?

"I grow weary of advancing one ridge and then retreating to the previous," Prydae replied.

"Three forward and two back," Laird Ethelbert agreed, for that was a fairly accurate assessment of their progress over the last three weeks of fighting. "But still, more than a few bloody caps met their end this day, thanks to the daring maneuver of the men from Pryd Holding."

"If Laird Grunyon and his men had closed from the south, more would lie dead."

Ethelbert shrugged. "Night is falling, and it will be a dark one. After this rout, the dwarves will not return before dawn. Take supper with me in my tent this night, my friend Prydae, and pray bring your champion with you."

Prydae watched the Laird of Ethelbert dos Entel as he turned and casually paced his mount away. Ironically, it was exactly that steadiness and solidity that for a moment unnerved Prydae. He couldn't dismiss the stark contrast of Ethelbert, in his shining and clean armor, so calmly walking his warhorse past the torn bodies of fallen men, some dead, others grievously wounded, some even reaching up toward him desperately. That's what it was to be a leader among men in Honce, young Prydae decided, the godly separation between laird and peasant, between noble and common. A rare gift it was for a man to be able to shine above the mess, beyond the touch of blood and mud and rain. Laird Ethelbert then stepped his horse right over one wounded peasant and paid the man no notice at all as he went on his way.

Ethelbert was above them, Prydae could clearly see.

The prince thought of the boy who had just died.

A peasant, a commoner.

Prydae shrugged and put the boy's dying words out of his mind.

Prince Prydae marveled at how adept this army had become in cleaning up after bloody battles. The Samhaist clerics accompanying the force went about their work with the dead, consecrating the ground in their ancient traditions before burying men of Honce, damning the ground below the bodies of powries, which would be left unburied. All of this was done under the judgmental eyes of the brothers of Abelle, who busied themselves with the wounded, not the dead, using their magical gemstones to bring some measure of relief.

The struggle between the two sects, a battle for the hearts of men, was not lost on Prydae. Nor were the various effects the two sects were having on the common soldiers. Those hopeful of returning home some day seemed to be favoring the brothers of Abelle, but as more and more died on the field, the Samhaists' promises and warnings of the afterlife seemed to be resonating more profoundly among those remaining.

Prydae looked to the west below the defended forward ridge, where screams and moans and sobs came forth continually, and he shook his head in amazement. For not far above the tents of the wounded sat a pair of Samhaists, staring down like vultures. The brothers of Abelle wouldn't give up the corpses easily to the clerics of the ancient religion, but they were too busy with those still living to prevent the taking.

The tug for hearts became a tug for bodies, a battle from birth that tore at every Honce citizen throughout his life, and even after, it seemed.

Neither Prydae nor Bannagran spoke as they crossed from the forward lines to the rear. They entered Laird Ethelbert's tent with little fanfare and, to their surprise, found none of the other lairds within.

Ethelbert smiled widely and warmly, bidding them to

enter and to sit opposite him at the opulent—relatively speaking—dinner table that had been set out. To either side of the laird sat his four military commanders, accomplished warriors all, men whose reputations had preceded them to this war.

"I am so pleased that you could join me, Prince of Pryd," Ethelbert said when Prydae and Bannagran had taken their places. Attendants moved immediately to put their food—a veritable feast—before them.

Prydae was too busy staring at the cutlery of shining silver and cut glass goblets filled with rich wine to even answer.

"A proper laird must always take his accoutrements with him," Ethelbert explained. "We owe that to our peasants, you see?"

Neither of the men from Pryd questioned that aloud, though both their faces, especially Bannagran's, asked the obvious question clearly enough.

"What the peasants need from us is the hope that their own lives might not always be so miserable," the Laird of Ethelbert dos Entel explained. "Or that their children will know a better existence. That is always the way, do you not understand? A miserable peasant with hope is a miserable peasant placated. We walk a fine line between breaking them altogether, which would lead to open revolt, and teasing them just enough to keep them happily working."

"Happily?" As soon as the word left Bannagran's mouth, Prydae jabbed him in the ribs with an elbow.

But Laird Ethelbert seemed to take no offense. He grinned and held up his hands.

"There is so much to learn about ruling the common folk," Ethelbert said at length. "I have spent forty years as leader of Ethelbert Holding and still I feel as if my initiation has only just begun. But the people of Ethelbert are happy enough, I would guess, and healthier than those in many other holdings, Delaval in particular."

Prydae perked up at the disparaging reference to the largest and most populous holding in all Honce. Set at the base of the great river that cut the main region of Honce off from the vast northern forests, Laird Delaval's city was more than twice the size of Ethelbert's. The river teemed with fish, the fields to the east of Delaval City were rich and fertile, and the wood brought in from the west allowed the Laird Delaval to build wondrous sailing ships that even Laird Ethelbert had been known to grudgingly purchase.

Laird Delaval's army, and his warships, were battling powries up the coast in the north, and with great success, by all reports. That success of his rival seemed to grate on Laird Ethelbert, from what Prydae could tell.

It all began to make sense to the warrior prince from Pryd Holding. The roads had brought the holdings of Honce closer together, had greatly increased trade and communication between them. Several lairds were rumored to be in secret alliance already. During this campaign, with so many armies marching side by side, Prince Prydae had come to envision a time, in his lifetime perhaps, when Honce would become a united kingdom under a single ruling laird. Of course, that presented the question of who that leader might be.

"We are scoring the greatest victories of all against the powries," Laird Ethelbert went on. "More of the vicious dwarves have died here than in the north, and I attribute that to the finer coordination between our forces." He lifted his goblet in a toast, and all the others followed suit.

"In the north, of course, there is little cooperation and a more-hierarchical command," Ethelbert went on, predictably now to Prydae, who hid his knowing smile. "Laird Delaval is not interested in the plans and movements of his peers, unless those movements follow his precise instructions."

Prydae thought to point out that Delaval's force was many times greater than the combined armies of the other lairds up in the north beside him, but he kept silent.

"This battle will be done soon," Ethelbert remarked.

"We can hope for that," said Prydae.

"Indeed." Ethelbert held up his goblet again. "And when it is done, we must all be aware that Honce will emerge a different land than the one of scattered holdings which began this campaign. The roads are nearly clear of powries and goblins, from the gulf to the mountains, and our people will be able to trade even more vigorously outside their communities.

Thus, we must anticipate the changes, my friends. We must prepare ourselves for the new reality that will be Honce. Smaller holdings, such as your own, will need allies, or perhaps even an overseeing laird of a greater holding to secure your defense."

So there it was.

Prydae felt Bannagran's stare upon him, and he turned to offer a comforting nod to his excitable and uneasy companion.

"An overseeing laird?" the prince calmly echoed.

"Various cities joined together in a greater and more powerful holding," Ethelbert explained.

"Are you asking permission to annex Pryd, Laird Ethelbert?"

The blunt question had Laird Ethelbert's commanders bristling and brought a slight gasp from Bannagran. But if Ethelbert was at all discomfited by it, he hid the fact. Again he seemed the calm man on a great horse, unbothered as he walked past the broken bodies of his inferiors.

"I am suggesting that you and your father begin to give consideration to your future," Ethelbert replied.

"We ever do. That is the duty of an independent laird above all, is it not?"

"Be reasonable, Prince Prydae. When this messy business with the powries is done, the world around you will be changed. You cannot deny that. Roads carry trade and they also carry armies."

"And Honce will no longer be a collection of separate holdings?"

"A few perhaps, or perhaps a single kingdom. We all see that. And you must understand that in the end, it will be Ethelbert or it will be Delaval. I offer you a peaceful alliance."

"You mean a subjugation."

"Not so. For all purposes, your land will remain your own

and under your control, though, yes, I will speak for you in the greater affairs of Honce. I will require some taxes, to be sure, and your share of the men to serve in the forces who will defeat all challenges. But for the family of Pryd, life will hardly change, and certainly not for the worse."

"And if we refuse your generous offer?"

Ethelbert shrugged. "Who can say what will happen? Will an army from Delaval march upon you?"

"Will an army from Ethelbert?"

The commanders bristled again, one even rising, but Laird Ethelbert merely laughed. "Of course not," he said. "We are comrades in arms, joined in common struggle. I admire your independence, young Prince of Pryd. It is one of the reasons that I come to you so early with my offer and the reason I do not wait until you have more wine inside of you to openly make this offer." He shrugged and laughed again. "The plague and the sea took my offspring, you have no doubt heard. I am childless. The line of Ethelbert will end with my passing. If I had a son as worthy as Prydae, I would die content."

Prince Prydae tried hard to keep his emotions from his face. Was Ethelbert hinting at a greater alliance here? Did he imply the lairdship of his holding would pass to Prydae?

"But enough of speculation," Ethelbert said jovially. "We have fine food to share and a fresh victory to better consume our conversation. Drink heartily and eat until your belly rumbles with content, I pray you!" He held up his goblet again.

"To Prince Prydae the Bold!" he declared.

Prydae noted that two of the four Ethelbert commanders seemed less than thrilled at that though they did lift their goblets to him.

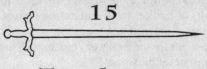

15

THE STORK

Bransen Garibond consciously thrust one hip forward and then the other, rocking his frail body so that his legs alternately dropped in front of him. He was small for his age and desperately thin. His unkempt hair was black as a raven's wing, and his eyes, too, favored his mother's southern heritage, showing so brown as to appear black. His skin was more brown than most in the region, but not enough to show that he had the blood of Behr running through him, particularly in a land where the peasants were almost always dirty. Besides, no one ever looked closely enough to notice, for the more obvious distinctions of Bransen—like his awkward walk or the purple birthmark that circled his right arm—separated him from the folk of Pryd more than the nuances of his heritage ever could.

Over the years, the young boy had learned to give a hasty glance at each footfall, to determine if the foot was firmly planted so that he could continue. He couldn't feel the ground beneath his feet, and if he stepped on an uneven surface or put his foot down on an edge, he would stumble and fall. Bransen hated when he fell in a public place, for pulling himself up from a prone position was no easy task, and showed little in the way of grace to the gawking—always gawking—onlookers.

Fortunately for the boy, he knew every step of every road in the eastern reaches of Pryd Town, and all the way out to his father's house by the lake. He rarely fell these days, unless of course one of the other boys ran over and knocked him to the ground, just so they all could laugh at him while he flopped around.

I don't like to drool. I can't feel the drool. I don't know when I'm doing it. But they laugh, and even the men and women stare or turn away in disgust. The drool and the snot. Always it is on my face, and crusting my sleeves. I don't like it!

He heard someone cry out, "Stork!" and he knew he was doomed.

That's what they called him.

Bransen locked his eyes forward and forced his hips to rotate faster, propelling him along at a great pace for him, one jerking, stiff-legged stride at a time, his head lolling and his arms flailing all the while. But still, within a minute or two, he heard the footsteps behind him, a pair of boys running up close behind, and when that rhythmic trotting changed suddenly, Bransen knew that they had taken up a mocking "stork" gait behind him, falling into line.

He didn't stop his forward-leaning walk. He had come into town to buy some grain for Garibond, and he was determined to push through this inconvenience. He brought his arm up in a jerky motion and wiped it across his face, and though he unintentionally smacked himself quite hard, he didn't blink or show it at all.

After another minute, the two boys apparently tired of imitating and ran around him, blocking his way.

"Hello, Stork," said Tarkus Breen.

Bransen kept moving, but Tarkus bashed him in the chest with his open palm.

Bransen stumbled and had to work his hips frantically to keep from falling. "Leeeave . . . m-m-me . . . alone," he cried, his mouth contorting painfully as he tried to form the syllables.

Both boys laughed. Most people did when Bransen spoke.

"I . . . have to . . . b-b-b-buuy . . ."

The laughter drowned him out, and Tarkus slapped him across the face, silencing him.

Bransen narrowed his eyes and stared intently at his nemesis.

In that moment, standing perfectly still, face locked in a determined and hateful grimace, Bransen did manage some measure of intimidation, did seem, for just an instant, as formidable and normal, as anyone else.

Tarkus sucked in his breath and even backed off a step. But the other boy came forward and shoved Bransen hard.

He wobbled and he scrambled, his hips swaying wildly, and then he fell, facedown to the dirt. He hadn't even been able to close his mouth as he hit, and now tasted dirt and blood.

Bransen fought hard against the tears welling up. He didn't want to cry; he tried not to cry in front of anyone anymore, other than Garibond. He could cry in front of his father; his father often cried with him.

I won't cry, he told himself over and over, but some sobs did bubble out. He heard someone shouting, but he was too upset to register the speaker or the words. He did take note of Tarkus mocking, "B-b-b-b-bye." Then he heard the boys run off.

His father, Garibond, had told him that his life would get better as he got older, but in fact, the last year had been the worst. Most of the menfolk, including the older boys, were away at the powrie war. Those older boys had never been kind to Bransen, but their abuse was usually more verbal than physical. Since they had left, though, the boys of around Bransen's age had taken free run of the town without restraint.

Bransen settled back down in the dirt, allowing himself to relax for a moment to get past his crying. He had to get up now that they were gone, and that was going to take all his attention and determination.

There was no time for tears and no use for them anyway.

But still . . .

As he started to rotate his shoulders so that he could roll to one side, his feeble arm finding a supporting angle in the dirt, Bransen felt a hand grab his shoulder. He stiffened immediately and closed his eyes, expecting a barrage of blows to rain down upon him, as so often happened.

The touch was gentle and supportive. "Are you all right?"

came a soft whisper in his ear, a voice he knew and welcomed. He allowed his helper, a girl his age, to turn him over, and he looked into a beautiful face.

"C-c-c-ca . . . dayle," he stammered, and he looked up at her, soaking in her every aspect. She was not tall for her age and was thin, like all the peasants. But she had a softness to her, a rich and smooth texture to her skin, that many of the other poor commoners lacked. Her blue eyes seemed to glow when she smiled. Her whole face seemed to glow, for Cadayle blushed often, and almost always when she smiled. Her hair was long and mostly straight, the color of wheat, and it flowed like tall stalks in a windblown field.

"Oh, Bransen," Cadayle replied, and her smile brightened the day for him and helped him push his tears away. "Every time I see you, you are dirty!"

It was not an insult. Bransen knew that from the tone of her voice, and simply because it was Cadayle who had said it. She never insulted him, never hurt him. She never judged him, and even wiped the snot and spittle from his face without complaint. And most important of all to him, she always waited patiently for him to stutter through his broken sentences.

With Cadayle's help, he got back to his feet, and managed to offer his thanks.

Cadayle gently brushed the dirt off him. "Pay them no heed," she said as she worked. "They're stupid, is all. And they know they're stupid and they know you're not."

Bransen smiled, but he didn't believe her.

Still, it was comforting to hear the words.

"You've blood on your shirt."

Cadayle looked down to see that her mother was right, for a dirty red-brown smudge marred the left shoulder of her tan shirt. She looked back at her mother and shrugged.

"Were you fighting?" the woman demanded.

"No, ma."

"Did someone hit you? Or did you trip and fall?" The older woman's voice went from suspicious to concerned as she approached her young daughter.

"It's not me blood, Ma," Cadayle explained.

Her mother began brushing at the smudge.

"It's Bransen's. The boys were beating him again. He cut his lip."

Cadayle's mother sighed and shook her head. "As if they've nothing better to do than beat the poor creature. The folk're nasty, Cadayle, meaner than you'd ever believe. How did you get yourself involved in it?"

"I yelled at them and they ran off. I just helped Bransen up, is all."

Cadayle's mother took her daughter's chin in her hand and forced the girl to look at her directly. "You listen to me," she said. "You did right in helping him. You always help him, or anyone else needing your help. I'm proud of you."

Cadayle was surprised by the sudden intensity in her mother's voice and the huskiness, as if her ma was holding back a flood of tears. Her mother pulled her in close, then, crushing her in a great hug.

"I'm proud of you," she said again.

Cadayle didn't understand why it was such a big deal to her ma, for she did not know that her mother had once been treated more horribly than she could ever imagine. She didn't know that her mother had once been thrown into a sack with a poisonous viper, then hung up by her wrists in the wilderness and left to die.

Only the generosity of strangers had saved her.

"Come inside and be quick about it," Garibond said to Bransen when the boy at last returned to the homestead. Garibond put his hand on the boy's back and ushered him along more quickly, the older man's gaze darting about the tree line surrounding his small fields.

Bernivvigar was out there, Garibond knew, watching

Bransen with sudden interest. Garibond wasn't surprised by that, other than the fact that it had taken the old and vicious Samhaist this long to take note of the crippled youngster. The Samhaists were not typically kind to such "inferior" people, for theirs was a brutal religion, ever searching for sacrifices to give their scowling gods, the dreaded Ancient Ones that haunted Honce. Like the second-born twin, cripples were considered appropriate gifts.

And now, Garibond suspected, Bernivvigar was watching Bransen.

Garibond watched the boy stagger across the room, pivot on one foot, and fall into a seat. His lip was blue and swollen on one side, and it looked as if he had chipped a tooth.

Garibond winced and silently berated himself for allowing Bransen to go into town that day. He had been against it, but Bransen, with his typical pigheadedness, had argued and argued. The boy was determined to live a normal life, but it would never be, Garibond knew. The folk of Pryd, the folk of any holding in all Honce, would never allow it.

The weary man thought back to the day of Bransen's birth, when SenWi had given her life to save him. She had thought it a generous deed, no doubt, but Garibond had to wonder. Many times during those early years when the extent of Bransen's infirmities had become clear, Garibond had entertained the thought of putting a pillow over Bransen's face and peacefully ushering him into the quiet realm of death.

It broke his heart to watch Bransen staggering around, to hear the insults hurled his way, to see the other boys mocking him with their "stork walks" behind him. It broke his heart to see the boy covered in blood day after day, whether from the bullying blows or from his own clumsiness. Would Bransen be better off dead?

The question remained inescapable for Garibond, but, in truth, it was already answered, and definitively. SenWi had answered it, with finality, when she had thrown her life force into the dying infant; and it was not in Garibond's province to go against that choice she had made.

He wanted only to protect the boy.

Bransen managed a crooked smile and said, "C-c-c-ca-ca-ca-Cadayle."

"Aye, boy," Garibond replied. "You lie down and rest and think of your little friend." He watched as Bransen settled down on his cot and on his pillow, which was formed of a folded and rolled silk suit of black clothing. In looking at that pillow, Garibond was reminded of how special, how magical, SenWi had been, and how magnificent were the works of the Jhesta Tu, for the pants and shirt and the soft, flexible shoes hadn't worn out in the least over the last decade, and Bransen's spittle and snot seemed to gain no hold on the soft and smooth material.

Garibond thought of the Book of Jhest and the sword of SenWi, both of which, like Bransen, had been entrusted to his care. He would protect them, as he protected the boy.

He looked at the frail figure lying across from him and wondered how in the world he could do that. He closed his eyes and tried not to think of the terrible fate that awaited Bransen if he should die before the boy. Or if wretched old Bernivvigar got his filthy nails on him.

The thought of the Samhaist had Garibond glancing back over his shoulder and out the door, which he quickly closed.

And barred.

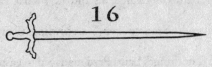

16

HIERARCHY

"**W**hat can you do for me?" Every word came out on a gasp of air, as old Laird Pryd lay on his bed, propped on a mound of pillows. Lying flat, the laird could not even draw breath; and even with the pillows, every inhalation was forced.

"We will pray," said Father Jerak. His head bobbed excitedly, as if he had just hit on a revelation.

Beside him, Brother Bathelais paled.

"Pray?" said Rennarq from across the room. "You will *pray*?"

"Yes, of course," offered Jerak. "We are priests, are we not? Praying is our wont." He chuckled as he finished, though no one else in the room was sharing his levity.

"Perhaps we might try again with the soul stone to make Laird Pryd more comfortable," said Bathelais.

"Perhaps you would be wise to do so," Rennarq replied.

Brother Bathelais nodded, but old Jerak—older than Laird Pryd even—scoffed.

"To what end?" he asked and turned to Pryd. "You are old, good laird. When we grow old, we die. The gemstones are no relief from the inevitable. They cheat not death, unless it comes for one wounded or prematurely ill." Again he laughed, apparently unaware of how out of place his words seemed. "Are you afraid of dying, Pryd? My old friend, I will join you in the next life soon enough, I am sure. As will you, Rennarq—and are you equally afraid?"

Brother Bathelais cleared his throat. "What Father Jerak means—"

"Has already been spoken," a scowling Rennarq interrupted.

"There is nothing?" Laird Pryd managed to gasp.

"My old friend," said Jerak. He moved very close to the bed and put his wrinkled hand on Laird Pryd's arm. He stared lovingly at this man who had been his liege for four decades. "Now comes the mystery. We are creatures of faith, for without it, we are nothing more than the goats and sheep that graze in our fields. I follow Abelle, and I believe his promise of redemption. You will find its truth before I do. Take heart."

Laird Pryd's face seemed as if it were frozen. "What can you do for me?"

Father Jerak fell back from the bed, and Brother Bathelais quickly replaced him. In one hand, he clutched his hematite, the soul stone, and he put his other hand flat on Pryd's chest. Bathelais concentrated and sent his healing powers through the stone, and it did seem as if Pryd did breathe a bit easier then, though only for a short time.

Behind Bathelais, Father Jerak began to pray, and behind him, Rennarq snorted and turned away.

"You raise their expectations," Jerak scolded his companion on their walk back from the castle to Chapel Pryd.

"I offer them hope."

"Where there is none, or at least, none for an outcome that cannot be. The laird will die within a week, likely this very night, and would so fail even if all the brothers of our order crowded about his bed, soul stones in hand." He glanced over at Bathelais, who was holding his arm in support but looking straight ahead.

"You disagree?" Father Jerak prompted.

"This is about more than the death of Laird Pryd, I fear. Prydae is off at war and you saw how Rennarq viewed us."

"Rennarq is a scowling idiot."

"One who will soon enough gain full power in the holding." Jerak shrugged as if it did not matter.

"We fancy ourselves to be healers."

"We alleviate as much suffering as we can," Jerak corrected. "If I could cure age, would I need your arm to get through a fifty-foot stroll?"

"Your bluntness . . ." Brother Bathelais sighed and quieted.

"Speak your mind."

"You offered no hope to them, even if that hope was a false one."

"You suggest that I should lie to my old friend?"

Bathelais's hesitation was telling. "Bernivvigar was at Laird Pryd's bedside earlier this day and last night," he reminded.

"Preparing him for death. That is all the Samhaists do, of course. Their entire religion is based on the inevitability of death. They mete out harsh justice so that the common fools can see death firsthand, offering them an illusion of conquering it. And the Samhaists dismiss the dead as inconsequential even as they pretend to consecrate the ground that holds the corpse."

"And are we not an alternative to the Samhaists? Is that not the message of Blessed Abelle, that we are the light to defeat their darkness?"

"We are. We are a hope for life after death, but we cannot prevent the passage of the body from this world."

"Rennarq wanted more from us."

"Rennarq is an old fool."

"Laird Pryd hoped for more from our gemstones."

"I hope for more from our gemstones!" Father Jerak laughed again and shook his head, though the movement, with his stiff neck, barely registered. "Laird Pryd is afraid, and who would not be? He goes to that place from which none has ever returned. He goes on promises and prayers and nothing more. That is faith, my friend. And it is a terrifying thing when at last we are forced to take the great leap from life."

Brother Bathelais at last let it go, for he did not want to speak his thoughts bluntly. He believed that Chapel Pryd should put on a grand show to try to save Laird Pryd, that every brother should be constantly at the old man's bedside, praying and healing. He had made that suggestion to Father Jerak when they had first learned of Laird Pryd's sudden ill turn, but the old monk would hear none of it. Perhaps, Bathelais mused, Jerak was looking not so far down the road, when he would find his own deathbed. Perhaps he was forcing the laird to face it without pretense, as if to bolster his own understanding that no pretense would alleviate his own fears when the time came.

In any case, Bathelais feared that Father Jerak wasn't looking at the implications beyond the immediate political situation. This was about more than the impending death of Laird Pryd: it was about the future standing of Chapel Pryd itself.

That very night, the monks of Chapel Pryd were summoned to the castle.

"He will not last the night," one of the guards, another old man in this town of very old men and very young boys, quietly explained.

The two monks hustled by, as fast as Father Jerak could manage. They crossed from the gatehouse and climbed the four flights of stairs to the largest tower and Laird Pryd's private chambers. They came into the anteroom of the laird's bedchamber to find Rennarq inside, pacing nervously, along with several of Pryd's attendants and a pair of guards blocking the door.

"We will offer the sacred rite of passage," Brother Bathelais explained, and he and Father Jerak started for the door.

Rennarq nodded, not to them but to the guards, who promptly blocked the way.

Bathelais and Jerak turned curious expressions upon the old adviser.

"Bernivvigar is with him," Rennarq explained.

Bathelais furrowed his brow, and Jerak argued, "Laird Pryd is of the Church of Blessed Abelle, is he not? As he accepted the sacred rite of birth and the sacred rite of second affirmation, the sacred rite of passage is expected, and expressly granted."

"The Samhaists have rituals of their own to ease the way into death."

"Ours is to prepare the dying for their meeting with Blessed Abelle. On his word alone shall a man know the joy of paradise."

Rennarq shrugged. The guards did not move aside.

The two monks looked at each other with concern.

"Perhaps in the end, Laird Pryd was persuaded by the honesty of your rival," Rennarq said. "You could not cure him and neither could Bernivvigar, but at least the Samhaist never pretended that he could."

"Nor did we, against your protests," said Father Jerak, and Rennarq shrugged again and seemed not to care.

"This is madness, Rennarq," Father Jerak declared, and he straightened more formidably than he had in many years. "Laird Pryd long ago embraced the Church of Blessed Abelle and commissioned our chapel to be built right beside his own castle. There can be no doubt as to the road of his faith."

"A dying man chooses his own path, father."

Father Jerak had to wonder about that. He was no fool, and was not unversed in matters politic. Jerak understood the reality of this moment. When Laird Pryd passed on, Rennarq would likely step in as ruler of Pryd until Prince Prydae returned from the powrie war—if that ever happened. This ending, right down to the call for the monks to quickly come to the castle, had been orchestrated by the shrewd old adviser for a very definite effect. Rennarq was sending a clear message to the brothers of Blessed Abelle—not one of outright rejection, perhaps, but one designed to remind them that they remained no higher than second in the hierarchy of Pryd—a very distant second.

"Let us go to him, at the end," Father Jerak said quietly, wanting to seem appropriately cowed for the sake of peace in the holding and the sake of the dying Laird Pryd. "Allow Laird Pryd the benefit of both blessings, Abelle and Samhaist. In the end—"

He stopped as the door to Pryd's bedroom opened. Old Bernivvigar stepped out, announcing at once, "The Laird of Pryd Holding has passed from this world to the ghostly realm. We are diminished as the ghosts about us grow stronger. Let us prepare an appeasement ritual to them."

Always it was about fear with the Samhaists, Father Jerak mused.

Bathelais, meanwhile, hardly registered Bernivvigar's words, so busy was he in scrutinizing and measuring the old Samhaist himself. The brothers of Abelle had a formidable opponent in him, Bathelais understood. Though no one really knew the man's exact age, Bernivvigar was at least as old as Jerak, and yet he was full of energy and the strength of life. By his own example of longevity and health, might Bernivvigar be silently enticing the folk of Pryd to lean the Samhaist way?

"The laird is dead, long live laird-guest Rennarq!" one of the guards proclaimed, and Bathelais's eyes went from the Samhaist to the new ruler of Pryd Holding. Never had Rennarq shown any love for the Church of Blessed Abelle.

Without another word, without a look at anyone— and pointedly none at all toward the brothers of Abelle— Bernivvigar walked past the monks and the others and left the castle.

"We will formally declare the transfer of power tomorrow morning," Rennarq said. He looked at the monks. "We are done here. You may return to your beds or your prayers or whatever it is you brothers of Abelle do at this hour."

"You and I must talk at length, laird-guest," Father Jerak replied, and Bathelais didn't miss the respect in his superior's voice, nor Jerak's insertion of the soon-to-be-formalized title.

"In time."

"Soon," Father Jerak pressed. "Most of your subjects are among the flock of—"

"In my good time, good father," Rennarq cut him off.

Father Jerak started to reply, but then just half nodded and half shook his head. He accepted Bathelais's arm and hobbled away.

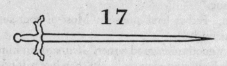

17

OFFSPRING OF TWO
RELIGIONS

Bransen watched Garibond at work on the small rock jetty one damp morning. The sky was low that day and soft with a misty rain. That heavy curtain kept the air still and only the slightest of waves lapped against the rocks.

Garibond sat hunched over, working with his nets and line. Every couple of minutes, he would straighten with a groan. He was getting older now—he had just passed his fiftieth birthday—and the toll of the hard work showed, particularly on wet mornings such as this.

Bransen knew that he should be out there helping with the lines and stitching the nets. Other boys his age were actually doing the fishing and the farming now, with so many of the older men off at war. That was why men had sons, after all, to take up the chores, that they could ease the toil on their old bones.

But not with me, Bransen thought. *I'm more trouble than I'm worth to him, and still he loves me so and never complains.*

At that moment, in that soft light and quiet air, Bransen wished that he could draw. He wished that his hands would stay steady enough for him to trace lines on a piece of parchment, that he could create a lasting image of his wonderful father out there, quietly toiling, uncomplaining, as constant and solid as the lake and the rocks. When he looked at Garibond, Bransen understood all that was good in the world. He felt nothing but unconditional love from the man and for the man; he would do anything to help Garibond!

But that was the rub, he knew, the source of his greatest frustration. For there was rarely anything at all that he could do to make the man's life easier—quite the contrary. Even when he went into town on errands, he knew that it was more for his own sake, for his expressed need to be independent, than for any true gain to Garibond. For more often than not, Bransen returned from town with goods spilled and lost in the dirt. He wasn't even ten years old, and he knew the truth of it.

How he wanted to go out to that jetty and help with the fishing nets! *I'd fall in, and Father would get wet pulling me out.*

The boy took a deep breath to throw aside the thoughts before more tears began to drip from his eyes. He swiveled his hips and did his stork walk back into the house, where he collapsed on his bed. Another day in the life of Bransen Garibond. Another day of unfulfilled wishes and of guilt.

He fell asleep and dreamed of fishing beside his father. He dreamed of walking, of running, even. He dreamed of telling his father that he loved him, without the spit flying and without turning a simple word like "love" into a rattling cacophony of half-bitten syllables.

"The clouds are lifting." Garibond's voice awakened him sometime later. "Do you mean to waste the whole of the day on your bed? Come along. I need to collect some vines."

Bransen managed to roll to one side and prop himself on his elbow. "I—I wou—wou—would just slo-ow you."

"Nonsense!" Garibond bellowed, and he walked over and helped lift the frail youngster from the cot to a standing position, and held on until he was sure that Bransen had found his footing. "And even if you do, I'd rather take three hours with your company than spend an hour alone."

The sincerity in that remark was all too clear to Bransen, defeating all his protests and arguments before he could begin to stutter them. He managed a smile and didn't even worry that parting his lips allowed a bit of drool to escape—because he knew that Father didn't care in the least. That mitigation wasn't complete within Bransen, though.

"Come on, then. I get lonely out there." Garibond ruffled

Bransen's dark hair and turned to leave, but the boy made no move to follow.

"You ch-ch-cho-ose this . . . l-li-l-l-life," he said.

Garibond, at the door, turned and watched him through the last half of the sentence, showing his typical patience with the painful speech but also wearing an expression of deep curiosity and concern.

"I did," he replied.

"You l . . . y-y-y-you . . . like alone."

Garibond sighed and dropped his gaze. "I thought I did," he clarified. "And now I prefer you."

"No."

Again Garibond put on that curious and concerned look. "What is the matter, Bransen?"

The boy gasped and sniffled, his thin chest heaving. "I should be dead!" he blurted; the words carried emotions so powerful that for once he didn't stutter at all.

Garibond's eyes widened in alarm and he rushed to tower over the frail boy. "Don't you ever say that!" he cried, and he lifted his hand as if he meant to strike out at Bransen, who didn't flinch in the least.

"Y—yes!"

"No, and don't you ever think that! You are alive, and that's wonderful, for all the trouble. You're alive because your mother . . . because . . ."

Bransen stared at the man, not quite knowing what to make of the twisted and confused expression. It wasn't often that he had seen sensible and stable Garibond ruffled, and never to this extent.

The older man took a few deep breaths and calmed, then sat down on the cot and pulled Bransen down beside him, gently draping his arm across the boy's shoulders. "Don't you ever say that or even think that," he said.

"B-b-but—"

Garibond put a finger over Bransen's lips to quiet him. "I once thought the same thing," he admitted, "when you were born. And the trials you face pain me every day—probably more than they pain you, you're such a strong one inside. The Samhaists say that any child born less than perfect is meant as a sacrifice, and that is still the way in many towns.

"But not for you, because of your mother. I haven't told you enough of SenWi, Bransen, and what a special woman she was. You know that you got part of your name from her, and that she died when you were born. The rest of your name came from your father."

"G—Gar—"

"No," Garibond interrupted. "I gave you that surname, as was my right. Your father's name was Bran. Bran Dynard, a monk of the brothers of Abelle."

The boy's jaw drooped open wide, drool escaping unheeded.

Garibond turned, and turned Bransen, so that he was looking the boy in the eye. "I am not your father, Bransen, though no man could love any child more than I love you."

The boy began to slowly shake his head. Tears welled in his eyes and rolled down his cheeks, and he began to tremble so fiercely that Garibond had to hold him tight to keep him steady.

"Please forgive me," Garibond said. "You are old enough now. You need to hear this, all of it. You need to know about Bran, my dearest friend in all the world. You need to know about SenWi." He couldn't help but smile as he said the name, and a wistful look came into his good eye. "She didn't just die when you were born, Bransen. She gave her life to you so that you could live."

Bransen, stunned already, was even more surprised when Garibond, who rarely showed any emotion, leaned over and kissed him on the forehead. The older man rose, then, and slowly moved across the room to the trapdoor leading to the tunnels below.

"You were dying even as you were born," he explained. "You were too weak to draw breath, and SenWi wasn't much better off after the birth. But she was no ordinary person, your mother." He reached down and lifted the door, and then removed one of the side boards of the solid wooden casing. He reached into the hidden compartment and pulled forth a thick book, held it up, and blew the dust from it. "She was a Jhesta Tu mystic," he said, and Bransen had no idea what that meant, and he let his expression show it, as much as he could manage to let his expression show anything purposefully.

"A magical person," Garibond explained, "more so even than those brothers with their gemstones. Your father went to her land to convert her people to his religion and wound up seeing the truth in SenWi's beliefs." He presented the book to Bransen. "It's all in here. All the secrets."

"M-m-my . . . fath-fath-fa-ther?" The boy trembled, tears flowing more freely. *What are you saying to me?* his thoughts screamed at Garibond, though he knew that he would never find strength to voice the words. *You are my father! You! Not anyone else! How can you say these lies? Why do you wish to hurt me?*

"SenWi knew that you both were dying," Garibond went on very slowly, making sure that Bransen was hearing him past the obvious turmoil his revelations had brought. "So she used her magic to give you what was left of her own life, so that you could survive."

Bransen seemed to simply melt then upon the bed, his tiny body bouncing with sobs, and assorted shrieks issuing forth from his tortured mouth. Garibond rushed to him and held him and let him cry it all out. For more than an hour, he sat with the boy, gently patting him and telling him that he loved him and that it would all be all right. For more than an hour, he told Bransen that he was old enough to learn of these unsettling things, and promised the boy over and over that he would understand just how special he was when he heard the full story of his mother and father.

Finally, Bransen composed himself enough so that Garibond could pull him back up to a sitting position, and then the older man truly began the story. He told Bransen of his younger days with Bran Dynard, of how Bran had entered the Church of Abelle but Garibond had not. He spoke of Bran's travels to the strange lands south of the southern mountains, relating all the stories Bran had told to him of the Behr and the Jhesta Tu. His good eye sparkled when he talked of Bran's return to Pryd Holding, SenWi at his side, determined to enlighten his brethren about the beauties he had learned among the Jhesta Tu.

"That first day back was trouble, though," Garibond said in more somber tones. "Your father and mother came across a woman who had been tried and convicted before Bernivvigar."

Bransen shuddered at the name.

"He condemned her to death, and so she was bitten by a deadly snake and hung up to die slowly and painfully out along the southern road. Powries were there with her, dipping their caps in her blood!"

Bransen sucked in his breath, eyes going wide, fully caught in the tale now.

"But your mother and father fought them away," Garibond said, his voice showing his eagerness in injecting some real drama into the story and to paint Bransen's parents in the heroic light they deserved. "And then your mother—what a special lass she truly was!—used her mystical powers to cure the poor girl. Aye, but in that, she brought the poison into her own body, and it was that same poison that so hurt you, and her, in the end. Your affliction is because of generosity, my son. That might make it seem harder, I suppose, but to my thinking, it makes you no less a hero than your mother."

"Is—is—is she st-st-still . . . a—live?"

"The poor girl? Well, I've no idea, to tell the truth. If she's not, then it has nothing to do with that day, ten years ago. She left here of her own accord, walking with strength. And all because of your mother."

Bransen sat quietly and let that sink in, then turned a curious look up at Garibond. "B-b-b-but . . . my . . . fa-fa . . ."

"Your father?"

Bransen nodded.

"He was sent away by Father Jerak. Jerak did not much like your mother, for her powerful religion threatened him, I think.

He didn't want to hear what your father had to tell him. So he sent your father away, to the north, to Chapel Abelle on the Gulf of Corona."

Bransen's curious look didn't abate.

"I don't know," Garibond admitted. "We never heard from him again. He may be up there at Chapel Abelle to this day, but Father Jerak's been telling me that he never got there at all. I do not know what to believe, Bransen.

"And I cannot believe that I told you all this in one sitting!" Garibond went on a moment later. "But you had to know— and you have to know that this changes nothing between us. You and me, we're family. Father and son, as far as I'm concerned. And don't you ever say to me again that you should die." He poked a finger threateningly at Bransen's face. "Don't you ever!"

Garibond couldn't hold the scowling pose, and he fell forward, wrapping Bransen in a tight and loving hug, and he held him there for a long, long time.

Garibond watched Bransen closely in the hours following their talk. He had placed so much on the shoulders of the frail boy—too much, perhaps.

Bransen, whose face was far too numb to show any but the most extreme emotions, seemed to move about with his typical posture and demeanor, giving Garibond few clues. He kept going back to the thick book, however. He'd stand beside it and run his fingers over the cloth cover, staring down, as if he were trying to somehow connect with his mother through those mystical pages.

"Do you know what a book is?" Garibond asked him on one such occasion.

Bransen jumped back from the tome, startled by the unexpected remark, and shifted to look curiously at Garibond.

Garibond smiled to reassure him, then walked over. "A book," he explained, gently pulling open the cover of the tome. He watched Bransen as he did, and was surprised at how the boy's eyes lit up, and at the sudden look of curiosity that crossed Bransen's face as he leaned in closer to see the gracefully curving letters.

"Your father penned it, one line at a time. It took him years." As he spoke, Garibond ran the tip of his index finger under the first line of the text, right to left as SenWi had taught him. When Bransen tentatively moved his hand toward the enticing letters, Garibond took him by the wrist and placed his fingers on the soft page. "Each of these lines is a letter," he tried to explain, and he scrunched up his face, wondering how in the world he might even begin to explain what a letter might be. He took Bransen's hand more firmly and moved it across one complete word, then spoke the translated word, "foot," out loud.

Bransen stared at him, then nodded and looked back at the page.

Garibond was tired from his long work that morning and even more from revealing so much painful information to Bransen. He wanted nothing more than to eat his supper and go to a well-deserved night's rest. But he could not deny the look on Bransen's face and, given his fears that he had overwhelmed the boy with sorrowful news, he understood his duty here.

Besides, after a few more minutes, after settling on the bed with Bransen sitting beside him, the book across their laps, Garibond found himself invigorated by teaching. He went through each of the letters, as SenWi had done with him. He pointed out and spoke aloud all the familiar words he could readily find on a page, then read complete sentences.

Garibond remembered SenWi's plea to him, that he teach the Book of Jhest to her child. He considered the high hopes, the promise held by the coming baby, and he had to fight back tears over and over again.

For now he considered the futility of this exercise. What might he really teach this idiot boy who could barely manage to walk and talk?

But Garibond quickly pushed those negative thoughts

away, even managing a wide and sincere smile when Bransen stuttered out the word for arm. This exercise wasn't about the boy, the lonely older man soon realized, but for him. This was a way to reconnect with those lost to him, to hear again the voice of Brother Bran Dynard and that wonderful wife of his.

Finally, the daylight faded too much to continue and Garibond rose to leave, closing the book.

Bransen clutched it close and would not let go.

Smiling, nodding, Garibond let him keep it. A short while later, candle in hand, Garibond checked on the boy, to find him sleeping restfully—more so than Garibond had expected given the revelations of the day—his arms wrapped about the book, holding it close to his chest, his head on the clothing of SenWi.

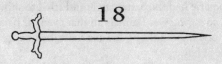

18

FOR THE LINE OF PRYD

The smell of brine hung thick in the air; they could hear the waves crashing against the rocks beyond the few remaining eastern ridges, and with great hopes and great hunger to be done with this awful campaign, the men of the many holdings pressed forward. The intensity of their charge drove the bloody-cap dwarves before them, spurred by the common cry to "push them into the sea!"

Led by their eager young prince and by the mighty Bannagran, the men of Pryd Holding drove hard from the southern end of the line. Bannagran charged out in front, his heavy axe clearing the way of powries with powerful sweeps.

One dwarf got past that flashing blade and rushed hard at the large man's side, short sword leading. It clipped Bannagran's hip, and the man grimaced and turned. Out snapped Bannagran's hand, catching the dwarf by the front of its leather tunic.

Up into the air went the powrie, soaring over the ridge line to bounce down the rocky eastern side.

Two other dwarves pressed Bannagran furiously from the front, whacking at his blocking axe with their spiked clubs. He was forced back and slipped down to one knee, and the dwarves charged in for the kill. But Bannagran scooped up a large rock and hurled it forward, smacking one powrie squarely in the face. Up came the huge warrior, prodding the spiked tip of his axe straight ahead to halt the charge of the second dwarf.

The powrie had the better angle and tried to shove that axe aside, but so strong was Bannagran that even off balance, even with only one hand holding the axe shaft, he managed to keep the powrie at bay.

Bannagran got his feet under him, and he stood up and lunged forward, his other hand now slapping against his axe handle. He forged ahead, and the powrie gave ground and slipped a step to the side. Instead of following the movement, Bannagran snapped his axe the other way. Suddenly free of the entanglement, the powrie stumbled on the uneven ground, putting distance between himself and the axe—and that gave Bannagran enough room to maneuver and strike, his axe plowing into the dwarf.

He had to reverse his swing immediately, though; and he took the head from a second dwarf that was clambering over the rocky ridge.

Propelled by the warrior's gains, Prince Prydae led the rest of his forces in a sudden charge up the ridge. The powries broke before them, affording them the high ground and offering a moment of respite from the nearly constant fighting of that morning. As soon as he was clear, the prince rushed up beside his friend and clapped Bannagran on the shoulder. "We have met our objective and the sun has not yet reached its apex," Prydae congratulated.

"Our comrades have not shared in our good fortune this day," Bannagran replied as both of them looked northward, where the men of several other holdings lagged, mired in heavy battle with the fierce and stubborn dwarves.

"If I could offer them sons of Bannagran to spearhead their charge . . ." Prydae said, and when Bannagran turned to regard him, he found his prince smiling.

"I hear the waves!" one man cried from behind them, and that brought a cheer from all the men of Pryd.

Prydae's smile became a wry grin. "Is our work done this day?"

Bannagran saw the answer clearly in the man's expression. "It came to us too easily," he replied with a shake of his head.

"Let us press on."

"We risk leaving our support behind," Bannagran warned.

"To the east a bit, but then north," Prydae explained. "Let us turn the end of the line so that the powries cannot flee around us."

Bannagran looked back to the battlefield in the north, across the broken and rocky terrain. All seemed quiet in the east, after all, and the day's fighting was not half done.

Prydae clapped him on the shoulder once more. "You take half our charges and move straight north in support of the men of Laird Ethelbert. I will hold your eastern flank with the other half."

Bannagran fixed him with a knowing stare.

"I will spread my forces out in a secure line north to south," Prydae promised, "to ensure that I am not flanked." He clapped Bannagran once again and moved off, calling his men to order.

"The daring young Prince of Pryd," Laird Ethelbert remarked when one of his commanders brought news of the unexpected northward curl of the army of Pryd Holding. "Ever out in front is that one."

"The powries break before his ranks," said the commander. "The men of Pryd have marked themselves well."

"Yes, particularly Prydae's large friend. One victory after another for the men of Pryd." Ethelbert smiled as he considered his own words. He wasn't jealous of Prydae's gains; quite the contrary: Ethelbert figured that Prydae's reputation would serve him well when he annexed Pryd Holding into the greater kingdom of Ethelbert, opposing Delaval. Though they remained far in the north, the men of Delaval had no doubt heard of Prydae's exploits here. What might their reaction be if Laird Delaval, attempting to take all of Honce for himself, ordered them into battle against the daring and cunning young prince and his soon-to-be-legendary champion?

"Tell your men to take the valor of Pryd Holding as their

example," Ethelbert instructed his commanders. "Let us press forward as Prydae and his forces seal the trap. The more powries we kill now, the fewer we will have to kill later. Perhaps this day will mark the end of our troubles.

"So valiantly, one and all of Ethelbert!" the laird cried loudly. "The completion of our task lies before us this day, and the road home is at hand!"

With cheers reverberating along the line, the men of Ethelbert Holding charged forward against the fierce dwarves. Their advance inspired those armies of the lesser holdings flanking them to fight on more courageously.

Laird Ethelbert shifted his gaze from his own men to the army of Pryd, who were forming a line east to west, up one side of a ridge and down the other. Still the powries broke before them as they made their way north.

Ethelbert wondered if he might be watching the champion he would name as heir to Ethelbert Holding.

The powries continued to break ranks and flee, and the men of Pryd, led by their new champion, Bannagran, eagerly gave chase. Even those at the end of the line looked ahead more than behind as they swept along the ridge line.

Which was exactly what the powries had anticipated.

Standing in the center of the two lines, Prydae clearly saw the first signs of the counterattack. Powries leaped up from concealment in the rocks and pressed against the trailing edges of the Pryd line.

"Turn, lads! Close up the line!" he cried. "Hold, Bannagran! Tighten the ranks!" As he shouted, Prydae moved south along his trailing forces, and each step more clearly revealed to him the urgency of the situation. For this was no disorganized and desperate maneuver by the dwarves. The prince had to wonder if all his army's gains that morning had been but illusion. Had the powries allowed him, even enticed him along on his sudden push?

There was no time for Prydae to stop and think about it, for the fight was on at the southernmost end of the line, his soldiers already sorely pressed by a score of dirty dwarves. Into their midst charged the valiant prince, his sword ringing hard against a powrie weapon.

He turned the powrie blade and, with a burst of rage, leaped forward and struck hard, driving his sword deep into powrie flesh. He cried out to bolster his men; but it was hardly necessary, for his presence alone had already stabilized their defense and solidified their determination. Not a man broke ranks and ran.

For a moment, the powrie attack seemed to waver, as several dwarves fell, and others shied from the sudden presence of the mighty prince. But then came further proof to Prydae that this was not an improvisation by the bloody caps; for the second wave came on the length of the Pryd line, locking his men into place as they tried to reinforce the weakness along their ranks. And from the south and west, behind Prydae and his men, came a second group of dwarves, howling and hungry; and some already seemed to reach for their berets, as if the spilling of human blood was inevitable.

Prydae batted aside one thrusting sword, then backhanded to clip off the head of a spear. Then he ducked to avoid a second spear, thrown from somewhere in the rear ranks of dwarves. Acting purely on instinct now, Prydae roared encouragement to his men and forced himself to press on. For he knew that to run was to die, that the dwarves had them caught, whatever the outcome might be. And he knew that without his example many men would turn and run and that would spell doom for them all.

"Hold strong!" he yelled, parrying another sword blow, then thrusting forward to send a powrie spinning down in pain. "Fight them, I tell you! Hold strong! Bannagran!"

Above all the turmoil, Bannagran heard his prince's call. He brought his axe high to intercept an overhand chop by one dwarf, then stepped in, his sheer strength forcing the powrie's axe over its head. He gave a sudden jerk, throwing the powrie off balance, then caught the dwarf by the front of its shirt and lifted it into the air.

"Bannagran!" Prydae called again in desperate tones, and the mighty warrior threw the dwarf back into its fellows, forcing that entire section of the powrie line backward just a bit— enough for him to turn and locate his prince amid the confusion of the melee.

The huge man winced as Prydae swiveled away from one thrust and barely pushed a second spear aside. Bannagran's hopes soared for an instant, when Prydae not only intercepted a third blade but also suddenly turned and sprang forward, his sword taking down one of a trio of powries. The prince landed in perfect balance and began to fend against the remaining two.

Bannagran's hopeful nod froze when he noted, and Prydae obviously did not, that the dwarf on the ground was not quite out of the action.

"My liege!" he screamed, and he broke ranks and charged toward him.

Prydae never heard him. Prydae never noticed the dwarf on the ground, reaching for its spear.

Suddenly the prince felt a fiery explosion erupting through his groin. All strength deserted him and his arms dropped and his sword fell.

He was already falling before the nearest powrie slugged him.

Prydae hit the ground hard, his loins torn and bloody, fires of pain coursing through his body. He knew that the powries were closing to finish him. He knew that all was lost, but there was nothing he could do.

He had no strength even to cry out for help, his voice stolen by the crashing waves of agony.

He saw only a blur as a large foot planted itself on the ground in front of his eyes. A hollow sound echoed through his fading senses, and only distantly did he hear Bannagran, though he was straddling his prone form, as he cried out for the men of Pryd to rally round their prince.

Finally, Prince Prydae slipped into blackness.

Bannagran set himself solidly, a foot on either side of the prone and unmoving prince. All around him, the men of Pryd tried to rally, but the dwarves came on in force from all sides. They smelled blood, Bannagran knew, and nothing lured a powrie more fiercely than the notion that it might get to dip its shining red beret in the blood of a victim.

One dwarf came at Bannagran hard from the side, and he brought his weapon up to meet the charge, holding his large axe out horizontally and catching the dwarf's axe as it chopped for him. Hands set wide on his axe handle, Bannagran jerked his weapon, hooking the dwarf's axe under its bulky head and lifting it. The stubborn powrie didn't let go even when the tall human brought his hands up over his head, forcing the dwarf to its tiptoes.

Bannagran turned his weapon and shoved it out to the side, sending the dwarf into a half turn. He saw that the powrie was already winding up for a second swing as it finally managed to plant its feet, but he was the quicker, kicking the dwarf hard in the ribs and knocking it several steps away. It swung anyway, its flying weapon falling far short of the mark, and Bannagran took a step forward and stabbed straight out with his own axe's pointed tip. Stuck, the powrie staggered away.

But Bannagran couldn't afford to follow and finish the task, for all around him, his men were falling.

And there remained Prydae, lying so still.

A roar of defiance escaped Bannagran as he set himself determinedly over his prince and began battling a pair of dwarves. He worked his axe furiously, stabbing and slashing, spinning to meet a charge from behind, and even hopping so that he dropped his feet on the opposite sides of the prone man.

He got hit hard in the ribs but shrugged the pain away. As he spun again, his axe flying, his weapon came together with a dwarf's axe at an awkward angle, and it rode right up the shaft. With a growl and his tremendous strength, Bannagran managed to wrest the axe from the dwarf's hands, but he clipped his own hand on the sharp underside of the dwarf's weapon, the blade cutting through his leather gauntlet and gashing deep into his skin.

Bannagran ignored the angle of his pinky finger, obviously severed and hanging in the torn glove. He couldn't afford to feel that pain at that time.

Not now. Not with dwarves flowing about him and his men, like water breaking over rocks.

Despite his roars of defiance and the brilliance and strength of his movements, Bannagran saw the truth. The men of Pryd could not hold back this force. Prydae was doomed, he was doomed, and all of Pryd's army was doomed.

He felt a twinge of regret and the guilt of failure, and he kept swinging and kept urging on his desperate companions.

Beside him, the powries took down another of Pryd's brave warriors and swarmed over him, chopping and stabbing, many already eagerly pulling off their berets.

The blare of horns rent the air suddenly, freezing man and powrie alike, and as he came to understand their source, Bannagran managed a sigh of tremendous relief.

"Ethelbert!" one Pryd man cried. "The Laird of Ethelbert is come!"

A great thrust, turn, and sudden swing had one dwarf flying away, giving Bannagran a moment to look back over his shoulder and regard the scene. Rolling through the rocky dale to the north came the forces of Ethelbert Holding, chasing the powries before them.

Hope suddenly renewed, Bannagran shouted to his beloved prince, "Hold strong, my liege! Our salvation is at hand! Laird Ethelbert is come!

"Fight on, men of Pryd!" the great warrior shouted, and he followed by cleaving a dwarf's head nearly in half. "The day is yet to be won!"

Powries swarmed Bannagran then, and he went into a fit of

battle rage, his axe swinging and stabbing. They hit him with clubs and chopped him with their fine blades and stabbed him with their fine swords, but he paid them back many times over.

And he held his ground, his legs as solid as if rooted deep into the earth. He was only half conscious when another mass of powries came by him, but enough aware to hold his strike.

The men of Ethelbert Holding flowed past their Pryd brethren, driving the vicious dwarves away.

19

THE WAY OF SAMHAINE

Thousands lined the streets of Pryd Town on the day the men came home from war. Bright banners waved and horns blew from every rooftop. Women put on their finest clothes and danced and twirled with abandon, children cried out in joy, and all the air was full of music and vibrant sound and bright colors flashing.

Prince Prydae led the solemn procession of returning warriors. He sat astride a large roan stallion, riding somewhat gingerly but holding his shoulders proudly squared. Bannagran, with a multitude of new scars, rode beside him, but other than those two, the procession consisted of footmen alone. Dirty and ragged footmen. Men weary of war and dirt, ill nourished and battered. Men with hollow eyes that had seen too much. Men with heavy hearts that had known too much pain and too much sorrow. They and their comrades of the other holdings had driven the powries to the sea and had all but eradicated the threat of the vicious bloody-capped dwarves, but the victory had been long and costly. When Prince Prydae had ridden out of Pryd Holding three years before, he had led a column of more than three thousand men.

Barely twelve hundred had returned, and nearly half of those carrying wounds that would follow them for the rest of their miserable lives.

Still, as the procession entered the southernmost stretch of the town and became almost immediately engulfed in the sounds and sights of the cheering throng, to a man they found their spirits lifted, and Prince Prydae rode a bit straighter in the saddle, and Bannagran managed a smile.

They continued their march through the town and toward the castle, where Prydae would be formally crowned as laird of Pryd Holding within the week. Couriers had told the prince of the death of his father; at the rear of the battlefield, Laird Ethelbert had even held a memorial for the lost Laird Pryd and a celebration for Prydae.

But Prydae hadn't yet been able to properly mourn his loss, and so his heart remained heavy as he moved along the road, despite the cheering and the dancing. These were his people now; this was his holding now.

He felt a twinge down low, an uncomfortable reminder that he would quite possibly be the last of his bloodline to hold the title of laird.

Prydae winced, and not from the pain.

"Are you all right, my liege?" asked Bannagran at his side, and Prydae realized that he had let his discomfort show on his face.

"It is all the same, yet all so different," he replied.

Bannagran nodded. "After the sights of war, it is indeed."

Even as he started to answer, Prydae's attention was caught by the spectacle of a young boy off to the side of the road up ahead. He was dancing, or moving at least, in an awkward manner, his head lolling from side to side, spittle glistening on his face. A man long in years, but still looking quite solid, sat on the ground beside him, obviously trying to calm him.

But the boy was clearly taken with the excitement and seemed on the very edge of losing control as he flailed about, cheering, or trying to, for the Prince of Pryd. Prydae made eye contact with the curious creature, and it seemed as if that link almost drew the boy forward as the prince walked his stallion by.

The boy staggered out; the man overseeing him tried to grab him, but the stiff-legged creature staggered forward suddenly out of the man's reach. The youngster lurched out into the road, arms flailing, legs striding this way and that without apparent control.

Prydae's expression turned to one of horror as the creature stumbled against the flank of his horse, against his own leg. He instinctively pulled his foot from the stirrup and kicked out hard, sending the boy staggering back.

"Control that beast!" the horrified prince said to the man who scrambled out to grab at the poor boy.

"Pardon, my laird," the man stammered. "We beg your pardon. He did not mean . . ."

Prydae wasn't even listening, and just marched his horse along.

A soldier from the ranks behind him rushed out and roughly pushed the man and the boy back from the road, both of them going facedown in the mud. Most of the nearby on-lookers laughed, though one woman and a young girl hurried to the side of the fallen pair.

"My people, oh, joy," Prydae said to Bannagran. "The pleasure of lairds to suffer the likes of the peasant rabble." Had the prince been watching the continuing drama along the roadside with any real interest, where the woman and girl were helping the strange creature, he might have felt a flicker of recognition. That particular woman, after all, was the first woman he had seen executed.

Bannagran laughed at Prydae's sarcasm, taking it as a sign that his prince was feeling a bit better.

Prince Prydae wasn't surprised to see Father Jerak and Brother Bathelais waiting for him inside the castle—though he had hoped that the old wretch Jerak would already have gone to his grave. Rennarq, lean and sharp as ever, sat at the front of the throne room in a seat set just to the side of the throne, as was the custom; and Bernivvigar, yet another remnant of a past age, stood nearby, tall and straight as always.

"My prince," Rennarq said as Prydae and Bannagran swept into the room. The old man pulled himself from the chair swiftly and bowed low. "Heavy are our hearts with grief at the loss of your father."

Prydae's eyes darted from man to man, finally settling on Bathelais. "Old men die," he said. "It is the way of things." In light of that comment, the fact that the other three awaiting Prydae were all well past their seventieth birthday was obviously not lost on Bathelais.

"We are glad that you have returned to us, warrior prince," Bathelais remarked. "Greater is Pryd Holding now that the line of Pryd is restored."

Prydae managed to hide the smirk that wanted to leap onto his face as he regarded Rennarq's slight scowl.

"The line of Pryd?" Prydae asked of Bathelais. "And how eternal shall that line be, pray tell?"

An uncomfortable moment passed between them all, with the two monks of Abelle looking nervously at each other and Rennarq looking at Prydae, his gaze inevitably lowering, then going to the floor and his own feet.

Yes, they knew, Prydae reasoned. Of course they did, for the monks at the front lines would have spread word far and wide of the battlefield casualty, that the gelded prince of Pryd would likely sire no children.

Off to the far side, Bernivvigar dared to chuckle, and all eyes turned to him.

Prydae felt Bannagran tense suddenly, and he half expected the man to leap over and throttle the impudent Samhaist.

"To put your faith in the trickery of the upstarts is to invite disaster," old Bernivvigar cackled, and Prydae shot a look at the two monks of Abelle.

"Our brethren have saved many lives at the front," Father Jerak protested. "Prince Prydae's among them."

"Limited miracles, then?" Bernivvigar replied. "An interesting concept."

"And what shall the Samhaists offer Prince Prydae beyond your clever insults?" Brother Bathelais charged.

Prydae could hardly believe that these men were vying so, right in front of him, and daring to speak of him as if he weren't even there. Rather than interrupt, the prince let them go on a bit more. It seemed obvious to him that the tension between the competing religions had heightened of late, as was logical, given the monumental changes in the land and the desperate and competing work of both Samhaist cleric and monk of Abelle at the battlefield.

"We shall see," Bernivvigar replied to Bathelais, and he offered a look to Prydae then, designed obviously to give the prince some ray of hope.

"My pardon, my prince, who is soon to be rightful laird of Pryd," Father Jerak interjected; and he stepped in front of Bathelais and fixed him with a scowl that silenced him. "The brothers of Blessed Abelle have prayed for you every day. We are pleased that your life was saved but sorrowful for your loss, which is a loss to all the lands of Honce. We have done all that we could, and will continue our efforts on your behalf. A collective of our most powerful brothers, with the soul stones of the greatest godly energy, can be called together at any time. Many would make the pilgrimage to the aid of Prince Prydae, no doubt, perhaps even some of our masters from Chapel Abelle."

"Though you know that you can do nothing," Bernivvigar immediately interjected. "Would you stretch out hope indefinitely to avoid the inevitable realization by Prince Prydae that there really is nothing your church has to offer him?"

"Perhaps you would do well to hold your tongue, old Samhaist," Father Jerak snapped back with uncharacteristic sharpness.

"I have held several tongues," Bernivvigar replied, and he brought forth his hand, palm up. "Cut from the mouths of undeserving fools, muting them so that others could be given back lost voices."

It took a moment for that remark, that notion of Samhaist doctrine which often used sacrifice for supposed medical purposes, to truly sink into Prince Prydae; and when he fixed Bernivvigar with a serious look, the old Samhaist merely offered him a meaningful stare.

"Father Jerak," Prydae began, still staring hard at Bernivvigar, "I am not without gratitude for the work of your brethren out on the battlefield. Surely I would have expired had it not been for them. Rest easy here, I pray you, and know that the brothers of Abelle showed themselves well in the east. Let us end this useless bickering."

"Yes, my liege," said Jerak.

"We have other matters to attend," Rennarq cut in. "Prince—Laird Prydae should be crowned within the week. The event will heighten the celebration of our glorious victory over the bloody caps! Their scourge is lifted from the land, and never again will the men of Honce have to fear powrie raiders along our roads."

That last remark had Prydae and Bannagran exchanging looks, for it wasn't quite true. Victory in the east had been substantial, and the blood of thousands of powries stained the coastal rocks and had turned the tides red for many days. But Laird Ethelbert and Laird Delaval, the two men truly in charge of Honce's arrayed forces, had stopped short of eliminating the powries altogether. And both Bannagran and Prydae knew well that it was not because of battle weariness and not because the two lairds simply could not have pressed farther. No, the decision to allow the powries some escape had been a calculated one, as almost all the lairds at the front had learned. The powrie threat had to be kept at a minimum to allow for trade and for the coming consolidations the two great lairds planned. But at the same time, the powrie threat had to remain, at the edges of awareness, so that all the lairds of the land could keep their people properly afraid of the world beyond their borders. With tales of powries and goblins lurking in the forests, the peasants would not question the demands of their protector lairds.

"You may leave us," Prydae said to the monks, and he pointedly turned to Bernivvigar and added, "but you stay a bit longer."

The old Samhaist bowed and flashed a superior look Father Jerak's way. Brother Bathelais muttered as if intending to protest the slight, but Father Jerak silenced him with an upraised hand.

"It is good that the brothers of Blessed Abelle were able to save your life, good prince," Father Jerak offered to Prydae as he shuffled past. "An empty place would be Pryd Holding without the proud son of Laird Pryd."

Prydae didn't respond, other than to offer a quick nod.

"We have much to attend to, my laird-in-waiting," Rennarq remarked, and Prydae stared at him as if listening, but the door had barely closed behind the departing monks when Prydae turned away from the old laird-guest to focus on Bernivvigar.

"You speak of the sacrifice of a tongue to restore the voice of another."

"Indeed, it has been done," Bernivvigar answered. "Other sacrifices have not been so successful, of course."

"To what does this apply?"

"To anything, if the sacrifice is appealing to the Ancient Ones. I have seen men slaughtered so that others could rise up from their graves. I have seen eyes plucked out to make more worthy blind men see."

Prydae lowered his head and sighed.

"As for your . . . infirmity," Bernivvigar said tactfully. "You fear that you are the end of the line of Pryd."

"There is little left to dissuade me from the conclusion," Prydae admitted.

"Castrating another might bring relief, depending on the extent of your injuries and depending upon the whims of the Ancient Ones."

"The whims?"

"That is the way of the gods, my laird," Bernivvigar answered. "Among men you stand tall. Among the folk of Pryd Holding, you are practically a god yourself. But among the Ancient Ones, we are all rather small."

Prydae paused and considered the words for a moment. He licked his lips and glanced over at Bannagran, who nodded. "What would we have to do?" the soon-to-be-laird asked.

"Find a sacrifice, of course."

"What requirements?"

Bernivvigar laughed. "That he has testicles, my laird. Any man will do, though I would not recommend an old and shriveled specimen." A smile widened on the old Samhaist's face that set Prydae back on his heels, so obvious was its wickedness.

"There is a rather odd boy about the town," Bernivvigar remarked.

"Not that stork creature?" put in Rennarq, and Bernivvigar blinked slowly, holding fast to his smile.

"Why that one was ever allowed to continue to draw breath, I do not know. The Ancient Ones surely show no favor to a creature so inferior and damaged as he," the imposing Samhaist said.

"The boy on the road?" Bannagran asked Prydae. "The one who staggers with every step and has a face full of snot and drool?"

"A wonderful specimen, is he not?" said Bernivvigar. "Perhaps when I am finished with him—with your permission of course, my laird—I can mercifully put an end to his thoroughly wretched existence."

Prydae's conscience tugged at him. Could he do such a thing? Any of it? Surely, if his virility could be restored, the line of Pryd secured, it would be for the greater good. But still . . .

He glanced around at his secular advisers, focusing mostly

upon Bannagran, who had become such a trusted companion under such difficult circumstances. The large man returned the look and nodded.

Prydae licked his lips nervously, then turned to Rennarq. "Do we know where this creature lives?"

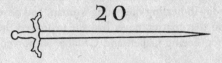

20

WHEN ALL THE WORLD
TURNED UPSIDE DOWN

Garibond watched as the woman he believed to be Callen Duwornay, who had stubbornly called herself Ada Wehelin, and her young daughter walked away from his house on the lake. "A good deed repaid," the man repeated, for that is what the woman had said when he had once more, upon their parting, thanked her and her daughter for their help in the town.

Garibond hadn't recognized the woman at first—Callen Duwornay was someone long out of his thoughts—and the truth of her identity hadn't even registered to him during their walk out to his house or during the short visit of the woman and her daughter. It wasn't until she was leaving, actually walking away, when she had uttered those words, "A good deed repaid." Even then, for a few moments, Garibond hadn't made the connection.

But watching her now, though her back was to him, the man understood the truth, beyond any doubt. That was her, Callen. Garibond was glad to learn that she was still alive, that she had gotten through her ordeal and had even managed, apparently, to remain in Pryd Holding—in Gorham's Hill, on the far western edge of the town proper, she had told him. Somehow seeing her alive bolstered Garibond's spirits, even beyond his simple sympathy and empathy toward her. Somehow, the fact that she had gone on, had even given birth to a beautiful daughter, made the sacrifices of SenWi and now poor Bransen, somewhat more tolerable.

All along, Garibond had known that SenWi had done right that day in healing the young woman, and never had she wavered on that matter, never had she expressed the slightest bit of regret. Seeing Callen and Cadalye reinforced the concept.

"Sh-sh-sh-she'sss—my frien . . . my frien . . . my friend," Bransen said to him, making his way over to join him at the window.

"What a beautiful little friend you've got there, Bransen," Garibond replied, and he draped his arm about the boy and pulled him close, in part to steady him but more because he just felt that he needed a hug.

"I-I-I'm going to m-m-marry . . . marry her."

Garibond's smile nearly took in his ears, and he squeezed Bransen up close to his side and continued to watch the departing pair. He knew that such a thing could never be, of course, but he simply said, "She'll be a fine wife to you." Why would he deprive Bransen of his dreams, after all? What else could the poor boy possibly have?

When he looked at Bransen then, his thought was only reinforced, for rarely had Garibond seen Bransen smile so widely. And Bransen didn't look back at him, didn't even seem to feel the weight of Garibond's gaze. No, he kept staring out the window at Cadalye, and he kept smiling.

Sometime later, when the mother and daughter were long out of sight, Garibond remarked, "Well, I must get myself cleaned up and get some dinner to cooking." He gave Bransen another hug, then moved off and went about starting a fire and heating some water for stew. As he stood there stirring the pot, Garibond wondered about the boy's smile. Glad he was to see it, after their humiliation in the town. How horrible that had been!

But more horrible for him than for Bransen, Garibond understood, if for no other reason than the fact that the poor boy was quite used to such humiliation. He second-guessed himself for all those occasions he had allowed Bransen to journey into the town on an errand. True, Bransen was always eager to go, and often begging to go, but had there been a single occasion in the last two or three years when the boy had gone to Pryd Town and had returned without mud on his clothing or blood somewhere? Given the experience today, Garibond realized more fully that many of those falls were far from accidental.

He thought of Dynard and SenWi as he stood there cooking, remembering his old friends. He watched the swirl of the stew, the thick liquid rolling back over to flatten the wake caused by the passing spoon, and that motion invited him to look more deeply into himself and his life. Garibond the hermit, he supposed, and he thought back to all the disappointments that had led him to this place. It hadn't been a sudden decision for him to move out here and settle in the abandoned shell of a cottage on the small rocky island. It had been a gradual drifting away from the disappointments he always seemed to find when around other people. He remembered when his sister had been killed by powries and how the soldiers of Laird Pryd, coming in just moments too late, had been more concerned with celebrating their victory than in worrying about Garibond's grief. While he had knelt there over his sister's body, the soldiers had cheered and danced, arguing over who could claim credit for which powrie killed.

"Aye, and what a wonderful life it's been," Garibond muttered over the stew.

The moment of self-pity passed quickly, as it always did with Garibond, and he turned his thoughts to the good things he had known, to Dynard again and SenWi, who had touched him deeply in so short a time. And of course, to Bransen, that awkward and fragile little boy. Garibond chuckled as he considered how frustrated other people always seemed to get when Bransen tried to speak, turning a simple statement into a long ordeal. Garibond didn't think of things that way with Bransen; to him, the boy's stuttering only lengthened the moment of revelation, like having a hooked fish put up a good and long fight or watching a refreshing spring storm roll in from far away.

He looked up from the stew to Bransen, then, and found that the boy had again taken out the Book of Jhest, and was now gently moving his hands across the pages. Bransen was always at that book, it seemed, ever since Garibond had shown it to him and had spent many days with him trying to explain the lettering. For some reason Garibond didn't understand, Bransen seemed to take a kind of solace in just looking at the flowery text. At first, the man had worried that the clumsy child would damage the book, but it had quickly become apparent to Garibond that Bransen was taking more care with the tome than anyone else ever could.

So he let the boy play with the book as often as he wished, and he never concerned himself with the well-being of one of the most important artifacts he had to tie him to SenWi and particularly Dynard.

The two sat down to dinner a little later, the room full of the rich aroma of the fish stew and wood smoke. Several candles provided the light, for clouds had thickened outside, hastening the onset of dusk.

"Good lettering in that book," Garibond remarked between bites. "You like looking at it."

Bransen's face twisted into a crooked smile.

"Does it take you away from all of this?" the man asked. "Can you forget what happened in the town when you focus on the letters in the book? Bah, what fools are those soldiers."

Bransen's smile twisted even more, finally settling into a perplexed expression, or the closest thing the boy could approximate. He started to respond several times, and Garibond caught on that more than his inability to quickly verbalize his thoughts was holding him back. Finally, Bransen brought one hand over the table, fingers outstretched and palm down.

"This iiiiis . . . take," he said. His arm shook from the effort as he forced the palm to turn upward without any wild flailing.

Garibond tilted his head curiously.

"Nnnnnnnth. Nnnnnnnth . . . th-this iiiis . . . re-re-re-receeeeive."

"Of course," Garibond said quietly, and he took Bransen's hand and slowly guided it off the table. He could see that Bransen was growing quite excited, and knew that type of emotion usually foreshadowed some wild movement from the damaged boy. Garibond had little trouble in imagining bowls of his fresh stew flying about the room.

But then, even as he brought the arm over the table side, it hit him, and he froze in place, staring wide-eyed at the boy. "What did you say?"

Bransen's face twisted as he tried to form the words, and he started to turn his hand over again, though Garibond still held it.

Garibond did it for him and brought the arm back up over the table. "This is take?" he asked, not willing to wait through the stuttered explanation.

Bransen nodded.

Garibond turned the hand over. "Receive?"

The boy's smile answered it all.

Garibond leaped up from the table so quickly that his chair skidded out behind him. He scooped up a candle as he went to the book, and bent low to study its open pages.

And there it was, on the very page Bransen had left open, one of the Jhesta Tu explanations of the differences of posture, the connotations of movement and position. Those acting in anger or superiority, the text explained, often reached for something from another with their palms down—the inference being that they took what they wanted without regard. Like the soldiers on the road, pushing Bransen and Garibond away, like the prince himself, kicking the boy without regard.

Those who lived a receptive life, an open existence in which they hoped to, and expected to, learn from others, must reach out with their palms up, inviting compliance and sharing.

But how had Bransen figured that out? Garibond had never read him this specific page!

The man turned to regard the boy. "Are you reading this?"

The twisted smile, the awkward nod.

"Reading?" Garibond asked with a gasp.

Bransen gulped for air, as if he was setting his jaw muscles so that he could try to answer. He did start to stutter something out, but it was irrelevant to Garibond, who had been thrown into complete confusion. How could an idiot read? How could Bransen, a boy who could hardly master the simple movement of putting one foot in front of the other, begin to decipher the intricacies of Dynard's flowing script?

He shook his head in denial, then gathered up the book and moved over to the table. He surprised and frightened Bransen as he swept the bowls from in front of him, caring not at all that they crashed about the floor. He placed the book down and flipped the pages, coming to one of the early lessons the Jhesta Tu placed upon their beginning students. A student would be bound by the ankles to a heavy weight, then dropped into a pool that was just deep enough to keep the student, fully extended, under water. As with most of the lessons and pages in the book, Garibond possessed only a rudimentary understanding. From what he gathered, the Jhesta Tu wanted to see if their students could free themselves without help.

The ending note of wisdom on this page—every page had one—went, "In the peace and solitude of the water, do we see ourselves."

"Re-re-reflec . . . reflecti . . . ti . . . tion."

"Yes," said Garibond. "Reflection. Like when you look into the lake with me. You see what you look like."

Bransen began shaking his head. "Nnnnnnno. No," he said, and he poked a finger at the text. "Innnn wa-wa-water . . ." The boy gave a great sigh and closed his eyes. He seemed deep in thought for a moment, looking inside himself, and then, in the clearest statement Garibond had ever heard him utter, he said, "In water we see ourselves."

So shocked was Garibond by the clarity of the words, that it took him a long moment to realize that Bransen was poking at the book, bidding him to look.

He read the indicated passage, and in light of what Bransen had just said, something dawned on him. The purpose of the

Jhesta Tu test of water was to measure the inner calm of a student. All the students had been shown how to extricate themselves from the binding weights; at issue was whether or not they could do it under the extreme pressure of being underwater. This test was of a person's inner strength, his calm under duress. Garibond had always seen that, somewhat, of course, but the revelation here was not what was on the page in the Book of Jhest, but rather, the reasoning power of Bransen!

That, and the fact that the boy could read! How could that be possible?

Garibond looked at him, and wanted to say something, wanted to pour out all of his amazement and joy. Never before had he looked at Bransen in quite this way, and he wanted nothing more than to shout with happiness.

But he couldn't. He felt the lump welling in his throat and he could force no words past it. He reached out and tousled Bransen's hair, and managed to motion toward the boy's bed.

Then he gently closed the book and blew out the candle and waited for Bransen to settle onto his bed, which was really just a cot piled with dry hay, before blowing out the other candles in the room.

Garibond didn't go straight to his own bed. He went to the window and stared up at the sky, which was caught in the last moments of twilight. In a patch where some of the clouds had cleared, he could see the first twinkling stars, framed by the rolling dark edges of the overcast.

It was a long, long time before Garibond managed to get to bed, and the room was beginning to brighten in predawn glow before he finally managed to fall asleep.

Garibond heard the knocking, but it didn't register in his mind, as if it were coming from far away, perhaps, or as if it were part of another world.

Even the loud crash that followed merely made him blink once and roll over.

But when he heard Bransen cry out, "Nnnnnnnno!" his eye popped open and he rolled quickly out of bed to his feet.

He took in the scene immediately: there was Prince Prydae and his companion, the warrior of note named Bannagran. Bannagran held Bransen by the shoulders, his great strength keeping the poor boy almost completely still.

"When your laird comes knocking, you would do well to open the door for him," Bannagran said to Garibond.

"I—I was asleep," the man stammered. "My liege, is there a problem?"

"No problem," Bannagran answered. "We came for the boy and now we have him." The large man wheeled about, jerking poor Bransen so forcefully that his legs swung out wide.

Garibond, dressed only in his flimsy nightshirt, rushed to the door before them. "What are you doing?" he cried. "You cannot take my boy!"

"Cannot?" Prydae said, holding a hand up to silence Bannagran.

"But, my liege—"

"Exactly," Prydae interrupted. "Your liege. Your laird."

"But why would you wish to take him? He is just a child. He has never harmed anyone. Please, my liege, I beg of you to leave him alone. Mercy, my liege. Sweet mercy."

"Oh, shut up, you babbling fool," said Bannagran. "And get out of the way before I throw you through the door. The Prince of Pryd is in need of your son, and so your son will come to his service."

"What can he do? He is just a child, and infirm—"

"Not infirm for our needs, I pray," said Bannagran. He wrapped one arm around Bransen's chest and leaned back, holding the boy easily from the floor, then reached his other arm around and down the front to the boy's crotch and gave a squeeze that brought a squeal from poor Bransen.

"Yes, he is secure."

Garibond's eyes widened with horror, and he charged

forward—or started to, for before he got a single step, Prydae had his sword out, its tip against Garibond's chest.

"I will forgive you that," Prydae said, "just once."

"Ah, I see that you have secured our sacrifice," came a voice behind Garibond, from the open doorway, and he turned around to see Bernivvigar standing there.

"S-sacrifice?" Garibond stammered, and then he steeled himself and straightened his shoulder. "You old beast! Begone from my home!"

"The boy will not be killed," Prydae assured Garibond, and there was something in the prince's voice, some bit of remorse perhaps, that made Garibond look back over his shoulder.

"He is needed," Prydae went on. "Take pride that this crippled creature will restore the line of Pryd."

Garibond's expression was one of pure incredulity. "What will you do to him? He's just a boy."

"The Ancient Ones oft accept such sacrifices," Bernivvigar said.

"You just said . . ." Garibond protested to Prydae.

"That he will not be killed," Prydae repeated.

"His life is not the sacrifice," Bernivvigar said, and there was obvious amusement in his tone. "This wretched little creature will restore to the new Laird of Pryd that which the powries took away."

Garibond's eyes widened, and he inadvertently dropped his gaze to Prydae's groin.

"If you utter a word of this, I promise that I will cut your face off," Prydae warned. "That for all of your life you will suffer the screams of revulsion, of children and women, and even men, who cannot withstand the horror of your ugliness. And if you utter a word of this, you will watch your wretched little boy die slowly and painfully."

Garibond hardly heard the words, his thoughts careening as he came to understand exactly what the old Samhaist had in mind. "You c-cannot," he stammered. "He is just a boy."

"The line of Pryd must continue," Prydae said.

Garibond's eyes darted all around, like a cornered animal. All the revelations of the previous day, all the wonderful realizations that there was actually some measure of intelligence within the stuttering Bransen, played in his mind, demanding an end to this sudden and unexpected tragedy. "Take me instead."

"Do not be a fool," Bannagran answered. "The boy is damaged and infirm."

"You should beg us to kill him when we are done removing his genitals," Bernivvigar said smugly. "He will have no need for his own virility, obviously. He should have been killed at birth—you know this to be true! So be satisfied that perhaps the little wretch will do some good with his miserable existence."

Bransen made a little mewling sound.

It was more than Garibond could take, and he wheeled around, fist flying, and connected squarely on the old Samhaist's jaw, sending him back hard against the doorjamb. As he started forward, Garibond heard Bransen cry out, and he turned about just in time to see Bannagran wading in.

The big man hit Garibond with a thunderous jab that straightened him and dazed him so that he could not even react to the wide-arcing left hook that caught him on the side of the face and sent him flying away to the floor.

Again he heard a voice, Bernivvigar's voice, as if it were far, far away, much like what he had heard before he had fully awakened that morning.

"Perhaps the older man would be better," Bernivvigar was saying. "How old is this boy?"

"Nine? Ten?" Bannagran answered.

"Not yet a man."

"Does that matter?" asked Prydae.

"It would be better if he had already reached manhood and was able to sire a child on his own," said Bernivvigar.

Garibond managed to turn to regard the Samhaist, standing in the doorway, leaning on the jamb, rubbing his jaw, and shooting Garibond the most hateful look Prydae had ever seen in all his life.

"Accept his offer and spare the boy," Bernivvigar advised.

A moment later, Bannagran's strong hand hoisted Garibond up to his feet, and the warrior began dragging him out. He managed to look back to the side, where poor Bransen was still trying to stand up after being shoved aside by Bannagran.

"Do not think your crippled son has fully escaped me," Bernivvigar muttered to Garibond as Bannagran hauled him past.

Poor Bransen spent all the day at the eastern window of the small house. He was still there when the sun disappeared behind the western horizon.

What will I do? How will I eat?

He wanted to rush out and run to the town to rescue Garibond—all the day, that had been his most pressing thought. But he couldn't rush and he couldn't run. He couldn't do anything. He couldn't even light a candle so that he didn't have to sit there helplessly in the darkness.

He wanted to stay awake, to stay alert, to be ready to do . . . whatever he could possibly do to help his beloved father. But eventually, Bransen's head dipped down to the windowsill.

His sleep was fitful, and he heard the approach of horses. He looked up, but they were already to the side of the window's view, splashing up the submerged walk to the front door of the cottage.

Bransen turned and tried to rise, but fell back repeatedly and was still sitting when the horses thundered away and the cottage door was pushed open.

In came Garibond, and he held up his hand to keep Bransen back. "Go to bed, boy," he said, and Bransen could tell that his every word was filled with agony.

Bransen started for his bed, while Garibond moved to the table and struck flint to metal to light a candle. Only then did Bransen see how bent over and haggard Garibond seemed; and when the man turned, candle in hand, Bransen nearly swooned, for the front of Garibond's nightshirt was drenched with blood, waist to knees.

"It is all right," the older man said. "You just go to bed."

Bransen fell onto his bed and immediately buried his face. He wanted all the world to just go away.

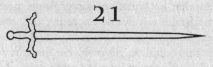

21

FOR THE BOY?

The rain splashed down all about him, spraying on the rocks and making the lake hiss in frothy protest. The drenching didn't bother Garibond but only because he couldn't remember a time over the last few weeks when he had felt anything but miserable. His wound had healed, or at least had scabbed over, but that was just on the outside. Bernivvigar's brutal work had left him sick inside as well, and he felt as if the festering sore were worming its way deeper into his body every day. Every morning, Garibond found pulling himself out of bed a trial.

The near-constant rain of the last days had added to his misery and had made his daily chores more difficult. The lake was up several inches, so that Garibond and Bransen had to abandon the lower house for the time being; that or watch their feet rot away from wading through ankle-deep cold water.

Garibond sat there and coughed through the morning's fishing. He didn't catch a thing, and knew that he wouldn't. The area of the lake near the island was not deep, a few feet at the most, and was not reedy; and the silver trout that normally could be hooked from the rocks of the small island wouldn't be milling about the shallows in this heavy downpour. Garibond stayed out there anyway, coughing and miserable, mostly because he couldn't find the strength in him to climb back to the house.

He knew that his situation was growing more dire. He knew that his health was fast deteriorating and, even with his stubbornness, he was beginning to recognize that he would not get through this ordeal on his own. He thought of going to Chapel Pryd to ask the monks for some magical healing. It wouldn't be easy to persuade them, and he knew it. His injury and illness were due to the order of Laird Prydae himself. Garibond wasn't a religious man in any sense of the word, and the distance he kept from the competing factions in Pryd Holding in many ways gave him a better understanding of each. Even from afar, Garibond understood the quiet war being waged between Bernivvigar and the brothers of Abelle. And the prize of victory, even more than the support of the peasants, was the sanction of Laird Prydae.

How could the brothers of Abelle help Garibond heal his current malady, given that?

Perhaps he should go instead to Castle Pryd, and beg the laird to ask the brothers for assistance.

The mere thought of it brought bile into the proud man's throat. Laird Prydae, as much as—or even more than—Bernivvigar had done this to him. Now was he to go and beg the man for mercy?

He slapped the wet rock next to him in frustration, and his hand was so cold and numb that he didn't even feel the sting. Was this numbness akin to Bransen's? he wondered.

That notion had him glancing back to the house, where Bransen was no doubt sitting on his bed with his nose deep in the Book of Jhest. That book had become Bransen's life of late, his tie to the past and . . .

"And what?" Garibond wondered aloud. Was Bransen finding solace within the pages of the Book of Jhest beyond anything he had ever expected of the boy? Certainly Bransen's apparent understanding of the text had been a surprise to Garibond, but what did the book—which Bransen claimed he had read cover to cover several times—now hold over him? Was he finding an escape within its pages from the misery of his tortured reality?

Garibond hoped that was the case. That was all he really wanted, after all. For himself, life had become a simple matter of survival, of getting through the days. His few joys were all tied up in Bransen's too-infrequent smiles. Garibond wanted nothing more, except for some relief from his pain. He didn't covet jewels or coins, and preferred to catch his own food over any banquet that Laird Prydae himself might set. He didn't want any companionship other than Bransen's.

As he considered these things, Garibond snorted and looked at the hissing water. Was there anything life could now offer him, to make him desire life? Responsibility for Bransen alone was keeping him going, he knew. And now, given his declining health, that, too, was beginning to worry him. What in the world would Bransen do once Garibond was gone? He couldn't fend for himself, and he had no real friends other than Garibond himself. At that moment, a crow flew past Garibond. He gritted his few remaining teeth, blinked his one good eye, and watched the black bird disappear into the film of heavy rain. A crow—a spy for Bernivvigar perhaps?

"Bah, you're just being an old fool," Garibond told himself, but he knew that he had reason to be suspicious. Bernivvigar's threat concerning Bransen had not been an idle one, Garibond understood, for Bernivvigar was not a man to make an idle threat. In the weeks since his ordeal under the Samhaist's knife, Garibond had seen Bernivvigar around the lake, often watching his house from afar, and he knew that the old wretch had never given up his desire to sacrifice Bransen.

He thought again of Callen Duwornay, or rather Ada, and her daughter who had befriended Bransen. Many times over the last few days had Garibond considered seeking her out and asking her to take in Bransen. But on every occasion, and now again, Garibond quickly dismissed the idea. How could he force this burden upon another, even one who owed her life to Bransen's parents? And how could Callen defend the boy if Bernivvigar came for him? Indeed, how could she defend herself, if the callous old Samhaist wretch discovered her true identity and that she had somehow escaped his punishment?

"Ah, what am I to do with you, then?" Garibond asked into the rain.

Some hours later, Garibond dragged himself back into the house, where he found Bransen sitting and reading, so engrossed that he didn't seem to hear Garibond enter.

"You like the book, don't you?" Garibond greeted, his typical refrain.

Shaking with every movement, Bransen turned his head and managed a half smile.

Garibond started to laugh, but caught himself short, feeling the crackling in his lungs. A wave of dizziness washed over him, but he caught himself on a nearby chair and managed to hide his weakness.

What was he to do?

"I know a place that has many more books you might enjoy," he said suddenly, hardly thinking of the implications.

Again Bransen turned, this time looking more confused than pleased or excited.

"Them monks in the chapel have shelves and shelves of books," Garibond explained. It had to be the monks, he knew, and it had to be soon—certainly before the next winter. "You would like that, yes?"

"J . . . Jh . . . J-J-J-Jhes . . . sst," Bransen stammered.

"Jhest? Yes, the Book of Jhest, penned by your father. But there are other books. So many more. Books of wisdom and history. You would like that, yes?"

Bransen nodded, but didn't seem overexcited about the prospect and turned right back to the Book of Jhest.

His reaction didn't matter. Garibond thought through all the options before him, and the only course possible seemed clear enough. He had to convince Father Jerak to take in Bransen and to care for him. That wasn't going to be easy. Certainly not. To Garibond's understanding, the monks of Abelle were not nearly as generous as they pretended.

Perhaps he could offer the monks something so they would take in Bransen. Perhaps that very book now open on the bed. Garibond quickly dismissed that notion, remembering the reaction of the Church to the book ten years before! Besides, how could he explain its existence, given that SenWi had made it appear as if the book had been burned?

Another thought came to him, an image of a marvelous sword wrapped in cloth in a dry place in his tunnels. Perhaps he could offer them the sword—a weapon unrivaled in all Honce. Yes, the monks could trade the sword to Prydae. Surely they would greatly appreciate its workmanship and the power it might offer to them in their battle for the affections of the young laird.

That was it, then, Garibond decided. The monks were his only option.

And it had to be soon, the crackling in his chest reminded him. For Bransen's sake. What would the young man even begin to do if Garibond dropped dead on the floor one morning?

He did hope that the monks would treat Bransen well, and that they would teach the boy to read the language of Honce and give him access to their books. Yes, he would have to make that a part of the bargain. Little in life other than reading offered pleasure to poor Bransen.

On the first break in the weather, a couple of days later, Garibond set out from his house, leaving Bransen, as usual, with his face buried in the Book of Jhest. The boy's single-mindedness toward that book continued to amaze the man.

Garibond walked a wide and careful circuit of his house before heading to the road to Pryd Town, for he wanted to make certain that Bernivvigar was not lurking about. What defense might Bransen offer if the old wretch came calling?

Once on the road, with no sign of the Samhaist anywhere, Garibond remained uneasy and reminded himself with every fast stride to be quick about his business. To his relief, he found that he did not have far to walk, for a monk from Chapel Pryd was out and about, standing before one of the town's outermost houses.

Garibond recognized the man, though he didn't remember his name.

"My greetings, brother," he said, moving up the short path toward the monk, who seemed to be just leaving the farmhouse.

"And to you," the monk replied. "I have no time to hear your woes, I fear, but must be straightaway back to Chapel Pryd."

"I know you," Garibond said in leading tones.

The monk paused long enough to look over the man carefully.

"I am afraid that your recognition is one-sided, friend."

Garibond tried hard to place the man, and finally, as the monk started away once more, just blurted out, "I was a friend of Brother Bran Dynard's."

Again the monk stopped and studied Garibond, his gaze soon dropping to the man's waist area, which told Garibond that he had been recognized. "You are the one the Samhaist took for Laird Pryd," he said.

"Aye, and that's a reputation to put forth, is it not?" Garibond said with a helpless laugh.

"I am sorry, friend, that you fell victim to the brutish old man," the monk said. "But there is nothing I can do to alleviate—"

"I'm not here about that, Brother . . ."

"Reandu. Brother Reandu."

"Ah, yes, I remember our meeting after my friend Brother Dynard left for the north. Has there been any word at all?"

"Brother Dynard is believed to have been murdered on the road," said Reandu. "That, or he rejoined the Behrenese woman and fled the land of Honce, as many brothers believe."

"He did not, for she did not survive." Garibond saw that he suddenly had Reandu's complete attention.

"What do you know of it?"

"I know that she is dead. Long dead, to the loss of the world."

"And yet you ask me of Brother Dynard?"

"Of him, I know nothing, beyond that he departed from your chapel ten years ago."

"Nor do any of us, master . . ."

"Garibond."

"Master Garibond. I feel for your loss, for your friend and for . . . well, your ill treatment by Bernivvigar."

Garibond nodded.

"I need the help of the Church," Garibond stated. "Not for me and my ailments—those I accept well enough. But for my son."

Reandu looked at him curiously.

"You know of him, no doubt," said Garibond. "He is . . . unique and difficult to miss."

"The damaged one? The one they call Stork?"

Garibond winced at the disparaging name, but let go his anger for the sake of Bransen. "Yes, for him."

"If we believed that there was ever anything our soul stones might do for one so damaged, we would have undertaken the task years ago, brother."

"You cannot heal his maladies, of course."

"Then what?"

Garibond gave a profound sigh, and was surprised at how painful this was. He had not considered how lonely his life might be, how much less fulfilled and fulfilling, without Bransen in it. "He is a lot of work, of course, and I am growing old—and more frail because of the Samhaist beast. I fear that I will soon not be able to care for Bransen."

Reandu's wide eyes betrayed his shock. "You would ask us to take him in?"

"I would. He needs protecting."

"We have not the means, brother. We are not a house for wayward—"

"Not wayward," Garibond corrected. "I do not ask you lightly to take this burden."

"You should ask a friend."

"I cannot, for I fear for the boy. Bernivvigar got me, aye, but that did little to satisfy his blood thirst. He wants the boy."

"Speak to Laird Prydae."

Garibond knew that he didn't even need to respond to that ridiculous suggestion. They both understood that Prydae wouldn't do much to go against Bernivvigar, not at present, at least. "I do not ask lightly you to take this burden," he repeated and then added, "nor without offering you gain for your Church."

Brother Reandu started to respond, but stopped short and looked curiously at him. "Gain for the church of Blessed Abelle? You are not a man of wealth or influence, good master Garibond."

"Rightly noted," he said dryly. "But I am in possession of an item that would prove quite valuable to you in your dealings with Laird Prydae."

He paused for effect. Reandu licked his lips and bade him, "Go on."

"Do you remember Brother Dynard's wife, the Behr woman named SenWi?"

"Yes."

"A mighty warrior, so it was said?"

"Her exploits against the powries were spoken of, yes."

"With an amazing sword, a sword more grand than anything in all the land of Honce?"

Reandu stared at him hard but did not respond.

"I assure you that if you heard any tales of that magnificent weapon, they were not exaggerated. Indeed, if anything, the people who saw the blade could not begin to understand its beauty and craftsmanship. It is a sword fit for a laird—indeed, it is beyond any weapon that any laird in all Honce now carries, or has ever carried."

"That is quite a claim."

"One I can back up, on your agreement to take Bransen into your chapel and care for him."

Reandu considered the words for a moment, then said, "I am not authorized to make such an arrangement."

"Of course, but you are capable of relaying my proposition to Father Jerak in the strongest possible terms."

"You would wish us to care for the boy until his death? For decades, likely?"

"Yes, but he is not without use. He can work for his meals, as long as the tasks are within his physical limitations. Oh, yes, and there is one more thing. I want you to teach him to read our language and to allow him access to books."

"The idiot?"

"He is no idiot," Garibond snapped back. "Do not confuse physical deformity with mental weakness—it was a mistake that I long made. He can read, I am certain. It is a skill that will allow him to transcend the limitations of his flesh."

Reandu kept shaking his head, his expression sour, but he did reply, "I will take this matter to Father Jerak and Brother Bathelais."

Garibond could ask for nothing more. He nodded and rushed away, hoping that Bernivvigar had not learned in the meantime that Bransen was all alone.

"He has her sword," Brother Bathelais mused aloud. He stared out the window of Father Jerak's audience chamber, overlooking the windy courtyard inside the chapel's outer front wall. Bathelais remembered Dynard out there sweeping the leaves. He remembered SenWi, a wisp of a thing, really, and quite beautiful in her exotic southern way. He had never seen this supposed sword, but he had met a few who had, and their description of it was nothing short of incredible.

"We are to take in this creature and care for him?" Father Jerak asked doubtfully. "Are we to throw wide our doors to all with maladies, then?"

"This is an exceptional matter, and an exceptional malady, perhaps," said Reandu. "And Garibond has assured me that the boy can do menial tasks and needs little care."

Father Jerak snorted.

"Perhaps this is an opportunity to display compassion," Reandu said.

"Have you not heard the chanting of the Samhaists at night?" Brother Bathelais interjected. "Do you not see Rennarq ever at Laird Prydae's side? What venom might he be whispering into Prydae's ear? This is the time for strength, brother, not compassion."

"Less than a century ago, a wise man proclaimed compassion to be strength, I believe," Reandu replied. He knew from Bathelais's immediate scowl that perhaps he had crossed a line in invoking the words of Blessed Abelle.

"It might well be compassion that costs us nothing," Father Jerak remarked. "This sword—you have seen it?"

"No, father."

"Then go to this peasant Garibond—both of you. Bid him to show it to you, and if you judge this sword as valuable as we believe, agree to his terms. I know this young Prydae, and if we are in possession of a weapon that will elevate his warrior status, it will prove a marvelous incentive to help us move the Samhaists from his side."

"This boy, this creature, slobbers," Bathelais reminded.

"And we have duties appropriate for one of his idiocy," said Jerak.

At that point, Brother Bathelais sighed, looked at Reandu, and said, "Let us go, then. I pray the sword will be naught but a line of rust, but we shall see."

Garibond held the package up before him and slowly unwrapped the cloth holding the fabulous sword of SenWi. And as he pulled the layers of cloth from the weapon, he saw the layers of doubt melt away from Brother Bathelais's face. The silverel steel gleamed in the sunlight and the snake-head hilt sparkled. Not a speck of rust marred the blade, not a sign of wear or age. It was as SenWi had crafted it, and as she had left it.

"It has no equal north of the mountains," Garibond said with great confidence. "Not in all of Honce."

"It seems thin," Bathelais said.

"Because the metal is stronger than bronze and stronger than iron," Garibond explained. He drew forth the sword completely from the wrapping and waved it, then nodded to the two monks and snapped it suddenly to the side, where it cut deep into the trunk of a tree. He extracted the sword, pulled it back, then stabbed the tree, and the fine tip dove in to an impressive depth.

Again Garibond pulled the sword out, and he rolled it over in his hands and presented it hilt first to Bathelais.

The monk took the extraordinary weapon and moved it around slowly, marveling at its light weight and balance.

When both Bathelais and Garibond looked at Reandu, they saw that he was smiling, and that drew a nod from the ever-doubting Bathelais.

"Do we have an agreement?" Garibond asked, taking back the weapon. "You take Bransen in and you keep him safe from Bernivvigar. He'll work for you, and without complaint. You give him a chance."

"There is nothing we can do for the . . . boy with our gemstones," Bathelais said. "We will not waste the time and energy in trying."

Garibond suppressed his anger and managed a nod. He handed the sword to Bathelais and went to the house, emerging a few moments later with Bransen, who was carrying a large sack, beside him.

"The Stork," Bathelais whispered to Reandu.

Brother Reandu didn't respond and didn't let Bathelais see his disdain at the remark. In truth, Reandu was hardly certain from whence that disdain had come or why the name, which he himself had often used, struck him as so unseemly coming from Bathelais. He watched Bransen's awkward but determined approach. The boy was afraid, he could plainly see, but he also appeared eager to please. Perhaps

behind the ungainly hip-swerving, stiff-legged strides and behind the smears of drool on his crooked face there was something else.

A boy, perhaps?

Just a boy?

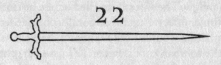

22

I WILL NOT FAIL GARIBOND

Garibond said this is important. He needs me to work here, so the brothers will heal him and feed him. I will not fail Garibond. Bransen let this litany repeat over and over in his head, leading him through his dreary days at Chapel Pryd. He had come there full of hope and excited at the prospect of having so many people around him who, Garibond had assured him, would not push him to the ground or laugh at him.

They hadn't done anything like that, and that was good. Unfortunately, they also weren't really *around* him at all. He had been given a room in the substructure of the chapel, a windowless, empty little square of stone and dirt. There was only one way in or out, a ladder and trapdoor that Bransen couldn't hope to operate on his own. Thus, every morning, one of the younger brothers came and opened the door, then reached in and lifted him out so that he could go about his chores, which amounted to carrying the chamber pots down to the river for emptying and cleaning, two at a time. It took him most of the day, and at the end of his journeys, another brother set him back in his hole, along with a single candle, a flagon of water, and a plate of food.

That was Bransen's day, his life, his solitude. *I will not fail Garibond,* got him through it.

He knew that his work here was making life better for his father, for the man who had given so much to help him.

I will not fail Garibond.

Bransen brought his mother's black outfit with him and

used it as a pillow. The soft silk smelled of her, he decided, and that gave him comfort. And it was comfort he needed, despite his resolve that he wouldn't fail Garibond, because as much as he missed the company of his father, he missed the company of his real father's work and of his mother's philosophy. He didn't have the Book of Jhest; he didn't have any books. He often tried to broach the subject with one of the brothers or another, but these men had no patience for his stuttering and never let him get the request out. In fact, they never really listened to anything he tried to say.

Every night as he lay there, every day as he made his uneven and awkward forays to the river, Bransen thought of that wonderful book and pictured its many pages. In his mind, he saw again the flowing script so meticulously copied by his father. In his mind, he recited the text, beginning to end, over and over again. He feared that he didn't have it perfect, but in the end, this was all he had.

As the days became weeks and the recital more rote, Bransen began to do something that had never before occurred to him. He began to roll the words in his thoughts and apply them to himself. He considered the source of Jhesta Tu power in the context of his own broken body, and searched for his *chi*. And he thought that he found that line of power, or what was supposed to be a line of power, for in him there were just inner flashes of energy, dispersing to his sides and his limbs, and no discernable and focusing line at all.

He thought that he must be doing something wrong in his inner search. Perhaps he was recalling the words of the book incorrectly. If only he could see it again, to compare his memory to its pages.

Several times, Bransen considered walking, along the riverbank to the little bridge that would lead him east to Garibond's house.

But suppose he angered the monks and they refused to help Garibond? Did he dare do such a thing?

If only they would listen to him long enough so that he could explain!

From a narrow window along the back wall of Chapel Pryd, Brother Reandu watched the boy stumble out through the mud, a pot sloshing and splashing at the end of each skinny arm. Strangely, those balancing chamber pots seemed to steady the Stork somewhat, though there remained nothing smooth about his movements and more than a bit of the contents of the pots wound up on his bare legs and woolen knee-length tunic.

Reandu sighed and wished that it could be different for this poor creature. He wished that he could gather up a soul stone and give the boy a more normal existence. That task was far beyond him, he knew. Far beyond any of them.

"But I will see to it that you are cleaned at least," the monk whispered, his words lost in the groan of the wind rushing through the narrow rectangular opening in the stone. He made a silent vow that he would begin assigning various brothers to take the last trip of the day to the river with Bransen, that they could scrub him clean before putting him back in his miserable little room.

He would have to get permission from Brother Bathelais, of course.

Brother Reandu gave a helpless laugh at that thought. Bathelais wasn't open to much of anything concerning the Stork. Keep him as far from the others as possible, give him enough to eat and drink, and make sure he doesn't freeze in his stone room at night. That was enough, by Brother Bathelais's interpretation, despite the fact that he, at the behest of Father Jerak, was preparing a grand celebration during which he would present the magnificent sword to Laird Prydae. Bathelais expected a large return for that gift—the brothers at Chapel Pryd who were knowledgeable about metals and weapons had told him that the sword was everything Garibond had claimed it to be and more.

But that optimistic outlook had done little to take the edge off Brother Bathelais concerning this poor, tortured creature.

With that in mind, and determined to at least help the boy wash the excrement from his legs, Brother Reandu went out from the chapel and quickly caught up with Bransen. The boy turned bright eyes upon him—and stumbled and nearly fell. In steadying him, Reandu got splashed by one of the chamber pots. He forced himself to hold back his automatic, angry response, reminding himself that it wasn't the poor boy's fault.

"Is this your last journey to the river this day?" he asked.

Bransen looked at him, as if in surprise. Of course he was surprised, Reandu realized. Had anyone asked him a question in all the days he had been at the chapel? Had anyone even spoken to him?

"Nnnnn-nyeah . . . nyeah, n . . . yes," the boy stammered.

Reandu had to take a deep breath to compose himself, the aggravating speech only reminding him all too clearly of why others like Bathelais simply could not tolerate being anywhere around this smelly one.

"Yes?"

The boy started to stammer.

"Just nod," Reandu prompted, and the boy did, and he managed a crooked smile.

Brother Reandu smiled as well.

"Uh . . . uh . . . I w-w-wa . . ." the boy stuttered.

Reandu shook his head and patted the air to try to calm the blabbering creature. Bransen responded and seemed to be trying to compose himself.

"B-book," he blurted suddenly.

"Book? What book?"

"Re-re-read b-b-boo-k."

"Read a book? You?"

The boy managed another smile and nod—or at least, something that approximated both.

"You want me to give you a book to read?"

Still the smile.

Then Reandu understood, as he remembered what Garibond had demanded of him as part of the deal. "You want me to teach you to read?"

"I r-r-re . . . re . . . read."

Reandu grinned and nodded and glanced back at the chapel. "Well, that was part of the bargain, I suppose. I should speak with Brother . . ." He turned back on the boy and winked. "I will see what I can do."

Bransen actually laughed at that, and the sudden jerk of his mirth overbalanced him and he fell to the mud. Reandu rushed over and picked him up.

"I cannot," Reandu started. "Do not expect . . . I must speak with Brother Bathelais. It is not my decision and I do not want to cause your hopes to soar."

Bransen was giggling with glee.

"You understand that?" Reandu asked, holding him steady and looking him right in the eye. "It is not my decision to make."

The boy stared at him—so stupidly, it seemed—and Brother Reandu thought himself a fool for even beginning to entertain such a thought as trying to teach this poor creature to read!

"Come along," he said. "The hour grows late and the river is still some distance." He hoisted one of the pots and helped Bransen gather up the other one, then took the boy under his arm and helped him to the river to complete his chores and so that both of them could get a much-needed washing.

Bransen was surprised, even frightened, when his overhead door opened unexpectedly late that night. A smile widened on the startled boy's face when he saw the face of Brother Reandu behind the glare of the candle.

"B-b-boo—" he started to say.

"No books, Bransen," Reandu replied.

The tone in the man's voice spoke volumes beyond the actual words to Bransen, a boy not unused to disappointment.

"Brother Bathelais will not be persuaded on this," Reandu admitted, and as Bransen's expression became crestfallen, he added, "You must understand, my boy, that our books are our greatest treasures. If you were to drool on them or dirty them—"

"No!" Bransen blurted.

"Even handling them causes damage," Reandu went on. "Please understand that it is not possible. Perhaps I can find some parchments on which a brother has spilled ink or otherwise damaged them. They might have words upon them. But you cannot read, of course."

Bransen started to stutter and pointed at the monk.

"Yes, Garibond wanted me to teach you to read," Reandu admitted. "But it would not be possible. I am sorry, boy. I wish that things could be different for you."

Bransen saw the true regret in Reandu's eyes, but that did little to fill the empty hole that had been dug in his heart. No books? Nothing at all but the dozens of walks to the river each day?

I will not fail Garibond, he repeated over and over and over as the trapdoor closed, leaving him with only the dim light of a single candle. Sobs and tears accompanied the litany.

He cried for many minutes, and only gradually managed to translate his heartbreak into anger. He picked up one of the many loose stones at the base of the wall and tried to throw it, but it slipped out of his hand and fell to the ground at his feet. He picked it up again, and again failed to propel it any distance. A third time he cocked his arm back to throw.

Symbols and curving script appeared in his thoughts, as if floating in the air before him. He held his pose and read the words, the words his father had meticulously copied, the words of *chi* and alignment, of the movement of muscles.

For one brief moment, it all came together for Bransen. For one beautiful and miraculous instant, one flicker of clarity in a decade of fuzziness, his core energy aligned and with a movement that could only be described as graceful, he threw the rock across the room to smack hard against the opposite wall.

Bransen stood in shock, staring into the darkness of the far end of the chamber. His legs quickly became shaky again as his line of life energy dissipated. But his mind held that moment of clarity.

Bransen shifted back to the wall and fell to his knees, then into an awkward half-sitting half-kneeling position. He lifted another stone and brought it against the wall and scratched out a shaky line.

No, that would not do, he realized as he studied the scratch.

Bransen concentrated more deeply. He remembered the writing in the book, the opening sequences. He could see them clearly in his mind, and his hand followed that guidance as he scratched out another line. He sat back and inspected his work. It was better than the first but still far from perfect.

The third line was a bit better.

The fourth line was better yet.

The hundredth line was almost perfect.

But the candle was gone soon after that, and Bransen allowed exhaustion to overtake him, there at the base of the wall on the cold, hard floor.

When he finished his chores the next day and was put back in his hole with another candle, he went right back to his real work.

And so it went, day after day, week after week.

Brother Reandu tried to convince himself that his inattention to Stork was merely a matter of his being too busy with his many duties. With several of the older brothers called away on missions or to Chapel Abelle, he was now the third highest ranking monk in Pryd, behind Father Jerak and Brother Bathelais.

His justifications held his conscience in check until one blustery, cold autumn night, the coldest by far since Stork had come to stay with them. Late that night, Reandu checked on the window hangings along the lower chambers of the chapel, making sure they were secured against the wind, while other brothers brought in wood to keep the hearth fires burning.

As he passed along the northeast corner of the building Reandu unconsciously glanced at the trapdoor leading to the substructure and to Stork's room.

How cold was it down there on a night such as this?

Brother Reandu took a torch from one of the nearby wall brackets and moved to the trapdoor, pulling it open gently and as quietly as he could so that he did not disturb the boy's sleep. He lay flat on the floor and poked his head through the opening, and was relieved to find that the room, though a little chilly, wasn't really uncomfortable and certainly wasn't dangerously cold. Hearing the boy's sleeping wheeze, Reandu brought the torch closer to the opening.

There lay Stork on his small cot, sleeping contentedly. The image warmed Brother Reandu's heart. Perhaps in sleep, at least, the tortured boy knew some peace.

He brought the torch back and began pulling himself up, but as he did the torch moved. Brother Reandu froze in place, his attention grabbed by the scratches, a hundred scratches, a thousand scratches, ten thousand scratches on the wall!

The monk blinked many times as the writing—it had to be writing!—became more clear, as the staggering scope of it began to be apparent. Now too curious to consider the boy's slumber, Brother Reandu climbed down into the underground chamber. He moved to the end of the wall nearest the boy's cot and found what had to be the beginning of this work: a large scratch, a squiggle, and nothing that made any sense to Reandu. Brother Reandu was no expert on linguistics; in fact, he had been among the worst of the scribes during his work at Chapel Abelle, but he instantly recognized patterns here, with words repeated.

"Amazing," Reandu said, and he was quite amused. Had Bransen, in his frustration, written his own book? Had he concocted a series of squiggles, a gibberish all his own?

Reandu's smile disappeared and he turned to consider the sleeping boy. Then he looked back at the wall, then back at the boy.

Then back at the wall again.

Even the first letter of the work was larger than all the others, a definitive beginning point. How had Stork possibly known to do that?

Shaking his head, Reandu slipped out of the room and went right to the door of Brother Bathelais.

He knew at once, as soon as Bathelais had squeezed into the cramped chamber beside him, that the older brother wasn't nearly as delighted. Bathelais stood there, staring at the markings, squinting and chewing his lip. He motioned for Reandu to follow, and they went back out of the hole.

"We will return in the morning, when we can study this without fear of disturbing the boy," Bathelais said.

"We should ask him about it."

"In time. I have little patience for listening to Stork stutter through some incomprehensible and ridiculous response."

Even though sympathetic Reandu always thought of Bransen as "Stork," hearing the name spoken by Brother Bathelais made him wince.

After more than an hour in the hole the next day, Bathelais's mood seemed to sour even more. He had brought with him some paper and charcoal and had done a rubbing of the work.

Reandu kept remarking that perhaps this was a miracle, but Bathelais just brushed him off over and over, muttering, "The boy has obviously seen a book."

"But to do such intricate work reveals an intelligence—"

"There are birds in Behr that can mimic human speech, brother. Should we kneel before them?"

Brother Reandu quickly realized that he would be better off remaining quiet as Brother Bathelais took over the investigation. He had little choice, in any event. He wasn't even invited to go along with Bathelais when he took the paper to Father Jerak later that day, and he only began to comprehend the level of Bathelais's disdain when the brother walked out of Father Jerak's room muttering, "Damnable Dynard, there were two."

Garibond was feeling particularly uncomfortable this day. He sat on the rocks beside the lower cottage, absently casting his line. He thought about Bransen; he was always thinking about Bransen, and he could hardly believe how lonely and empty his days had become since the boy had gone off with the monks.

But it was for Bransen's own good, he had to continually remind himself. That, or he would simply sit and cry.

He heard the horses, but was so entangled in his thoughts of his lost boy that the sound didn't register for several moments. When he finally glanced to the side, the riders—three monks and a pair of soldiers—were almost to the stones leading to his front door.

Garibond hurried to set his pole down and meet them. He recognized two of the monks and one large soldier that he knew to be Bannagran, the close friend of Laird Prydae. His presence more than anything warned Garibond that something was amiss, and he immediately thought of the Samhaists. Had they gotten to Bransen?

"Greetings to you, Brother Bathelais," he said, trying to keep the fear out of his voice.

"Where is it?"

"It?"

"Apparently, Brother Dynard kept another secret, did he not?" Brother Bathelais said.

Garibond rocked back on his heels, his mind spinning.

"You would be wise to speak openly and truthfully," Bathelais added. "For your sake and the sake of the boy."

"He is Bran Dynard's son," Garibond blurted, and he was surprised at the shock that came over Bathelais, as if he had caught the man completely off guard with the admission he believed the man to be anticipating.

"Bran Dynard," Brother Reandu said. "And SenWi." With both names, he emphasized the first syllables. "Bran and Sen," he clarified to those astride the horses about him.

"Bransen," said the third monk, whom Garibond did not know.

"When was the boy born?" Bathelais demanded. "Soon after Dynard departed?"

"Or soon before," Garibond admitted.

"And so the mother was here, all the while," reasoned the monk. "When all the holding was searching for the outlaw SenWi, she was kept safe through her pregnancy in the home of Garibond Womak." As he spoke, Bathelais looked at the soldiers, particularly at Bannagran, whose lips went very tight and whose dark eyes bored holes in old Garibond.

"She was no outlaw," Garibond managed to whisper, and his voice grew even weaker as all the riders began to dismount.

"Save yourself more trouble, and more for the boy, do not doubt," Brother Bathelais said to him. "Tell us where it is."

"SenWi is dead."

"Not the creature of Behr. The heretical book that Brother Dynard scribed. We know that there were two."

Garibond shook his head. "Two? No, there was only the one."

"Destroyed in the hearth in Father Jerak's room?" asked Bathelais.

"So I have heard."

Bathelais's smile became that of a predator that had finally cornered its meal. "And pray tell me how you heard of such a thing?" he asked. "Certainly few even in Chapel Pryd knew of the destruction, for few even knew of the work. How could Garibond Womak, who lives out here on the edge of the wilderness, know of such a thing as that?"

Garibond swallowed hard. "Word spreads quickly."

"Not that word!" Bathelais snapped. To the others, he said, "Tear out every stone of the walls if you must. I will have that book."

He looked back at Garibond, his scowl increasing. "Make it easy, master Womak. Your trouble has only just begun, and it will soon end, I assure you, but if you make it easy, then I will make your passing easy."

There it was. Bathelais had just branded him a heretic, and from that, there could be no appeal. He felt his knees go weak beneath him, but he stubbornly held himself up.

"For the sake of the boy, then?" Bathelais added.

The weakness was gone, replaced by a wall of anger. Garibond tried to respond with a barrage of insult and accusation, tried to scream out that this Church of Blessed Abelle was a sham under the leadership of Father Jerak, that Bran Dynard was the finest man he had ever known, and SenWi the finest woman, that all of the monks' pretense could not hide the awful truth.

He wanted to say all that, but all that came out was a wad of spit, aimed at Brother Bathelais's face.

The monk didn't flinch, and he slowly brought his arm up to wipe his face. He stared at Garibond hatefully all the while, and that was the last image he knew before a sudden burst of pain erupted on the side of his head and he fell away into blackness.

He awoke much later—he knew not how much time had passed—to the sound of voices and the crackle of wood. Immediately he was assaulted by a wave of smoke, stinging his eyes and throat.

And he felt the pain suddenly in his feet and shins. He squirmed and realized that he was lashed tightly, his hands behind his back and around a stake.

"I had hoped you would not awaken," came a sympathetic voice. Garibond managed to open his eyes enough to see Brother Reandu, with Brother Bathelais lurking right behind.

The waves of heat and smoke engulfed him. He heard himself screaming as the fires of Church justice curled the skin of his legs, as his woolen tunic ignited, and a million points of pain screamed out in protest.

He thrashed and he cried. And he choked and gagged, and couldn't find any air at all to draw into his burning lungs.

Just beyond the pyre, the soldiers, the monks, and a few curious neighbors watched the man pass from life.

"You could have made a grand spectacle and example of him," Bannagran said to Brother Bathelais.

"That is what Bernivvigar would do," Bathelais replied, and his voice was subdued and full of regret.

"It teaches proper respect."

"Respect?" Bathelais said, turning to regard the soldier. "This is an unpleasant necessity. This"—he held up the book the soldiers had found in a secret cubby in Garibond's tunnel complex—"is not an issue for public discourse." He looked down at the book for a long moment, then tossed it into the fire.

"This all ends here," Bathelais instructed. "All of it. Garibond is gone and the pagan tome is finally destroyed. We will speak of it no more."

And he went to his horse, and the others followed.

And the neighbors were left to watch the flames roar against the late afternoon sky and to bury the husk of Garibond's body the next day.

PART III

—

GOD'S YEAR
74

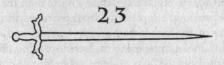

23

WALKING—AWKWARDLY—
IN PLACE

Bransen stood in the growing darkness outside Chapel Pryd. At just under five and a half feet he was smaller than most men, and since he could not stand straight, he seemed even shorter. His battered, bony frame barely topped a hundred and twenty pounds, making him closer in weight to the average woman than man. His hair hung long and black and his beard was scraggly, unkempt whiskers dotting his chin and cheeks, along with splotches of angry-looking hives. The unique and purplish birthmark on his right arm had not diminished, yet another mar on a body so full of imperfection.

His teeth were straight and white, his best feature, but they were rarely seen, for Bransen didn't smile often. Every day of every week led him on the same journey through Chapel Pryd to the river. Every night found him in his underground chamber, whose walls were smooth and unmarked—as the monks had moved him to another room and regularly inspected his walls.

Only three things sustained Bransen: his memories of the Book of Jhest, whose words he recited in his mind every day as he went about his chores; the conversations and lessons of the brothers in the room above him, particularly when they used the formal speech of ancient times as they read stories of legendary heroism and valiant deeds; and finally, the few scraps of mostly illegible parchments that Brother Reandu had generously obtained for him, pages ripped from old and decrepit tomes and errant works produced by tired brothers. Reandu hadn't been able to teach Bransen any more than the basics of this form of writing, but playing with those pages and trying to make sense of the words had greatly benefitted the curious young man, at least in relieving the boredom of his life.

It was the Book of Jhest, transcribed in his mind, that truly sustained him.

Especially at moments like this. These few minutes each day, after his last trip to the river, afforded Bransen the privacy and opportunity to further explore those words of wisdom implanted in his mind.

Very slowly, Bransen visualized his *chi*, starting at his forehead. He moved his internal eye down the line, collecting all the scattered flashes of life energy as he went. His lips stopped quivering, the drool held back. His head stopped lolling and settled in balance. His shoulders straightened and his arms stopped twitching and flailing. He couldn't see it, but the red splotches that so marred his face disappeared, although the birthmark on his right upper arm did not.

He took a deep and calming breath as his inner eye moved down the line between his lungs and to his belly.

Bransen stood perfectly straight.

Bransen stood perfectly steady.

Slowly, he lifted his arms before him, then above his head. He brought them down to his sides as he rooted his feet into the ground. In that moment, Bransen, the boy they called Stork, was so strong, and he believed that he could hold his ground and footing even if Laird Prydae charged into him!

The young man took a few strides forward—not awkward and stiff-legged strides but real steps, powerful steps, balanced steps. "I am the son of SenWi and Bran Dynard," he said, and he did not stutter. "I am the child of Garibond, the boy he loves, the boy who loves him."

A wobble of Bransen's hip belied his calm posture. The moment of clarity was quickly passing, and a wave of exhaustion was following.

In another few moments, he was just Stork again, stuttering and gangly, drooling all over himself. But beneath that slimy and shiny covering and those crooked and twitching jaw muscles, Bransen was smiling.

Every day, he escaped the bonds of his infirmities. Only for a moment, perhaps, but that moment was more than he had ever dared to hope.

One day, he mused, he might tell Brother Reandu of his secret, and tell him in a voice strong and stable.

Perhaps that fantasy would take place, but Bransen remembered all too well the monks' reaction to his writing the Book of Jhest on his walls. He remembered the panic and the anger; and though he had not been punished, he saw the flash of hate and outrage in Bathelais's eyes, the implication and threat all too clear.

But he wanted to tell someone, and Reandu was probably his best friend. Or maybe he would get stronger, and maybe he would learn to sustain the power offered by his forcefully composed *chi* for longer periods—forever perhaps—and then he could go to Garibond and show him.

That was Bransen's deepest wish and hope: to return to his beloved Garibond, not as Stork but as a whole man. Wouldn't Garibond be proud of him! And if he could become whole, even if he were to continue working for the monks, he should be able to find enough time each week to go back and visit his beloved Garibond!

The young man picked up the empty chamber pots and staggered toward the chapel's back door, his simple dreams sustaining him through each labored step.

"Has he spoken at all today?" There was no missing the contempt in Master Bathelais's tone, a simmering revulsion that seemed to be growing almost daily.

"No, master," replied Brother Reandu. "Father Jerak sits, staring into emptiness. It is almost as if he is looking at the past."

"He is, and seeing events as if they are only now unfolding. Last week, he demanded that I go to Laird Pryd to insist that he ease the burdens of those working on the road."

"The road?" Brother Reandu echoed, and then he grew even more startled as he added, "Laird Pryd?"

"It is an argument twenty years old," Master Bathelais explained.

"It is good that the masters at Chapel Abelle saw fit to convey the powers and title of master upon you, dear brother," said Reandu. "If we were at the discretion of Father Jerak now—"

"Father Jerak has no discretion," said Bathelais, and when Reandu started to balk at the bold statement, he held up his hand. "I say that with great sadness, brother. Long have I considered Father Jerak my friend—more than my friend. He has been as a father to me in more than Church ways."

Brother Reandu nodded. Father Jerak had ruled Chapel Pryd wisely and compassionately for many decades.

"You will need to formally announce your position as presiding father of Chapel Pryd very soon," Brother Reandu advised. "Our superiors offered you this at your discretion."

Bathelais rocked back on his heels. "You ask me to unseat my beloved friend."

"Will Chapel Pryd survive the weeks, months, even years we may have to wait for him to go and sit with Blessed Abelle? Master, Rennarq whispers in Laird Prydae's ear in favor of Bernivvigar even as the people shout the same, all the more loudly every day."

Bathelais's look turned icy.

"The Samhaists had more than a thousand people gathered at their bonfire last night." Bathelais winced at that.

"The people are angry," Reandu went on. "How many men are dying in the south? How little have they to eat, and less now that Laird Prydae has been forced to pay taxes to Laird Delaval."

"We are not responsible for the policies of Laird Prydae."

"But neither are we fulfilling our promises to the people of

Pryd. We cannot heal their illnesses when so many of our resources are caught up in the greater issues of the holding. We cannot continue to tell them that our God is a benevolent God when their sons, husbands, and fathers die in the south. We cannot continue to tell them that our God is a bountiful God when their stomachs pinch with hunger."

"What would you have me do to alter the realities of our life in these dark days?"

"We are in need of a stronger voice in Chapel Pryd, with no confusion. Retire Father Jerak with all honor and respect, and speak out with a voice bold and full of conviction."

"And what will this voice say?" There was no missing the skepticism in Master Bathelais's tone.

"Speak out against the policies of Laird Prydae," Reandu pressed. "Against the conscription and the taxes. Against the suffering of the common folk. Bernivvigar embraces that suffering and says it will make the people more prepared for their ultimate fate. Are we any different from the Samhaists if we remain silently by the side of an oppressive laird?"

Bathelais's eyes flashed with anger for just a moment. "We are here at the sufferance of Laird Prydae," he reminded. "Prydae understands that if Laird Delaval is not successful in his campaign against Laird Ethelbert, then Ethelbert will annex Pryd Holding."

"And Laird Delaval will do the same if he wins," Reandu argued. "He already has, in everything but name."

"Name is an important factor to a man like Laird Prydae."

"Is that what all this is about, master? The pride of one man? It is well known that Laird Prydae was ready to throw his sword to the side of Laird Ethelbert when he believed Ethelbert meant to place him in the line of succession of Ethelbert Holding. It is only because of Ethelbert's rejection, since the line will now end with the gelded Prydae, that our laird saw Delaval's offer as more tempting. And even that offer calls for the annexation of Pryd by Delaval upon the end of the line of Pryd!"

"You involve yourself too much in politics, brother."

Reandu was a bit taken aback by the tone of warning clear

and present in that statement. "The matters of politics are the only reality the people of our congregation know," he said.

"I do not recall Laird Prydae asking our opinion, brother."

"Then what is our purpose?" Reandu blurted, but his bluster dissipated quickly under the threatening scowl of Master Bathelais. Reandu suddenly found his breath hard to come by, as so many implications of his continuing resistance flashed across Bathelais's eyes. Fear, frustration, and anger all rolled together within Reandu, gathering into a single, tangled ball that left him speechless.

"Go to your duties," Master Bathelais instructed. "If you truly wish to help me now, then help me find a way to positively distinguish us from the Samhaists. I will take your words concerning Father Jerak under serious advisement, as I believe that you might be correct in your observation. Father Jerak cannot openly oppose Bernivvigar at this time. Father Jerak cannot properly clean himself at this time! But I warn you, and only this once, beware your words against Laird Prydae. I prefer a tentative hold on the people of Pryd to no hold at all, brother, and your indignation is a sure way to the expulsion of the Church of Blessed Abelle from Pryd Holding."

Reandu continued to reel in unfocused anger and frustration, and could barely mouth out, "Yes, master," as Bathelais walked away.

24

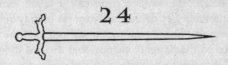

THE LAIRD'S MANLY
SWORD

Bannagran banged on the wooden door, his huge fist nearly dislodging it from its frame.

"You would be wise to open the door," he called. "You may need it when the battle comes north!" He hit the splintering wood again with a resounding thump that made the door lean into the hovel.

Finally, the door opened a crack, and the dirty face of an old woman appeared.

"If ye're coming for coins for yer laird, we got none left, master," she said.

"Not for coins," Bannagran replied. "And I trust that if you happened upon a few, you would know to deliver the proper amount to Castle Pryd."

"Then what? More food's what ye're wanting? Oh, but ain't we to keep enough to feed our own skinny bodies?"

"Not food," Bannagran replied. "A regiment of Laird Ethelbert has been sighted in the east. Men are needed."

The woman gave a cry and fell back, trying to close the door tight, but Bannagran's heavy fist knocked it open. He and the two soldiers accompanying him strode into the one-room hovel.

"Bah, ye took me husband and now who's knowing if he's dead? Ye took me brothers and not a one's to be found! What more are ye asking?"

"You have a son of fifteen winters," Bannagran replied.

"He's dead!" the woman shrieked. "I killed him meself. Better that than he get all chopped in some bloody field!"

As she spoke, Bannagran motioned to one of the soldiers, who moved to the hanging curtain that divided the room. A tug pulled it down, revealing a small cot, really no more than a wooden frame covered in hay.

The soldier looked back at Bannagran, who nodded for him to proceed.

"Dead, I tell ye!" the woman continued, her voice rising with obvious terror. "I put a pillow over his face while he slept. A peaceful way."

"If I believed your tale, then I would have you executed," Bannagran said matter-of-factly.

"For murder? He's me son, and I can kill him if I'm choosing."

"For stealing from Laird Prydae," the large man replied. "All the folk are the property of the laird, and you've no right to deny him his possessions. Whether he is your child is not important." He nodded and the soldier upended the cot, revealing a teenage boy and a younger girl, huddled together on the floor against the wall.

"Come on," the soldier said, and he reached down and hooked the boy under the arm and roughly pulled him to his feet.

The girl started crying; the woman rushed past to intercept.

But Bannagran caught her by the back of her tunic and easily held her in place. She tried to turn and swing at him, but he had her quickly wrapped in one powerful arm, and she couldn't begin to wriggle away.

"Ye can't have him!" she cried. "Ye can't be taking him! Oh, ye dogs!"

Bannagran squeezed her more tightly and hoisted her up so that his scowling face was barely an inch from hers. "Foolish woman. If we do not go out and meet the threat of Ethelbert, his soldiers will knock down your door and knock down your house. They'll kill your boy when he hasn't even a weapon in hand to defend himself, and they'll take you . . ." He paused and offered a wicked smile. "Might be that you're too ugly to interest them, but that wouldn't be your gain. They'd take your daughter instead, every one of them would, and leave her torn and bleeding and broken. Perhaps she's old enough to bear a child—is that what you're wanting, old fool? Do you wish upon your daughter a bastard child whose father you'll never know?"

The woman was crying so violently now that she couldn't answer. Nor did she offer any more resistance. Bannagran released her and shoved her back, then followed the two soldiers, who were flanking the subdued boy, out of the house.

"That makes twelve," one of the soldiers said when they were outside.

"Enough for this group, then," Bannagran explained. "Get him to the castle and fit him with leather armor and a weapon." He looked more closely at the boy, even reached over and felt the skinny biceps. "A spear for him. He couldn't hit anything hard enough with a sword to make a difference."

Bannagran quickly climbed onto his horse and turned the mount away, not wanting the others to see his continuing scowl. He found this duty distasteful, and he was quite weary of pulling men—and now boys—from their families. He heard the woman's frantic shrieks and prodded his horse on more swiftly, wanting to put the noises far behind.

He rode away from the others and moved closer to Pryd Town, trying to ignore the haunted stares of the many people in the streets. Not a family had escaped the last six months of the war unscathed. Bannagran wondered if Pryd Holding would survive this wave of battle; an entire generation of menfolk could be wiped out if Laird Ethelbert persisted in his designs for conquest. Already, more than three hundred of Pryd's menfolk were known dead—a hundred and fifty alone in the battle of Bariglen's Coe.

As he rode toward Castle Pryd, Bannagran thought back to those days of battle against the powries in the east, when Laird Ethelbert and his legions had held the flanking ground north of the men of Pryd. The laird of the great holding in southeastern Honce had rescued him, Prydae, and all the others when they had been caught in a powrie web. Even then, though, Bannagran had seen the first signs of coming trouble. The roads were complete, crossing Honce from Delaval City to Ethelbert dos Entel, through Pryd and Cannis and all the way to Palmaristown on the mouth of the great river, the Masur Delaval. With that network came the march of armies to push the powries back, and with that network came the march of armies to expand the influence of their respective lairds. Already, Palmaristown was under the rule of Laird Delaval, and all the Mantis Arm heeded the commands of Laird Ethelbert.

It was Pryd Holding's bad fortune to rest halfway between the two dominating lairds.

Castle Pryd's drawbridge was down over the newly constructed moat, and the great champion of Pryd, the most recognizable warrior in all the land, didn't slow as he thundered across the wooden bridge and between the gate towers—also newly built—and into the lower bailey of the rapidly expanding castle. He pulled up short and leaped down as attendants moved quickly to tend to his strong mount.

To his right sat the Laird Prydae's private chapel, with an open garden behind it for those occasions when Bernivvigar came into the castle proper to offer his prayers and blessings. This was the oldest building in the castle, dating back many generations, and was of a stone more gray than the main castle structure. The architecture of the chapel, too, was more primitive, with thicker walls and smaller windows. Past the chapel lay the only predominantly wooden building in the complex, the barracks, nearly empty now, as most of the men were off patrolling.

Directly ahead of Bannagran, opposite the main gate, sat the great keep, the tower of Laird Prydae, connected at its base to the castle's dining hall and audience chamber.

The two men standing guard at the keep's heavy wooden door moved quickly when they saw Bannagran's approach, pulling wide the double doors, then standing at attention, eyes ahead and unblinking, as their commander walked through.

The bottom floor of the keep, the only square room in the tower, was sparsely appointed, with only a pair of chairs set before the large hearth, a thick rug beneath them. Bannagran's eyes were drawn to that hearth and to the empty hooks above it. Not too long ago, Laird Prydae's magnificent sword, a gift of the brothers of Abelle, had hung there. But the laird had recently moved it to his private quarters, safely out of sight whenever any of the noblemen of Laird Delaval's court came calling. For when they came, they did so with their hands out, seeking money or goods, and Laird Prydae knew well that his sword, a creation far beyond anything any blacksmith in Honce could hope to forge, would be greatly desired.

That was the one treasure in all his holding that Laird Prydae would not surrender.

Bannagran was surprised that his friend wasn't down here taking his breakfast, as was Prydae's custom at this hour. The warrior moved for the stairs on the left side of the room but paused at the base when he heard a woman crying up above.

Somewhere behind her, Prydae cursed, "Harlot!" and then, "Rotfish!"

Bannagran put his head down and drew a deep breath. He knew the insults well enough, had heard Prydae launch them at women for a decade now. As ruler of Pryd, it was Prydae's privilege to take any woman in the holding, married or not, a tender child or an old hag, as his lover. "Lover" wasn't quite the right word with regard to Prydae, Bannagran supposed, for the scars of the laird's powrie wound would not permit it, despite the work of the monks with their soul stones, despite the many sacrifices of other men's genitals old Bernivvigar had offered over the years.

Inevitably, when he failed to perform, Prydae would blame the woman, calling her harlot and other similar insults, and "rotfish," a term usually reserved for a woman of no sexual imagination, who would lie still as a receptive, yet unmoving, vessel.

The woman, a pretty enough thing—as long as she hid her three-toothed smile—in her mid-twenties, came out on the top balcony and rushed to the highest of the four visible staircases, her clothing bundled about her, hardly hiding her ample charms. Her bare feet slapped on the wide wooden stairs as she scurried down to the next balcony, her face wet with tears.

Bannagran recognized her—he remembered the day he had taken her husband away to join a group marching south to battle.

She hardly glanced at him as she rushed past, sobbing at every step.

Bannagran watched her go, then looked back to the top stairs, where Prydae stood naked and half erect, his face red with frustration, his fists clenched in rage. "Rotfish!" he cried again, and he banged his hand hard against the wall, then moved back.

Bannagran shook his head and sighed, then moved to one of the chairs before the hearth and poured himself a drink of Prydae's wine. He took a seat and stared into the embers, some still showing lines of orange, wisps of smoke slipping out from the ash and drifting lazily up the chimney.

It was some time before Prydae came down to sit beside him.

"Useless bitch," the laird said, and he filled, drained, and refilled his wine goblet before offering more to Bannagran. "A sound other than a whimper, a movement beyond her drawing of breath—is that too much to ask?"

"You were close this time?" Bannagran asked.

Prydae set his goblet down on the arm of his large, upholstered wooden chair and rubbed both his hands over his still-red face. "Better if the powrie had taken it all," he said, "and taken, too, the desires that burn within me."

"You seek the treasure of a dragon," Bannagran remarked, "and have found its footsteps on several occasions. Is not the hunt worth your time, my liege?"

"I seek the honey of a woman," Prydae corrected. "And have seen the sweets before my eyes and within my reach, and yet I cannot grasp them! Is not the frustration more than any man should bear?"

Bannagran chuckled as he brought his goblet up to his lips and tasted the smooth red wine from the grapes of Laird Delaval's western fields. "The honey will be sweeter for your wait," he replied.

Prydae joined him with a chuckle of his own, but they both knew that this was much more serious than the frivolous pleasures of an overamorous laird. If Prydae could perform—and he had come so close on several occasions—and produce an heir to the line of Pryd, then the politics of all the regions would dramatically change, and for the betterment of Pryd Holding. The only reason Laird Ethelbert had not named Prydae as his successor and heir of all his holdings was because it had become apparent that the line would end with Prydae.

Conversely, that fact had brought Laird Delaval to Prydae's side; and the pact between Pryd Holding and the most powerful laird in all Honce was quite specific: when the line of Pryd ended, Delaval or his heirs would annex Pryd Holding, by contract and treaty.

A son to Laird Prydae could change the dynamics all across southern Honce, and positively on every account for Pryd Holding.

"How much less would be the frustration if the coals below weren't showing signs of fiery life," Bannagran said. He knew that he was, perhaps, the only man who could speak in such a manner to proud Prydae, for he alone knew the intimate details of Prydae's attempted liaisons.

"So close," the laird muttered, and he drained his wine, then moved to refill his goblet.

"Prince Yeslnik is fighting in the south," Bannagran remarked. "His banners have shone on the field—word has it that he is leading charge after charge."

"Your voice says that you do not think this likely."

"Prince Yeslnik is no warrior. Likely, his champions are riding forth in his stead, while he sits in the comfort of his carriage far behind. It would seem that outside of the small holdings, places like Pryd, the nobleman warrior is fast becoming a lost notion."

"Delaval was a great warrior, as was Ethelbert, who put his sword to the task only a decade ago, beside us in the east."

"Was, my laird," Bannagran replied, and he looked at Prydae doubtfully, for both of them knew the laird's last remark to be an exaggeration. In truth, Ethelbert's armor was rarely dirtied and never bloodied in all the months of their campaign. "Was," Bannagran repeated. "Among the lairds of Honce, I doubt that any could stand in battle more than a few moments before you."

"Ah, but in the bedroom . . ." Prydae replied with a mocking laugh, and he lifted his goblet in toast.

Bannagran didn't drink to that.

"Yeslnik will make a name for himself," Prydae said.

"Yeslnik's *champions* will make a name for him," Bannagran corrected.

"Can any less be said of Bannagran and Prydae?"

"Yes," the champion answered immediately and with complete sincerity. "The name of Bannagran is known—not once did Prydae claim the credit for the successes of Bannagran. Not once did Prydae need the achievements of champions to heighten his own claims to glory."

"You are kind, my friend." Prydae lifted his goblet to Bannagran for another toast, and this time, the warrior did lift his own. "There were occasions when I wore your powrie trophies as if they were my own."

"And more occasions when you wore trophies of your own victories."

"Perhaps it is nearing time for me to put the Behrenese sword to use," Prydae said. "Will we ride south, my friend? Two warriors, side by side, to help drive back the hordes of Laird Ethelbert?"

Bannagran paused and considered the words carefully, then slowly shook his head. "We will have all that we can handle should Ethelbert turn a portion of his force north and strike at us from the east. The work on Castle Pryd is not yet completed, and five thousand men would press us hard, even behind our walls. Laird Ethelbert has twice that to spare."

"True enough," Prydae admitted.

"You will find the opportunity to bloody the silver blade of your sword, I suspect and fear. Battles rage across the width and breadth of Honce." Bannagran needed yet another drink as he considered the truth of his words. All the land was in chaos. The roads had been built with the promise of greater trade and a greater ability to rid the land of the powries and the goblins. And at first, that promise had been realized, with the powries thinned to irrelevance and pushed to the sea, and the goblins all but eradicated throughout the land east of the Masur Delaval and south of the great Gulf of Corona.

But now the holdings were warring. Now Delaval and Ethelbert fought for dominance on a wide scale, while minor holdings battled over small pieces of valuable land. Even the powries had returned, or were beginning to, as reports of bloody cap murders seemed to increase daily throughout the land.

Bannagran drained his goblet. He didn't mind battle, didn't mind killing powries or slaughtering goblins.

But killing other men was something quite different, something that left him sour and empty.

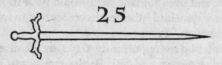

25

STRAINING THE QUALITY
OF MERCY

It was a day like any other day. The same routines and chores, the same time for waking and eating and collecting the refuse from the previous night. A light rain fell through the humid early summer air, making the dirt clump about Bransen's sandaled feet as he staggered out from Chapel Pryd toward the river, a chamber pot in each hand.

He hardly felt the weight of the two buckets, though they were nearly full, for his grip had grown strong and sure. That much of his muscles, Bransen could control. As for the rest, he stumbled and had to realign himself continually after each awkward step, certainly living up to his nickname. It had been a rainy spring, and so Bransen was used to the muddy ground, and he was managing well enough, though with great concentration, his eyes set straight ahead, his every thought locked on his forward movement.

He didn't notice a figure move silently up beside him, or the foot that went out in front of him.

Bransen tripped and stumbled; the chamber pots at his side sloshed and splashed him. He caught himself and would not have gone down, but the foot kicked hard against the back of his locked knee, buckling it.

He heard the laughter as he crashed to the ground, the contents of the pots splashing over him, mixing with the mud on his face and sliding up his nostrils.

Bransen fumbled and finally managed to come up to one elbow and lift his head, spitting with each movement. Then he froze, seeing four legs—strong legs, the legs of young men—planted before him.

"Aye, Stork, you fell down hard that time," came a voice that Bransen knew, a taunting voice he had heard on many occasions for more than ten years: that of Tarkus Breen, who had been away at the war, so Bransen had thought. Now he was back, apparently. As Tarkus finished, he stamped his foot down hard, spraying Bransen's face with muddy water.

"Take care, Tarkus," said his companion—Hegemon Noylan, Bransen knew. "You'll bury Stork where he lies and only make it all stink worse."

"Bah, all right, then," Tarkus conceded. "I'll pick him up." The strong young warrior reached down, grabbed Bransen by the front of his tunic, and hoisted him to his feet. But then he shoved Bransen hard as he offered a phoney "oops!" and the poor helpless young man stumbled back and fell in a painfully twisted manner.

He had barely hit the ground when a boot came in hard against his back, jolting him.

"Hey, you nearly tripped me with the dolt," said the third of the group, a younger boy of about fifteen, Hegemon's little brother Rulhio. He gave another kick, this one more vicious, that set off an explosion of pain in Bransen's shoulder. Bransen grabbed at the wound and tried to cover up, but his inability to curl onto his belly made him roll back before Rulhio in a vulnerable position.

Bransen tried to scream as a muddy foot lifted over his face, ready to stamp him flat. The poor young man couldn't even manage to cry out properly, his face twisting and his voice gurgling. He couldn't even manage to bring his arm back across to block the blow. A moment later, he tasted blood with the mud—his blood, running from his nose.

Then he was up again, suddenly, hoisted by Tarkus.

"Aw, you hurt him," Tarkus said, and he threw Bransen forward.

Rulhio caught him roughly, turned him, and shoved him to the waiting grasp of Hegemon.

"Well, I don't want the wretched thing!" Hegemon proclaimed, and he sent Bransen hard at Tarkus.

And so it went, around the triangle of bullies, the three of them taunting, pinching and punching, and throwing him in turn. Bransen couldn't begin to put his feet beneath him, couldn't even twist his mouth to shout a protest. On one throw, he tripped as he started ahead toward Tarkus, and he toppled forward, crashing hard against Tarkus's waist and knocking Tarkus off balance so that he followed Bransen to the muddy ground.

Of course, though that made the other two howl with laughter, it infuriated Tarkus, and he punched Bransen even harder in the face, then hauled him back up. Before Bransen realized that he was standing again, Tarkus slapped one hand between his legs and grabbed him by the front of his tunic with the other. A twist and heave had Bransen horizontal and in the air, Tarkus lifting the thin little man right over his head. With Bransen up high, the powerful Tarkus began to turn.

Only then did Bransen realize that the commotion had brought a crowd of onlookers—men, women, and children.

Tarkus stopped short, then threw Bransen down. He landed on his back, dazed and out of breath. He heard the crowd, and it brought an ache to his heart that far exceeded any of the pain the three bullies had caused him. For most were laughing, while one or two expressed their sympathy for "the ugly little creature," mostly in the form of whispers along the lines of, "It's a pity that such a beast should have survived birth."

Tarkus's foot stamped on Bransen's stomach, and Bransen jolted into a curled-up position.

"Hey, we're not done with you!" Tarkus said, and he grabbed Bransen again and pulled him to his feet, violently shaking him.

Crying, bleeding from his nose and gums, Bransen offered no resistance as Tarkus wound up to pound him some more.

"Stop it!" came a cry. "You leave him be!"

Before Bransen could register the identity of the speaker, the distant familiarity of the female voice, a woman crashed hard into him and Tarkus. Bransen slipped and would have fallen, but Tarkus held his ground and held Bransen upright; and the free hand that was about to launch a heavy punch at Bransen instead shoved the woman back.

Bransen tried to cry out, "Cadayle!" but only managed something that sounded more like "Cc . . . c . . . ca-daaaa!"

Cadayle pulled herself up from the mud and came right back in—or tried to before Hegemon and Rulhio intercepted her and held her off.

"You leave him be!" she continued to shout. "He's done nothing to you! He's just a—" She stopped short, and Bransen saw that something had caught her attention and had caught the notice of both men holding her. He followed her gaze back to Tarkus and saw him looking back over his shoulder. And Bransen realized that the crowd had gone silent.

When Bransen finally managed to turn his head to see what the others were looking at, he understood, for there stood Bernivvigar.

The Samhaist towered over Tarkus and all the others, making them all seem insignificant. He stared hard at Bransen mostly, and there was no mercy in his awful glower.

Bernivvigar curled up his withered old lips and chuckled menacingly. Out of the corner of his eye, Bransen noticed the transfixed expressions on the faces of the three bullies and noted that Cadayle had apparently shaken off the trance. She twisted suddenly, pulling free of Hegemon. Her arm came forward suddenly, slapping Tarkus across the face.

That brought the three to action. Rulhio moved quickly to grab the young woman. Tarkus Breen reacted even more directly, stepping forward and punching Cadayle square in the chest. She tumbled backward and would have fallen had not the other two regained solid grips upon her.

"Oh, but you're to pay dearly for that, witch," Tarkus remarked.

A moment of clarity, in the form of outrage, surged through Bransen, and he cried, "No!" and lashed out with both arms, flailing away. He heard the laughter erupt all around, even from Bernivvigar, but that didn't slow him. He felt Tarkus's grip tighten on the front of his tunic and knew the man was regaining his composure and balance, but that didn't stop him.

But then his face exploded in pain, spraying blood, again and again as Tarkus pumped his free arm. Cadayle screamed; many in the crowd gasped, while others laughed; and Tarkus growled like some rabid animal.

Bransen's senses were fast deserting him under that barrage, but he did hear a distant shout of protest and then a sharp and thunderous report, as if from a thunder bolt.

People stumbled and people screamed, and Tarkus stopped punching.

"Let him go!" cried Master Bathelais, and he extended his hand and opened it, showing the gray graphite stones, crackling with power.

When Tarkus didn't immediately respond, Bathelais dropped his arm and fired another lightning blast into the ground, jolting them all.

"I said let him go, and I warn you that I will not offer any more warning blasts." Other monks scrambled behind Master Bathelais, several of them, including Brother Reandu, showing gemstones of their own.

Tarkus Breen eyed Bathelais defiantly, but he did release Bransen, giving him a shove that had him tumbling to the ground.

"You protect this wretched creature," Tarkus shouted loudly enough for all to hear, and he gave a derisive snort.

"We are measured by the welfare of the least among us, not the strongest," Master Bathelais said.

From the side, old Bernivvigar laughed.

So did many others.

Bransen saw that Master Bathelais was not amused, and when the master's gaze locked with his own for just a moment, he saw little true compassion there. In fact—and it hit Bransen hard—even Tarkus Breen had not looked at him with as much hate as Bathelais did now.

Bransen didn't dwell on it, though, as he tried to pull himself back up, especially when he heard Tarkus say to Cadayle as he walked by her, "This is not over, whore. I know where you live."

Cadayle spat at him, and she rushed to Bransen, helping him to his feet. She began brushing him off, to the catcalls of the crowd and in the face of the obvious disdain of Bernivvigar.

"Get back from him," came an unexpected assault from an unlikely source. Both Cadayle and Bransen looked at the approaching Master Bathelais. "Shoo, girl," Bathelais fumed. "You have no place here."

"B-b-but," Bransen started.

"Shut your mouth," the master commanded, and he grabbed Bransen by the shoulder and pulled him away from Cadayle, shoving him into the arms of the waiting Brother Reandu.

"Easy, Bransen," Reandu reassured him. "It's over now."

Bransen managed to turn to face Cadayle, and she smiled at him. Then she motioned to indicate that Bransen should go along with the monks.

"B-b-b . . ." Bransen stammered, trying to point out Tarkus and the threat to Cadayle. "B-b . . ." he stuttered, spittle flying everywhere.

"Oh, be silent," Master Bathelais scolded as he walked past, and then he added to Reandu, "Get him inside before I lose my compassionate humor and give him to the anger of the crowd."

Reandu kept reassuring Bransen and led him off toward the chapel.

Clearly, Master Bathelais was not pleased. Bransen heard him shouting long before he neared the room to which he had been summoned by Brother Reandu; and as he approached, the master's words became clearer.

"So now we are using gemstones to threaten the populace away from this . . . this . . . this abomination?"

"Master, we are brothers of Blessed Abelle. Blessed because of our capacity for compassion," Brother Reandu countered. "When we took him in, we discussed this very matter."

"We took him in to secure the sword, that we might strengthen our position with Laird Prydae," Bathelais corrected. "Never forget that."

Bransen froze in place and found his breathing hard to come by. The sword? His mother's sword?

"He is our charge," said Reandu.

"Then keep him inside from this day forth. Have him collect the pots and put them out by the wall, where a younger brother can take them to the river."

"Do you justify the actions of the three ruffians?"

"Can you blame them?" Bathelais argued. "In these times? They go off and fight and die, while he stays here and—and what, Brother Reandu? While he stays here and eats the food for which others toil in the fields or hunt in the forest?"

"Master!"

The room went quiet for a moment, and Bransen dared to peek in. Bathelais stood there, before one of two chairs set in front of a desk. His eyes were closed, and he finally seemed to settle down with a series of deep breaths, his large chest heaving.

"Once, I vowed never to use the magic of a gemstone in anger, unless it was against a powrie or goblin," Bathelais said.

"You hurt no one."

"But I scared them. I scared them all." He gave a little snort. "That has always been the difference between us of the Church of Blessed Abelle and Bernivvigar and the Samhaists. They held power through fear, but we . . ." He gave another disdainful snort and shook his head. "I believe now that when it comes down to the moment of crisis, our two religions are not so different."

Brother Reandu stiffened defiantly in his chair. "I refuse to believe that."

Bathelais snorted yet again. "Keep the pitiful creature inside," he said again, and he turned and walked away, heading for the room's other door.

Bransen waited for some time before staggering into the room.

Brother Reandu smiled widely as soon as he saw the young man.

"Come along," the monk said cheerfully and he moved to a small desk and brought forth a pouch. He dumped its contents, a cache of various gemstones, onto the desktop and produced a gray hematite. "Let me tend the wound that young man gave you."

Bransen moved over and managed, with Reandu's help, to get into the chair opposite. Reandu cupped Bransen's chin in his hand and tilted his head back.

"He hit you hard, didn't he?"

Bransen wanted to say that he didn't care, but he grunted. Too many thoughts swirled in his head for him to even begin to sort them out at that time. He was angry at the bullies and deathly afraid for Cadayle. He was terrified of Bernivvigar and very confused about the words of Master Bathelais and his simmering anger, apparently directed at him.

It was all too much, and it was all that Bransen could do to hold back his tears.

Then he jumped in pain as Brother Reandu touched his nose.

"Ah yes, he hit you hard," Reandu said, and he gave a comforting laugh. "This will not hurt you," he promised as he brought the soul stone up to Bransen's face.

Bransen instinctively pulled back as Reandu began to chant, putting himself in a state of focus and meditation as he gently brought the stone against the other's broken nose. Bransen's slight discomfort from the pressure of the stone lasted only a moment and was replaced by a warm feeling spreading through his nose and face. He felt the healing powers of gemstone magic for the first time, and he closed his eyes and basked in it.

And something wholly unexpected happened. Bransen saw his line of *chi* react to the soul stone, just in the upper areas of his body. He pictured it clearly, a lightning line of crackling energy suddenly coalescing and aligning to the call of the gemstone!

Bransen's eyes opened wide.

"Yes, it does feel good, doesn't it?" Reandu asked.

The moment passed quickly—too quickly—and Bransen slumped back.

"There, done already," said Reandu. "That feels better now, does it not?"

Bransen gave a head-lolling nod.

He was too surprised to begin to elaborate.

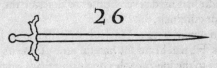

26

PARALYSIS OF ANOTHER SORT

When the trapdoor slammed shut, its reverberations felt to Branscn as if someone had driven a stake right through his chest. He sat in the near darkness of his barren and cold room, the light of a single candle the only barrier between him and a blackness so profound that he could not see his own hand if he waved it an inch in front of his face.

He was in emotional tumult, his thoughts flying from Tarkus Breen to Cadayle. Cadayle! Bransen could hardly believe that she had arrived in his moment of need. He hadn't seen her in years, and there she was, right when he most needed her, just as she had so often been before Bransen had come to Chapel Pryd. And as if all that turmoil and confusion, elation and fear weren't enough, Bransen saw the scowl of Bernivvigar and the trembling rage of Master Bathelais.

And one more thing swirled through his roiling emotions: the feel of the touch of hematite.

In his deepest dreams, in his moments of the purest concentration over the Book of Jhest, Bransen had not imagined anything as crystalline as the sensation that gemstone had provided.

Now he had to consider the hematite in a different light, and for a different purpose. He had tried to warn Brother Reandu that Cadayle was in danger. He had heard Tarkus Breen's whispered threat. But he hadn't succeeded and Reandu had merely reassured him that everything was all right, that bluster was just that and that the boys were "feisty"—yes, that was the word Reandu had used several times to describe the bullies—but were not criminals.

Bransen knew better. He had seen the look in Tarkus Breen's eyes. He had heard the hateful tone of Breen's voice. All that led him to the inescapable conclusion that Cadayle was in danger.

And no one would help her. And he was here, in a hole in the dark, hardly able to help himself.

Bransen forced himself to stand on his wobbly legs. He recalled the head to groin, conscious alignment of the energy line, of *ki-chi-kree*. Even though Bransen could hardly hope to achieve or sustain such a state, the effort to do so allowed him to throw aside his jumble of thoughts, one by one.

He dismissed the humiliation he had suffered outside. He dismissed Bernivvigar's threatening glare. He dismissed the unsettling comments of Master Bathelais. He dismissed the implications of the reference to his mother's sword. He even put aside his thoughts of Cadayle.

Temporarily.

Now he was in control of his tormented body. Now he stood straight and strong, and he stretched his arms out, then brought them in slowly and in perfect coordination, working through some of the Jhesta Tu exercises.

With a deep breath, Bransen fell into stillness and let thoughts of Cadayle come back to mind, hearing again the threat from Tarkus Breen. He focused the inevitable rising anger into his meditation, into his determination.

He knew he had to do something, but how could he even begin?

He thought again of the gemstone, of the moment of not just physical wholeness, but of *easy* physical wholeness.

Bransen stepped forward, walking swiftly before this effort of smooth movement weakened him. He went below the trapdoor and pushed it open, hoping that no brothers were around in the lower levels of the chapel at this late hour.

Bransen lifted his arms and planted his hands firmly on the lip of the opening. Only as he pulled himself up did he come to understand that his years of torment, of twisting and struggling for every movement, had actually done something wonderful: his muscles were strong. Now moving with coordination, his often-flailing arms easily hoisted him out of his hole.

He was beginning to tire, though, as he walked across to the desk and he nearly fell with exhaustion, his mind beginning to lose focus, his *chi* beginning to scatter once more. With great effort, Bransen pulled open the small side drawer, where Brother Reandu had dropped the gemstone-filled pouch.

He pulled it forth and carefully emptied its contents onto the desk, then sifted through the stones to find the one he needed. As soon as he had the smooth gray hematite in hand, Bransen felt the cool pull of its depths. He had never been trained in gemstone use, and he had only rarely seen the brothers of Abelle employ them. He wasn't sure how to begin to access and employ the magic.

But he found himself in the swirl of the stone almost immediately, and he understood its properties clearly. Amazed, Bransen quickly realized that the mental state that permitted gemstone use was almost identical to Jhesta Tu concentration.

His arm was shaking again, so much so that he actually punched himself in his still-sore nose—which sent a wave of nausea rolling through him—as he lifted the soul stone to his forehead. Finally he got it in place, and he let his thoughts flow through its inviting depths and then back into his *chi*, starting right there at his forehead.

Bransen's breathing steadied, and his arms and legs stopped shaking almost immediately. He saw his line of energy coalesce and straighten, and he felt a harmony within.

A perfect harmony, even more complete than he had achieved in those few moments when Brother Reandu used the stone on him. The combination of Jhesta Tu and gemstone magic held his life energy, his *chi*, strong and tight.

Bransen stood straight. He wanted to move through some of the Jhesta Tu exercises, for all weariness had suddenly flown, but he couldn't bring his arm down. He wanted to revel in this feeling of freedom, this feeling that all healthy people took for granted. He wanted to stand there and bask in the moment or to jump for in joy in an impromptu dance.

Could Cadayle wait for him to calm down?

He began replacing the other stones in the pouch; with each one he handled, he felt its magical energy, and its knowledge of its various properties flitted through his mind. He felt the tingling of the lightning-inspiring graphite and the weightlessness afforded by malachite. He felt the inner heat of ruby, the protective shield of the serpentine, and the warmth and light of diamond. The stones seemed strangely familiar to him. He couldn't dwell on it now, though. He put the pouch away and returned to his chamber. He fumbled with his bedding and pulled forth the black silk suit. It was still in amazing condition, but a seam at the right shoulder had begun to open. Bransen knelt on the main part of the black shirt and with his free hand pulled the right sleeve off. Then he wrapped it around his head, using it to secure the hematite in place.

Gingerly Bransen tied the ends together and brought his hands down to his sides, then breathed a huge sigh of relief: the gemstone effect was continuing even without his hand holding the stone. The connection remained, and it was strong.

Bransen smiled as he considered the expressions he might elicit if he walked out of his hole and to Master Bathelais's private quarters! What would Bernivvigar think of him now? Would he apologize? And what of Tarkus Breen and his cohorts? Bransen was free of his limitations; Bransen was also schooled in the martial ways of Jhest. He felt confident that Tarkus Breen couldn't even hit him, let alone hurt him!

Indeed, what might the world think of the Stork now?

Bransen's smile disappeared and a wave of fear nearly buckled his legs, every hopeful possibility fast replaced by dread.

With that in mind, he removed his bandana. Working carefully, one hand holding the gemstone, the other manipulating the material, he brought the fabric over the candle and held it there, once and then a second time. When he put the bandana back on his head to hold the gemstone, he spread it over his face so that it covered his nose and all the way to his upper lip. An adjustment showed him that he had burned the eyeholes correctly.

Cadayle.

That one thought stayed with him. He quickly pulled off his tunic and began donning the black silk suit. He recognized one error almost immediately, though, for he had removed the right sleeve, showing his bare arm and the unique birthmark. Thinking quickly, Bransen removed his bandana and tore a narrow strip off it. He put his mask back in place, then tied the strip around his right arm, hiding the mark.

When he put on the soft shoes, he felt as if he could leap to the stars or run faster than any deer. He was complete, dressed in his mother's outfit of station and blessed by the powers of both Jhest and the Abelle gemstone. He blew out the candle and scrambled out of his hole, closing the trapdoor behind him; and he quietly crossed out of the chapel, across the courtyard, and out into the night. As he tried to get his bearings, he moved from shadow to shadow, though there were few people milling about anyway. Cadayle lived at the western end of town, he remembered from long ago, or at least she *had* lived out there.

Bransen ran off.

He *ran* off!

His legs moved swiftly and he didn't have to throw them by jerking his hips forward. His legs strode in balance, his feet planting firmly with each long running stride. Bransen couldn't believe the feeling of freedom, of elation, and pure joy. He had never imagined this release from the bonds of his infirmity. He had never imagined the feel of the wind in his hair quite like this. He almost felt as if he were flying; and to him, this ability to run was almost as much of a leap as true flight would have been to a normal man.

So rapt was he that he nearly forgot his purpose, and he had gone quite a long way before remembering Cadayle and the possible danger. He slowed—how he hated doing that!—oriented himself, and realized that he had no idea where he was, for never in his life had he been west of Castle Pryd.

The farther he got from the castle, the more sparse lay the houses, scattered about small fields, clusters of simple houses separated by walls of piled rocks. All the structures looked the same, one- or two-room hovels of plain stone with thatched roofs. A few had small gardens under their windows, flowers and vegetables with colors dull in the pale moonlight. Some cows lowed and a few goats skittered past Bransen as he made his way along the winding roads. Some of the houses had candles burning inside; and whenever he noted the lights, Bransen slipped to the window and peeked in, hoping every time that he had at last found Cadayle's house.

He walked for hours, all the lights going down, even the moon setting in the west, so that he was alone in the quiet dark. He went farther out than he had intended, out to where the houses were even more widely spaced, out where fields and forests dominated, and cows and chickens and goats far outnumbered people. Bransen had no idea that Pryd Town was this big, for there were certainly more houses here in the west than in the east where he had grown up, where Garibond lived quietly with few and widespread neighbors around the small lake. Given the scope of the town, the young man only then realized the magnitude of the task before him in even finding Cadayle, let alone protecting her.

Frustrated, but with the eastern sky beginning to brighten with the first light of dawn, Bransen sprinted back along the roads toward Castle Pryd, whose massive dark outline could be clearly seen even from this distance. The light was growing by the minute, and Bransen realized that he might have erred. He understood clearly that he did not want to reveal his new secret, he did not want the monks or anyone else to know that there was another side to the Stork.

Each stride became more desperate as Bransen realized that he wouldn't make it back to the chapel before the brothers had begun to stir. How would he explain himself? He thought of running right by, of going all the way out to Garibond's house, but his place was Chapel Pryd, especially since he had one of their prized possessions, a magical gemstone, with him.

Bransen sprinted. He thought of the Book of Jhest, about its lessons concerning breathing and stamina. He loosened his fists and let all his muscles relax, save those pumping his legs.

He passed Castle Pryd and moved to the side of the chapel, sidling up to one window in the room above his chamber. He peeked in and saw a couple of brothers sweeping and dusting. "Come along, Stork," one of them called.

Bransen fell back against the wall and held his breath, trying to figure out some escape. He thought that perhaps he should just slip in and tell them the truth.

And then he thought of the Book of Jhest, the book that seemed to have the answers to everything buried in its graceful lines of script.

Barely making a sound, Bransen turned back and studied the two working brothers, soon discerning their patterns, soon predicting their turns and movements. He found his timing and slipped over the stone sill and in the window, sliding down to the floor and crawling along it like a snake. He reached the trapdoor and paused, silent and still, watching the two brothers moving in the dim light. As one brother lifted a candelabra from the desk, Bransen lifted the trapdoor, just enough so that he could slither through the opening. He touched on the floor below hands first, and held himself there, his feet slowly descending and quietly lowering the trapdoor closed as they did.

Bransen dropped to all fours and breathed a sigh of relief.

"Stork!" he heard one of the brothers call more insistently.

Now he moved fast, to his bed, where he stripped and pulled his woolen tunic on. Last, and with great remorse, he removed his mask and the gemstone it held. He worried about keeping the stone for just a moment, until he realized that there had been several of the soul stones in the pouch, after all, and the brothers didn't seem to keep close watch on them.

Bransen tucked everything out of sight, and not a moment too soon, for his trapdoor banged open. "Come along, Stork," said the monk. "Daylight is wasting."

Bransen rose from his bed, or tried to, and only then did he understand the toll his previous night's exploits had exacted upon his tortured body. A wave of such weariness came over him that he staggered forward and dropped hard to the floor, blackness engulfing him. Only distantly did he realize that he was being hoisted from the hole. Only distantly did he hear the calls of the monks.

He awoke much, much later, with darkness again settled on the land. He was on a blanket on the floor of the room above his own, a monk sitting in a chair above him, his head to one side, his breathing rhythmical in slumber.

Cadayle.

The thought stabbed at him. Had he failed her? Was it too late to go back and find her house?

Bransen tried to roll over and rise, but before he even really began to pull himself up, the monk grabbed him by the shoulder.

"Easy, Stork. It's almost dawn. Come on, now, go back to sleep. You had us all worried. We thought you had just decided to die!" The monk gave a chuckle, and Bransen hardly paid him any heed, but he did clearly hear the man's next words.

"I suppose that might be a good thing for you, though, eh, Stork? Poor wretched thing. Might be that we'd all be better off, yourself most of all, in just giving you to Bernivvigar. Ah, you poor thing."

Bransen wanted to scramble into his hole and gather up the soul stone, then come back in a rampage and teach this fool better!

But he didn't and he couldn't. He slumped back and hoped desperately that Cadayle was all right.

He went through his duties absently the next day, and was glad that the monks had reduced his workload since the incident with Tarkus Breen. When he finally managed to get back down into his hole, he was relieved to find that the monks had not found his hastily hidden black suit and the stolen soul stone. A crooked smile crossed Bransen's face as he considered that. Why would they find any of it, after all, since none of them ever came down to see him? On the one occasion when he had found visitors in his subterranean lair, they had been too consumed by the writing he had done on the wall even to notice the roll of black material that had so long served him as a pillow.

Realizing his limitations, Bransen dared to slip out earlier that night. He had to move more carefully, as there were people around, but the sky was heavily overcast, and the darkness gave him ample opportunity to hide.

And he used the lessons of the book, the deeper understanding it offered of how individuals perceived their surroundings. As he fell into those words, it almost seemed to Bransen as if he could see the world through the eyes of those from whom he wished to hide; and moving past them without being noticed presented very little challenge.

Bransen felt as if he were truly Jhesta Tu, as if the secrets of the mystics were more than simply known to him but actually were a part of him. How could he move so gracefully with his newfound freedom so fresh? How could he run, and fast, when he had never done anything like that before? And yet, he knew how, as if he saw every movement of his muscles, as if he understood every twist and its result, as if his thoughts, his *chi*, had so perfectly aligned that his body had become a perfect extension of that life energy, perfectly guided.

As he walked to the west end of Pryd, Bransen moved through the various routines of Jhesta Tu fighting, working his arms in a series of movements both defensive and offensive. He thrust his hand forward or sideways, precisely snapping at the end of each strike as if to crush a windpipe or stiffening his fingers as if jabbing them through flesh.

Many more lights were on as he moved through the western reaches of Pryd Town, affording him a better chance to locate Cadayle. The shadow that was Bransen drifted through the lanes and small yards, one by one, peering into house after house. And finally, he found her.

She lived with her mother at the end of a lane in a small stone house with flowers all around the yard. She was inside going about her nightly routines. Bransen's heart leaped at the sight. He watched the two eat their dinner, laughing and talking. He listened as they sat before the small hearth later, sometimes talking and sometimes sitting silent, taking in the meager heat on this unseasonably chilly night.

When at last Cadayle rose and moved to a small cot and began to undress, Bransen froze and nearly panicked.

She pulled her tunic up, and Bransen turned away, putting his back to the wall and fighting for every breath. How he wanted to watch her, to bask in the beauty of her soft curves and delicate limbs! His curiosity and something deeper, something he didn't really understand, something deep in the base of his line of life energy, in his loins, tugged at him to watch.

But he knew that it would be wrong.

He stayed by the house until late in the night, protecting his dear Cadayle. And while he was there, he practiced the Jhesta Tu exercises, the precise movements designed to instill memory and precision into the muscles of a warrior.

Any Jhesta Tu mystic watching him would have thought he had spent years at the Walk of Clouds.

No trouble came to Cadayle that night, nor the next, nor the next after that. And through each night, Bransen was there, outside her house, keeping watch and examining, too, his new-found physical prowess and the implications that it might hold.

"How will Master Bathelais and Brother Reandu accept this change?" he asked himself quietly. The young man found himself speaking aloud quite often these nights. The sound of his voice, without the stuttering, without the wetness of unwilled saliva, without the tortured twists and tugs of uncontrolled jaw muscles, amazed him and pleased him in ways he had never imagined. "Or Bernivvigar? Yes, the old one will be surprised and not pleased. What will he say when I look him in the eye and declare him a criminal? What will he say when I knock him down and kick him hard for the pain he brought Garibond?"

Bransen's eyes gleamed as he considered that, as he pictured Bernivvigar helplessly squirming on the ground before him. He shook the dangerous fantasy away, when he reminded himself that Bernivvigar had acted on behalf of Laird Prydae. Would he challenge the whole of Pryd?

"Garibond," he whispered to the night. "My father of deed, not blood. You will see your efforts rewarded. You will see your prayers answered. You will see your son stand straight. I will tend to you as you did for me all those years. Never again will you have to sit huddled in the cold rain, trying to catch a fish or two to silence your growling belly. Never again will you stagger toward the house, an armload of firewood in your weary arms.

"Never again, my father."

As he finished, Bransen leaped high into the air and spun one leg flying out in a circular kick, muscles working in perfect harmony, joints moving smoothly and without pain. He heard the crack of wind at the end of that kick, so sharp and swift was its motion. He landed easily in a crouch, arms flowing side to side before him as if fending off enemies.

He stopped abruptly and looked back at the house. "Cadayle," he whispered. He tried to imagine the look upon her face when he revealed himself to her, when he showed her that he was the Stork no more—or at least, not all of the time. "My love, my all."

A sudden stab of fear stole his voice. He thought he would rush forward and profess his love to her, tell her that there was nothing in all the world more precious to him than her smile and her gentle touch, that there was nothing warmer to him than the feel of her breath.

He realized that she wouldn't reciprocate. He knew in his heart, then and there, that she would never be able to see past the shit-covered Stork, wallowing in the mud. How could someone as beautiful and perfect as Cadayle ever hold any feelings other than compassion and pity for the wretched creature he had been all his life?

"How could I begin to think myself worthy of you?" he asked the empty night.

No, not empty, he only then realized, as his senses reached outward and caught the movements of several forms, distant laughter, and the crash of a bottle thrown to the road.

Bransen ducked into the shadows of a tree a dozen yards to the side of Cadayle's house. He stared back to the east, back down the lane, and noted the approach of five dark forms. He couldn't make out any details from this distance, but he knew at once that it was Tarkus Breen and his friends, come at last to make good on their threat. Bransen's hands trembled so hard that his fingers tapped against the rough oak bark. His legs turned weak beneath him and his mouth went suddenly dry.

"This is why you came out here," he reminded himself, but the words sounded hollow against the fear, the terror that was welling within him. He thought himself a fool, a pretend hero who kicked at the air and imagined he could do anything.

Anything at all.

For he was just the Stork, just a boy, who had never been to war, who had never fought back against anything other than pounding his dirty hand into the dirt after being thrown down.

A movement before him brought him from his thoughts, and he caught a flash, a reflection of glass in the starlight, as the bottle soared and smashed against Cadayle's door.

The three walked right past, taking no notice of him.

"Cadayle," Tarkus Breen called. "Come out and play, girl. I've a weapon too long sheathed!"

The others laughed.

The group strode right up to the house, one going left, another right, to ensure that no one got out.

Bransen wanted to shout. He wanted to charge at the group and demand they leave. He wanted to run back to town and call out the guard.

He couldn't bring himself to move. Not an inch. He couldn't bring himself to swallow, let alone cry out!

Everything seemed to move before him so slowly and yet very quickly as if his mind couldn't properly take in the unfolding scene. He saw candlelight inside the house. He watched a large man walk up to the door and kick it hard, and then again, knocking it wide open.

He heard a protest—Cadayle's mother.

And Tarkus Breen and two others went in.

He heard a scuffle, saw the two other men coming back around the house; and the sound of a slap jolted him straight.

Cadayle appeared in the door, wearing only a white nightshirt. She started to run out, but Tarkus himself caught her by her thick hair and tugged her back. She fell to her knees right there in the doorway.

Bransen shook violently. He silently cursed his cowardice. How could he watch this and not go to her? How could he stand here, ready to pee in his pants?

"Shut up, you old hag, and be glad that you're too ugly to feel the sting of our weapons!" one of the brutes shouted from inside. And Bransen jumped at the sound of another slap.

Cadayle crawled out and started to rise, but Tarkus's foot planted on her back and sent her sprawling to the ground.

In a moment, four of the five were around her, taunting her, while the fifth remained inside with her mother.

"You should know your place, girl," Tarkus Breen said. "You interfere where you're not wanted."

Cadayle looked up at him. Even at this distance, Bransen could see her eyes full of hate and fear.

"You defend that creature," Tarkus Breen said, and he spat upon her. "Do you not understand who we are and what we have done for you? We fight in the south and we die! We defend you, whore, and you side with that creature over us?"

Cadayle shook her head.

"You should welcome us with your legs wide," Tarkus Breen said, and he kicked her and started to roll her over. "You should be honored that we think you worthy of our seed!"

"Take her!" one of the others eagerly prompted, and the other three laughed.

Bransen told himself to move, ordered his legs to take him out there and intervene. And yet, he stood huddled against the tree, hardly breathing.

He looked at Cadayle, offering a silent apology for his weakness.

She didn't see him, but as if in response, she seemed to go suddenly weak, all defiance falling into hopelessness, and she began to cry.

Those tears, lines of wetness glistening in the starlight, crystallized Bransen's thoughts. All his personal emotions fell aside in the face of that sight, of dear and wonderful Cadayle crying and broken, the surrender of the woman who had been one of the pillars of strength in his life.

Bransen was moving without even thinking. Bransen's subconscious and muscles were falling into the martial lessons of the Book of Jhest. He hardly realized that he was approaching the group; he hardly even saw the closest man, the big one who had kicked in the door, turn and stare.

Bransen slid to one knee as he came up on that man, who was just beginning to cry out in surprise. Without breaking his momentum, Bransen drove the heel of his right hand hard into the big man's groin, lifting him up to his toes.

Bransen sprang up, snapping his foot up to kick the man in the face. As the victim straightened, Bransen hit him a left, right-left-right combination, finishing with a left hook that had the man flying sideways. Bransen leaped forward going right past the reacting attacks of the two men at the sides of Cadayle and going right over her to land before Tarkus Breen.

Breen's arm flashed out, a knife in his hand, but to Bransen he almost seemed to be moving under water. Bransen turned his fingers upward and pushed the striking arm harmlessly wide.

Reacting on instinct, he leaped straight in the air, tucked his legs beneath him, then kicked out on both sides, stopping the charges of both men beside him. He landed with his arms crossed over his chest, then flung his arms out, the backs of his hands smashing against the faces of his attackers. Bransen slipped to the right, bending his right arm, then lashing out once and again with his elbow. He felt the crunch of the man's nose with the first blow.

He dropped as that man fell and snapped out his leg into the kneecap of the other attacker, stopping him short. The man stiffened and stumbled backward, and Bransen used the distance to begin a charge of his own, easily deflecting another stab from Tarkus Breen. Two short steps and he leaped and spun, turning nearly horizontal in the air, adding even more weight behind his kick to the man's midsection.

As one leg flew out hard, Bransen lowered his other leg. He landed, absorbing the impact by letting his knee bend deeply and using the movement to regain his center of balance as he dropped nearly to the ground.

Then, with all his strength, he came up hard and threw all his strength and weight into the move to gain enough momentum to again lift him from the ground. Around he went as he rose, sending his free leg into a circle kick. It was too high, and cut the air above Tarkus Breen's head as he ducked and charged ahead, arm extended.

But Bransen's kick had been too high on purpose, in accordance with the movements taught in the Book of Jhest. As Breen ducked, Bransen launched his intended attack, his other foot snapping straight up into Breen's face.

Bransen landed easily on both feet, Tarkus Breen staggering backward. To Bransen's left, an attacker was rising but scrambling away, one leg broken. To his right, a man squirmed on the ground and clutched his broken face. Behind him, Cadayle cried; and beyond her, the big man lay very still.

"Who are you? What do you want?" Tarkus Breen said, the confidence long gone from his voice.

"I am . . ." Bransen paused, as if awakening from a dream, as if for the first time actually realizing what he had done. While his body had come in here, fighting perfectly, his thoughts were stalled back at the tree. Now he was waking up.

But what was he to say? He recalled some of the brothers at the chapel complaining that the roads were becoming unsafe again, with powries and highwaymen. He recalled pieces of their stories of older times and great deeds. He seized on that without even thinking.

"I am the Highwayman," he said, hardly considering the implications.

Tarkus Breen wasn't listening, Bransen then realized, but had used the pause only so that he could gather himself for another attack. He came forward hard, slashing his knife back and forth.

But Bransen, though he had regained his awareness of himself, was no longer afraid. There was no paralysis in him, and the lessons of the Book of Jhest flowed through him as easily and fully as if he were reading the book. His line of *chi*, formed so solidly by his discipline and by that soul stone set under his black mask, held tight and straight, relaying his thoughts to his muscles perfectly, and calling them to action.

Breen's knife slashed, left to right, then back again, but Bransen retreated and veered, so as not to trip over Cadayle. Tarkus Breen followed, stabbing straight ahead. Bransen's hand pushed the strike out wide, but then his attacker surprised him by breaking off and turning back to Cadayle.

Tarkus Breen stabbed the knife out toward her.

He never got close to connecting.

For Bransen rushed back to Cadayle, catching Breen's wrist with his left hand. He lifted Breen's arm and went under it, turning it and forcing the bully to come up straight. Bransen kept twisting as he stood up straight. He lifted his right arm and drove his elbow against Breen's.

The snap of bone sounded like the breaking of a thick tree branch.

Bransen hardly heard it and hardly slowed, ducking under the shattered arm and turning to come face-to-face against the agonized man, the twisted and broken arm between them.

The look in Breen's eye—somewhere beyond pain, somewhere in the realm of shock and horror—was the first indication of something serious to Bransen. He leaped back, letting go, and Tarkus Breen stood still, his right arm hanging at his side, his left hand coming in slowly, trembling every inch, approaching the hilt of his knife, which he had driven hard into his own diaphragm.

Shaking fingers moved around the hilt and started to close, but Tarkus Breen seemed to lose all strength then. He looked at Bransen. His arm fell to his side.

He fell over dead.

Cadayle screamed, but Bransen hardly heard it. He knew his enemy was dead. He knew that he had killed a man.

He searched through the Book of Jhest for an answer to this sudden realization. He tried to remember to breathe.

Another woman's cry behind him took it all away, and Bransen spun and charged into the house.

A moment later, Callen staggered out, crying, one eye swollen. She caught the door with one hand as she passed and managed to pull it partially closed behind her. She stumbled to Cadayle, who rose to embrace her, and the two turned back to the house, to the sounds of fists connected repeatedly, to the sound of grunts.

The door slammed closed then exploded outward, the assailant flying through it backward. He hit the ground hard, groaned, and rolled over, giving the two women a view of his bloody face.

The Highwayman appeared at the door.

"Be gone, all of you!" he demanded of the beaten attackers. "Be gone and return to this place only on pain of death."

They staggered and scrambled, hoisted their friend with the shattered kneecap, dragged Tarkus Breen's body, and managed to move away.

"They'll not return," Bransen said to the two women.

"How can we ever thank you?" Cadayle said to him breathlessly as she continued to hug her crying mother.

Bransen went to her and helped both women to rise. "No need, of course," he said, trying to show some measure of calm so that the two would follow that lead. "I consider it an honor to be able to help."

Despite his cool demeanor, Bransen was churning inside.

How he wanted to pull off his mask and proclaim his love for Cadayle! How he wanted to kiss her and hold her and tell her and her mother that everything was all right. How could he blend this moment of heroism into a moment of personal revelation?

The sound of a neighbor's call defeated any hopes he might have. No doubt, the defeated gang were beginning to draw attention.

Bransen smiled and tapped his hand to his forehead in salute.

"Good evening to you, beautiful ladies," he said. "Blessed am I to be granted the good fortune to aid you this night."

"But—" Cadayle started.

"The look on your face is all the gratitude any man would ever need, and more than any man would ever deserve, milady," he said, and he thought himself clever in sounding like the monks when they told their great tales of old heroes. Stealing a line directly from one of those overheard stories, Bransen added, "In all a man's life, might he hope to see a single instance of such pure beauty as your face. I am the fortunate one this night." He saluted again as both Cadayle and her mother looked to the road and the neighbors' approach. When they looked back, he was already gone, melting into the night.

The road back to the chapel was a long one for Bransen. So many truths assailed him from every side, so many conflicting emotions. He had performed brilliantly. He had saved Cadayle and her mother, had beaten the bullies.

He had killed a man.

Out behind the castle, in the darker predawn shadows within a copse of trees, Bransen Garibond, the self-proclaimed Highwayman, fell to his knees and threw up.

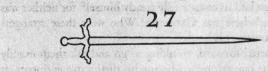

27

CATCHING HIS
MOTHER'S SPIRIT

The thrill of being out in the daytime had Bransen smiling widely, almost giddily, below his black mask all the way out to the small lake in the west. When he had heard—so soon after his return just before dawn—that all the monks had been summoned to the castle for the day, Bransen couldn't resist the chance to finally go out to his dear father's house. Now he could hardly contain his joy when Garibond's house came into view. Gray lines of smoke rose from each chimney, which struck Bransen as unusual, since Garibond typically only kept one hearth burning.

He skipped from tree to tree, moving through the shadows and even up in the lower branches as he went. He had been spotted a couple of times on the way out, as indicated by the shouts of distant people, but he thought nothing of it. Now, though, as he neared, he saw several forms moving around the small island: a pair of children and a pair of women, one of about his age and the other older, possibly her mother.

Had Garibond taken a wife?

Bransen swallowed hard, not sure what to make of it all. Were these Garibond's children running about his island? And who was the girl of his own age, for surely she couldn't belong to his father? He moved even closer and rushed past the house to a pile of rocks on the shore, affording him a view of the southern side of the small island. Both women were heading that way, and now he saw why. A pair of men sat on the rocks down by the water, fishing.

Bransen had to consciously steady himself, for neither was Garibond. Where was Garibond? Who were these strangers that had come to his house?

He started forward, thinking to go and ask them exactly that, but he paused, remembering his distinctive garments. It was one thing to be spotted running along the distant fields but quite another to go right up to someone. And if he asked about Garibond, wouldn't he be implicating his father as an ally? He knew not what retribution might be in store for him for his actions at Cadayle's house. Was he to be branded a hero or an outlaw?

He couldn't risk it, for Garibond's sake.

He stayed in place for some time longer, taking a look at each of the six people on the island, committing their faces to memory. If they came into town, he would find a way to ask, he decided, or he would come back out here dressed in his woolen tunic and walking in the awkward guise of the Stork. Yes, that might work. With the gemstone hidden, he could pretend to be the creature that everyone believed him to be.

It was all too surprising and all too confusing, and the sun was low in the western sky. The monks would be returning soon after dinner, so he had heard.

He sprinted back to the west.

"Do these problems never lessen?" Prydae said, and he threw down his gauntlets upon the desk, stamped his hands upon the wood to steady himself, then turned his angry look back at Bannagran. "One man?"

Bannagran shrugged.

"One man, unarmed, defeated five?" Prydae pressed. "Five who served with our warriors in the south and are not new to the ways of battle?"

Again, the big man shrugged.

"There were spearmen in the trees, perhaps?"

"There were no spear wounds, my liege," said Bannagran.

"Nor were any cut, except Tarkus Breen, who died on his own dagger."

Laird Prydae rubbed his face. Powries were all around once more. Bandits had been seen on the roads to the south and to the west, and now this—a daring attack by a single man against five! Here Prydae was, trying to focus on the titanic events in the south, on the war between lairds Delaval and Ethelbert and the implications to his sovereignty, if not his very survival—and trying to discern how best to collect the heavy taxes Delaval was demanding—and these minor distractions would not lessen at all.

"What of the other four?"

Bannagran shrugged again. "Keerson will not walk again without a limp, but beyond that, they will all recover with time. Except for their wits, perhaps, for they claim the martial prowess of this one to be beyond belief. He was possessed of the strength of ten men, they said, and he fought so quickly that it seemed as if there were three of him."

"They would say that to save their drunken pride, though, wouldn't they?"

Bannagran shrugged.

"Who was it?"

"He called himself the Highwayman."

"Wonderful." Prydae slammed his fists down on the desk.

"He is one man," Bannagran reminded.

"Who defeated five—unarmed when they were not."

"Five staggering drunks."

Prydae nodded, having to accept that.

"Our guests are waiting," said Bannagran. "We should not linger; I doubt that Father Jerak will be able to remain much longer."

"Does he even know where he is?"

"Doubtful. And if we don't get him out of here, it is likely he will shit himself soon enough."

Prydae laughed, then moved to the hearth at the side of the room and pulled the fabulous sword from its perch and slid it into his belt at his left hip. "Lead on," he bade his friend, and he fell into step behind the man who would announce him. Before they even began to descend the stairs of the tall keep, Prydae reached out and grabbed Bannagran's shoulder, stopping him. "We should go out in full splendor in the morning," he said. "It has been too long since I worked my chariot team."

"A show of strength to assure the people?"

"And to warn this Highwayman. Let him realize the terrible end of the road he has chosen to walk."

Chapel Pryd was strangely quiet the next day as Bransen went about his chores, collecting the chamber pots and setting them by the back wall. Not a monk seemed to be anywhere, except the one who served as attendant to Father Jerak, and the old man himself, apparently worn out from the excursion of the previous day.

Bransen wasn't using the soul stone, though he missed it dreadfully, as he missed walking straight and missed the sensation of running. Secretly, he never wanted to assume the posture of the Stork ever again. But playing his alter ego, this Highwayman, was physically exhausting to him, and, beyond that, he had no idea of how the brothers might react to his newfound health, nor to his pilfering their sacred gemstone. He had noticed, however, that even without the soul stone firmly secured against his forehead, he was finding a bit more control of his movements with every day. In Jhesta Tu terms, and using Jhesta Tu technique, Bransen was finding more and more solidity to his line of *chi*. With his meditation and focus, he could form that line and hold it, albeit for only short periods; but even when he was not consciously engaged in such Jhesta Tu disciplines, he found that his line of life energy wasn't dispersing quite as widely and wildly as before.

Given that, Bransen found himself in the strange position of consciously exaggerating his storklike movements. He wasn't quite sure why he should not reveal the changes he was experiencing, but he had a feeling that his cover as a helpless creature would serve him well for the time being.

On his fourth trip to the back wall, a chamber pot sloshing at the end of each arm, Bransen found the six previous pots still sitting there untended and unemptied. He put the two new additions down and looked about curiously. Where was his helper?

Bransen moved back into the main areas of the chapel's first floor and was struck again by how empty the place seemed. Not a brother was to be seen or heard. He staggered through all the main rooms, finding them unoccupied. He went to the front door of the chapel, which was opened wide, and glanced out into the courtyard, with its twin trees, left and right of the cobblestone path.

He was about to go back in and head right up to Father Jerak's attendant to inquire about it all, but then he heard the bells ringing and the trumpets blowing out in the town. Curious beyond any fear of breaking the rules, or of simple good judgment, Bransen moved down the chapel steps and across the courtyard to the open outer gate.

He saw many of the monks lining the main road of Pryd Town. He picked out Bathelais and Reandu among the throng, and it was indeed a throng, with all of the folk out there, waving and cheering. The Stork made his awkward way to Reandu and reached the brother just as the trumpets began to blow with even more urgency.

"Stork," Reandu greeted. "What are you doing out here?"

Bransen couldn't tell if the man was angry or merely surprised. "I-I-I . . . I didn-didn-didn't kno-kno—"

"Never mind," said Brother Reandu and he put his hand on Bransen's shoulder to quiet him. "Perhaps it is better that you came out. You should see the glory of Laird Prydae revealed!" As he finished, he pulled Bransen forward and helped him settle in place right at the road's edge. He even helped Bransen to steady his head and look toward the castle, where the procession had begun.

First came the soldiers of Pryd in their full regalia, bronze armor dully shining in the sunlight. They carried long spears, holding them vertical, gleaming tips up high and in perfect alignment with one another, showing the splendor of the discipline of these best-trained soldiers of Laird Prydae. The laird's various commanders walked along the side of the tight formation, calling orders and warning back any peasants who stepped too far out from the roadside.

Bransen watched in amazement as the procession paraded by, boots thumping the ground in unison.

Behind the common soldiers came three horsemen, including one Bransen knew well enough in the center. Bannagran seemed even more huge and more imposing on his armored mount! And clearly the legendary warrior commanded the attention of all the onlookers.

That is, until the man behind him appeared. In a chariot more grand than the one he had lost in the war all those years earlier, and with a team of two large and strong horses, Laird Prydae seemed the most splendid of all. He wore a new breastplate, replacing the many-nicked one that had gone off to the powrie war. This one, again of bronze, and again emblazoned with the running wolves, was studded with jewels that caught the sunlight in bursts of radiance. He wore an open-faced helm with a horsetail-like plume, dyed red. But armor, helm, and chariot seemed not to matter much when he drew forth his shining steel sword. He held it aloft and the crowd gasped and cheered and as one pointed at the marvelous weapon.

That sword could cut through a plate of bronze armor, so it was rumored, and it could fell a small tree with a single powerful stroke. That sword, it was whispered all around Bransen, would keep the powries at bay and make any imperialistic-minded laird tremble at the mere thought of warring with Pryd Holding.

That sword . . . was the sword of Bransen's mother.

The emotions sweeping through Bransen as he watched the procession and the proud laird were very different from those of the people around him. They saw inspiration; they showed awe. But for Bransen, there was only the sudden realization that this sword did not belong with the Laird of Pryd. This sword, his mother's sword, was his own to claim.

And so he would, he determined, and that very night.

When the chapel monks had all settled into their beds, the Highwayman, dressed in black, a soul stone pressed against his forehead by his tight mask, slipped silently out of Chapel Pryd and moved through the shadows to the wall of the great castle itself.

Bransen watched the wall top for signs of sentries, trying to spot their dark silhouettes against the moonlit sky. All seemed quiet.

He fell into his meditation, recalling the lesson in the Book of Jhest, recalling the day he had spent at the desk when first he had taken the soul stone. He considered the many revelations of the various gemstones, recalling the properties of malachite. Bransen gathered his *chi* and lifted it, replicating the levitational energy of malachite. He felt almost as if he were floating, though of course he was not. But he was lighter, his life energy battling against the pull of gravity.

Bransen lifted a hand to the stone wall, found a slight fingerhold, and propelled himself upward. Hand over hand he went, easily and spiderlike, needing no more than the ridge between two stones to provide him enough of a grip to move past.

He reached the top of the wall in short order and glanced all around. With no guards in sight, he moved silently along the wall to the point where it joined with the large keep. This tower was Prydae's own, Bransen had learned from various discussions among the monks over the years, and so this was likely where he would find his mother's precious sword. Again, he fell inside of himself and lifted his energy skyward, walking up the wall.

He passed one window and peered in, but saw nothing of interest in the candlelight. *Up higher*, he decided, and he moved along. As he neared the next window, this one along the back of the tower, he heard voices from within.

"A fine show, my liege," said a deep voice. Bannagran's, perhaps, Bransen thought.

"Every now and then, they need to be reminded," came the reply, a voice that Bransen did not know, dour and serious and gravelly with age.

"Perhaps it is a reminder that I need, as well," said a third, whom Bransen recognized as Laird Prydae. It also struck the young man that the laird's voice was quite somber. "I do not miss the sound and smell of battle," Prydae went on. "Yet I cannot dismiss the thrill that courses my body when I drive my chariot and draw my sword."

"It gives hope to the people," said the voice Bransen believed to be that of Bannagran. "You are their protector."

"And their laird, with all the privileges that entails," said the old voice. "The woman you chose along the parade route awaits you in your chambers, my liege. Use her well."

"My blood is hot with the sound of trumpets and cheers," Prydae said. "Perhaps this, at long last, will be the night for consummation."

Bransen heard the tink of goblets tapped in toast, and a moment later, the sound of footsteps receding, followed by the bang of a heavy door closing. He waited a bit longer before edging toward the window and peering in.

The room was dark, with only the glowing embers of the fire remaining to add to the slanted rays of moonlight that were sliding in through the narrow window.

Bransen held his position and glanced all around and down. Still he saw no guards walking sentry. After a few more moments of silence, he slipped into the room.

He moved away from the window, crouching in the darkness and allowing his eyes to adjust. Gradually, the distinctive shapes within the room came into clearer focus: the closed door across the way, the chairs before the hearth off to his left, the hearth itself.

And something set on the wall above the hearth.

Bransen sucked in his breath. Had good fortune shone

upon him? Had he wandered into the very room that contained his mother's sword?

Silent as a shadow, he slipped to the hearth and saw the outline on the wall. It was a sword, a long sword, too long for bronze or iron.

Behind him to the right, the door banged open, and he saw the steel of the fine blade flash with the sudden intrusion of torchlight.

Bransen swung around to see a surprised Bannagran standing just inside the door, torch in hand and wearing only a tunic and loose breeches. The man's eyes were so wide that they seemed as if they might roll out of their sockets, and his jaw drooped open. But that dumfounded expression fast twisted into a wicked grin.

"Was it the Ancient Ones of the Samhaists or Blessed Abelle that put you here in my grasp?" the large man asked as he quickly set the torch into a bracket beside the door. "For truly such good fortune as this falls within the realm of divine miracle!"

He balled his huge fists and rushed forward.

Bransen sprang over the chair behind him, putting more ground and now two chairs between himself and the charging warrior. He landed in a defensive crouch and easily ducked away as Bannagran lifted one of the chairs and threw it at him. Then he hopped aside as the second chair flew through the air, swept away by the wrath of the powerful Bannagran.

The mighty warrior waded in with a wide-arcing left hook that the nimble Highwayman easily ducked, then came with a straight cross. Bransen's hand knifed up to deflect the blow, but Bannagran would not be so easily deterred. He launched a straight left and followed with a right, then back and forth in a sudden and vicious flurry, barreling forward like an angry bull.

Up came the Highwayman's hands one after the other, slapping left and slapping right, and ducking and swerving. A couple of glancing blows clipped him, but only at first, only while he was acting with his conscious mind instead of letting himself fall into the teachings of the Book of Jhest.

As the rhythm of the book flowed through his body, as his concentration became a pure interaction between mind and body, a fusing of the mental and the physical, and again it almost seemed to him as if his opponent were moving under water. Even the expressions of Bannagran's face as he roared in increasing frustration seemed an exaggerated, slow-moving thing, as the roar itself seemed to stretch out in the Highwayman's ears.

Now Bransen dared to counter, getting his hand up inside Bannagran's punch, deflecting it and launching one of his own. He hit the big man once, twice, thrice about the head with short, snapping jabs.

But Bannagran pressed on, ignoring the blows. And as he stepped forward, he dropped his right shoulder and launched a roundhouse punch that seemed to come from his ankle, his heavy right hand swooping in for the side of the Highwayman's head.

A right jab smacked into Bannagran's nose, but the big man didn't flinch. The Highwayman, in trying to drive his opponent back, didn't duck but bent his arm, his wrist against his ear to cover.

It was a perfectly executed block, a detailed maneuver in the Book of Jhest. But neither that book nor the Highwayman had taken into account the strength difference between the diminutive Bransen and the giant and powerful Bannagran. Bransen's arm blocked the punch, but the weight of the blow sent him flying sideways. He staggered and nearly fell, but instead threw himself into a sidelong roll that brought him back to his feet near the wall.

In charged Bannagran, fists flying, but suddenly Bransen wasn't in front of him. Bannagran only began to understand how completely Bransen had out-maneuvered him when he felt the weight of the man in black crashing against his legs, tripping him headlong into the wall. He managed to get his arms up to absorb some of the jolt.

He spun immediately, launching a wide-flying right hook.

Bransen ducked it, dropping so low that his butt nearly touched the ground. Up he sprang into the air, lashing out with his feet, one and then the other.

But as he landed, he found that he had done little damage to Bannagran, for the big man went right back to the attack. And now he was altering the angles of his strikes, high and low, and seemed perfectly willing to accept Bransen's stinging counters.

Bransen's ear ached from the last blow, and he understood that it wouldn't take many hits from Bannagran to drop him!

The flurry intensified; Bannagran snapped off a series of crosses, then dropped and repeated with three left jabs in a row, though Bransen brought his knee up to block. Up went Bannagran, and Bransen jumped back a step, then came back in, his hands rotating in overlapping circles before him, offering no openings.

A left jab snapped in, and Bransen turned it, retracted his hand, and started to counter. Then he saw the blood pouring from his fingers, and then he noticed that Bannagran's hand was no longer empty. Bransen leaped back, glancing from the cut to Bannagran, to the long knife that the man now held.

A sweeping crosscut had Bransen sucking in his gut and leaping backward. Bannagran charged ahead, stabbing hard, but Bransen went around the outstretched arm in a quick roll, then sprinted past the man for the wall.

Bannagran cried out in victory and turned to pursue, then watched in amazement as the Highwayman seemed to run right up the wall, springing directly over him in a twisting somersault. The Highwayman landed lightly, and a second leap brought him to the top of an overturned chair. He sprang away again, gathering momentum, in a great leap that sent him flying across the room.

He landed right before the hearth, grabbed the magnificent

sword by the pommel, and turned to face Bannagran. With a grin, Bransen yanked the sword in an upward and sliding motion, its fine edge easily severing the two leather ties securing it to the upturned hooks.

Bannagran skidded to a stop.

"You drew first," the Highwayman chided. "I was content to embarrass you with open hand. Now it seems I must kill you." As he finished, the Highwayman leveled the deadly blade Bannagran's way. "Which will you pray to, mighty Bannagran? The Ancient Ones or Blessed Abelle?"

The Highwayman took a fast step forward, thrusting the blade; but Bannagran leaped back, caught a chair by the arm, and whipped it across to block. Then, with strength beyond anything Bransen had ever seen, the big man stopped his swinging arm suddenly and threw the chair.

The Highwayman dodged it, barely, and spun in a pirouette, then fell into another defensive crouch.

But Bannagran hadn't pursued; he had run back to the open door, shouting for the guards. Bransen heard a commotion out there.

He ran to the window, turned to salute the big man, and promised, "We two will fight again, sword to sword or fist to fist!" Then he went out.

But not down.

Like a spider, the Highwayman moved to the side of the window and then up. He reached the top and pulled himself over even as the head of a guardsman poked out the window and began looking all around at the ground. "Did he fall?" the man cried.

Bransen put his back against the crenelated tower top and lifted the gleaming sword before his eyes. He felt the smooth steel and the keen edge and marveled at the beauty of the etchings running the length of the blade. This was the work of his mother as surely as the copy of the Book of Jhest had been created by his father. Bransen didn't know the technique that had gone into making this sword, of course, the folded steel and precise and disciplined toil. He didn't know that it had taken his mother years to craft it.

But he understood completely that this was no ordinary weapon, and from more than the exotic feel of the materials. The balance, the delicate work along the pommel, the light yet solid feel of the blade all hinted to him of the marvels within and of the discipline required to create this. He knew that his mother had made it, for he could feel her residual energy within the blade. The Book of Jhest had referred to weapons such as this and spoke about the bonding between the craftsman and the weapon, but only now could Bransen truly come to appreciate that truth. For in holding this magnificent sword, Bransen felt as if he were touching the mother he had never known.

Could she have foreseen this day? Could she have guessed that her sword would outlive her and would be handed down to her son?

A weight of responsibility fell upon Bransen then. His mother was a Jhesta Tu mystic, an accomplished warrior and philosopher. He had a lot to live up to.

He heard the commotion below him as Castle Pryd came fully awake, but he paid it no heed. Not now. Now, he was with the spirit of his mother as he had been with his father in those moments when he had possessed the Book of Jhest. This was so much more than a weapon, Bransen knew at once. This was a work of art, an extension of Sen Wi herself, imbued with her skill and her love.

As he continued to hold and contemplate the sword, he felt a warm, clear sensation that his mother was pleased, that she was looking down at him now and was glad that her sword was in the hands of her son, the child for whom she had willingly offered her own life force.

A long time later, the commotion around the castle died down, but Bransen could still see groups of soldiers with torches scouring the area. He poked a loop for the sword in the tied waistline of his trousers, gathered his inner strength, and climbed down the wall. Moving from shadow to shadow, the Highwayman was soon back in the chapel, and soon back in his little room.

And now he had one more thing he knew he must keep hidden.

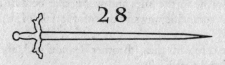

28

ALONE, AND SO BE IT!

The lines were not as intricate and flowing, but the patterns of the words were much the same. Bransen focused hard to keep his head from lolling about so that he could study those patterns and try to make some sense of them. It wasn't often that Bransen got any opportunity to view the writing of the monks. On those occasions when he was the Highwayman, he spent very little time in the chapel, only enough to get in and out along a direct route from his trapdoor to the window and back again.

So this morning, going about his rounds, when he saw the parchment unrolled and weighted down on the desk, Bransen quickly moved to inspect it.

How he wished that the monks had taught him to read their language. How he wished that so many of his empty hours could be spent engrossed in a tome filled with words of wisdom. Did the words of Blessed Abelle mirror those of the Jhesta Tu? He had already clearly seen and felt the similarities of Jhesta Tu meditation and the powers afforded by the sacred stones, and he had to believe that those commonalities extended into the relative philosophies of the holy men. Bransen suspected that the books of the monks would enhance his understanding and control of his life force, but, alas, Brother Reandu had made it quite clear to him that the brothers would not teach him to read.

He stood there for a long time, staring down at the script and wondering if he might somehow teach himself. So immersed was he in the lines and words that he didn't hear the door open across the way and the soft footfalls of an approaching monk.

"Take care with that," Brother Reandu said, and Bransen staggered and nearly fell.

Reandu steadied him.

"Taking respite from your work?" the monk asked.

Bransen stammered, trying to formulate an answer, but Reandu calmed him and quieted him quickly.

"Still intrigued by words?"

Bransen nodded.

"Well, please do not drool on this, my little friend. Do you know what this is?"

Bransen tried to shake his head, but it went in a circular motion instead, and sent his eyes spinning.

"It details instructions from the masters of my order," Reandu explained. "From Chapel Abelle itself, where the prophet taught and where he died. Perhaps one day I will find the means to take you there. Yes, you would like Chapel Abelle." Reandu's eyes sparkled and he began to wave his arms out to show the vastness of the place and to dramatize his nearly breathless words as he continued. "It is set on a high cliff overlooking the dark, rolling waters of the ocean. Waves smash against the rocks continually, like the thunder of God himself! You cannot stand atop that cliff without seeing the beauty of God, Stork. You feel small and great at the same time, as if you are part of something larger and more wonderful than yourself, than your life itself. The thunder of the waves pounds like the heartbeat of God, I tell you!"

He paused and looked back at Bransen. "You would like to see that place, wouldn't you?"

Bransen nodded eagerly and grinned from ear to ear, but the smile went away almost immediately as he came to consider what any journey away from Chapel Pryd might do. How could he take his clothing, the sword, and the stolen gemstone with him? How could he keep his secret, or find the hours of freedom in the guise of the Highwayman?

He caught himself in those thoughts and glanced anxiously at Reandu, who, thankfully, had not noticed his changing mood. Quickly, Bransen shifted the focus and the conversation by pointing emphatically at the parchment.

"An order from Chapel Abelle," Reandu explained, and he gave a sigh. "The world is a difficult place right now, Stork. Men are warring across the land of Honce as the lairds vie for supremacy and allegiance. And we of Blessed Abelle are caught in the middle. We are healers, not warriors, but some of the lairds wish us to use our gemstone powers to help them in their battles—and, indeed, many of the brothers are doing just that. And, of course, after the battles, we toil endlessly over the wounded."

Bransen understood that the man was not really talking to him, but rather was simply thinking out loud, as if he were trying to clear up things in his own mind.

"Thus come the troubling decisions concerning the disposition of the wounded," Reandu went on. "Are we to heal only those men who fight for our own lairds? Are we to ignore the cries of the enemy wounded? I do not know if I could do that, Stork. I do not know if I could allow a man to die, knowing that I might have healed his wounds.

"But it is not my decision, so declare the masters of Chapel Abelle. The decree before you states that we are to heed the desires of our laird regarding the wounded. If Laird Prydae insists that we let the enemy wounded suffer and die, then we must abide by his decision."

Reandu gave a shrug. "Do the colors a man wear so determine the value of the man? Does allegiance to a laird mean anything more to a peasant than the happenstance that he was born in the holding of that laird? Would a man of Pryd serve Laird Ethelbert with equal fervor if he had happened to be born in Ethelbert Holding? I think so, Stork, and so I am saddened by the choice of my masters."

Bransen looked back at the parchment, seeing it, suddenly, in a very different light. If the monks of Blessed Abelle were truly God inspired, as they claimed, then how could they abrogate their moral imperatives to the decisions of a secular man? It seemed a cowardly thing.

"Practicality has its place, I suppose," Reandu said, as if reading Bransen's thoughts or, at least, as if sharing Bransen's concerns. "Fortunately, the battle has not yet reached us here in Pryd Town, and with good fortune and the aid of Laird Delaval's thousands, it never will."

Bransen glanced over to see Reandu standing calm, his tirade ended.

"Come along, Stork," the man said. "You cannot avoid your duties."

Bransen lifted the room's chamber pot with one hand and offered his free arm to accept Reandu's guiding hand, and he shuffled along beside the monk toward the room's open door. Not willing to let go of this rare encounter with Reandu—at least, rare when they actually had time for a few words— Bransen stuttered out the name of his father and protector.

He made sure that he watched Reandu closely as he spoke Garibond's name, knowing, as was detailed in the Book of Jhest, that a man's initial reaction was often more telling than his subsequent words.

And, indeed, Brother Reandu's eyes did flash and widen for just an instant before he got himself steadied.

"Garibond?" Reandu echoed. "Ah, yes, old Garibond! A good man. A good man."

He was stalling, Bransen could tell, given his initial reaction.

"He went to the south, I believe. Yes, yes, to Ethelbert, from what I have heard. The sea air would be gentler on his aching bones, so he said."

Bransen wasn't entirely convinced, and he only half listened, focusing instead on the man's expressions and inflections as Reandu continued to tout the healing aspects of salty air and went on about the better, warmer, and sunnier climate of Ethelbert compared to Pryd.

Of course, Bransen knew, the monks could simply have offered Garibond healing sessions with their gemstones.

He didn't press the point, and he showed no outward sign of his doubt as he and Reandu exited the room and moved along toward the next door in the hallway. But then monks were rushing all around, responding to a commotion down the hall the other way, near the main chamber of the chapel's first floor. Immediately Reandu reversed direction, pulling Bransen along with him. They came to the end of the corridor to see many of the brothers assembled in line before Master Bathelais in the main chamber, with Laird Prydae himself and several soldiers facing them.

"Stay here," Reandu told him, and he rushed out to join Master Bathelais.

Bransen watched as Bannagran moved along the line of monks, lifting and inspecting their hands. The young man's eyes widened as he realized what was transpiring here, and he lurched over, placing the chamber pot down hard, then dipping his hand into its brown contents. He came back up as fast as he could, holding the pot once more in his filthy, shit-covered fingers—fingers that had been cut by Bannagran's knife the night before. How glad was Bransen that Brother Reandu had not apparently noticed the scar, the cut healed by the stolen soul stone and the meditation of Jhest, but still visible.

Bannagran finished with the monks then, and noticed Bransen as he turned back to his liege. He paused and studied the damaged young man.

He thinks I am the right size, Bransen thought, and he immediately staggered and lurched, accentuating his infirmity.

Bannagran started to approach and Bransen fought hard to remain calm. He wished that he had his soul stone with him, that he could become the Highwayman, if need be, and flee this place. He thought he was surely trapped.

But Bannagran stopped suddenly and looked down at Bransen's hand and the chamber pot. The large man crinkled his nose in disgust and gave the Stork a dismissive wave, then went back to join Prydae, Bathelais, and Reandu.

Bathelais dismissed the monks then, and they began to disperse, talking among themselves.

Bransen used the distraction to shamble along the general direction of the leaders, and he perked up his ears as he neared.

"Surely you do not believe any of the brothers hold any complicity in this theft," he heard Master Bathelais say.

"There was no rope," Bannagran answered, his voice low and grave. "No sign of a rope."

"It is hard to believe that anyone could steal the sword and so easily flee the forty feet down the side of the tower," Laird Prydae added, "unless of course the thief had the aid of a magical gemstone."

"Malachite," said Brother Reandu. "We have but two, I believe, in all of Chapel Pryd."

"And where are they?" asked the laird.

Reandu looked at Bathelais.

"I will order a complete inventory of all of our gemstones," the master said. "All of them, and I assure you that if any are missing, our aid will prove invaluable to you. There are ways to detect the usage of gemstone powers, my laird."

Laird Prydae nodded slowly, but he didn't seem very happy at that moment. "Are you so careless with your sacred gemstones that you know not even where all of them are now placed?"

Bransen took note of the embarrassed scowl on Master Bathelais's face. Of course, Father Jerak's unorganized ways were legendary among the brothers of the chapel, and the implication now was that perhaps Bathelais was not only inheriting but furthering the carelessness. That possibility seemed not to sit very well with him at that moment.

"We are no less vested in our gemstones than you are in your magnificent sword, my laird," Bathelais declared suddenly, with renewed vigor in his voice. "We will account for all of them, I assure you. If an outside contraband stone has been brought into the region by this man, this . . ."

"Highwayman," Bannagran spat.

"This Highwayman creature," Bathelais agreed. "There is no tolerance for this within our order. Any man found with a contraband gemstone will suffer the full wrath of the Church of Blessed Abelle."

"A man not of the Church in possession of a stolen gemstone is declared a heretic and burned at the stake," Brother Reandu added.

Bransen heard the contents of the chamber pot sloshing below his trembling fingers.

"Perhaps I will allow you that pleasure, if indeed this thief holds such a stone," Prydae said. "But not until I am finished with him. And know that he will welcome the consuming flames when I have shown him my wrath!"

Bransen nearly tumbled to the ground and felt as if he would throw up. Somehow he managed to get out of the room without attracting any more attention to himself.

What was he to do? Had he gone too far? Could he possibly explain to the brothers why he had borrowed the soul stone?

Unsure of himself, not knowing what to do next, the terrified man continued with his duties. The guise of the Stork would protect him, he tried to convince himself. How could they suspect him of anything when he could hardly walk?

He knew then that he had to be very careful. He could bring no attention to himself, and could not give any of them, not even Reandu, any reason to believe that there was any kind of intelligence inside his damaged physical form. And he had to take care in using the soul stone, apparently, if Master Bathelais's claims of being able to detect such magic were to be believed.

He had to be the Stork—just the Stork. His frailty would protect him, he hoped.

He desperately hoped.

Several days passed before Bransen dared to go out as the Highwayman again, days made longer by his burning desire to test his mother's magnificent sword. Now that he had it firmly in hand, moving through the training movements he had learned in the Book of Jhest, Bransen began to understand just how wonderful the weapon truly was. It felt as if it were an extension of his arm as he swung it; its balance remained perfect at nearly every angle, making it seem even lighter than it was—and although it was much longer than the average Honce bronze or iron sword, the thin steel blade of SenWi's creation *was* far lighter.

Bransen spent an hour and more playing with the blade, weaving cuts against imaginary opponents, defeating attacks and quickly countering with killing strikes.

Even when he finished the most taxing of practice routines, he was full of energy and brimming with eagerness. He had no destination in mind this night, so he glided through the shadows, taking in the sights, the sounds, and the smells of Pryd Town. It was generally quiet: a bird calling, some cattle lowing, a mother shooing her children into the house, an owl hooting. But Bransen stopped when he heard a sharp cry among the soothing sounds of the town winding down.

"But what am I to feed my children this night?" came a woman's voice.

"You have more," a man replied. "You know you do. I told you three days ago to be ready for this."

"But me husband's not returned from the south!"

"Then get on without him! Do you believe that any are having an easy time of it with the war, selfish woman?"

Bransen came up over a small grassy mound to take in the sights of the argument. A peasant woman, dirty and dressed in rags, was practically on her knees before one of Laird Prydae's soldiers, who had a bulging sack slung over one shoulder while he kept her at bay with his other arm.

"Just give me food for the night, then, so I won't be going to bed hungry," the woman begged, and she came forward suddenly, lunging for the sack.

The man slapped her aside.

Bransen, the Highwayman, started over the knoll, but

stopped short and held his ground. Anger welled up inside him, but he suppressed it, reminding himself that anger was a warrior's worst enemy. Anger denied calculation. Anger led to errors.

He watched the soldier kick the peasant woman as she scrambled back toward her hovel, whining pitifully all the way.

Laughing, the soldier turned away. He pulled the sack from his shoulder and fished his free hand about inside, bringing forth a shiny tomato, which he promptly bit into as he started back toward Castle Pryd.

The Highwayman circled him, moving to a tree and up it and onto a branch overhanging the road.

"A fine night of thievery, I see," the Highwayman said as the soldier approached. Bransen hardly took note that he had slipped back into that peculiar way of speaking, emulating the monks when they told their stories.

The man stopped and threw aside the remaining piece of tomato, quickly drawing his short sword. "Who said that?" He glanced all around, even hopped in a circle, waving his weapon.

"An admirer," the Highwayman replied.

The soldier stopped and followed the voice to the tree that held the Highwayman.

"Truly," the Highwayman went on. "I do admire one who has found a way to so easily steal that which he desires. It shows cunning and efficiency, I think."

"Steal? Bah, I'm no thief! This is the laird's business and none of my own."

"Laird Prydae bids you to eat your booty?"

The man laughed. "Get yourself gone, and be quick. I've no time to suffer a fool. You interfere with the laird's tax collectors on penalty of death."

"Oh, but I am already so marked," the Highwayman said, and he dropped from the tree, landing a few paces in front of the soldier. The man fell back a step, surprised.

"Do you not know who I am?" the Highwayman asked.

He drew out the sword that had recently been hanging in the private quarters of Laird Prydae, the sword that had incited a search of the whole town.

"You!" the soldier cried.

"Curiously said," replied the Highwayman. "Could I not claim the same of you?"

"You're . . . you're him!"

"Again, my point holds."

"You come with me!" the soldier demanded. "In the name of Laird Prydae, I arrest you!" He dropped the sack and presented his sword in a menacing manner.

The Highwayman suppressed a chuckle and instead backed off a cautious step.

"Come on, then," said the soldier. "I've been fighting in the south for a year now and think nothing of cutting you up."

The Highwayman glanced around as if he meant to run away. The soldier, predictably, rushed ahead, the tip of his sword barely inches from the Highwayman's chest.

"Now!" he said with a growl. "Last chance to surrender before I run you through."

The Highwayman sighed, feigning fright, and presented his sword horizontally before him. When the soldier reached for the offered blade, the Highwayman tossed it up into the air.

The soldier's eyes followed the ascent.

A right cross from the Highwayman staggered him backward, tumbling to his knees.

The Highwayman caught his blade as it fell and leaped forward in a spin, whacking the soldier's feebly presented sword across, then rolling behind the blade and up the man's arm, timing his turn perfectly so that he could drive his left elbow into the side of the man's face. He felt the soldier's sudden halt and reversal, and he dropped as the man cut a fast backhand, the short sword whipping above his head.

And the Highwayman came up fast, inside the soldier's reach, bringing the tip of his sword under the soldier's chin and forcing the man up on his tiptoes.

"I will hear your sword hit the ground, or I will hear the

last breath of your life," the Highwayman calmly stated, and he inched his sword up just a bit to accentuate his point.

The short sword fell to the dirt beside them.

Up came the Highwayman's knee into the soldier's groin, as the Highwayman retracted his blade and stepped back. Again he spun, a foot flying to smash the lurching, bending man's jaw, sending him falling to the side and to the ground.

"The first rule of battle is to know your enemy," he explained, though the man was far from hearing him, or anything, at that moment. "The second is to prepare the battlefield. And the third, one you apparently have not read, my sleeping friend, is to make certain that your enemy thinks that you are less formidable than you are."

The man stirred and groaned and pulled himself up to his elbows and shook his head.

"Although I admit, such a tactic would be difficult to present, for one of your lack of skill."

The man growled.

"But you have learned, perhaps. I suppose that if we meet again, you will not be so easily deceived," the Highwayman said to him. "On that occasion, regretfully, I will likely have to kill you." He ended by putting his foot on the soldier's shoulder blades and stamping the man flat to the ground, adding the warning, "Of course, if you stubbornly persist now, we will never meet again in this lifetime."

Sometime later, the naked soldier, his arms twisted and bound behind his back with his own torn clothing, a tight gag tied in place, stumbled to the front gates of Castle Pryd.

Sometime later, the peasant woman found a cache of food inside the one small window of her house, as did several of her equally hungry neighbors.

Sometime after that, a voice awakened Cadayle. When she went to the window to investigate, she saw a bright smile below a black silk mask.

"Here, eat well with your mother this evening," the Highwayman said to her, and he handed in a worn sack of food.

"What are you doing?"

"I met with one of Laird Prydae's thugs," the Highwayman explained. "The laird has enough to eat, I think."

"You stole?"

"Well, it sounds harsh when you speak it in like that. I prefer to think of it as seeing to the laird's flock in the name of Prydae himself, and representing his better and more generous side."

Cadayle rubbed a bit of the sleepiness out of her eyes and took the offered food, then glanced back into the darkness of her small house. "If we are caught with this . . ." she started to warn.

"Then eat it!" came the easy answer. "Laird Prydae's men cannot see into your belly, now can they?"

"You play a dangerous game."

"That makes it more fun."

He finished with another wide and bright smile, and added only, "Eat well, beautiful Cadayle!" before he spun away from the window and disappeared into the night.

She pressed the food close to her breast, and she could feel the excited flutter of her heart.

The Highwayman danced away through the shadows, spinning his sword and leaping into battle against imaginary foes. He knew not why he had acted as a thief this night, knew not why he had suddenly taken this more dangerous fork in the road. But he couldn't deny the lightness of his step, the rush of blood throughout his body, or the thrill of his mischief.

Yes, he knew, he was the Highwayman, who defended the woman he loved, who took back his mother's stolen sword, and who, it now seemed, would not suffer the unfairness of Prydae's rules.

The image of gratitude on the faces of those he had fed this night was better than wine as he danced his way across Pryd Town and back to the quiet chapel.

29

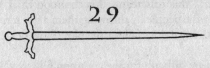

ALMOST HONEST

"All the town speaks of him," Prydae said, grinding his teeth with every word. He moved to the hearth and roughly threw a log onto the fire, for autumn was in the air, the wind chill and from the north.

More than a month had passed since the theft of his precious sword, which was now being used weekly—at least weekly—by the outlaw Highwayman, usually in stealing from Prydae's tax collectors and even some of his soldiers. The lone bandit was striking haphazardly, without any discernable pattern. Every time, he seemed to simply appear out of the darkness, quickly dispatch of any offered defenses—and thus far in a nonlethal, though usually painful, manner—take what booty he could, and melt away back into the night.

"They exult in the glory and cunning of the Highwayman!" Prydae growled.

"Not openly," said Bannagran, standing across the room and stripping off his cloak and wet boots.

"No, and that is all the more troubling. He is feeding them, you know. He is taking the requisitioned food from lawful collectors and distributing it among the peasants."

"We do not know that, my liege. And if we find any such evidence, rest assured that the offending peasant will be punished."

"You know that he is doing that!" Laird Prydae retorted, turning sharply on his friend.

Bannagran shrugged, not arguing.

"This . . . this miscreant, this common thief, becomes a hero among the people by throwing them a few scraps of food. And these disloyal dogs fall for the ploy. How fickle is their allegiance!"

"Times are difficult for the common folk, my liege," Bannagran reminded as he took a seat and began to rub his sore feet. "So many are off to the south, never to return, and our demands sorely press those remaining. Many families are headed now by the mother alone, without even an older son to help her in the fields."

"Laird Delaval presses me hard," Prydae argued.

"They have little to eat."

"They have as much as our warriors battling Ethelbert in the south!" shouted the Laird of Pryd. "Should I deny food and clothing to men spilling their blood so that these peasants, hungry though they are, might live more comfortably?"

"I am not arguing, my liege, but merely trying to explain why this Highwayman creature has so easily found the hearts of many."

"I want him caught." The words were accompanied by another crash as Prydae threw a second log into the fireplace. "I want him dragged to the castle and burned alive."

"The people will frown upon you," Bannagran warned, and it occurred to both men that Bannagran was the only man in the world who could have so bluntly said that to Laird Prydae.

"Upon me?" the laird asked. "Nay, the execution of this one will fall to our Abelle brothers, or to Bernivvigar, if not them. Either way, he will die."

"Deservedly so."

"Prince Yeslnik, favored nephew of Laird Delaval, is on his way," Prydae said. "Double the scouts upon the road and send patrols of the castle guard out to the ends of Pryd Town each night. Offer a reward for any whispers that lead us to this knave. We must put an end to this before the legend of the man grows and before Laird Delaval comes to know that we harbor such a secret."

Bannagran kept his expression impassive as Laird Prydae fell into the chair across from him, drawing a curious stare from his liege.

"What?" Prydae asked.

A slight smile turned up the corners of Bannagran's mouth.

"What?" Prydae asked again, before he took the cue from his friend and managed a smile of his own, which kept widening and became a burst of laughter that Bannagran shared.

"You are right, my friend," said the laird. "He is one man, one prickly thorn, that we shall pluck and discard soon enough."

"He strikes in the dark, from behind and by surprise, and against men ill prepared to defeat him. We learn from his every attack, and we will become better prepared."

Prydae took a deep breath and settled more comfortably in his chair.

"What will Yeslnik Delaval ask of us?" Bannagran inquired.

"More food, more gold, more iron, and more men, likely," Prydae answered. "The fighting in the south has not let up at all, and there is word that Laird Delaval has sent warriors to support the people of Palmaristown and their battle against the wild tribes of the north and west."

"He should focus his strength against Ethelbert first, and drive the man back before offering any truce," Bannagran reasoned. "This has gone on far too long already."

"Would that he would," Prydae agreed, and he went silent and turned back to the hearth, which had flared to life, hungrily eating the two new logs.

Bannagran folded his large and calloused hands behind his head, stretched his legs before him, wriggling his cold toes near the flames, and said no more.

Cadayle walked along the road to her house one dark night, her stride easy and her posture showing that she was unafraid. That calm demeanor was not unnoticed by the people in the neighboring houses, most of whom dared not venture outside after dark.

For the young woman, her own realization that she was unafraid struck her suddenly. Bandits were all around the roads of Pryd, and powries had been seen in several areas—one group had attacked some men not far from this very area. But Cadayle knew that she was not alone.

A small sack plopped to the ground before her, hitting with the jingle of coins. It fell open and an apple, shiny even in the starlight, rolled out.

Cadayle looked up to the tree, to see a now-familiar and not unexpected figure sitting astride a low branch, leaning back against the trunk.

"You should not be out after dark," said the Highwayman. "You never know what knaves might find you and ravish you."

Cadayle blushed, and was glad of the darkness.

The Highwayman, though he was at least fifteen feet up, swung his leg over the branch and dropped down, landing easily, knees bending to absorb the impact. He stood up straight before Cadayle, his smile wide—as it always seemed to be when he was with her.

"Well, are you not going to accept my gifts?" he asked, and he bent down and retrieved the bag and the apple. His grin became mischievous when he stood back up, and he held the apple out toward her, then pulled it back and took a large bite of it when she reached for it.

Then he offered it once more.

Cadayle put her hands on her hips and stared at him defiantly.

"You'll not share your ill-gotten goods with the man who ill got them for you?" the wounded Highwayman asked.

Cadayle couldn't resist, her expression brightening, and she took the apple and the sack. She looked inside the bag, confirming her suspicions when she noted the glisten of shiny coins among the remaining food.

"Money?" she asked.

"I have no need of it."

"If I go to market and spend it, I will draw suspicion. No one has extra coins, with Laird Prydae's tax collectors all about. Not unless they are hiding it from the laird, and that is not wise."

"People spend money in the market every day," the Highwayman replied with a shrug.

"But not so much."

"Then spend it a bit at a time. Buy something for your mother."

Cadayle paused and smiled, then lowered her arm to her side and lowered her gaze. A moment later, she looked back at the Highwayman. "Why do you do this?"

"Do what?" he replied. "You need the food, so I give it to you."

"No, I mean, why do you do all of this?" Cadayle clarified. "You live in the shadows of the night. What of the day?"

"I am alive every day."

Cadayle blew a frustrated sigh. "Do you serve with Laird Prydae's garrison? Are you a farmer? Did you fight in the war?"

"Are you an agent for the laird?"

Again she sighed and declared, "You're impossible."

"Not so, my lady. I am here." He dipped a polite bow.

"The laird is not happy with you."

"I would not expect him to be. In fact, I would be disappointed if I learned that he was."

Cadayle was about to remark that the soldiers were everywhere, it seemed, but the point was made for her with the sound of horses coming down the road behind them. Before she could react, the Highwayman grabbed her by the shoulder and pulled her from the road, the two of them rolling into the depression off to the side.

And not a moment too soon, Cadayle realized as a trio of soldiers came galloping past. Alarmed, she looked at the Highwayman—to see him smiling and to hear his laugh.

"The laird is not happy with me," he said with a grin. "I thought it best that you not be seen speaking with me."

Cadayle started to respond, but suddenly realized how

close she was to this man, their bodies intertwined, his breath warm on her face. He, too, seemed suddenly caught up in the moment, and Cadayle wondered if he would kiss her.

And she realized that she hoped he would.

But he didn't. He rose and helped her up, then brushed himself off as she did likewise.

"Why do you do this?" she asked him again.

He stared at her for a long while, his face sober, his eyes, so dark and sparkling, locked onto her. "Because it is right."

Cadayle had no idea of how to take the conversation from there. *Because it is right.* She rolled those words over and over in her mind. She had heard many of her neighbors say such things, had even seen a few of them do such things on occasion. But never, in all her life, had Cadayle heard or seen that particular concept expressed by a man in power.

Because it is right. So simple, and so elusive.

"Sleep well this night, my lady," the Highwayman said. "Dare I hope that you might dream of me?"

The bold question had Cadayle back on her heels, but as it was accompanied by one of the man's typical sassy smiles, she let it go with a grin of her own.

He took her hand and kissed it, then bowed to her and danced away, leaping into the night and disappearing.

This was how it usually had gone between them over these last few weeks and their few encounters. Was that the real reason she had offered to take some eggs to a neighbor for her mother, and then tarried with the neighbors before heading home after darkness had fallen? Had she been hoping to see the Highwayman again? She knew the truth of it, of course—and was finding it harder and harder to deny that truth to herself—for Cadayle found herself thinking of the man more and more.

And as he had boldly asked, she was indeed dreaming of him.

Because it is right.

The words followed Bransen, too, as he made his way

across the town and back to Chapel Pryd. It had been a good answer, he knew, and one that had certainly seemed to impress Cadayle.

But was it true?

Bransen chewed his lip as he considered that. The teachings of the Jhesta Tu demanded introspection and honest self-evaluation, and the Book of Jhest had shown him many techniques to strip away the inevitable defenses that any person would construct against such painful personal intrusion.

Bransen studied his feelings honestly. He recalled how he felt during all his actions these last weeks as the Highwayman. He knew, and came to understand even more with every step, that his efforts weren't quite as magnanimous as he had made them seem with that answer.

There was the matter of his pride.

There was the matter of his love for Cadayle.

Yes, he felt proud when he rescued someone from bandit, powrie, or tax collector alike, or when he saw the smile of gratitude on the face of a peasant after the heroic Highwayman had offered some food to quell the grumbling of his belly. He knew that pride was a failing—the Book of Jhest often referred to it as the downfall of great men—but there it was.

When he had answered Cadayle, Bransen had to fight hard to resist blurting out the truth. How he wanted to tell her that he loved her, and had loved her since he was just a boy, when he was the Stork and she would help him off the ground, when she chased the bullies away. He had almost said it, but he was too afraid. What would Cadayle think of the dashing Highwayman if she knew that he was really the dirty Stork?

So perhaps there were some personal reasons for his choices of late.

Because it is right.

"Well, it is right, is it not?" the young man asked when the chapel was in sight. "I am helping people desperately in need, as some have helped me. Would Garibond do any less?"

Satisfied with that, Bransen crept back through the window, across the room, and into his hole. He had defeated the demon of introspection and self-evaluation, and fell to his cot with the warm memory of Cadayle beside him.

He hadn't reached for the deeper self-evaluation, however, hadn't gone to the dark place in his heart where festered his frustration and anger, memories of his years of torment, thoughts of the missing Garibond and the horrible Bernivvigar who had once mutilated the man, and resentment at his continuing ill-treatment by the brothers who had taken him in and would not teach him to read.

It all sat there, buried within, quietly waiting.

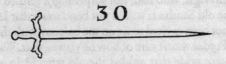

30

IN THE HEARTS OF
EVERYMAN

"An impressive turnout," Prince Yeslnik of Delaval said to Laird Prydae as the two ate on the balcony of Castle Pryd's grand dining and audience hall, along with his wife, Olym, Bannagran, and Rennarq. The prince from the huge city at the mouth of the great river, the Masur Delaval, was, in Prydae's estimation, a fine example of Honce nobility. Tall and lean, physically fit and deceptively strong, young Yeslnik sat with perfect posture, and was perfectly groomed, head to toe. His blond hair was trimmed in the fashionable bowl cut, halfway over his ears, and he kept his light beard and goatee trimmed close. His clothing, of course, was of the finest cut and the rich hues of expensive dyes, and he wore rings, bracelets, and a necklace of glittering precious metal and gems. It did not escape Prydae's notice that among the four rings Yeslnik wore, three were sparkling gemstones of obvious value, but the fourth was a set with dull gray soul stone.

Likely, it was an enchanted item, one of the sacred stones that had escaped the Church of Blessed Abelle, and probably as a gift from the brothers. Had they used this item to gain the favor of Laird Delaval? Certainly a soul stone ring, with its healing powers, would be a valuable asset to a nobleman.

Prydae made a mental note to speak with Master Bathelais about that.

Below the foursome, the dining hall brimmed with activity. All the brothers were in attendance, as well as the many substantial landowners within Pryd Holding. Notably absent was Bernivvigar, who had, not surprisingly, refused the invitation. The old Samhaist would not bend to secular leaders, and he had not been invited to sit on the balcony with the laird and prince. Prydae wasn't sure of how he viewed that. Was it principle or mere pride that guided the old wretch? In any case, it wasn't practical. The Samhaists had dominated the ways of Honce for centuries, and still held great power over the ever-fearful peasants. The only reason the Church of Blessed Abelle had leaped so greatly in stature among the lairds was their monks' accommodating attitude toward the nobility, the true power among the folk.

That, and the gifts they could bestow, like the ring Yeslnik wore and the sword—

The mere thought of his missing sword made Prydae wince, and he quickly covered it up by raising a goblet of wine to his lips.

"And I was pleased by the roadside reception, Laird Prydae," Yeslnik went on; and if he had noticed Prydae's soured expression, he did nothing to show it. "I see that your people understand the role Laird Delaval has played in securing their freedom from the grasp of greedy Laird Ethelbert."

Prydae thought it wise to not point out that his holding was pouring money, men, food, and other supplies into those efforts against Ethelbert. "They, we, are grateful that Laird Delaval has seen fit to side with us against the intrusions."

"Laird Delaval respects the sovereignty of the smaller holdings."

Laird Prydae didn't respond, but Bannagran nearly choked hearing that and covered up by coughing, and Rennarq merely rolled his eyes.

"Of course, Laird Delaval cannot settle all of the problems of Honce alone," Yeslnik continued.

Prydae wasn't surprised at the leading statement, of course. He knew that Yeslnik had come here to exact more resources. "More than half the men of Pryd Holding over the age of twelve are dead or off fighting in the south," he answered.

"There is more to fighting a war than soldiers."

"And we are, in every respect, thin, Prince of Delaval," replied Prydae. "Every belly in Pryd growls with hunger, and many of the peasants growl with mounting anger."

"How you control your peasants is no concern of Laird Delaval," said the prince.

"Kill a few and the others will quiet," his wife added, surprising the other four at the table. Rennarq gave a chuckle—one appreciative of Olym's understanding, it seemed to Prydae—and Bannagran cleared his throat.

So did Yeslnik, and he seemed a bit disconcerted by the bluntly callous statement. "Forgive my wife, I pray you," he said.

"For speaking that which we all know to be true?" Rennarq asked. "That which the Samhaists have understood for centuries?"

"Yes, well . . ." Prydae cut in, trying to change the subject, especially since peasant servants were coming to the table often. "My good prince, you must understand that our demands on the people of Pryd Holding have pushed them to the very edge of despair."

"Then push them over," Yeslnik was quick to answer. "Ethelbert is a stubborn foe and for every Pryd man killed, Delaval has lost two."

The fact that Delaval Holding had a population more than twenty times that of Pryd—plus a fishing fleet that easily kept its people fed—was yet another of those troubling details that Prydae thought it best to not mention.

"Bernivvigar will keep the peasants in line, my liege," Rennarq offered, and it was obvious to Prydae that he wasn't the least bit concerned with the common folk or their troubles.

"Our warriors die in the south for the sake of your holding, Laird Prydae," Yeslnik added. "Need I remind you of that? Men of Laird Delaval do battle with those of Laird Ethelbert for your good! Laird Delaval has sent me here because more is needed. More coin and more supplies. And we will expect you to keep your ranks well stocked with soldiers to replace those who fall. This is the critical moment in our struggles with

Laird Ethelbert. His lines are near to breaking, and he has found more resistance to his plans of conquest and domination than he expected from the various lairds along the Mantis Arm."

Prydae kept his face emotionless. He knew that the resistance Ethelbert was facing was simply due to the deep pockets of Laird Delaval, who had made many of the other lairds a better offer, as he had done with Prydae. He also understood that Yeslnik's estimation of Ethelbert's weakness was more than a bit exaggerated. Many of Honce's lairds understood the truth of Delaval's offers: that autonomy was such only under the continued willingness and the fluctuating interpretations of Laird Delaval himself. If Delaval proved victorious in the struggles with Ethelbert, then, yes, Prydae would retain his power in Pryd Holding.

But that wouldn't stop the occasional visits from Prince Yeslnik or some other Delaval nobleman. And there were always demands to be met, after all.

"Bannagran here will lead the tax collectors out at the break of morn," Prydae assured his guest. "Your wagon will leave laden with supplies."

"With coin and other valuables," Lady Olym corrected before her husband could speak.

Yeslnik only confirmed that anyway, adding, "Your own wagons may deliver the mundane supplies to the south. I expect to remain another three days. Will that suffice for your collection?"

Prydae looked to Bannagran, who nodded.

"Three days, it is," Prydae confirmed. Noticing that Yeslnik wasn't even looking at him as he replied, he followed the prince's gaze to the man's wife, who sat there seeming perfectly giddy and glowing.

A moment later, not unexpectedly, Yeslnik said, "You will pardon me and my wife for a few moments, good Laird Prydae. We have something we must discuss at once." He rose up swiftly and took his wife's hand. He bowed, she curtsied, both abruptly, and they hurried off toward their private quarters.

"I expect there will be little conversation between them," Rennarq said dryly.

Prydae chuckled at the lewd innuendo, but Bannagran did not. "Laird Delaval's forces do battle for the good of Laird Delaval, not for Pryd Holding," he said.

Prydae disarmed that ire with a smile and a wave of his hand. "It matters not at all. For whatever reason, the army of Laird Delaval serves our purposes in their struggle with Laird Ethelbert; and so we do well to support our friend."

"In the end, we all see to our own needs," Rennarq added.

Prydae looked at the old man and thought that had been a perfectly Samhaist thing to say.

Bransen loved days like this, when all the brothers, with the exception of Father Jerak and one—usually sleeping—attendant, were away. He tied the soul stone onto his forehead and finished his duties in a matter of minutes, then took up a sack with his highwayman garb, removed the soul stone, and went out of the abbey in the guise of the Stork.

He made his way to the river, and there, when he was sure that he was alone, became his true self.

The Highwayman looked all around, feeling strange in this guise when the sun was still bright in the sky. He knew that he'd have to be careful every step of his way, but he couldn't deny the thrill he now felt—as intense and exciting as the night when he had gone to Cadayle's rescue.

Bransen knew that he shouldn't be enjoying the danger so profoundly. The Book of Jhest didn't allow for such thrills. But he didn't deny it; and the young man, whose life had been so empty for all these years, didn't push the excitement away.

Courting disaster and basking in the glow of danger, the Highwayman set out, circling the town to the north, the one region of Pryd Holding he did not know.

He kept imagining that he would find his true sire on the road—hadn't Bran Dynard left Chapel Pryd on a northerly route?—but of course, he did not. He kept thinking of Cadayle as well, and he knew that his roundabout course would take him to her eventually. It always did.

He crossed fields of grain, and followed the aroma of a baked treat very near to the windows of one cottage. He glanced all around and approached. The yard was unkempt, the fields overgrown, and the garden ill tended. But the smell kept Bransen moving for the window, where he even dared to peek in.

A peasant woman perhaps ten years older than he went about her chores, a pair of young children yapping at her feet. She wasn't particularly beautiful, but neither was she ugly, with the blond hair and blue eyes so common among the folk of the region and a body still relatively shapely despite the obviously difficult conditions around her. Bransen studied her for a few moments, but then his nose drew his eyes to the middle of the room. On a small table sat a pie, steaming in the morning air. Blueberry, by the smell of it.

The Highwayman considered how he might get to that treat and take a slice, but it was just a mental exercise, for he had no desire to take anything from the peasants of Pryd, who had next to nothing.

He was still musing about the pie, glancing left and right and trying to figure out how he might get in the front door without being noticed, when he realized his error. For the woman turned around and gave a shriek.

The Highwayman looked at her and held up his hands, bidding her to silence and trying very hard not to seem threatening to her in any way.

"Oh, but ye're to scare a sort to death!" the woman proclaimed. "I thinked yerself to be a goblin or a powrie!"

Bransen stared at her, hardly believing the obvious relief in her tone as she apparently recognized him.

"And what's bringing yerself to me house, Mister Highwayman?" she asked, seeming completely unafraid.

Bransen's mind whirled around corners he didn't know existed. Had his reputation spread so quickly among the peasants that he was considered by them to be a friend? For surely, this woman, helpless if he chose to attack, was showing no more fear of him than she might show to her own farm dog.

"Ah, it was me pie, wasn't it?" she asked with an exaggerated wink. "Come on in, then. I'll cut ye a good piece to fill yer belly."

Bransen looked all around to make sure that no one else was in the area, then with a shrug pulled himself through the window and took an offered seat at the table.

"I came to steal a scent of your pie, not to take food from your family," he said.

"Bah, ye've earned that and more."

"What do you know of me?"

"I know that ye kicked them beasties bothering poor Cadayle. I know that them tax collectors—Bestesbulzibar take them all!—keep looking over their shoulders for fear that ye'll strip them naked and run them into town! Hah, what more am I needing to know than that?"

As she finished, she pulled out a knife, cut fully a quarter of the pie, and heaped it onto a wooden plate. "Eat up, Highwayman. And if ye're still hungry, I'll chop ye another slice!"

Bransen couldn't deny the growling in his stomach and so he did begin to munch on the wonderful berry pie.

The woman sat across from him and shooed her children off into a corner. She stared at him all along, only turning her head to yell at the children whenever they became unruly. After a minute or so, she began telling him all about her miserable life, of how she rarely had enough to eat, of how her husband was off in the south and probably dead, of how her neighbors wanted to help her—and some were helping to tend the fields—but they were almost all in similar straits. She had few kind words for Laird Prydae, Bransen noted, and few for the Church of Abelle, though if she harbored any ill feelings at all toward the Samhaists, she kept them to herself.

She rambled on and on as he ate the pie, and she gradually shifted the conversation to the subject of her missing husband, repeatedly saying that he'd "been gone so long. So terribly long," and how lonely she was. Naive Bransen didn't even catch on to her leading statements until he finished the pie and she moved to cut him another piece, insisting he stay.

He politely declined and started to rise.

"Ye don't have to be going," she said, and she put her hand on top of his.

For a moment, the dashing Highwayman found that he couldn't draw his breath.

"I knew ye wouldn't hurt me the moment I saw ye at me window," the woman went on, her voice husky. "But there be a part of me that was hoping ye might be wanting more sweets than pie."

Bransen lifted her hand to his lips and kissed it gently. "My sweet lady," he said, "would that I could. But time is short and I've much to do." He kissed her hand again, then on impulse, moved in close and kissed her on the cheek—or started to, but she grabbed his face and brought her lips to his, and with an urgency he had never known before.

Finally Bransen extracted himself from her clutches.

"Let me see that face!" the woman purred, reaching for his mask.

But he was too quick, and ready for her now. With a jump and a spin, he was back at the window. "Truly a lovely pie," he said with a salute, and then he leaped outside and ran off.

He looked back a short while later to see the woman, face flushed, staring at him from the window.

Many emotions coursed through Bransen at that moment, not the least of which was a warm feeling that went from head to toe. It wasn't just the passionate kiss that had excited him but the mere fact that this woman, this ordinary Pryd peasant, knew of his deeds and obviously approved!

Full of spirit and full of confidence, the Highwayman dashed across the outskirts of Pryd Town, moving from shadow to shadow as always, but not too concerned that he might be seen—which he often was, peasants pointing and calling his name, and a couple even cheering from afar.

He came in sight of Cadayle's house at long last, approaching the lane from the north. He saw her before he got close, for she was out in the fields, down the long sloping hill behind the cottage, with the family's donkey.

Bransen looked all around, at last spotting some wild-flowers, and he pulled them from the ground and hurried down the hill to join his love.

Cadayle nearly jumped out of her worn leather shoes when she finally saw him, standing there calmly and leaning on the donkey.

"Greetings this fine noon, fair lady," he said, grinning mischievously, one hand on the donkey as the beast contentedly munched the grass, the other behind his back.

"What are you doing about in the light of day?"

"Do you think that I vanish with the sunrise? A creature solely of the night, am I?"

"You've made few friends among the soldiers of Laird Prydae."

Bransen shrugged. "They are not the friends I want," he said, and he pulled his hand from around his back, presenting Cadayle with the flowers.

Her eyes widened in surprise, but she did smile and gradually reached for them.

Bransen teased and pulled them back away. "For a kiss?"

Cadayle's smile disappeared and she stepped back. "A kiss?" she echoed. "For my own flowers?"

"Your own?"

"You just picked them on the hill."

"How could you know that?"

"Because they're still dripping of dirt, and I saw them on my way down here. I kept Doully here from eating them, for I could see them from my window. Pretty they were in sunset, but now I'll not have that pleasure again, will I?"

Bransen could not have been more crestfallen, and it showed on his face; but Cadayle just laughed and jumped forward, taking the bouquet. "You are an easy one to tease," she remarked, and she brought the sweet-smelling flowers to her nose and inhaled deeply.

"But, fair lady," Bransen said, regaining his composure, "I

named a payment." He started forward, but Cadayle held him at bay with her outstretched hand.

"A kiss is not a payment," she said. "It's given by choice. My own choice."

Bransen stepped back and studied her. "Then it is true," he said, feigning sudden and complete despair. "There is another man who calls Cadayle his lover!"

"What?"

"Ah, I have heard the rumors, my lady. All about town speak of them."

Cadayle waved him away dismissively.

"They speak of Cadayle and a queer little man who works with the monks," Bransen pressed, thinking himself quite clever.

But Cadayle's face went very tight.

"Yes, a creature they call the Stork," Bransen went on, not reading the signs. "Cadayle loves the Stork!"

He finished with a wide smile, one that Cadayle's hand promptly wiped away with a stinging slap.

For a moment, Bransen's heart fell and broke. Had the mere notion of Cadayle with his other self so disgusted her?

But the truth spilled forth in a burst of venom from her that shocked the Highwayman. "Do not ever speak of poor Bransen in such a manner ever again!" she demanded. "Do not mock him!"

"I—I did not," Bransen tried to reply.

"I thought you a better man than that!" Cadayle fumed. "Bransen Garibond's infirmity is no matter of jest, nor is it his fault in any way. You mock me by calling me his lover—but I would be, do not doubt, if he were a healthy man!"

Those simple words nearly knocked Bransen from his feet and had his heart thumping in his thin chest.

"I thought you different from the others," Cadayle continued, despite the Highwayman's holding his hand up to try to calm her. "When you fought Tarkus Breen and his bullies, when you slew him, I thought it in defense of Bransen as much as in the defense of Cadayle."

"It was," he managed to interject.

"But you mock him."

"I do not."

"Then what?"

"I feared that I was walking over a line in trying to court you," Bransen improvised. "I thought it prudent to discern your true feelings for the one called Stork."

"I hate that name. He is Bransen."

The Highwayman conceded the point with a low bow and asked in all sincerity, "Then you do not love him?"

"Perhaps I do."

"But you will not marry him?"

"Marry him?" Cadayle echoed with obvious incredulity. "He can hardly care for himself. How is he to care for a family? Bransen will stay with the brothers of Abelle. It is the only place for him, I fear."

"And what for Cadayle, then?"

"That is for Cadayle to decide."

He dipped another conciliatory bow. In the middle of it, it occurred to Bransen to pull off his mask and reveal himself to her. How he wanted to!

But he could not. He could not so endanger Cadayle as to reveal himself, and he realized that he had not the courage to do so. She had not declared her love for him, after all, but had merely not denied the possibility.

Bransen wished that he were a braver man.

"You are not the only one who cares for Bransen," he said.

Cadayle didn't seem convinced, but neither did she remain overtly angry.

"Do you wish me to leave?"

Cadayle paused and stared at him for a long while, then said simply and soberly, "No."

"But no kiss for the flowers?" Bransen dared to tease.

"Next time, perhaps," she said, and she managed a smile. When his grin widened, though, she added, "Perhaps not."

"My lady, do not play with my heart."

Cadayle laughed.

"You dare to mock me?"

She laughed again, and he joined in.

A moment later, Bransen remembered the monks had planned to begin returning soon after lunch. "I must be on my way," he said. "But I will visit again, on my word."

"Day or night, it would seem."

"A man's heart forces him to take risks."

It was tough for Bransen to turn away from that smiling face, but he knew that time was running short. He ran with a spring in his step, flush with hope and joy, all the way back to the river, where he changed back into his woolen tunic and shuffled his awkward way back to Chapel Pryd.

Brother Reandu was already back at the chapel, waiting for him, seeming very afraid and more than a little angry. "What are you doing out beyond the chapel wall?" he scolded, and he grabbed Bransen by the arm and rushed him inside. "And what have you got in that sack?"

A wave of panic swept over Bransen. The game was over, he realized.

But a call from across the chapel's courtyard caught Reandu's attention.

"Come along and be quick!" Master Bathelais ordered Reandu. "Laird Prydae has ordered a sweep of the town to collect funds for Prince Yeslnik!"

"You go and finish your chores," Reandu said to Bransen, and the monk hurried away, apparently forgetting about the small sack.

Bransen breathed a deep, deep sigh of relief.

He made his way back to his room and fell upon his cot. The laird had ordered yet another round of taxes to be collected?

Bransen lay down and closed his eyes, seeking sleep.

He thought that the Highwayman would be busy that night.

Sweet dreams of fields and flowers and Cadayle swept through him. His body felt again the warmth of the peasant woman's kiss, but his mind substituted his love for the farm woman. Somewhere deep inside, the sleeping Bransen knew that her kisses would be sweeter.

The exertion of the day, the tumult of emotions, and the energy used in maintaining the harmony of his life energy, were more than Bransen had bargained for, and he was awakened not later that night, but the next morning, by the calls of a brother for him to get up and get to his chores.

So he did, and during the course of that day, he learned that Laird Prydae's collectors had been especially energetic the previous night.

Perhaps the Highwayman had missed an opportunity.

But the visiting Prince Yeslnik still had to get the treasure out of Pryd Holding.

When Yeslnik's carriage left Castle Pryd to great fanfare two days later, all the monks were in attendance.

And with the chapel emptied yet again, the Highwayman, too, was out and about.

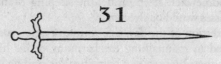

31

THE SPARKLE IN HIS EYES

Bannagran tried hard not to laugh, but his chuckles kept slipping past his tightly closed lips.

"Do not underestimate the seriousness of this," Laird Prydae warned. "Men like Prince Yeslnik do not take well to embarrassment." Despite his obvious sincerity, Prydae couldn't help but chuckle also. Prince Yeslnik's coach had rolled back to Castle Pryd. The angry young man had leaped from it, running screaming to Laird Prydae that he must capture and kill this "Highwayman beast!" Yeslnik had quickly recounted the encounter with the Highwayman, how this mysterious figure dressed in black had leaped atop his royal coach and had robbed him at sword point of all the monies Prydae had just collected.

Princess Olym had added that this robber had initially dispatched the powries who had initially stopped the coach.

"Do not forget that the prince's wife was quite smitten with the beast," Bannagran replied. "Or that Harkin, the driver, was quite grateful. Had the Highwayman not arrived, the three of them would have been slaughtered by the dwarves and Harkin's wounded friend would surely have died—I noticed that Prince Yeslnik made no mention of the powries at all."

"The man is angry."

"Wounded pride will do that to you."

"He will take that anger back to Laird Delaval. That and an additional tax exacted from Pryd."

"My liege, we cannot go back to the people for more

money and goods," Bannagran warned. "They will not stand for it. Every tax collector would need a band of warriors to accompany him on his rounds, and there would be bloodshed, I warn you. Much bloodshed."

Laird Prydae considered those words carefully, knowing their truth but knowing, too, that he could not send Yeslnik back to Laird Delaval empty-handed. How he wished that the young prince had just kept going, all the way to the great river. That would have bought him some time, at least, before he needed to go and collect more revenues for his protecting Laird Delaval. Now he understood the truth, and that realization only made him even more angry at this Highwayman. He would have to take the money for Delaval out of his own riches.

"Post a reward," he told Bannagran.

"The people love the Highwayman."

"The people love money more. Post a reward, a substantial one. Promise that anyone who provides information leading to the capture of the outlaw will dine at the castle for the rest of his life. Offer a thousand gold coins. Offer complete access for the informant and his family to the brothers of Abelle and their healing gemstones."

Bannagran raised an eyebrow at that.

"Master Bathelais will not refuse me in this."

"I will spread the word through every tavern and every road," Bannagran promised.

Prydae walked over and dropped a hand on the sitting Bannagran's shoulder. "You have been my friend and companion for as long as I can remember," he said. "I need you now. I charge you with capturing and killing this outlaw. He is undermining my rule, Bannagran, and this latest theft jeopardizes the very life of Pryd Holding."

Bannagran's eyebrow arched again, showing that he thought his friend might be exaggerating a bit on that last point. There was no doubt, however, that the mere presence of this Highwayman was raising the ire of the common folk against Prydae.

"The people will not be pleased when he is dragged in and executed," Bannagran noted.

"Bernivvigar will kill him for us, I am certain. And the people will forget, soon enough. But we must get him, and soon. He has embarrassed us—could it be that he will attempt to attack me? To murder me in my sleep?"

Bannagran furrowed his brow. After all, the Highwayman had only killed one man in all of his exploits, and that with the man's own knife.

"Destroy him, my friend," Prydae ordered. "Use every soldier and every resource at our disposal. Find him and kill him, and very soon."

Bannagran nodded.

"You should not be here," Cadayle said. "You should not be anywhere near the town this night. Laird Prydae's men are everywhere, searching for you."

"How do you know that I was the one who saved Prince Yeslnik this day?" Bransen asked.

"Saved? Robbed, you mean."

"Robbed? Nay, I call it a reward, my lady. First I killed all the powries that would have killed the good young prince, then I took a reward."

"That is not what they are saying."

"Do you believe that any nobleman would be brave enough to admit that he was rescued? And by an outlaw highwayman?" Bransen said with a laugh. "No, Prince Yeslnik's pride will not allow him to include that little detail in his recounting of the encounter."

Cadayle managed a smile—and her smile truly lit up Bransen's heart!—but she glanced all around nervously, as if expecting Laird Prydae's soldiers to leap upon her.

"Perhaps I should have let the powries finish him and his wife before taking my reward," Bransen went on. "But then, of course, the innocent drivers would have been slaughtered as well, and that I could not allow."

"But you would have allowed the prince to be killed?"

The Highwayman shrugged.

"And his wife?" Cadayle pressed, clearly distressed.

"Well, perhaps not, though I am not very fond of the lairds of Honce and their ignoble henchmen."

"They are our protectors."

"They protect themselves," the Highwayman argued. "I have seen Laird Prydae's castle, and I assure you, the man wants for nothing."

"He is appointed by God, so say the priests. His line is blessed, as are the lines of all the lairds."

The Highwayman laughed at her, but inside, Bransen thought her words no laughing matter. He had come to understand the "sanctity" of the lairds, anointed by both monk of Abelle and Samhaist alike, each trying to gain favor with the powerful noblemen. The Book of Jhest had told Bransen a different story. The Jhesta Tu mystics outright rejected any special relationship between the secular leaders, of tribes and kingdoms and holdings, and God. But the peasants of Honce didn't see that; not even Cadayle, whom Bransen considered very intelligent and aware—mightily so, compared to the other peasants.

"Then I suppose that God will not be pleased with me for taking . . . this," Bransen answered, pulling forth the jeweled necklace he had pilfered from Olym.

Cadayle sucked in her breath, and the glittering of her eyes rivaled that of the stones in the starlight.

"Lady Cadayle," Bransen began. "Beautiful Cadayle. If you are to try to convince me that Princess Olym Delaval's neck is more fit for this than your own, I pray you save your breath and your effort. If God has blessed any woman with the beauty to properly complement this necklace, then surely that woman is you."

She raised her gaze to match his stare, and still she said nothing.

Bransen moved forward slowly, unthreateningly. She was afraid, he could tell; she was even shivering a little, and not from the chill night air. Bransen reached up and draped the necklace about her thin neck, reaching behind with both hands, and even moving closer to look over her shoulder as he worked the clasp.

He could feel her breath on his neck, so warm, and after he had secured the clasp, he stayed in place for a while, basking in the feel and smell of Cadayle.

Finally, he leaned back so that he was right before her, his hands still upon her shoulders.

"I cannot keep this," she said, and he put a finger to her lips to silence her.

"Of course you cannot," Bransen agreed. "But wear it this night, and secretly for as long as you desire. No doubt Laird Prydae and Prince Yeslnik will offer a fine reward for the piece. When they do, say that you found it at the side of the road, and collect your due. For your mother, if not for yourself."

"I cannot."

"Of course you can," said Bransen. "I will scatter a few coins near to the oak at the forward end of this very lane. Say you found the necklace there. The fools will believe that I dropped some of the booty."

"But—"

"What else am I to do with it?" Bransen interrupted. "I have no need of coin, am well fed and well housed."

"Then why do you steal?"

"Because I know that I am among the few who can so make such a claim of health and comfort. Because I know that Laird Prydae and all the other noblemen live in luxury while the rest toil for their benefit, even die for their benefit." He wanted to add, "And because it's fun," but he thought it better to keep that a secret.

"And I do appreciate beautiful things," Bransen added, and he stared intently at Cadayle, grabbing her eyes with his own, and he would not let go. "And truly that necklace is a pale bauble beside the beauty I now see. Upon you, it shines so much the brighter."

She blushed and couldn't hide her smile, and she started to look away. But Bransen wouldn't let her. He brought his hand up beside her cheek and slowly turned her to face him directly. He couldn't resist her, then, her smell, her warm breath, her beauty in the starlight, and so he leaned forward and dared to press his lips against hers.

To his amazement, she did not pull away from him, and her arms came up around his back, pulling him closer.

For Bransen, there had never been a moment as sweet.

Cadayle pulled back after a long and lingering moment. "I should not have done that," she said, and she broke free of his embrace.

"Oh, but I want to do it again!" Bransen blurted, and Cadayle put a hand over her mouth and giggled.

"But I do," Bransen said, and it was his turn to be embarrassed.

"Have you never kissed a woman before?"

Bransen thought on that for a moment, in light of his encounter with the farm lady. "One kissed me, once."

Cadayle giggled again. "Only one? A rogue like you?"

"And how many men has Cadayle kissed?" Bransen shot right back at her.

She grew very serious suddenly. "None before like that," she said.

Bransen felt his legs go weak. "One more kiss before I go?" he asked.

"Just one, and just a kiss, and then you must be on your way, Highwayman."

Bransen came forward in a rush, but Cadayle held him back long enough to calm him. Then she kissed him, long and soft and sweet.

The taste of her followed him all the way back to Chapel Pryd, all the way back to his dark and dirty hole.

Callen brought her hand to her mouth to hide her gasp, and she felt for a moment as if she would simply fall over. Never in her life had she ever seen any piece of jewelry as fabulous as the necklace Cadayle was wearing.

"You saw him again," Callen breathed.

"I found it by the side of the road," Cadayle said. "Along with these." She held out her hand, showing the few coins the Highwayman had given her to seed the story.

Callen's eyes went narrow. "You didn't find anything."

Cadayle squirmed, the observant mother noted. "Under the tree, mother. There might be more. You and I can go look in the morning's light."

"Cadayle . . ." Callen said in even and controlled tones, her best mother's voice. "You've not ever lied to me before."

Cadayle seemed to visibly break, then, her shoulders slumping.

"The Highwayman came to you again this night."

"Yes."

Callen took Cadayle's chin in her hand and lifted her face so that their stares locked. "And what did you give him for the necklace?"

Cadayle's eyes went wide in shock, which brought a wave of relief to the older woman.

"I did kiss him," Cadayle admitted a moment later, and Callen scowled. "But not for the necklace. I kissed him because I wanted to."

"Would you have kissed him if he hadn't given you the jewels?"

"Of course!" Cadayle blurted, and then she seemed embarrassed and lowered her gaze once more. "I mean, it wasn't the necklace that made me choose to kiss him."

Callen pulled her close for a hug, then pushed her back to arms' length. "But you cannot keep it. You know that."

"He told me to turn it over to the laird and prince for the reward they will likely offer. Still, I feel as if I'm stealing. Perhaps I should just give it back for no reward."

"You're to do no such thing!" Callen snapped, and Cadayle shot to attention. "No, you do as the Highwayman bade you. Laird Prydae and Prince Yeslnik aren't to miss any reward, and God and the Ancient Ones know that we could put the coin to better use, for our sake and for that of all our hungry neighbors."

Cadayle brought her hand up to the precious necklace and her look went wistful, revealing to the observant Callen that her daughter wasn't truly enamored of the idea of parting with the gift.

"You know that you cannot keep it," Callen said softly. "Wouldn't Bernivvigar be happy to find you wearing such a thing?"

"I know," Cadayle replied halfheartedly.

The younger woman went to the other side of the small house then and began undressing, then slipped into her bed under the blankets.

Callen noted that she was still wearing the necklace. Callen just smiled about it, however, and was both glad that her daughter had apparently found love and terribly afraid of this man who had become the object of Cadayle's affections.

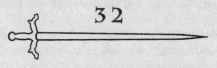

32

TRINKETS AND REVELATIONS

Any feelings of levity Bransen held about his exploits and the frustration he was causing to Laird Prydae were lost the next day when, out in the courtyard of Chapel Pryd, he saw the results of that frustration. Soldiers were everywhere, it seemed, moving about the streets and banging on the doors. The Stork overheard one conversation along the roadside not far away.

"What do you know of him?" the soldier roared, and he grabbed a young woman by the front of her simple tunic and lifted her up to tiptoes. "You'd be smart to tell me all!"

"I know nothing, me lord," the woman cried.

"You haven't met this Highwayman?"

"No, me lord. Please let me go. Ye're hurting me poor neck."

The soldier roughly shoved her back, and she stumbled and nearly fell. She ran off, crying, while the warrior moved along to the nearest door and began banging on it.

Anger welled inside Bransen, and it was all he could do to suppress his urge to don his black outfit and have a word with that man and all the others.

The Stork bit his lip and forced himself to calm down. The laird was angry and his soldiers were bullying some folks, but it was nothing serious, he told himself. A smile wound its way onto the Stork's crooked face, and suddenly he found that he was thrilled that he was so troubling the powers of Pryd Holding, and even those beyond. He used the recollection of Prince Yeslnik's face to block out the image of the frightened young woman. Yes, that was a pleasing memory.

Bransen vowed to himself that he would step up his pace, that he would infuriate Laird Prydae beyond reason. How far could he push it? he wondered. How long would he have to go to force the laird to make concessions to him? He fantasized about that, about being called to a meeting wherein Prydae offered his surrender. Wouldn't he be a hero to the common folk then! And wouldn't Cadayle love him all the more?

That last thought brought a frown to him. Was it him she loved? Bransen? Or was it someone else entirely, the mysterious rogue named the Highwayman?

It was all too confusing, and so Bransen let go of the troubling questions and fears and focused instead on the kiss. He could still feel Cadayle's warmth; it had taken him through a night of wonderful dreams. There was nothing about her that wasn't perfect in his eyes. Her face, her soft skin, her softer lips. The feel of her against him, the sound of her voice, her gentle touch.

All of it stayed with him as he finished his chores that day—a day in which he kept glancing to the west, willing the sun to hurry and sink behind the horizon. For in the night, he would see her again.

She couldn't deny her excitement as she noted his approach. She had known that the mysterious Highwayman would come out to her this night. She had seen his face after their kiss and had heard the sincerity in his voice. Even with all that, however, Cadayle couldn't help but doubt, and fear, that he would not return. That fear, above everything else, revealed to her the truth behind her jumbled thoughts. For she was indeed afraid that he would not come to her this night, and if that fear was realized, it would be a painful thing.

But the Highwayman did not disappoint. He approached

the field behind Cadayle's house with a visible spring in his step, and Cadayle knew that he had seen her long before she was aware of him.

He danced up before her, dipped a quick and polite bow, and produced a small sack from behind his back, handing it to her.

"You and your mother will eat well this week," he said with that mischievous grin of his, one made more mysterious by the fact that he wore a mask above that toothy grin, and one that Cadayle was beginning to see in her mind long after the man had gone.

Cadayle fished about in the sack, discovering an assortment of meat and fruit and bread. She hid her excitement and her smile, and she wasn't really surprised. Almost every night, the Highwayman came to her bearing gifts, from the mundane, like the food, to the fabulous necklace she still wore upon her delicate neck.

When she looked up, she noted that he was staring at that necklace. "They've posted no reward," she said, bringing a hand up to it.

"They will soon enough," he assured her. "Their searches around Pryd Town have brought them nothing but the enmity of the peasants. Their frustrations will lead them to try to turn commoner against commoner because there are simply too many of you for the noblemen and their few warriors to inspect or to control, if it ever came to that."

That last line hit her hard. "Do not speak of such things," she said.

"It is a reality the lairds understand well."

"Please do not speak of it," Cadayle said again.

"If the common folk rose up—"

"Then many of them would be slaughtered," Cadayle interrupted. "Whether the lairds fall or not would be of little consequence to a man killed in the street. And I would rather live under the press of Laird Prydae than bury my ma in trying to defeat him. What we've got is not perfect, but it's what we've got, and nothing more."

The Highwayman paused, then started to say, "But," then just paused again and seemed to shrug it all away.

"They will post a reward soon enough," he did say.

Cadayle wanted to reply that she hoped it would be a long time before Laird Prydae did so, but she held her thoughts to herself. She liked wearing the necklace—more than she understood at that moment. It made her feel pretty. It made her feel, for just a few moments of conscious delusion, rich and powerful.

And it made her feel, most of all, as if this mysterious stranger, this hero who had saved her and her mother, this good man who was trying to help the lot of the always-overlooked rabble of Pryd, cared for her. Cadayle wasn't even sure how she felt about the Highwayman. Did she love him? She hadn't even seen him without his mask!

Cadayle looked at him then, carefully, and what she did know was that she was glad, truly glad, that he apparently cared for her.

"Are all the people feeling your generosity?" she asked. "Or just a few, like me and my mother?"

"All the people? I would be busy indeed in even trying to visit the homes of half! I share what I can and do not distinguish among the people—well, except for you, of course. For you, I always save the best that I find."

Cadayle was certain that she was blushing fiercely, and she lowered her gaze.

"The laird must be seeking you."

"With all of his men," the Highwayman answered.

Cadayle looked up at him with concern. "If he catches you, he will kill you horribly."

The Highwayman shrugged. "I have killed no man who did not deserve it, nor have I taken anything that did not rightfully belong to the people."

Cadayle's hand went back to the necklace.

"Well, the lairds should not so hoard the wealth, then," said the Highwayman. "They live in splendor, while all else suffer in squalor."

"They are the chosen of God."

The Highwayman snorted and Cadayle took a reflexive step back, not quite understanding what it was about her last statement that had irked him. Was it the concept relating to the lairds, or the concept of God? At that moment, Cadayle began to understand just how shallow her growing feelings for this man truly might be.

"Are you of the Church of Blessed Abelle?" she asked.

He seemed surprised. "Well, no . . ." The answer was less than definitive in tone.

"A Samhaist?"

"Never that!"

Cadayle looked at him curiously, hiding her great relief. She certainly had no love for Bernivvigar and his horrible followers. Her mother had never told her anything good at all about the Samhaists, and though neither had she overtly attacked Bernivvigar in her remarks to Cadayle, her voice when speaking of the man or his religion had always been tight, as if holding back visceral hatred. Cadayle had gotten that impression, at least.

"Do not think me a godless man," the Highwayman stated, drawing her from her contemplations. "I see good in much of what the brothers of Abelle attempt to accomplish, and many of their actions are wrought of generosity. But there is more to the world than they know, I am certain, and so I do not limit myself to the beliefs they present."

"You know better than the Church?"

The Highwayman shrugged in that confident way of his.

Cadayle let it go at that.

They talked some more, about nothing in particular, and nothing of any real importance, and Cadayle soon began to understand that the Highwayman was just stalling, stretching out the conversation in the hope of . . .

He was nervous.

So was she.

Her mother began to call for her, and she glanced back at her house, then turned to her masked suitor. "I must be going," she said suddenly, and she came forward and offered him another kiss, thinking to make it just a quick peck.

But he caught her and he held her, held them pressed together, and for a long and wonderful moment, Cadayle didn't try to wriggle away.

She skipped all the way home, like a little girl dancing in the sunshine after a spring thundershower.

Thoughts of Cadayle followed Bransen as he made his way across Pryd Town. Once again this night, many of Laird Prydae's soldiers were about, as well as tax collectors moving from house to house and pestering the peasants. Bransen was in no mood for violence that night, no mood for catching one of those money-grubbers in a dark corner and striping him of his ill-gotten coin and foodstuffs.

He did veer from his course at one point, however, when he noted firelight far to the east. He headed toward the campfire out of the main town, moving through a copse of trees and then across a small field to a second copse.

Several men sat around the fire, over which a pig was roasting. They were vagabonds, Bransen knew, dispossessed by the many battles and the weight of their disappointment. All had wild beards and all were incredibly dirty. These were the outcasts of Pryd Holding, the forgotten men wandering the shadows at the edges of the civilized town. Bransen had seen many such men, perhaps some of these very ones, at Chapel Pryd, coming in to beg for food or magical gemstone relief from their maladies.

Bransen crouched just outside the radius of the firelight and listened, his smile widening as he came to understand that they were talking about him and the inconvenience he was causing Laird Prydae.

"Bah, good enough for Laird Prydae, I say," one roughly grumbled, and he tore a piece of meat from the bone and popped it into his mouth.

"Tired I am of fighting," said another. "Watched three of me friends fall to the swords of Ethelbert. Three's enough."

"Three's too many," another agreed.

"Well, I'm not seeing how this Highwayman's to help us from having that number go up," the first came back. "Nor am I seeing how he's to stop meself from going back to the south at Laird Prydae's bidding."

"But ye're not for crying over Prydae's money losses, now are ye?" said the second, and they all laughed.

"Laird Prydae can afford the losses," Bransen heard himself saying; and without even thinking of it, the Highwayman rose and stepped into the firelight. How the men scrambled! One even drew out a small knife and waved it ominously in Bransen's direction.

"Hold, I pray you," the Highwayman said. "I come not as any foe but simply as another traveler this night."

"Ye're him!" one of the men cried.

Bransen shrugged.

"Ye're the one stealing everything," the first said.

"Not everything and not for myself, of course," Bransen replied. "Laird Prydae has more than enough food and coin, I know, and so I am merely helping him to distribute his goods to those in need."

The men all looked at each other, and the one with the knife lowered it and put it away.

"Sit down, then," said the first of the group. "Take some food with us and tell us yer tale."

Bransen did take a seat on one of the fallen logs that formed the seats in their camp, and he did take a chunk of the offered meat. He didn't tell them any tales, however, and he just answered their barrage of questions with grunts and shrugs. To him, it was enough to simply enjoy the company, and he couldn't deny that he didn't mind at all the expressions of admiration, even awe, that were aimed his way. Again, the Book of Jhest's warnings about the failings of pride came to him, but he easily pushed them away.

For it all seemed like an innocent encounter of little importance, and so what matter if he indulged himself a bit by basking in their admiration? But then one of the men asked, in all seriousness, "Are ye looking for hire ons, then, Mister Highwayman? Are ye needing some strong men to help ye with yer work?"

The others all grunted and nodded and began whispering excitedly among themselves, but Bransen was too taken with the question to even begin to listen to those side conversations. This was a possibility he hadn't foreseen, and one that he found hard to dismiss. Could he form a band and lead it? Could he take these ragtag men, and so many others just like them who loitered about Pryd Town, and turn them into a formidable force?

He didn't know, and before he could explore it more seriously with some questions of his hosts, he noted something else, something that one of the men was holding: a skinning knife with a dull white bone handle.

"May I see your knife?" Bransen asked, holding out a hand.

"What?" the man replied, and he followed Bransen's gaze to the implement, then brought it up. "What, this?" He handed it over. "An old one and not much to see, but holding a fine edge, don't ye doubt!"

Bransen took the blade, thinking how much it resembled the one Garibond had always used back at the lake. That thought amused him, until he rolled the knife over and noted a stain on its handle, just below the blade, and a nick in the blade itself. Bransen froze, his eyes going wide. There could not be a second knife like this one, with such a similar stain and nick.

Bransen stared at it, remembering the many times he had seen this very blade, this exact knife, in Garibond's hand. He could picture his father putting it to use to cut the tasty flesh from a bass or trout; he could see it as clearly as if he were watching it then and there.

"Where did you get this?" the Highwayman asked, his tone changing dramatically.

He could tell that the vagabond caught the seriousness of that voice when the man stuttered, "W-what? That old thing? Had it all me life. Me da, he give it to me, he did."

Bransen turned a scowl upon the man. "I know this knife," he said. "And it was not your father's."

"Oh, ye're m-meaning the knife," the man stammered in a ridiculous correction. "No, no, the knife's not from me da. Found it, I did, years ago."

"Where?"

"Well, I'm not for remembering."

Bransen's sword seemed to leap into his hand, and he leveled it at the trembling man. One of the others screamed, a second shouted for him to be at ease.

"Come from the lake," the frightened vagabond stammered.

"From a house near the lake, you mean. The house of Garibond Womak."

The man shook his head and stuttered a few incomprehensible sounds.

"Aye, it was old Garibond's house," said another of the group. "I knew that one, Garibond Womak, and as good a man as ever I knew, he was."

Bransen lowered the sword. "Was?"

"Aye, Garibond once lived in the very house where come that knife."

"Where is he now?"

"Garbond Womak?" The man shrugged. "He's dead, from all I heard, and so he must be. Many went to the house and took what was there."

Bransen's eyes flashed with sudden anger.

"Aye, that's the way of it," another of the group insisted. "So many have so little. When one's dying, we're not to let his belongings go to waste."

"Garibond is not dead!" Bransen insisted.

"Then he's been gone a lot of years, and so it's the same," the man with the knife argued back.

Bransen shook his head. None of it made any sense to him.

Garibond couldn't be dead. What had Brother Reandu said? That he had moved south . . . But Bransen remembered, too, that Brother Reandu would not meet his eyes. And Bransen thought of his last visit to the houses on the lake, of the strangers he had seen there, fishing and going about their business as if that was their home.

A fit of trembling began at the base of Bransen's spine and worked its way steadily up. Garibond dead? The thought hammered at him, for never had he even considered such a thing. Garibond was the foundation of all his life; and for ten years, Bransen had held fast the fantasy of going back to him, of showing him that his son was all right, after all.

"What more do you know?" he demanded of the group.

"I know that ye're holding me knife."

"Garibond's knife," Bransen corrected with a growl that told them the issue was not up for debate. But he noted the expressions coming at him from all the men, and most of those looks registered disappointment. They had invited him in to dine with them, though they rarely had enough to eat, he knew. They had offered to join with him.

They thought him a hero of the common folk.

Bransen tossed the knife down before the man. "Garibond is not dead," he said. "And when I find him, I ask that you return his knife."

"Bah, it's me own now," the man said defiantly, and he scooped up the blade. "Had it for ten years!"

The words nearly floored Bransen, and he staggered back as if struck, then turned on his heel and rushed out of the trees and across the field, running fast for Chapel Pryd, running away from the horrible thoughts that were dancing in his mind.

But they followed him, every step.

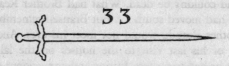

33

A WOMAN AND HER JEWELS

Bannagran walked through the streets of Pryd Town muttering to himself, remembering his last conversation with Laird Prydae. He had not often seen his friend so animated and agitated. The continuing war threat to Pryd Holding had the laird on the edge, and this Highwayman character was threatening to push him right over. Every day at breakfast, Prydae spoke of nothing else, feverishly working with Bannagran and Rennarq to try to find some clues as to how they might apprehend the rogue. Every day, they related the same stories over and over again. Prydae had even bade Rennarq to ask Bernivvigar for help, something the secular ruler had always been loath to do.

Bannagran tried a rational approach now, focusing on the patterns of the attacks, from the first sighting of the Highwayman to the last. His thoughts and instincts kept going back to the first incident, the only one in which anyone had been seriously hurt, other than one of Yeslnik's drivers in the powrie attack. As chance would have it, with those very thoughts in mind, he spotted Rulhio Noylan—who had been among the five that the Highwayman had defeated—walking along the road by the market square.

The large warrior moved to intercept, and Rulhio saw him coming and abruptly turned.

"I would speak with you, young Noylan," Bannagran said, moving fast to catch up.

Rulhio's expression showed great fear when he glanced back at Bannagran, but no more so than Bannagran was used to seeing on the faces of young men, for usually when he spoke to them, it meant a trip to the south and the battle lines! Still, the young man did skid to an abrupt stop and stood waiting for the imposing warrior.

"You were there that night when Tarkus Breen was murdered?" Bannagran asked.

Rulhio swallowed hard and managed a slight nod.

"I wish to hear the tale."

"I told it in full," Rulhio replied shakily. "We all did."

Bannagran sensed suddenly that the man was a bit too defensive, and his instincts told him that there might be more to this than had previously been explained. Knowing aggression to be the arbiter of truth, the imposing warrior grabbed poor Rulhio by the front of his tunic. "And you will tell me again," he too-calmly explained, and he half carried, half dragged the terrified man off the main road, down a side alley where fewer witnesses could be found.

So the cringing Rulhio recounted the tale of that fateful night, a story that seemed strained now to Bannagran and not completely in line with what he had heard those weeks before. Bannagran purposely doubted every word, and searched for weaknesses in the logical chain of events.

"You and your friends were drunk?"

"Aye, he could not have defeated us if we were not," the terrified young man replied.

"And this happened out on the west road, out by Gorham's Hill?"

"Aye, as we told you. Way out there."

"Where did you come by the drink?"

"Inkerby's," Rulhio replied, naming a well-known tavern in Pryd Town, under the shadow of the castle and often frequented by soldiers.

Bannagran tried to hide his smile as he caught on. Why would five drunken men—troublemakers all, he knew—wander from Inkerby's, which was frequented by many of the local whores, all the way out to the western edge of Pryd Town. To his knowledge, none of the five in question lived out that way.

"Gorham's Hill is a long walk from town," he remarked, and he saw the sudden flash of panic in Rulhio's eyes.

"Well, we were drinking and needed to walk it off a bit. Me ma's not in favor of me—"

"You are often drunk," Bannagran interrupted. "And your mother knows as much."

"Just walking, is all."

"To Gorham's Hill? From Inkerby's?"

"Aye."

Bannagran went with his instincts. He came forward suddenly and brutally, grabbing poor, frightened Rulhio and lifting him off the ground. Two strides put them across the alley, where Bannagran slammed Rulhio up against the wall and held him in place, his feet a foot and more off the ground.

"W-what are . . . ?" Rulhio stuttered. "Why are—?"

"You tell me why you were out by Gorham's Hill."

"I just—" Rulhio started to reply. Bannagran brought him out and slammed him against the wall again, and Rulhio cried out.

"Hey there!" someone shouted in protest from the entrance of the alleyway, but when the newcomer saw who was down there—the legendary Bannagran—he ran off.

"My polite questioning fast approaches its end," Bannagran warned, and he pulled poor Rulhio out from the wall again, as if to slam him.

"Was the wench Cadayle!" Rulhio cried, and Bannagran froze, holding him aloft with ease.

"Cadayle?"

"She lives out there. Nothing but trouble for all of us. Teasing all the town men with her charms and protecting that ugly Stork beast who hides in the chapel."

Bannagran put him down, and Rulhio slumped back against the wall, which seemed the only thing holding him up at the moment.

"What are you blabbering about, man?" Bannagran demanded.

"We just wanted to teach her some respect."

"Who? Cadayle?"

"Aye, the wench."

"I know not of her."

"She's living out by Gorham's Hill with her ma," Rulhio explained. "Was Tarkus Breen's idea to pay them a visit. She fought him, here in town, defending that ugly little Stork."

"And so you went out there to teach her a lesson."

"Someone had to!"

Bannagran didn't argue the point with the fool. "And did you? Teach her, I mean?"

"We was going to."

"Did you find her?"

"Aye, we knew where she lived, her and her ma. We had her ready to learn, but then the—the Highwayman, he showed up, and . . ."

Bannagran pulled the man out from the wall. "He showed up and defended the women?"

"Weren't any of his business."

"And he beat you up and your brother?"

"Aye, and he murdered Tarkus!"

Bannagran nodded and roughly pushed Rulhio toward the alley's exit. "Show me this house by Gorham's Hill," he ordered. "I would like to see this woman, Cadayle."

Rulhio started to protest, but Bannagran shoved him again, hard enough to send him sprawling, and he got the message that this was not the time to argue.

Later that day, after sighting the house and Cadayle, Bannagran went back to Castle Pryd and alerted his spies. He thought to go to Laird Prydae with his hunch but changed his mind. Perhaps Rulhio's admission was important. Perhaps not.

Guldibonne Cob rested back against the trunk of a tree, relaxed and quite pleased with himself. For months the slender soldier had worked hard to get in Bannagran's favor, and now his efforts at last seemed to be paying dividends. All those who had fought in the ranks beside Guldibonne were back in the south, warring with the savages from Ethelbert.

But not Guldibonne. Bannagran hadn't sent him back, for he had given Bannagran reason to keep him around. Any errand, asked or unasked, the man had jumped to complete. He had scouted out the most tempting ladies in all the taverns of Pryd Holding, and even beyond Pryd Holding, and had brought them to his commander. It was all in the details, Guldibonne knew, and his attention to those little things had landed him this wonderful duty, watching the house of a pair of pretty women, mother and daughter, while his former comrades were off again at war.

He had gotten to know the lay of the land about Gorham's Hill very well during that first day and had found what he considered to be the perfect observation post, tucked in the boughs of a thick evergreen, with a view of the house, the lane before it, and the rocky field running wide behind. So comfortable was he that he even dared to take a bit of a nap that afternoon while the women were out tending their garden.

Guldibonne awoke soon after sunset, when the lights of candles and fires were just beginning to glow through the small windows and cracks in the wooden doors of the nearby cottages. The spy waited a bit, then carefully looked all about before heading to the window in Cadayle's house. He crept up right below the sill and slowly lifted his head to peek in.

The younger woman was there before him, partially dressed and unknowingly showing him much of her curving charms. But Guldibonne, as much of a lech as he was known to be, found his eyes drawn away from Cadayle's breasts, and up to her neck, where she was placing one of the most magnificent jeweled necklaces he had ever seen.

No peasant could possess even a single one of those glittering stones!

Trembling, Guldibonne finally managed to tear himself away from the amazing sight, and he lowered himself to the ground and slunk away. He hit the road and began walking, even started quietly whistling, in an attempt to appear casual and draw no attention. But this was too much to suppress—wouldn't Bannagran reward him magnificently for this information!

The man began to run full out, all the way to Castle Pryd.

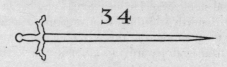

34

BEHIND TWO DOORS

So consumed was Bransen by the discovery of Garibond's knife that he did not go to visit Cadayle the next night. Of course he wanted to see her—he always wanted to be by Cadayle's side—but he knew deep in his heart that something simply wasn't right. Garibond would never have willingly parted with that blade, Bransen knew, for the knife was more than a utensil to him. It was a piece of Garibond's identity, a tool he had clearly valued because of how well it served him throughout his daily routine. He used it for cutting line and skinning fish, for taking small branches for firewood, and for eating his meals. He always carried it. Always.

Yet the man at the campfire claimed that he had possessed it for ten years. Doubts clouded Bransen's thoughts. Was it really Garibond's knife? Or was it, perhaps, that his own memory was not quite as reliable as he believed? He had seen Garibond's knife every day, practically, in the decade he had lived with him. But it was, after all, just a knife, of a simple and common design. And that was, after all, a decade ago, when Bransen was a child.

But why, then, Bransen wondered as he watched from the shadows of some trees, were these strangers living in the two houses of Garibond Womak? He could see them in the firelight behind the small windows of the lower cottage, milling about and making themselves perfectly at home. But how could they be at home in there? And where was Garibond?

He would find out, he decided. He would walk up and demand an explanation. But in what guise? As the Stork? The Highwayman?

He sat and he waited, so many questions spinning about in his thoughts. He watched as the scattered houses all around the area went dark, one by one, and as the upper house on the island similarly dimmed. All the forms moving in the lower house were adults, he could see, the two couples—two generations of a family, he believed. Gradually, the candles burned down and the windows darkened and the fire died out.

But even after the house was dark and quiet, Bransen sat there. He clenched his fists repeatedly at his side; he squinted against the stinging possibilities. He kept hoping that Garibond would walk up to the house, but he knew deep in the truthful recesses of his heart that it would not be.

The night deepened around him. No use in going to Cadayle now, he knew, for she was likely fast asleep. Almost all the town was fast asleep.

He watched the moon—the goddess Sheila to the Samhaists—pass her apex above him and wind down to the western horizon. And still he sat there, paralyzed by a fear more profound than any he had ever known, more so even than on that night he had first watched Tarkus Breen and his cohorts at Cadayle's.

"I must," he whispered to the night wind, and he pulled himself to his feet. "I must," he repeated, more loudly and assuredly, when he realized that his feet were not moving.

He thought of Garibond, recalling images of him as clearly as if he were seeing them all over again: at the lake; showing off a large catch; flashing one of his rare smiles; tousling Bransen's hair; splitting firewood; or just sitting calmly at the window, watching the world flow past.

Bolstered by the memories, the young man began to move, forcing one foot in front of the other. He owed this to Garibond, he reminded himself. He had to find out what was going on and where his father had gone. Outwardly, he just kept repeating, "I must."

Then he was at the door, and never had he seen a more solid barrier. He lifted his fist to knock, but lowered it, and then repeated the movement several times.

And then he began banging on the door, softly at first, but growing in intensity with each frustrated rap. "Answer me!" he called, and his fist slammed hard against the wood.

After several minutes, he had made up his mind to kick the door down, but just then he saw a light come up inside, and a form appeared at the window.

"Open the door," he demanded. "I must speak with you."

" 'Ere, who are you, then?" asked an older man.

Bransen slammed the door hard. "Open the door or I shall knock it down."

" 'Ere now, you be gone, knave!" the man at the window cried.

In response, Bransen leaped over, flashed out his sword, and put its tip near the man's face. "Knave it is," he said. "And growing angrier by the moment. Open the door, I ask and demand."

"You be gone!" the man shouted, and behind him, Bransen heard a woman cry, "The Highwayman!"

"We've got no coin for you to take," the man said, backing safely out of the sword's reach and sounding less sure of himself.

"I want not your coin," Bransen replied, and he lowered his sword. "Answers I need, and nothing more." He forced all sounds of fury and impatience out of his voice and calmly added, "My apologies, good sir. But please, it is important."

"If talk is all you need, then do it out there," said the obviously terrified man.

"How did you come by these houses?" Bransen asked.

"What do you mean?"

"We been here near to ten years now," the woman added.

Bransen heard other voices from inside, off to the side and out of sight.

"How did you come by these houses?"

"Why is that your concern? You're not to take them from us!" the man answered.

"I've no need of any such thing. But I once knew a man who lived here on this lake. He was a friend, and I wish to know why I find you here now, where he should be."

There was some murmuring from within, a whispered conversation that Bransen could not follow.

"His name was Garibond," Bransen said, daring to utter it, though he was concerned about making any connection between Garibond and the Highwayman. But his mounting desperation would not allow for caution at that time. "Garibond Womak. A good and fine man."

More whispering ensued, and then, to Bransen's surprise, the door opened a crack. He moved over to see the two couples standing there in the light of a pair of candles, with the older pair just inside the door and the younger in the shadows behind them. None of the four seemed pleased at that moment.

"Ye knowed Garibond, did ye?" asked the younger woman, a short, plump, and dirty thing with a pug nose and dark rings under her sullen eyes.

"Aye, a good and fine man," said the man standing beside her, his arm draped across her shoulders. "From what I knew of him, I mean, and that weren't much."

"He had that damaged boy," said the older woman. "The one the monks took in when . . ." Her voice trailed off and she looked away.

"This was his house," Bransen blurted, growing nervous.

"For all his days," replied the older man who had addressed Bransen through the window.

Bransen started to nod, and then the words hit him hard as he came to understand their clear implication.

" 'Twas Taerel, me da there, that buried him them ten years

ago," said the younger woman, and she indicated the previous speaker.

"You must be mistaken," Bransen managed to say, trying hard to keep his jaw from quivering. "Ten years, you say?"

"Aye, was ten years," said Taerel.

"Garibond was dead when the monks came and took this . . . this damaged boy?" Bransen asked, trying desperately to destroy the logic of their claim.

"Was a few weeks later that the monks returned for Garibond," said Taerel, "with the soldiers."

The hairs on the back of Bransen's neck began to stand up.

"Aye," the younger man added. "I was just a boy then, but I'm never to forget that day. They went all through this house, tearing it up, and then they took him." He stepped forward and pointed down the lakeshore to Bransen's right. "Right over there's where they did it."

"Did what?" Bransen's words were hardly more than a whisper.

"They burned him," said the man, who was just a few years older than Bransen.

"Staked him up, branded him a heretic, and burned him alive," Taerel added.

"Bah!" snorted the younger woman. "And them's the ones who're saying that theirs is the gentle way and the gentle god, and not like old Bernivvigar. Bah!"

"The m-monks?" Bransen stuttered. "The monks from the chapel murdered Garibond?"

"Aye, Master Bathelais and the others. With the help of Laird Prydae's soldiers, of course. And it weren't murder if Garibond was guilty of heresy as they claimed, I'd say," said Taerel.

"Murder's murder," muttered the younger woman.

Bransen felt his knees go weak and he knew that he had to get out of there. His stomach began to churn. He half turned.

"Highwayman, you've got quite the tale growing about you," said Taerel. "All the town's talking of you, and glad they are that someone's telling Laird Prydae that he cannot keep taking all of our food and . . ."

The man's voice drifted off behind Bransen as he staggered away, back toward the trees. He couldn't believe what the four had just told him—Master Bathelais and the others would never do such a thing! But Bransen's inner denials rang hollow. He pictured again the knife held by the stranger at the campfire. He wondered suddenly why Garibond had never once come to Chapel Pryd to visit him. Never before had he even considered that fact, but why *had* his beloved father stayed away for all these years?

A sense of profound aimlessness washed over Bransen, a complete unhinging of all his focus and purpose that manifested itself in his lifeline of *chi*. He staggered and stumbled and fell more than once as he made for the copse, finally leaning heavily on one tree.

And still there was nothing but the confusion, the scattering of his life energy, the sporadic bursts and twitches—a profound aimlessness. Not even hopelessness, for hopelessness inferred some design and forward thinking, and in Bransen there was none of that. For all his life, he had lived with daily tragedy, with bullying and his helplessness, with the frustration of having a keen mind trapped in a damaged body. For all his life, the dominant feature had ever been pain.

But not like this. Garibond was dead. Branson knew it, he believed it, he held no doubt of it. Garibond, the uncomplaining man who had given so much to him, was simply no more. And all the fantasies that Bransen had entertained of returning to his beloved father whole and strong were no more. All the hopes that Bransen had about living again with Garibond—but in a completely different relationship, one in which he could care for his father as his father had always cared for him—were no more. But Bransen couldn't even focus on any of those things specifically. They were all there, spinning and intertwining in the scattered jumble of his mind, finally settling to a sense of emptiness, a hole he knew he could never fill.

He slipped down to the ground, all strength gone, tears filling his eyes.

The knock startled the two women, but before either could begin to react, a second, more impressive banging burst the door askew. Behind the kick came Bannagran, commander of the laird's garrison, the most notable and feared warrior in all central Honce.

Cadayle fell back, as did her mother, and the two started for each other suddenly, needing the comfort of each other's arms.

But Bannagran cut in between them and shoved them apart. And before the women could react or protest, a second unexpected figure strode into their house, one that froze them in place.

"A fine day to you, ladies," said Laird Prydae. Hulking soldiers moved behind him, blocking the morning sunlight as it tried to stream in through the now-open door. "I forgive your lack of preparedness for my visit."

"My liege," said Cadayle's mother, and she fell to one knee and lowered her gaze. Cadayle took the cue and did likewise—or started to, until Bannagran grabbed her by the hair and pulled her back upright. She reached back and pulled at the big man's wrist, but his mighty grip did not weaken at all.

"You were awake late into the night, I expect," Laird Prydae went on. "Meeting the Highwayman, no doubt."

"No, my liege," Cadayle started to say, but she just shrieked instead as Bannagran reached over with his free hand, grabbed the front of her nightdress, and tore it from her, leaving her naked in the room—naked except for a jeweled necklace.

Cadayle looked down at the floor and quickly lifted her hand to cover the stolen necklace.

"You leave her!" her mother cried from across the way, and Cadayle glanced over just in time to see Callen's approach stopped suddenly by a backhanded blow from Bannagran, which sent Callen flying to the floor. Cadayle instinctively started to react, but the big man pulled all the harder on her hair.

"Enough of this foolishness," Bannagran said. "You are fairly caught, young lass. Make your death an easier thing with a bit of cooperation."

Callen shrieked at the blunt remark and charged again, only to be thrown aside once more by the giant Bannagran.

"My liege, pray you get those soldiers in here to control this wench," Bannagran said with a chuckle, but he bit the words off suddenly, noting Prydae's transfixed expression. "My liege?"

Prydae stood there staring at the naked Cadayle, at the softness of her curves, at their odd familiarity. The laird was no stranger to the sight of a naked woman, and so he was not leering like some giddy adolescent. But he was transfixed, by a memory the sight of Cadayle had inspired. The curve of her belly, the way her wheat-colored hair cascaded in layers across her lowered face. He thought of a bonfire, of an adder, of an adulteress and a knave. His gaze went from Cadayle to her mother, who, like Bannagran and Cadayle, was now staring at him curiously.

"Callen Duwornay," Laird Prydae remarked, the name springing from memories he didn't even know he possessed.

The woman blanched, something that neither Prydae nor Bannagran missed, and fell back a bit.

"N-no, my liege," she stammered.

"Callen Duwornay," Prydae said again, more confidently. "Not the poison of a snake nor the powrie dwarves could kill you."

"No, my liege, I am—"

"You are Callen Duwornay, and that is your daughter," Prydae interrupted. He looked back to Cadayle, at her curves, as images of that long-ago night began to stir within him. He remembered Callen in the firelight—remembered her looking exactly as this young woman now appeared to him. He remembered her curves, and the regrets he had that he would never bed her; and as that last thought played in his mind, he felt a stirring in his loins.

"That one," he said breathlessly, pointing to Cadayle. "She comes to Castle Pryd."

"What of the old wench?" asked one of the soldiers moving into the room past the laird.

Prydae fixed his gaze upon Callen, who seemed too afraid to say anything at that terrible moment.

"What do you know of the Highwayman?" Prydae asked sharply.

"She knows nothing!" Cadayle blurted, and Prydae turned a fierce scowl upon her.

"But you do," he said.

"My liege, I will tell you everything I know," Cadayle pleaded. "But please, do not hurt my ma. She's done nothing. She knows nothing. She's innocent. Please, my liege."

Prydae motioned with his head, and Bannagran dragged Cadayle from the room as the other two soldiers descended upon Callen. Only when Cadayle was long out of sight did Prydae turn on the woman.

"How you survived is of no concern to me," he said. "I admire it, I would say."

"Please, gentle Laird Prydae, do not harm my girl," Callen said, her voice a whimper, her body seemingly broken by the weight of it all.

"Harm her? Nothing could be further from my intentions, Callen Duwornay."

Callen began to cry.

"My liege?" asked one of the soldiers flanking her.

"Give her to Bernivvigar," Prydae said, turning and exiting, hardly seeming to care about Callen. "Perhaps he will be merciful, perhaps not. It matters not at all to me."

The woman, too broken by the suddenness of it all, by the

shock of being discovered and the horror of having her daughter so unceremoniously dragged away, offered no resistance, offered nothing at all, as the two men hoisted her up. She didn't, couldn't, walk as they started out, but that hardly seemed to matter.

They just dragged her.

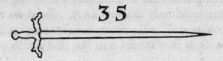

35

THE DOWNWARD SPIRAL

He stayed near the edges of town as the sun climbed in the eastern sky. He knew that he should return to the chapel, knew that he was taking a giant risk in remaining out and about. The monks would go to his room when they noticed that he was not doing his daily chores.

But none of that mattered to Bransen now; nothing beyond the reality of Garibond's death mattered. He couldn't believe the tale those living in what had once been his home had told him. He couldn't imagine that Master Bathelais, scowling as he often was, could be so despicably cruel as to have murdered a man as fine as Garibond. And what of Brother Reandu? Perhaps Reandu wasn't as powerful in the order back then as he was now, but certainly he would have protested the execution. It made no sense to Bransen as he wandered through the shadows under the many trees that marked the outskirts of Pryd Town, and yet, he found that he could not deny that which was obvious.

The man at the campfire had Garibond's knife. The people in his house were sincere, and why would they lie, given that such a lie might well mark their doom at the hands of this masked stranger who had come banging on their door? Bransen knew that they couldn't be telling the truth, that Garibond couldn't be dead, and certainly not by the hands of the brothers who had been his protectors all these years. And yet he knew that they certainly were speaking honestly. He had seen it in their faces.

At one cluster of trees, the weary young man plopped down in the shade and leaned back against a white birch. He tried to sort through every memory he had of every encounter even remotely relating to Garibond these past ten years. He remembered Brother Reandu's face on the one occasion when he had mentioned his father, the initial shock Reandu had shown, the obvious discomfort behind his stuttered responses.

But what did it all mean? If Garibond was dead, murdered by the brothers of Blessed Abelle, what did it all mean to Bransen and for Bransen?

A myriad of emotions rolled through him, everything ranging from anger to despair to the feeling that he had to run and hide somewhere, somewhere dark and deep, where no one would ever find him. All the confidence of the Highwayman flew from him, and he felt again the helpless little boy he had been. But what did it matter, after all? He thought again of his absence at the chapel, and of the implications should he be discovered, and he shrugged them away. How could he go back there, knowing the truth? He would have to face Master Bathelais and Brother Reandu. He would have to demand the truth from them, though he already knew it, in his heart at least. And then what? What could he say to them? What explanation could they possibly offer that would make any difference to the realities of their actions? For Bransen knew Garibond's heart as well as he knew his own, and if that man was a heretic in the eyes of the brothers of Abelle, then the brothers of Abelle were simply entirely wrong.

Bransen found a stream of sunlight flowing in through an opening in the trees, and he lay down, staring up at the fiery orb. He wanted the rays to permeate his corporeal form, to cleanse him of the impurities and anxieties, to empty him of his rage and his pain. He closed his eyes, and exhaustion overcame him.

He knew at once, when he awoke, that the day was nearing its end, and that any hope he might hold of sneaking into the chapel unnoticed was long lost. Instinctively, he began concocting possible explanations and excuses to explain the absence of the Stork.

But then he stopped himself, coming to understand clearly that he truly had no intention of ever returning to the chapel as the Stork, of serving the wretched brothers of Abelle ever again. He would go back, perhaps, but as the Highwayman, formidable and angry and demanding the entire truth of Garibond's fate.

He wasn't ready to travel that mental course, and he winced against the tear in his heart. He wasn't ready. Not yet.

But what was he to do? Bransen glanced to the west and the lowering sun, its rim just beginning to brush the horizon. The world seemed so huge to him and so imposing. And he felt so small and so empty, without anywhere to go, without anyone on whom he could lean his weary frame.

No, that wasn't true, he realized, and before he even sorted out the emotion, his feet were already moving, propelling him to the south and west, toward the house of the one person in all the world Bransen felt he could still trust.

But when he got there, Cadayle was not at home. Nor was her mother, and the broken door spoke volumes to Bransen as he hesitantly stepped across the threshold and into the dark house.

He knew she wasn't there. Her smell wasn't there, the freshness she brought wherever she walked wasn't there, leaving the place dark and cold and empty. His eyes adjusted to the dim light and he slowly and deliberately scanned the room, afraid as his gaze roamed over every inch of space that he would find the body of his beloved.

Nothing was amiss, save the broken door. He saw no signs of struggle, no blood.

But they were gone.

Bransen's breath began to come in heaves, as he steadied himself and strengthened his resolve. He had come here thinking to lean on Cadayle; now he began to understand that it was she who likely needed him.

He would not, could not, fail her.

He turned and realized his error immediately as he found a pair of iron swords pointing at his throat.

"Easy now, Highwayman," one of the soldiers said.

The Highwayman noticed a third and then a fourth soldier moving around the sides of the small house.

"We knew you'd return, and now you're fairly caught," said the other, and he prodded his sword forward menacingly. "Laird Prydae will be speaking with you."

"Indeed," the Highwayman replied, the irony lost on the pair. He brought his hands up, palms out, in apparent surrender.

And then his foot flashed up, before him; and though the soldiers were but inches from him, so nimble was the Highwayman, so in control of his every movement, that his foot struck unerringly into the face of one, then the second, so quickly that neither registered the movement but just felt the sudden jolt.

Both staggered a step, though the blows were not heavy. It was no more than a momentary distraction, but that was all the Highwayman needed. Before his flashing foot even came back to the ground, his other leg propelled him backward, putting some distance between them, and in the same fluid movement, he drew his fabulous sword.

The soldiers hardly realized what had happened, but found themselves facing a swordsman with a blade twice as long as their short iron weapons.

One moved fast, coming forward before the Highwayman could bring that amazing sword to proper angle—so he hoped.

With a sudden surge, the Highwayman slashed down diagonally, driving the soldier's sword low and wide. A reversal brought his elbow smashing into the man's face. The Highwayman changed his angle so that the pommel of his sword connected squarely with the attacker's nose, shattering it. The man was out on his feet, but as the Highwayman squared up again, he launched a left hook that sent the unconscious soldier flying away.

Even as the man fell, the Highwayman came forward. The

second soldier, obviously unsure, waved his sword around defensively.

He was too slow, and the Highwayman's blade slipped past, screeching as its tip connected with the man's bronze breastplate. A subtle twist and turn snapped the blade up, forcing the soldier to lean backward fast to avoid getting his face creased.

The enraged Highwayman pressed the attack, turning his sword and using it to keep the soldier's weapon at bay while he plowed forward, pushing the man right over. The soldier hit the ground and rolled immediately, trying to get up, but the Highwayman crossed to the side and kicked him in the face, once and then again. As the man flattened on the ground, the Highwayman stamped hard on the back of his neck, stilling him.

Then the Highwayman turned right, sword leading the way. He meant only to deflect the stabbing spear coming at him from the charging soldier, but his sword sheared the spear in half and scraped the man's breastplate, opening his throat as he came forward, unable to stop in time.

The soldier staggered past, clutching at the gushing blood, and fell to his knees and then to his face in the dirt.

The Highwayman had no time to concern himself with the man. Not then, for he completed his circuit and fell into a crouch facing the fourth and last attacker.

The soldier skidded to a stop, clearly terrified. He threw his sword to the ground and lifted his hands in surrender.

The Highwayman came forward suddenly, sword setting itself right on the top edge of the man's breastplate, poised to drive through his throat.

"Where is she?" the Highwayman demanded.

The man shook his head, looking stupid and out of his mind with fear.

"Cadayle—the young woman who lives here," the Highwayman demanded. "She was taken! You tell me where, or my sword will free your ugly head from your shoulders!"

"I do not know!" the man cried.

"You lie!" the sword jabbed in, forcing a squeal from the man.

"No! No!" the man begged, and he began to cry. "Please do not kill me. A wife I have, and children. Please, I beg of you!"

The words, so full of sincerity and terror, hit the Highwayman and reminded him that these men, these soldiers, even the tax collectors, were more than a part of the oppression that weighed upon the people of Pryd. They were individuals, real people with real lives and families and concerns.

But those concerns found no real hold on the Highwayman in that moment of outrage, overwhelmed by his fears for Cadayle and her mother and by his frustration at the loss of his beloved Garibond. He came forward suddenly and forcefully, bowling the soldier over onto his back and setting his sword once more at the man's throat.

"Your family will bring your body to the brothers of Abelle to be put cold in the ground or to the Samhaists for burning," he warned. "I'll not ask again."

"They took her and her mother," the soldier gasped. "I know not where they took the girl, but the mother was given to Bernivvigar. She will be tried and killed this night by the adder or the flames."

The Highwayman moved his sword tip back and stepped away from the man, his thoughts spinning. He glanced to the west, where the sun was almost gone, then back to the east and south, toward where he knew Bernivvigar held his audiences, his trials, and his murders.

He looked back down at the soldier, still crying, still lying there with his hands up defensively.

"Collect your companions and herd them into the house," he instructed, and when the man didn't immediately move, the Highwayman kicked him hard in the leg. "Now!"

The man scrambled to his feet and did as he was bade, while Bransen moved fast to the soldier whose throat he had cut. He turned the man over, fearing the worst, and was relieved to see that he was not dead, and that the wound, though still bleeding, wasn't gushing forth blood any longer. Still, it was a vicious gash, one that would need tending.

Bransen brought one hand to the wound, the other to the soul stone set under his mask on his forehead. He recalled the lessons of the Book of Jhest, the Healing Hands, and fell even deeper into the swirl of the gray gemstone. He felt warmth in his hands and was amazed to see the wound sealing. He stopped short, though, for he found that the effort was taking from his own control, from the solid line of his own *chi*. A wave of dizziness came over him, followed by a profound weariness.

But he shook it away, reminding himself of Cadayle. With a growl, he rose from the soldier and called to the man's companion to hurry up.

A short while later, the Highwayman ran off, leaving the four soldiers bound and gagged inside the house's dark walls.

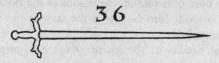

36

BUZZING IN HIS HEAD

The spinning thoughts followed Bransen away from Cadayle's house, but as he met every different emotion with the reality that Cadayle and her mother were in trouble, anything other than simple rage was pushed away. Step by step, one thought by one, Bransen's mind became focused, crystalline clear, sharpening and narrowing his vision so much that it seemed to him as if he were looking down a long and straight tunnel. The tumult within his mind became something more like an internal buzzing, as if the top end of his life's line of energy were spitting jolts into his head.

Moving with a singular focus and complete determination, the Highwayman increased his pace, running purposefully but without any clear idea where he was going. And then he arrived, his head thrumming, the edges of his vision limned in red. Hardly formulating any plans, hardly considering any move he might make, the Highwayman looked out through a tangle of twigs and logs at the front of a tall, flat stone.

The buzzing did not relent.

Sometime later, he felt the heat growing around him, but it was as if the flames were not in proximity to him, but were distant. Without any conscious decision, the Highwayman's mind went to the drawer in the desk in the room above his hole. His fingers began to wriggle as if he were rolling a small stone in his palm, but he wasn't even aware of the movement. He felt the power of the gemstone as if he were holding a serpentine in his hand, though of course he was not. But somewhere within the buzz of his mind, the lessons of the Book of Jhest resonated, showing him the way to the same energy the magical stone provided.

And he needed it, though he wasn't even aware of the flames leaping all around him, devouring the twigs and logs. He sat there and stared out at the Stone of Judgment, peering around the yellow sheets of fire that flared barely inches from his face.

He knew the time drew near. He could hear the voices of people gathering around the bonfire, could see flashes of movement through the red shield at the edges of his vision. But they didn't matter. All that mattered was the stone before him and the man he knew would soon appear atop it.

The sight of the great bonfire roaring to life elicited horrible memories in poor Callen, a clear reminder of that night so long ago, a night that she had hoped she would never, ever have to recall. The crowd was comprised of different people but it all seemed the same to Callen, the jibes, the spit, the almost gleeful shouts.

As if in a dream, she allowed the guards to shove her out to a spot halfway between the fire and the large, flat stone. Bernivvigar's stone.

The hoots behind her told her that the snake handler had arrived with the sack and the snake, and Callen felt her knees go weak. Darkness filled her thoughts, memories of the confining sack, and the slithering serpent crawling over her, sharp fangs hooking into her tender flesh and pumping in their deadly, burning poison.

With a growl of defiance, Callen dismissed those recollections and divorced herself from her terror. This was not about her; she was not important. And so she would die this night, and for a crime that she had committed two decades before, a crime of passion and not cruelty, a misjudgment of her heart and nothing of malice.

But so be it, because this wasn't about her.

This was about her poor daughter. Nothing else mattered to Callen. Not her pain, not the viper that would await her in the sack, not her own death.

Were her previous crimes now being visited upon Cadayle? Callen knew that her daughter had played a dangerous game and had, in fact, brought this tragedy upon them both. But Callen couldn't so easily dismiss her own guilt. Had she passed more than her appearance to her daughter? Was there something in them that allowed for such mistakes of the heart? The irony of it all wasn't lost on Callen, because, indeed, hadn't Cadayle's foolishness with this outlaw Highwayman been much the same thing as Callen's behavior when she had cuckolded her husband?

Strangely, a wistful smile made its way onto her face as she considered that long-ago encounter. She had been given in marriage to a man she did not love and had been offered no say in the matter. That was often the way of things in Pryd, in all Honce, where practicality almost always overruled love. Her affair had not worked out well for her, or for her lover, but did she really feel that it had been an error? That affair had produced Cadayle, the beauty of her life. How could she consider that a mistake?

The wistful smile disappeared in the blink of an eye. Cadayle, the beauty of her life, was in trouble, likely to be executed, and there was nothing, nothing, that Callen could do about it. Cadayle had allowed her heart to lead her into a place of beauty, perhaps, into the warmth of love and the tingling expectation of merely seeing the Highwayman. But it had also led her into danger, a deep and deadly hole from which there seemed no escape.

Callen didn't know who to blame; Callen didn't care about blame. All that mattered was that she was never going to see her Cadayle again and that her daughter, her beautiful child, was in danger.

And there was nothing she could do.

Her contemplations fell away as a tall and straight figure walked out to the edge of the flat rock, towering over the gathering, seeming identical to the man he had been twenty years before and certainly with as much, and more, power than he had then commanded. At his appearance, the crowd fell into a fearful silence.

Bernivvigar spent a moment surveying them, his cold gaze freezing with fear any it fell upon. He nodded to the side, and she heard the scramble as men behind her began to ready the sack and the viper.

"Callen Duwornay," the old wretch began, not a quiver in his powerful voice, "we gather to execute the sentence imposed two decades ago. You did not admit your guilt then. You were given your chance to speak, though you said nothing. Now, we will not ask you again. You are doomed by your harlotry, and may the Ancient Ones forgive us all for delaying their proper justice and the gift of your corpse."

He snapped a wave in her direction, and the men flanking her yanked her back so forcefully that they pulled her from her feet.

But they stopped abruptly, and Callen followed their looks to Bernivvigar; and then, with them and with all the others, she followed Bernivvigar's gaze to the bonfire, rustling and shaking and taking on a life of its own.

Callen's eyes widened in shock as she saw the dark form step forth. Surely the old Samhaist had summoned a demon! One of the dreaded Ancient Ones had come to Honce to take her body away!

He saw the tall form of the old Samhaist but only in a strange silhouette, for sheets of fire rose up before his eyes. Even with his understanding and mimicry of the powers of the magical serpentine stone, Bransen realized that he could not remain within the inferno. If his concentration faltered for just an instant, the fires would set his hair and clothing ablaze and consume him.

But he did not falter. He thought of nothing but Cadayle, conjuring an image of her at the mercy of Laird Prydae. The buzzing in his head didn't lessen—quite the opposite—and even with the fiery yellow glow before his eyes, there remained that red haze at the sides of his vision, focusing him, directing the course of his rage.

That focus now was the solitary figure before him. Bransen stood up and the pile trembled, fiery branches falling down before him.

He thought of Garibond and the hideous wound inflicted on him by Bernivvigar, and the buzzing in his head intensified even more, like an angry bee trapped within him, prodding him with its sound and its stinger. Bransen's breath came in sudden gasps; he felt as if he would scream. His lungs burned as if they were on fire, as indeed he knew that they soon would be!

But he found his focus again, and he forced himself forward through the fire, ignoring the burning branches, ignoring the painful licks of flame. None of it mattered. None of his discomfort, his pain, his potential death mattered. All that mattered was that figure, now the focus of his ire, the symbol of all the injustices and all the hatred, of all the bullying and all the torture.

There he stood before Bransen, high on his rock.

Bransen crashed through the side of the bonfire. He heard the screams all around him; out of the corner of his left eye he saw Callen gasp and fall back, along with the guards supporting her.

But he strode forward, clearing the edge of the bonfire, stepping into the open in all his Highwayman glory right before Bernivvigar the Samhaist, right before the gasps and wide eyes of all the gathering.

He heard them crying out and whispering, "Highwayman."

They didn't matter. Nothing mattered, except that one figure.

"You dare interrupt this sacred ceremony?" old Bernivvigar roared down from on high. "You dare?"

Bransen drew the sword from his rope belt, but even without the weapon, the murderous intent was very clear in his eyes.

He strode toward the rock, and Bernivvigar surprised him, for the old man did not back away, did not show fear.

"To challenge me is to challenge the Ancient Ones!" he proclaimed, and he lifted his skinny arms up before him and uttered a quick incantation, the likes of which Bransen had never before heard. Bernivvigar's voice sounded like guttural grunting, but in a rhythm, as if someone were rolling stones down a jagged rocky slope in perfect timing.

Bransen didn't care. He drove forward, thinking to run up to the base of the stone and leap atop it, cutting the old wretch down in a single movement.

But he wasn't running fast, was suddenly barely moving, as if he were wading through deep mud. He glanced down at his feet, to see the grass itself reaching over his soft black shoes, grasping at him, knotting above the top of his feet. With a determined tug, Bransen tore one foot free, then the other. He swung his sword down in frustration, slicing a line in the grass, but any freedom he found was temporary as Bernivvigar's weeds and grass slapped and grabbed at him.

And the man was still chanting, and was no longer before him, Bransen realized. He followed the voice to the side and saw that Bernivvigar was standing on the grass not too far away, chanting and leering at him crazily, hungrily.

"Too long has the wrath of the Ancient Ones been bound inside the earth!" Bernivvigar cried; all about him, the people fell back in fear, for his voice was no longer that of a man, no longer that of a mortal creature. Somehow, Bernivvigar had gone beyond the bounds of his corporeal body, beyond the reach of the lesser beings about him.

Bransen, too, nearly swooned under the power of that voice.

"Feel the fires of the Ancient Ones!" Bernivvigar proclaimed, and he thrust both his hands out before him, his old, gnarled, and twisted fingers sparking and trailing wisps of smoke.

Bransen braced himself, falling once more into his concentration to deny the expected fires. But Bernivvigar was not aiming his strange magic Bransen's way, at least not directly. The ground beneath the Highwayman's feet began to slide and churn, and Bransen looked down in terror, noting that what had seemed ordinary grass was now smoldering with swirling red lava!

He didn't know what to do; he didn't know how to react. He scanned his memory of the Book of Jhest, looking for some clue, some hint as to what this old wretch was doing to him.

And then he heard a cry, sharp and shrill and full of a primal, tearing energy. His gaze slipped to Callen, who was on the ground on her back, the deadly viper coiled and ready to strike, just inches from her face.

Bransen wanted to call out to her, to tell her not to move. He wanted to leap before her, to take the strike if necessary, for he believed that with his training, he could withstand a snake's poison.

But the buzzing screamed in his head, a nest of bees, it now seemed. He knew that his shoes were smoking, knew that his feet were blistering, but he felt no pain: not even the bite of Bernivvigar's molten fires could penetrate the wall of his rage.

Without thinking, Bransen jerked his arm up and then snapped it forward, throwing his sword as if it were a spear.

He heard Bernivvigar's gasp, and the incantation stopped, before he registered that his sword had struck right through the Samhaist's chest.

Bernivvigar staggered backward, but did not fall to the ground. It hardly mattered to Bransen, for he charged at the man, in a great leap that brought him clear of the lava. His arms worked like the hooves of a charging horse, pumping and pounding, smashing Bernivvigar in the ribs, but strangely Bernivvigar was not grunting under the blows, and his skin seemed not to give at all beneath the weight of Bransen's punches, nor did his old bones crack in protest.

Bransen looked up to see Bernivvigar staring down at him and smiling, as if Bransen were but a child, an inconvenience.

Bernivvigar lifted a hand and balled it tightly, and lightning-like energy crackled from his fist.

Bransen slugged him hard in the jaw, snapping the old man's head to the side. But Bernivvigar kept smiling and punched back. Though Bransen blocked the blow, he felt the jolt of energy surge through his body, stiffening him. Only his studies saved him, for he instinctively arched his body in just the right manner to serve as a conduit for the jolt, so that it ran down to the ground and left him relatively unscathed.

He punched again, and Bernivvigar swung.

Bransen ducked, leaning low, and with perfect balance, managed to kick his foot against the hilt of the sword protruding from Bernivvigar's chest.

A wince broke through Bernivvigar's mask of calm and confidence; and Bransen snapped off three quick kicks, all smacking the hilt and changing the angle of the blade.

Now the Highwayman found his rhythm, coming forward suddenly and popping off a series of short punches at the Samhaist. None connected heavily, and none would have done much damage anyway. But that wasn't the point.

Bransen was setting his feet; balance was the measure, he knew.

Bernivvigar swung again, and Bransen, knowing better than to block the enchanted fist, ducked. But even though the fist did not connect, it sent a jolt of lightning into him.

But that didn't knock the focused Bransen off balance, that didn't diffuse the buzzing.

He stepped sideways at Bernivvigar, grabbing the sword hilt, and accepted another powerful jolt and then another as he stepped away, turning his back as he tore his sword free.

Bernivvigar cackled mockingly behind him, but Bransen didn't hear it, didn't hear anything but the anger in his head.

Bransen started left, reversed the sword flow suddenly, and spun back right so quickly that Bernivvigar was still looking the other way when Bransen came whirling around, the sword high and horizontal, level with the old Samhaist's neck.

High into the air flew Bernivvigar's head, still wearing a smile of calm confidence.

Bransen was already moving the other way when the body crumpled behind him, when the head bounced down to the ground with a wet thump.

He dropped his sword and slowed his movement as he approached Callen and the snake, motioning at her to keep still. The snake hadn't struck yet, and it seemed as confused and overwhelmed as everyone else in the area—now far fewer people than when Bransen had emerged from the bonfire!

The buzzing continued, but within it, Bransen found a place of calm as he slipped between Callen and the viper, moving low and staring the frightened snake in the eye.

He moved his right hand across before him, and the snake's head swayed in concert.

His left hand snapped out, quicker than an adder's strike, seizing the creature right behind its triangular head.

Bransen allowed the snake to wrap itself around his left arm as he stood up, offering his right hand to the woman and pulling her to her feet.

He blew in the snake's face several times, and it seemed to calm. He gently set it down, where it rushed into the forest.

"You and you!" the Highwayman called to the two soldiers who had dragged Callen onto the field.

The men looked at each other and both edged away, as if thinking to run. But Bransen lifted his sword as if to throw it, and both froze in their tracks.

"On your head—if any harm comes to this woman, I will see you dead. All of you!" he shouted in rage, spinning to encompass the crowd. "Any who harm this woman will feel the wrath of the Highwayman! That wrath is boundless, I assure you!" He turned back to the two frightened soldiers, locking their gazes with his own. "I know your faces now. I know."

He turned to Callen. "Where is Cadayle?"

"Laird Prydae took her," she replied, her voice and body trembling. "He took her!"

"To the castle!" someone in the crowd called out.

"I seen him drag her in," said another.

Bransen looked all around, amazed once more at the reaction to the Highwayman. He pulled Callen close and hugged her tightly. "On my life, she will not be harmed," he whispered, then he turned and ran off, heading straight for Castle Pryd.

But then he veered as he saw the other structure beside the great castle.

The place he had called home for a decade.

The place, he now knew, that had never been his home.

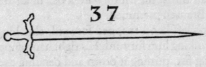

37

THEIR PET IDIOT

He sprinted through the streets of Pryd Town, chased only by the calls of those who spotted the man in the distinctive black outfit. He charged into the courtyard of Chapel Pryd, hardly slowing and brushing aside the one young, startled monk who made a move as if to try to stop him.

The main doors were open, but the Highwayman, knowing this building intimately, moved to the right-hand wall and to the small door set at its far end. This one, too, was unlocked, and Bransen charged through. He crossed the room above his own dungeon, to the door to the main corridor, and paused there, hearing voices in the hallway beyond and calls echoing.

With a growl, a memory of Callen at Bernivvigar's stone, and a mental image of the pains that Cadayle might then be suffering, Bransen kicked the door open and leaped out into the hall.

A pair of brothers confronted him at once, one holding high his shaking fist—clenching gemstones, Bransen understood—and the other waving an iron short sword, so ill cared for and infrequently used that it showed rust all along its black blade.

"You would be wise to escort me to Master Bathelais," he warned, his voice even, calm, and controlled. "And if you try to use that gemstone, I assure you that your head will bounce to the floor beside it."

The man thrust his fist forward a bit, in an attempt to be menacing, Bransen presumed.

Bransen's left hand snapped forward, clutching the man's wrist and yanking him forward. His right hand cupped over the gem-holding fist, turning it down and bending the wrist. The man shrieked in pain, all strength fleeing from his hand, and Bransen shoved him back—and now it was Bransen's fist that held the gemstone.

Even as he pushed the monk away, the other, inspired by the sudden action, perhaps, leaped forward and plunged his sword at the intruder's chest. A slight turn by Bransen had the blade going harmlessly by, and Bransen locked the man's sword arm tight against his side and sent his free hand, his fist balled, crunching into the monk's nose. He pumped his arm three times, connecting solidly with every punch, then brought his knee up hard into the poor man's groin. As the man lurched over, Bransen let go of his trapped sword arm and hit him with a right cross that spun him to the side and slammed him hard against the corridor wall, where he folded down in a heap.

The other young monk stood there transfixed and obviously terrified. That fear only heightened when the Highwayman snapped his magnificent sword out, putting its gleaming tip close to the trembling monk's bare throat.

"To Bathelais, at once, or I leave you dead on the floor," the Highwayman promised, and to his surprise, Bransen realized that he meant every word.

The terrified young monk scurried away, Bransen close behind. Bransen paused just long enough to turn and throw the gemstone at the head of the groaning, prostrate monk.

"What is the meaning of this?" Master Bathelais shouted, leaping from his chair when the door of his audience room burst open and a younger brother came stumbling in, to fall hard on the floor. Bathelais's eyes narrowed, but he did not back down as a second figure entered, one dressed in black clothes that proclaimed his identity.

Bathelais was not alone; Reandu, sitting across the hearth from him, also rose, sucking in his breath with the movement.

Closer to the hearth, Father Jerak sat slumped in a chair, appearing oblivious to it all. One other brother was there, an attendant to the infirm Jerak. He had been standing just inside the door and to the side, though now he faded farther from the door, inching out toward his master and Brother Reandu.

"You dare to enter this holy place?" Bathelais said, and he squared his jaw and straightened his shoulders.

"It is no place that I have not been many times before," the Highwayman responded.

Bathelais stared at him hard, searching for a clue, but he needn't have bothered, for in that moment, Bransen reached up with his free hand and pulled the mask, and the gemstone, from his head.

"Do you not recognize your pet idiot, Master Bathelais?" Bransen asked.

Bathelais's composure couldn't hold any longer, and he widened his eyes, staggered back half a step, and nearly toppled over his chair. Across from him, Brother Reandu gasped and fell back into his chair, and the other monk cried out, "Stork!"

"It is imposs—it is impossible," Bathelais stammered, and the irony of listening to him stuttering was not lost on Bransen. "How? How can this be?"

Bransen came forward suddenly, sword tip lunging close to Bathelais's throat. "I have not time for explanations."

"We took you in!" Bathelais roared back. "We showed you mercy when—"

"Shut up," Bransen said, and he prodded the deadly sword ahead. "Mercy?" He spat the word, and then spat upon the floor at Bathelais's feet.

"You dare—" Bathelais started to protest, but he learned then that a sword tip against his throat was a sure way to silence him.

"Mercy?" Bransen echoed again. "You allow me to clean your chamber pots, and I am to fall to my knees in gratitude?" As Bathelais started to respond, Bransen poked his throat again with the sword, and then snapped the blade across, in line with Reandu, when he began to answer.

"None of it matters," Bransen explained. "I need you now, and you will help me."

"You are a fool," Bathelais managed, before Bransen prodded him again.

"An idiot, perhaps, if I was to believe the opinion of Master Bathelais," Bransen replied. "But it matters not. None of it. You are going to help me now, to repay me for the murder of Garibond Womak."

Bathelais's eyes widened so much that Bransen wondered if they would just roll out of their sockets.

"Yes, I know all about it," he said. "I know what you did soon after taking me in as your slave."

"He was in possession—" Brother Reandu started.

"Shut up," came the interruption. "I know everything there is to say on that matter, and the only reason that your heads are not rolling on the floor now is because I need you. Fail me in any way, and you die and all of your brethren in this chapel die also. Every one."

He studied Father Jerak as he finished—the man who had been in charge of the chapel on the day when Garibond had been murdered. Bransen thought to go over and cut the man's throat to show these others how serious he was, and he did take a step in that direction. But just one step, then the Highwayman stopped and pushed the thought out of his mind. To what gain?

Having passed that test, Bransen turned back to Bathelais and noted that the man shifted his glance, just briefly, to glance over Bransen's shoulder.

Alerted, the Highwayman dipped suddenly and lashed out with his foot, catching the creeping monk in the stomach and doubling him over. As soon as his foot came back to the floor, Bransen spun, his other foot connecting squarely with the side of the lurching monk's face, sending him flying away, crashing over a table and into a wall, where he lay very still.

Both Reandu and Bathelais started for Bransen at that moment, but they hadn't a chance and were backed again by the gleaming tip of the leveled sword.

"I am long past mercy, Master Bathelais," Bransen warned. "Hesitate again, and a monk will die." He pointed his sword at Father Jerak. "Hesitate again, and *he* will die."

"What do you want?" Master Bathelais asked.

"You and you," Bransen added, waving the sword at Reandu, "and the Stork are going to pay a visit to Laird Prydae."

As he spoke, Bransen pulled the black armband from his sword arm, revealing his birthmark, and began unfastening the black silk shirt.

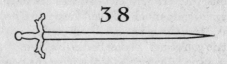

38

THE WATERFALL AT
RIVER'S END

"You should not be here, not at this time," the sentry at the gatehouse of Castle Pryd said to the three unexpected visitors late that night. The man looked at the two monks—for all purposes, the two leaders of the Church in Pryd Holding—and then scrunched up his face in obvious disgust as he turned to regard the third visitor, the Stork, swaying and drooling and leaning on a long, narrow canelike implement that was wrapped in cloth.

"We have information regarding the man who has put this castle and town in a state of frenzy," Brother Reandu replied, and Bransen did not miss the not-so-subtle look that Bathelais shot him.

The sentry perked up at that, and stepped aside, calling to his companions to hold his post so that he could escort the trio into the keep.

The sentry and the monks huddled as they crossed the open courtyard, for a shower came up then, suddenly, with a crackle of lightning splitting the dark sky and big heavy drops splashing down.

Bransen shambled along behind them, trying his best to mimic the walk that had been his natural step all his life. He held his soul stone firmly in hand, his other hand tight on his "cane," which was, of course, his sword. He lolled his head and thrust each hip out before waving the respective leg forward. He babbled and moaned and let the drool flow from his mouth. In that moment, despite all the vital events that were churning about him, it occurred to Bransen how unpleasant a creature he was, how awkward this damaged physical coil appeared. Surely the outside world cringed at the sight of him, and while he did not relinquish his disdain for that shallow and unsympathetic attitude, he understood it more fully now. That thought only made him appreciate more acutely the one person who had fought against that flow, only made him realize the depth of kindness Cadayle had shown to him all these years.

He didn't let the steeling of his determination to rescue her interfere with his awkward gait. His focus held firm, and he kept to the course.

They entered the well-guarded keep at the rear of the castle, and those guards who met them moved back at the unexpected sight of the Stork. Bransen looked up at them and smiled stupidly, his head rolling, and that only intensified their disgust and drove them further aside.

"The laird is . . . engaged," the sentry reported back to the monks a moment later.

Bransen gave a grunt and secretly nudged Master Bathelais.

"This is more important," the monk replied, offering a quick glance back at Stork. "Take us to Laird Prydae at once."

"It would not be wise to interrupt—" the sentry started to protest, but Reandu cut him short.

"Do you begin to understand the importance of this?" the younger monk snapped. "The Highwayman is within our reach, right now, and any hesitation will cost us this one chance we have to put things aright."

"We understand fully," the man retorted. "The death of Bernivvigar is no small thing!"

"The death of Bernivvigar?" both Bathelais and Reandu asked together.

"His head lopped from his shoulders this very night by the Highwayman," the sentry explained. "He appeared out of the Samhaist fire, as if summoned from hell itself, so said the onlookers—half the town saw it! He walked through Bernivvigar's magic, and not even the Ancient Ones themselves could stop him!"

"Bernivvigar dead this very night," Master Bathelais murmured, and both monks widened their eyes at that remarkable news; both turned again subtly to regard Bransen.

Bransen managed to slip them a look reminding them that they, too, could easily find such a fate this night.

"That only strengthens our need and desire to speak with Prydae!" Bathelais said suddenly, with great animation. "Admit us at once, you fool, before all the holding is destroyed by the hands of this outlaw!"

The sentry babbled some protest, but he eventually led the monks past the surprised and curious looks of the other soldiers. A grand stairway swept up from the ground floor to a balcony that lined the left hand wall. From the other end of that balcony, the stairs climbed to the higher levels of the tower.

The foursome climbed the first flight to the balcony and started along, with the sentry pausing at the door in the middle of the wall and knocking hard as the monks and Stork moved past.

Bransen turned as he heard the familiar voice booming behind him, to see a man well known to him come out of the room. Bannagran gave him only a cursory and disgusted glance, then turned to the soldier; but Bransen could not tear his eyes from the imposing warrior.

The monks moved away from him, but he didn't notice.

Brother Reandu called for him to keep up, but he didn't notice.

Finally, he broke the spell and turned, just as Master Bathelais swung around, fist up high. "Bannagran, to arms!" he cried. "The Stork is your Highwayman! Seize him!"

Bransen's eyes went wide in the face of the deceit, and he lifted his cane and waved it in tight circles to free its of its cloth casing. Or at least, he started to, for then a streaking bolt of lightning erupted from Master Bathelais's hand and slammed him hard in the chest, throwing him backward.

Bransen heard the cries of Bannagran and the sentry, heard the protests of Brother Reandu, and heard most of all, the continuing fury of Master Bathelais. He collected his wits and his focus immediately—he knew that he had to—and fell inside himself, visualizing the line of his *chi*. That spark of energy, that focus of life, was exactly the attack point of the lightning, as Bransen could see by the dispersing flares. He tightened his focus and forced his *chi* back into alignment. He used his Jhesta Tu understanding and his soul stone, countering the effects of the jolt.

And he did it all in the blink of an eye.

On instinct, Bransen dropped low, and the sentry who was charging him from behind flipped right over his bent back and tumbled down, but not before intercepting Master Bathelais's second lightning blast.

Bransen went around and thought to stand to meet the charge of Bannagran, but then stayed low instead, kicking one foot right into the leading foot of the warrior.

Bannagran tripped off to the side of the moving Bransen and stumbled forward, but recovered quickly, purposely running into the wall to secure his balance. He spun around, ready to meet Bransen's charge.

But Bransen wasn't charging. He hadn't come here to do battle with Bannagran or with the monks. He hadn't come here to exact revenge or to punish anyone.

He remembered all that keenly with battle so clear before him, and instead of charging forward to stab Bannagran or to thrust his sword into the treacherous Master Bathelais, the Highwayman leaped onto the railing of the balcony and then sprang from it just ahead of another of Bathelais's searing lightning bolts.

Bransen's muscles propelled him up and out, as he lifted his *chi* to lighten the resistance against that great leap, making it seem as much a flight as a jump. He soared across, catching the railing of the next ascending staircase and pulling himself over it in one fluid movement. He glanced back to see the commotion he had left behind: the man shivering on the floor from the sting of Bathelais's second lightning bolt; Bathelais shouting and pointing his way; Bannagran, with other soldiers now in his wake, running along the balcony to the base of the staircase.

Bransen ran to the top of the stairs and then a few steps along the next balcony before again leaping to the top of the railing and springing across, leaving his pursuit behind.

Below him, as Brother Reandu tended the wounded sentry, Master Bathelais watched that second flight with as much amusement as awe. He lifted his fist, holding the graphite gemstone, and followed the Highwayman's course.

"And now you die," the monk growled, thrusting his arm forward—or starting to, until something slammed against him hard, driving his arm across his chest.

With a great heave, Bathelais shoved back and extracted himself from the grasp of Brother Reandu. "What are you doing?" he demanded.

"Master, do not!" Reandu said. "He is just a boy."

"You idiot!" Bathelais growled, and he lifted his arm again. And again, Reandu crashed against him, defeating his aim.

"Brother!" Bathelais roared, and he swung back and shoved Reandu away. But Reandu came right back at him, wrestling him away from the ledge and toward the wall.

Bathelais turned as he fell back, yanking Reandu around him and slamming his attacker into that wall first, then crashed hard against him. Bathelais jumped back, pulling Reandu from the wall, then slammed Reandu into the wall once more.

"I warn you," Bathelais cried.

"This is not the way!" Reandu argued, his words popping out in an explosion of breath as Bathelais rammed him hard into the wall. Dazed, he hardly noticed as Bathelais let him go and whirled, rushing back to the railing.

All the world was spinning for Brother Reandu, all his

buried notions about right and wrong. Images of Stork flashed through his mind, of the boy's pleading with him to teach him to read, of the filth and disrespect the boy had long suffered at the hands of the "generous" brothers of Abelle.

He saw Bathelais lifting his arm to loose another lightning bolt, lifting the edges of his mouth in a smile that struck Reandu as very wicked.

He pushed himself out from the wall, shouting at Bathelais to stop. And indeed, the master did hesitate and half turned to regard Reandu's charge. Master Bathelais tried to get out of the way or to brace himself, but wasn't successful.

Reandu plowed into him, both of them going hard against the balcony rail, which buckled under their weight.

Bathelais tumbled over the edge and Reandu stood, waving his arms in a effort to keep from falling. He did manage to do that, then looked down in horror at his superior lying on his back on the lower floor, groaning and barely moving.

Out of the corner of his eye, as he leaped to the next balcony, Bransen saw the fall of Bathelais. It hardly registered because it hardly mattered to him. He saw a figure on the last balcony above, rushing through a doorway and heard from within a woman's cry.

The Highwayman leaped out and high, lifting his *chi*, lifting himself toward the heavens. He caught his balance on the railing of the top balcony just as the dark figure disappeared into the room and the door started to close. Two strides and a dive had him there in time, shouldering the door open before the locking bar could be secured, and Bransen tumbled into the room. He came up fast, kicking the door shut, the locking bar falling in place.

Bransen jumped up, his back to the door, his sword at the ready.

There stood Laird Prydae before him, stripped to the waist and easing behind the side of a great canopy bed. Bransen could have had him dead in one leap, he knew, but he had to hold, for on the other side of that bed stood Cadayle, wearing only a sheer nightdress, her hair disheveled, her face streaked with tears, and her head back awkwardly, twisting to avoid the knife that was firmly held at her throat.

Behind her, eyes gleaming with open hatred and a wildness that Bransen had never before witnessed, stood Rennarq.

"Could it be?" Rennarq rasped.

"Let her go," Bransen demanded.

"The Highwayman is this creature?" Laird Prydae asked, his voice full of mocking disbelief. "All my holding has held its breath in fear of this damaged, half-goblin . . . thing?"

Bransen kept his eyes locked on Cadayle, ignoring the insults, trying to find some way out. He thought of throwing his sword, but Rennarq had Cadayle locked tight as a shield, with only part of his face showing around her tresses.

"A dangerous little boy, now aren't you?" said Prydae, and he reached subtly toward his mattress, under which he always kept a dagger.

Bransen noted the move and pointed his sword at Prydae threateningly, but held his advance.

"He loves this one, my liege," Rennarq noted, and Bransen glanced the old man's way to see a wicked smile splayed across his wrinkled face. "Yet another victim claimed by the weakness of the heart."

Bransen steeled his expression at that.

"Is that not so?" Rennarq teased him. "Will you charge at me, brave Highwayman, and cut me to death? Will you slay the Laird of Pryd Holding? No doubt that is your desire, but is it above the price that such an action must cost?" As he finished, he slapped his free hand across Cadayle's forehead and pulled her head back, revealing more of her vulnerable neck and the dagger firmly pressed against her tender skin.

Bransen found it hard to draw breath.

He jumped, they all did, when something or someone slammed hard against the door behind him. The locking bar held, and the door did not burst open.

"My liege!" they heard Bannagran cry outside, and he began to bang hard on the heavy wooden door.

"I'll have your sword, Highwayman," Laird Prydae said, and he extended his hand.

Bransen didn't move, didn't breathe. He stared at his helpless love, who shook her head, or started to, before Rennarq tugged her head back viciously and pressed in the dagger.

"Be reasonable, boy," Laird Prydae went on. "Surrender your sword to me and I will let the woman live. Else she dies, and you will live with that image for the rest of your days, short though they will surely be."

Bransen looked at him, at his extended hand, though he was too far away for Bransen to hand him the blade.

"Come along now," Prydae prodded, motioning with his fingers. "Put it on the floor and slide it across to me."

"Let her go or you die!" Bransen growled.

"Do you think we are afraid of death, foolish boy?" Rennarq answered, stealing Bransen's bluster before the young man could even begin to gauge Laird Prydae's reaction to the threat. For when Bransen glanced back at Rennarq, he saw a wildness there that laughed at his threat and a determination that Cadayle's throat would soon be open wide. There was no hope for negotiation to be found in those dark and angry eyes, Bransen knew, whatever Prydae might say.

The pounding intensified against the door behind him. The buzzing in Bransen's head began anew.

"Your sword!" Prydae demanded sharply.

Bransen had no answers. Cadayle was doomed if he lunged for either the laird or Rennarq. He couldn't get to the old man quickly enough, and he knew without doubt that Rennarq would put his knife to deadly use without hesitation.

"Boy, on my word, the woman will live," Prydae shouted at him, above the crack of wood that now sounded behind Bransen, as if someone had taken an axe to the door. "Surrender your sword now, before my patience comes to its end!"

Bransen's breath came in gasps. He searched his thoughts and his recollections of the gemstones, but found no answers.

Because there were no answers.

He forced himself to stand straight, then bent and placed the sword on the ground and kicked it across to Laird Prydae.

Cadayle whimpered at the sight, and that, too, was cut short by another tug and press by Rennarq.

Bransen stared at the pair, hardly paying attention to Prydae who scooped up the fabulous sword and readied it.

"Now move away from the door," Prydae demanded, and another sharp rap and the crack of wood accentuated his words.

But Bransen hardly heard them, keeping his focus on his helpless love and on the wretch who held her and who seemed so full of glee at the thought of tearing out her beautiful throat. A spasm nearly knocked Bransen from his feet then, as his emotions threatened to break the concentration that allowed him to hold himself in check. He tightened his grip on the soul stone and forced himself, for Cadayle's sake, to regain his complete control.

His line of *chi* burned brightly within him, excited by anger and terror, vibrating and humming. He could see it clearly as he closed his eyes and looked inside.

"Move aside," he heard Prydae demand, "away from the door."

He kept his eyes closed, kept his focus on that line of burning energy. He brought his hands down together in front of him, cupped his free hand, and clenched the soul stone all the tighter. His *chi* was a tangible thing to him at that moment, a real line and not an imagined one, like a wire that held him together, like a strong cord that kept him upright.

Like a spear.

With a deep exhalation, Bransen fell even further into himself.

"I'll not tell you again, boy!" Prydae screamed, but Bransen didn't hear him.

Behind him the door broke apart under another heavy blow, but Bransen didn't hear it.

Another deep exhalation, and the young man pictured a

part of his life's energy blowing out from him, into his cupped hand. He collected it there, and felt its weight, felt its tingle.

"Move, boy!" Prydae screamed, distantly, it seemed to Bransen.

Cadayle's gasp sounded more keenly and more closely, but that, too, he pushed aside, as he breathed deeply yet again.

"Kill her!" he heard Prydae command.

Bransen's eyes opened, and he thrust his hands out toward Cadayle and Rennarq; and with that movement he threw his collected *chi*, a javelin of his life energy, a bolt of his inner strength.

Rennarq gave a gurgled cry as that tangible energy crashed into him, and his legs buckled, pulling Cadayle down behind him, hard to the floor.

Prydae leaped ahead with a shout, sword jabbing for Bransen's chest.

Bransen's left hand slapped the tip aside at the last moment and he turned to counter, but this was no novice he faced but a trained and seasoned warrior.

Prydae retracted the blade and thrust again, and though Bransen again managed to slap the side of the blade, the laird deftly twisted it, cutting a gash in Bransen's forearm.

Bransen heard a gurgled whimper and realized that Cadayle was hurt.

Prydae struck again, and this time he got the blade through enough to poke a hole in Bransen's side, forcing him to leap back—and he felt a jolt behind him that nearly had him flying forward to impale himself on Prydae's blade as the door got smashed again, this time with the axe driving down to crack the locking bar.

Prydae thrust the blade and Bransen fell back against the door and snapped his foot up to deflect the blade. Ahead he charged, thinking he might have an opening, but even as his foot first connected, Prydae was already moving out of reach, falling back and low in a defensive crouch.

"Well fought, boy, but you have no chance!" Prydae cried. To drive his point home, he tried to drive the sword home and might well have succeeded, had not the door burst open behind Bransen, startling them both.

Prydae fell back; behind Bransen, Bannagran roared.

Bransen turned, purely on instinct, leaning back, arms out wide, as he came around. He only half registered the flying, spinning axe, soaring in now for his chest as he came around. And still he leaned, bending his knees, head going back so far that he looked through eyes turned upside down and saw Prydae coming in at him.

A darkness flickered before his eyes, but Bransen did not consciously register it as the spinning axe.

He went down so low that his shoulder blades brushed the floor, and then every muscle in his body reacted to his demand, swinging him back upright, his legs straining to pull.

He immediately went to a defensive stance and started to turn sideways, expecting an assault from Bannagran in the front and Prydae behind. But Bannagran, his eyes and mouth opened wide in a silent scream, did not approach; and before Bransen even glanced back at Prydae, he understood why.

For there staggered the Laird of Pryd Holding, mortally wounded, Bannagran's axe buried deep in his chest.

Bransen dove to the side of the room, to Cadayle, whose throat was pouring blood. Beside her, Rennarq gurgled and twitched, and Bransen absently pushed him aside. For he posed no threat, the young Jhesta Tu knew. Bransen's spear of energy had ruptured Rennarq's *chi*, had shattered the line and sent it into uncontrollable spasms. The irony of it, that Rennarq was doomed to become the very storklike creature he so detested, made no impact on Bransen at that moment—not with Cadayle lying so still before him.

He could feel her life energy, her warmth, flowing out of her as he fell over her in a hug. He tried to compose himself, tried to bring the soul stone to bear and find some way to heal her.

But it was too personal, too horrible, and Bransen couldn't find his focus! And he knew that the soldiers were coming in and that Bannagran would fly into murderous rage. He pressed the soul stone to her wound and sent his thoughts, his heart and soul, into it.

But it was too little, he feared, and his trembling hands could not focus the power.

Then he felt a hand on his shoulder, and he nearly swooned, nearly broke apart on the floor.

"Bransen," Brother Reandu said quietly in his ear, and he placed his hand over Bransen's hand that held the soul stone. "Together, my friend," Reandu assured him. "Calm. Calm is the key."

Reandu kept talking to him, whispering to him, reassuring him. Bransen felt Reandu's energy flowing into his hand and into the soul stone, and used that flow as his own guide.

Bransen felt his hand grow warm.

The blood slowed to a trickle, then stemmed altogether.

Cadayle seemed so pale and so still. . . .

"Please," Bransen whispered, but Cadayle did not stir.

Reandu patted Bransen on the back as the young man fell over his beloved sobbing, and the weary monk rose to his feet and turned. Prydae was dead, he knew, and had known as soon as he had pushed his way into the room. Over by the body, Bannagran rose, his face twisted in a knot of rage and confusion. He started toward Reandu and Bransen, but the monk stopped him with an upraised hand.

"There has been far too much tragedy this day," Reandu said.

"One more will die," Bannagran promised.

"Because he was protecting the woman he loves?"

The simple question stole some of the bluster from Bannagran, and stopped his approach.

"Would Bannagran, loyal Bannagran, have done any less?" Reandu pressed.

"Laird Prydae is dead," the large man proclaimed. "Bernivvigar is dead. Rennarq lies torn on the floor, and your own Master Bathelais lies broken below. All because of this man, this Highwayman!"

"We gain nothing by continuing this," Reandu said.

Bannagran glowered at him, then glanced down at the sword on the floor. "Perhaps my satisfaction at killing him will be enough," he growled, and he started to bend for the sword.

He jerked back, as a rolling body rushed past, and when it went by, the sword was gone; and Bannagran glanced behind to see the Highwayman standing there, sword leveled and ready to plunge it through Bannagran's chest.

"You speak of satisfaction?" Bransen asked him. "Like my own satisfaction in killing those who maimed and murdered my father Garibond? Like my own satisfaction in watching Bannagran's own axe tear open the chest of Laird Prydae? Like my own satisfaction now, when I see mighty Bannagran fall dead on the floor? For, yes, I know that you were among those who murdered Garibond. Pray to whatever god you serve, Bannagran, and be quick!"

He ended with a movement that seemed the start of a thrust, but the shout of Reandu stopped him.

"No!" the monk cried. "No, Bransen, do not do this!"

Reandu came forward in a rush, pushing past to stand between Bannagran and Bransen. "I beg of you, my friend. This is not the way. You gain nothing by killing him, by killing anyone."

"And was Brother Reandu among those who murdered Garibond?" Bransen snapped back.

Reandu paled, all the answer Bransen needed, and for a moment, everyone, including Bransen himself, expected him to drive his sword through the monk's chest.

"Bransen?" Cadayle called.

The Highwayman looked past the helpless Reandu, past Bannagran, to see Cadayle propped on her elbows, her pretty eyes open and staring at him.

And judging him, in this critical moment. And the weight of that judgment forced him to judge himself.

He looked back at the terrified Reandu and the subdued Bannagran.

He lowered his blade.

Early the next morning, Bannagran studied the frail-looking young man standing before him, his mind flying between confusion, pity, and hatred. This man's actions had led to the death of his dearest friend, and for that, the mighty warrior demanded revenge.

To the side of the room stood Cadayle and her mother, Callen, holding each other, both crying, for they knew what would transpire here. Bransen had surrendered, on agreement that they would be spared, but that noble action did not lessen the blow they knew was about to fall.

"Do not do this, I beg you," said Brother Reandu, standing at Bransen's side. "There is no gain to be found here in continuing the senseless tragedy."

"We have already had this discussion," Bannagran said, cutting him short, and the warrior's eyes bored into Bransen, who did not look away, did not look down, and did not blink.

It all seemed so simple to Bannagran; he was willing to let the young woman and her mother go free—the Samhaists were in complete confusion and leaderless now, after all, and so there was no one to demand the death of the mother. As for the Highwayman, he was fairly caught and guilty of great crimes against Pryd Holding, indeed crimes that would undermine Pryd Holding!

Yes, the Highwayman had willingly surrendered to Bannagran, with the agreement that Cadayle would be spared. And so it all seemed a simple matter of beheading the fool or throwing him to the flames.

But that simplicity was undermined by the spectacle that Bannagran knew was unfolding right before Castle Pryd's closed gates. Hundreds, thousands, had turned out that morning to show their grief at the loss of Laird Prydae and to shout their support for the Highwayman.

Dangerous support, Bannagran knew, and he remembered his own warnings to his friend, Laird Prydae, when Prydae had expressed his determination to kill the Highwayman. Beyond that, Bannagran understood keenly that with the power vacuum, religious and secular, in Pryd Holding, the state of the holding would be his to wear as mantle or weight when Laird Delaval came to claim the land as his own. Bannagran's standing would greatly depend upon his actions this very morning.

He looked hard at the Highwayman and wanted to hate the man. He thought of his dead friend, killed inadvertently by his own hand, and he wanted to blame this man and to hate him all the more.

And yet Brother Reandu's words—of sympathy and understanding, of seeing poor Bransen's perspective in all this tragedy—had not fallen on deaf ears. Would Bannagran be honoring or doing a disservice to the memory of Prydae by executing this young man?

Or did it even matter?

He looked at Bransen for a long, long time, then barely believed his own words as he said, "Get out of Pryd."

EPILOGUE

Brother Reandu stood at the gate of Chapel Pryd long after the carriage had rolled out of sight, contemplating the momentous changes that he would have to steward. Master Bathelais had succumbed to his injuries, leaving Reandu as the highest-ranking monk in Pryd, behind the shell that was Father Jerak. Already, brothers were on the way from Chapel Abelle to discuss the disposition of their Church in Pryd Holding, which, it was commonly believed, would soon cease to be Pryd Holding.

For even as Reandu was preparing himself for the inquisitors of Chapel Abelle, Bannagran and the others at the castle made their preparation for the arrival of Laird Delaval himself, along with Prince Yeslnik, who, it was widely assumed, would be granted the holding as his own, under the auspices of Greater Delaval.

Reandu couldn't help but smile a little as he considered how greatly the old wretch Rennarq would despise this takeover by Laird Delaval. But Rennarq, after all, was now a babbling idiot, a storklike creature who could not control his movements. He could hardly eat, by all reports, gagging on every bite, and was likely to choke to death soon. Reandu had tried to help with his gemstones, but whatever the surprising Bransen had done to Rennarq was far beyond Reandu's meager powers to correct.

Good enough and proper justice for the brutal Samhaist,

Reandu supposed, though he was not completely without sympathy.

He could not follow any course of sympathy at that time, though, for Reandu had much to accomplish in the short time before his superiors arrived. They would demand of him a complete report, and he knew that the report would not be viewed favorably if the chapel was not in perfect order. Every brother was hard at work, Reandu knew, and that thought reminded him that he, too, had much to do.

He turned toward the chapel, away from the road, but not without one last wistful glance at the long and empty lane. He missed Bransen already and lamented that he had not tried to learn more from the surprising young man. He hoped that the brothers from Chapel Abelle wouldn't take too close an inventory of Chapel Pryd, because he knew that he couldn't begin to explain his decision to allow Bransen to keep the soul stone he had stolen.

But Reandu, despite his fears, was still smiling as he considered his decision. Had he ever met a person in all his life as deserving of a gift from God?

"Farewell, Bransen Garibond," he said softly to the empty lane.

The simple wagon bounced along the flagstone road, the bumps rolling and soft as the wagon moved along at a leisurely pace. Holding the reins, Bransen didn't prod the horses, for he was in no hurry this day, no more than were Callen and Cadayle, flanking him. Tied to the back of the wagon, old Doully the donkey meandered along in step.

"I never knew the world was so wide," Callen remarked every so often, and her eyes were filled with a sparkle of adventure that backed up her claim.

"Wide and scary," said Cadayle, and she hooked her arm under Bransen's and moved a bit closer.

"Scary?" Callen replied doubtfully. "With the Highwayman here to protect us?"

Bransen smiled widely. He didn't look much like the Highwayman at that moment, in his simple woolen tunic and sandals and with not a weapon to be seen. But the black suit was there, tucked neatly under the wagon's bench, and beside it rested his mother's sword. His sword.

"And where shall we go in this wide, wide world?" Callen absently asked. "To where the wind begins and the gods do battle?"

"To whatever lands we find that are free of battle," Cadayle answered. "And few are those, these times in Honce."

"Then to Behr," Bransen answered, and both women looked at him in surprise.

"To the wide blowing sands of the southern lands, to the temple of the Jhesta Tu in the Mountains of Fire."

"You speak of places I do not know," Callen said. Bransen smiled, for in truth, he was merely spouting names that Garibond had told him in his youth and distant references in the book he had committed to memory so long ago.

"Are there any places we do know, beyond the boundaries of Pryd Holding?" Cadayle asked. Though her tone was light, there was substance to that question that was not lost on any of the three.

"To where the wind begins, then," said Bransen, and he gave the reins a little snap. "And where the gods do battle. That is something I wish to see."

And so they rode from the only place any of them had ever known as home, into new lands and new adventures.

An excerpt from

The Ancient

the next book in

R. A. Salvatore's

Saga of the First King.

•

Coming to hardcover in Winter 2008

TOR® A TOR HARDCOVER

ISBN-13: 978-0-7653-1789-6   ISBN-10: 0-7653-1789-3

www.tor.com

ROCKS, ALWAYS ROCKS

Rocks, rocks, it's always rocks!" the strong young man complained, his muscular bare arms glistening with sweat. He was tall, more than six and a half feet, and although he had lost considerable weight on this multiyear journey, he did not appear skinny and certainly not frail, his lean muscles taut like ropes. A mop of blond hair covered his head, bespeaking his Vanguard heritage, and he wore a scraggly beard. Even though his superiors disapproved of it, they would not enforce their rules against facial hair when they possessed no implement to easily be rid of it. He stood on a slope of brown dirt and gray stones—fewer near him now, since he had already tossed scores over the ridge so that they would roll down and bounce near the wall the man and his companions were repairing. He hoisted another one, brought it near his shoulder, and heaved it out, but it didn't quite make the lip and began to roll back his way. He intercepted it with a few fast strides, planting his foot against it and holding it in place before it could gain any real momentum.

"Catch your breath, Brother Cormack," said an older monk, middle-aged and with more skin atop his head than hair. "The air is particularly warm this day."

Cormack did take a deep breath, then gathered up his heavy woolen robes and pulled them over his head, leaving him naked apart from a bulky white loincloth.

"Brother Cormack!" the other monk, Giavno by name, scolded.

"Always rocks," Cormack argued, his bright green eyes flaring with intensity, and he made no move to retrieve his heavy robe. "Ever since we came to this cursed island, we have done nothing more than pile rocks."

"Cursed?" Giavno said, shaking his head and wearing an expression of utter disappointment. "We were sent north to frozen Alpinador to begin a chapel, Brother. For the glory of Blessed Abelle. You would call that cursed?" He swept his arm up to his left, beyond the ridge and in the direction of the small stone church the brothers had constructed. Though the square structure was no more than thirty feet in length on any side, because they had placed it on the highest point of the small island, it dominated the view.

Cormack put his hands on his hips, laughed, and shook his head helplessly. They had departed Chapel Pellinor in Vanguard more than three years before, full of excitement and a sense of great purpose. They would travel to Alpinador, home of the pagan barbarians, and spread the word of Blessed Abelle. With their gemstone magic and the truth and beauty of their message, they would save souls.

But they had found only battle and outrage, and their every word had sounded as insults to the proud and strong northmen. Running for their lives more than proselytizing, the band had in short order become quite lost and had stumbled and bumbled their way along for weeks, while the freezing winter was closing in around them. Surely the nearly twoscore monks and an equal number of their servants would have found a cold and empty death, but they had happened upon this place, a huge lake of warm waters and perpetual steam, a place of islands small and large. Father De Guilbe, who led their expedition, proclaimed it a miracle and decided that here, on these waters, they would fulfill their mission and build their chapel.

Here, Cormack mused, on a lump of rock in the middle of the water.

"Rocks," Cormack grumbled, and he bent low and picked up the heavy stone again. This time he heaved it far over the ridge line.

"The lake teems with fish and other food, and have you ever tasted water so fine?" said Giavno, his voice wistful. "And the heat of the water saved us from the Alpinadoran winter. You should be more grateful, Brother."

"We were sent here for a reason beyond our simple survival."

"Patience," Giavno argued—a predictable answer and oft given, but something about Giavno's inflection as he spoke the last word gave Cormack pause. He looked over at his Abellican brother, then followed the older monk's wide-eyed stare to the water behind them.

Cormack saw the powries—bandy-legged and -armed, barrel-chested dwarves—floating in on their flat raft just an instant before they began springing into the water near the shore, bursting into a wild charge, brandishing their weapons.

Cormack whirled about, took a few running strides, and leaped high into the air, crashing into a pair of dwarves before they cleared the surf. One went down, the other staggered back, and Cormack set himself quickly and launched a circle kick that caught the standing dwarf on the side of its chin before it could fully recover from the unexpected assault. Its dull red beret—the headgear that defined the powries, who were also known as "bloody caps"—went flying away, and that dwarf, too, tumbled under the water.

"Out, or they'll be sure to drown you!" Giavno cried, and he accentuated his point by thrusting forth his hand and loosing the power of the stone he clutched: graphite, the stone of lightning. A bright blue bolt sizzled past Cormack to strike the raft, sending powries tumbling, but as the bolt dispersed into the water, Cormack felt a nasty sting about his legs.

Behind Giavno and beyond the ridge another pair of monks cried out a warning.

Cormack sloshed toward the rocky shore with all the strength he could muster. He half turned as he went and managed to somewhat deflect the barrage of clubs that came spinning his way. More than one hit home, though, and by the time he got out of the water, he sported a large welt on one arm and a bruise on the side of his face that threatened to swell his right eye closed.

"To me!" Giavno called to Cormack and the other pair, and just ahead of the dwarves the young monk ran. Reaching his companion he skidded low, grabbed up a stone, and turned as he rose, launching it at the nearest pursuer. The missile hit the dwarf squarely in the chest, briefly interrupting its howl. But only briefly, for the tough creature slogged through the strike and closed fast, smacking wildly with its club.

Cormack didn't retreat; in fact, he surprised the dwarf by coming forward within the weight of the club, rolling as he went to better absorb the blow. It still blew his breath out, but Cormack fought through that and caught the club as he turned, then turned again, taking the club with him and yanking it from the surprised dwarf's hands. He snapped off a quick smack against the dwarf's head, then pivoted the club fast and sent it out spearlike at the next powrie in line.

That one waved its arm to deflect the missile but misjudged and whipped its hand past too quickly. The redbearded dwarf did block the throw, however, with its face—its nose, more specifically—and its head snapped back.

"Yach, ye mutt," the powrie growled, reaching up to grab its busted proboscis, and taking away a palm covered in blood. The dwarf sneered and growled louder and started for Cormack with more purpose.

But it stopped suddenly, looking confused, and staggered down to one knee.

Cormack had neither the time to acknowledge his luck nor pat himself on the back for a perfect throw, for powries were made of tough stuff and such a strike wouldn't normally bring one down, temporarily though it might prove. As soon as he had let fly the missile he retracted his throwing arm and drove it down to the side, slugging the initial target in the head.

The dwarf wrapped its strong arms about Cormack's waist and drove him to the side, intent upon bearing him to the ground. The monk worked his legs frantically, trying to stay upright, and repeatedly hit the creature with his pumping right hand. Blood flew out from his knuckles and not the dwarf, for surely Cormack felt as if he was punching stone instead of flesh!

The monk didn't relent, though, nor did the powrie, taking him far aside from Brother Giavno and the other two monks, and the group of a half dozen powries bearing down on them. Another lightning bolt shook the ground, and the lead powrie began to dance wildly, arms and lips flapping, his thick red hair and beard straightening to full length and shivering in the air. He danced and hopped, managing another step forward, but then fell over.

The other five rumbled past, ignoring rock missiles, and the club fight began in earnest.

Cormack continued to work his legs frantically, continued to punch at the dwarf, but on one slug the stubborn little creature turned about, purposely putting its face in line with the man's flying fist. Cormack scored a solid, stunning hit, but square dwarf teeth clamped onto the side of his hand and bit down hard.

Cormack thrashed and tore free his hand, breaking out of the dwarf's vicelike grip in the process. Even as he jumped backward with the powrie following in immediate pursuit, the monk launched a heavy left hook that snapped the dwarf's head to the side.

A right cross staggered the powrie even more and gave Cormack the opportunity to square up against the dwarf.

"Yach, but I'm to scrape the skin from yer pretty face!" the stubborn powrie promised as it came on.

A trio of stinging left jabs put the dwarf back on its heels.

Cormack retreated a bit more; his reach was his advantage, he knew, and when he looked at his opponent, who seemed like a walking block of rock, he figured it might be his only advantage.

Giavno swung hard with his makeshift wooden mace. He scored a solid hit, but the powrie pressed him relentlessly. How the monk wished that he still had the mace he had carried when he had left Chapel Pellinor, a spiked weapon of wonderful balance and weight. But, alas, that mace was lost to him, as were all of their other metallic items, corroded by the constant steam that floated about the islands of this hot lake.

Giavno hit the powrie again, cracking the block head of the weapon against the back of the dwarf's shoulder as he turned. The monk rolled his shoulders, thrusting forth his free hand in time to deflect the dwarf's smashing response. And as that powrie's staff slipped by, the monk wrapped his arm over the dwarf's hands and bore in hard against his enemy.

This was a big mistake, Giavno realized as soon as he slammed against the dwarf, who didn't budge an inch. For now his advantage—the length of his arms—was lost, and the powrie squirmed fast and twisted free its hands, clamping them about Giavno's waist and tugging him down as it fell into a roll.

Another powrie closed in on the wrestling pair, whacking away at Giavno with a weighted stick, raising welts under the monk's heavy brown robes.

Giavno grimaced in pain and managed to turn about to see his two companions, both fighting valiantly and fiercely against a trio of dwarves, trading punch for swat. At one point in the roll the dwarf loosened its grip, and Giavno quickly set his feet and thrust forward, scrambling toward his friends. As he had hoped, one of the powries broke away to intercept, launching a flying tackle at the monk and bearing him back to the two pursuing dwarves.

Still clutching his graphite stone, Giavno got smacked with a staff and punched on the side of his head. The dwarf who had tackled him twisted him about as if to break him apart. But Giavno held his concentration and sent his energy into and through the stone, and jolting sparks of electricity fired out in all directions around him.

The powries fell back, or were thrown back, and Giavno sprinted for his companions. He glanced over at Cormack with sincere, almost fatherly concern, but reminded himself that Cormack had secured his position on this mission to

Alpinador precisely because he had shown himself to be the finest young fighter at Chapel Pellinor.

Cormack would get back to the three brothers, Giavno told himself, and prayed.

"Ah, ye're that one," the dwarf said, nodding and smiling, and spitting a line of blood at Cormack's feet. "Yer blood'll make me beret shine all the brighter, then."

It howled and brought its staff up above its head, leaping forward.

But Cormack had anticipated the move and was moving as well, diving down to the side and lashing out with his top leg. He didn't hit the dwarf but slid the kicking foot past him, then bent his knee and brought the leg back in behind the dwarf's knees. The powrie halted its swing and overbalanced backward for a second as Cormack's calf drove in hard against it.

That was naught but a ruse, though, as the unfortunate dwarf soon learned. Cormack tumbled out farther to the side, then reversed his flow, throwing his hips over and locking a scissors grip on the dwarf. The powrie tried to fight the inevitable pull but had no leverage against the prostrate and rolling man, and Cormack's trailing leg drove the dwarf over, forward, and to the ground. The staff went flying and the powrie hit hard, getting a hand underneath just in time to stop its face from smashing against the stones.

Cormack continued the roll to his back, extracting his legs on the last turn. He arched, put his feet under him, and snapped his muscles, lifting himself up to stand over the prone, facedown dwarf. He moved fast into position so that he could stomp the powrie's face into the stone, and even lifted his foot over the back of the still-stunned dwarf's head.

He hesitated.

He heard splashing and turned in time to see the charge of the first dwarf he had decked, from the water. It came out with fury—no, not fury, Cormack realized, but with terror.

For behind it emerged another creature, its smooth, bluish, almost translucent skin gleaming in the dull and hazy light, its black eyes peering at its prey intently under a protruding brow. A glacial troll, Cormack realized at once, and so too had the powrie, judging from the look of terror on its face!

No taller than the dwarves and far lighter, the glacial trolls were nevertheless the bane of all the island societies. Their thin limbs were deceptively strong and their teeth pointed like little knives. And where came one troll, inevitably, came many. Cormack saw them clearly now, the long waggling ears of the ugly goblinoid creatures poking from the surf all about the rocky beach.

The dwarf at Cormack's feet grabbed him by the ankle and tugged hard. He didn't resist but let himself fall into a backward tumble, one that took him right over himself and back to his feet.

"Trolls! Trolls!" he cried, and he started toward the beach, yelling at the dwarf, "Faster!"

The dwarf threw his head back as he broke free of the surf and seemed to come on more quickly. Momentarily, though, for when the powrie jerked again Cormack saw the truth of it.

The dwarf staggered forward, slowing, then slumped down to his knees and gave a great exhale.

"Yach!" cried the powrie on the ground before Cormack, and that one leaped to his feet. "Bikelbrin, me friend!"

That call had all the powries pausing and turning, as the truth of their predicament fell fully on man and dwarf alike. Ten of them stood against more than a dozen of the trolls, who were armed with spears tipped with sharpened, barbed shells rather than the relatively benign sticks that the island inhabitants generally used to batter each other about the skulls.

The trolls closed in on the kneeling Bikelbrin, but so did Cormack, leaping across the stones in full charge. He heard Brother Giavno shout, "To the abbey!" and understood that his three brethren would take that route, but he could not ignore the wounded powrie.

The glacial trolls neared, reaching for their spears. Cormack put on a burst of speed, closing ground, and leaped, turning himself sidelong in midair as he cleared the dwarf. He was over the spears before the trolls could fully retract them. One let go of the shaft and threw its hands up to block, while the other stubbornly, and with a sickening wet sound, drew free its spear. That one took the brunt of the flying body-block as Cormack bowled over both of the trolls.

He landed atop them hard, smacking his hand painfully against a stone and his forehead against the back of that hand. A wave of dizziness washed over him, but he knew better than to succumb to it while in the midst of vicious trolls. He rolled sidelong, right off the two, who scrambled and bit at him, one catching a tooth on his bare forearm.

Cormack tugged that arm free immediately and managed to slam it down hard on the troll's face for good measure as he regained his balance.

No faster than the other troll, however, which lowered its spear for Cormack's belly and thrust it forward.

The trained monk dodged aside and slapped the spear away with the flat of his hand. He started for the opening to strike at the creature, but instinct stopped him and turned him about.

Just in time to deflect the thrown spear of another troll.

Cormack jumped back, three on him now and a fourth approaching. To his left came a sharp retort, and one of the trolls he had bowled over stumbled forward and to the ground. Behind it the furious powrie was running headlong and empty-handed, for he had thrown his staff, spearlike, into the back of the fallen troll's head. He called for Bikelbrin but ran right past his wounded friend, leaping onto the second of the trolls Cormack had tackled, pinning it under his thrashing and kicking form.

Cormack stomped hard on the back of the neck of the first fallen troll, ending its squirming. No mercy for glacial trolls or for everyone on that beach, he thought, human and powrie alike, knowing that the trolls would show none. Up on the ridge all of the powries had disengaged from Cormack's Abellican brethren and were charging down. To the monk's relief he saw Brother Giavno extending his clenched fist.

"To the abbey!" Giavno yelled again, and Cormack understood that it was for his benefit alone, a warning to him that his three friends would desert him here. A lightning bolt followed that warning, off to the side where it sent a trio of trolls hopping wildly and weirdly, the residual jolts waggling their spindly limbs in a frenetic dance.

One troll leaped at Cormack, another went for the powrie and its wrestling companion. The young monk dodged a spear thrust, then a second. He turned sidelong, bent back and down as the third thrust angled high, past his head. Cormack's left hand, his inside hand, grabbed the shaft, and he wrapped his right arm over it just below the seashell tip as he brought it down. He turned to face the troll and thrust his right forearm, now under the shaft, upward at the same time he drove his left hand down. The sudden movement and Cormack's redistribution of his weight snapped the spear at midshaft. As soon as he heard the break, Cormack tugged the remaining troll's weapon aside and crashed against the troll, grabbing firmly on the broken piece of the spear as he went. He felt that sharp piece drive into the troll's torso, and he wrapped his left hand about the creature, boring in harder.

The troll went into a frenzy and tried to bite at him, but Cormack stayed too low for that. The frantic creature wasn't done, though, and it used yet another of its many weapons—its long and pointed chin—and repeatedly drove the bony edge hard against the side of Cormack's head.

Both fell to the ground, Cormack on top, and he shoved himself up immediately to his knees, his movement pulling free the spear shaft. He flipped it in his hands as he rose and came right back at the troll, this time with the seashell head leading.

The troll scrambled and thrashed, slapped and squirmed, but to no avail. Cormack fell atop it again, pushing the spear right through its chest. He tugged left and right, ensuring that the wound would be mortal, and finally he fell aside—only to see the other troll, the one who'd been hit in the back of the head by the thrown powrie staff, standing over him, a rock in its hand.

An explosion of bright white light filled Cormack's head as the troll struck. He covered and tumbled and somehow even managed to regain his footing without being hit again too badly.

But the troll was there, punching and biting at him, and all the world was spinning.

Cormack found his sensibilities just long enough to punch a stunning right cross that, through good fortune alone, connected solidly on the troll's jaw, snapping its neck and sending it to the ground.

Cormack tried to straighten up, staggering left and right. He saw the powries and the trolls as one big pile of confusion and fury.

Then he saw the ground rushing up to swallow him.

The sounds receded, the light disappeared in a blink, and Cormack drowned in a cold and empty darkness.

Mail this coupon with your original store receipts for your purchase of the special $4.99 edition of *The Highwayman* and the new R. A. Salvatore hardcover *The Ancient* and receive $5.00 US back!

Mail to: Tom Doherty Associates, LLC/Tor Books
Dept. KM
175 Fifth Avenue, 14th floor
New York, NY 10010
Attention: *The Ancient* **Rebate**

The Highwayman and *The Ancient* must both be purchased by **April 5, 2008**.

I loved *The Highwayman* and bought *The Ancient*. Purchase receipts for both books, with the price of each circled, are enclosed. Please send me $5.00 US back.

Send $5.00 US to:

Name: _____

Address: _____

City: _____

State: _____

Zip: _____

E-mail: _____

Please send info on Tor/Forge authors.

I purchased *The Ancient* at _____ (retailer)

_____

Enclose this coupon with your original store receipts for *The Highwayman* and *The Ancient* **and a self-addressed, stamped envelope (SASE may be omitted by Canadian residents)**.

Coupon, receipts, and envelope must all be received by July 5, 2008. One rebate per person, address, or household. No copies of coupons or receipts allowed. US and Canadian residents only. Allow 6–8 weeks for delivery of your rebate. Tor is not responsible for late, lost, or misdirected mail. Void where prohibited.